Under Siege

Under Siege

EDWARD MARSTON

First published in Great Britain in 2010 by
Allison & Busby Limited
13 Charlotte Mews
London W1T 4EJ
www.allisonandbusby.com

A CIP catalogue record for this book is available from
the British Library.

10 9 8 7 6 5 4 3 2 1

13-ISBN 978-0-7490-0817-8

Typeset in 12/16 pt Adobe Garamond Pro by
Allison & Busby Ltd.

Paper used in this publication is from sustainably managed sources.
All of the wood used is procured from legal sources and is fully traceable.
The producing mill uses schemes such as ISO 14001
to monitor environmental impact.

Printed and bound in the UK by
CPI Mackays, Chatham ME5 8TD

By Edward Marston

THE CAPTAIN RAWSON SERIES

Soldier of Fortune
Drums of War
Fire and Sword
Under Siege

THE RAILWAY DETECTIVE SERIES

The Railway Detective
The Excursion Train
The Railway Viaduct
The Iron Horse
Murder on the Brighton Express
The Silver Locomotive Mystery
Railway to the Grave
Blood on the Line

THE RESTORATION SERIES

The King's Evil
The Amorous Nightingale
The Repentant Rake
The Frost Fair
The Parliament House
The Painted Lady

To our lovely new granddaughter,
Imogen Rose,
in the hope that she will one day read it.

CHAPTER ONE

July, 1708

'Will you think of me, Daniel?' she asked, gripping his hands.

'Every day,' he replied.

'Will you write to me?'

'I'll try to, Amalia, but it's not always possible.'

'Promise me that you'll take care to stay out of danger.'

He laughed. 'That's something I can never guarantee.'

'I worry about you so much.'

'There's no need. I can look after myself.'

She tightened her grip. 'Oh, *why* do you have to be a soldier?'

'I like the life.'

'How can you like all that pain and suffering and death?'

'Army life has its redeeming features,' he said with a smile. 'Remember that it's only because I'm a soldier that I had the opportunity to meet you. Do you have any regrets about that?'

She beamed at him. 'No, Daniel,' she said, 'I don't.'

Daniel Rawson's visit to Amsterdam was necessarily a fleeting one. Having ridden to The Hague to deliver news of another startling victory by the Grand Alliance, he galloped north to pay the briefest of visits to Amalia Janssen. Delighted to hear of the success at the battle of Oudenarde, she was even more thrilled to see the man she loved. The seemingly endless war against the French had drawn them closer that summer because Amalia had been kidnapped by the enemy and was only rescued from their hands by Daniel's skill and audacity. The experience had strengthened the bond between them to the point where it was unbreakable. They now lived for each other.

Duty, however, could not be ignored. The doting swain had to remind himself that he was also a captain in the 24th Regiment of Foot and a member of the Duke of Marlborough's personal staff. He was needed by the captain-general both as an interpreter and as someone entrusted with assignments that always flirted with dire peril. A final kiss from Amalia had sent him on his way and the exquisite taste of her lips stayed with him for a whole day. He'd first met her in Paris where he'd been sent to rescue her father, Emanuel Janssen, a celebrated tapestry maker imprisoned in the Bastille when unmasked as a spy. To get them safely back to their own country, Daniel had had to call on all of his daring and resourcefulness. During the hectic flight, he'd got to know father and daughter extremely well.

Until Amalia came into his life, Daniel had taken his pleasures where he found them and broken more than a few hearts in the process. Tall, slim, well featured and with an easy charm, he'd had no shortage of conquests and took them in his stride. All that had now changed. He'd at last found a woman he adored and to whom he felt obliged to be faithful. The notion of permanence had entered his head. He'd started to think seriously about marriage, children and family life. Nevertheless, tempting as they were, such delights would have to wait until the War of the Spanish Succession eventually came to an end, and nobody could predict with any certainty when that might be. He and Amalia would have to wait, enduring the loneliness and anguish of being apart.

It was a long ride back to Oudenarde and Daniel was grateful that, for the bulk of the journey, he would have the company of a squadron of Dutch dragoons sent as reinforcements. He joined them as they were crossing the border into Flanders, his bright red coat in striking contrast to their sober grey uniforms. Daniel fell in beside a lieutenant who was intrigued by the newcomer's history.

'You live in Amsterdam yet fight for the British?' he asked.

'My father was English, my mother was Dutch.'

'Then our army should have taken precedence. After all, you were brought up in the United Provinces. You left England when you were still a boy.'

'I'm content to fight with a British regiment,' said Daniel.

'Well, you've obviously fought well, my friend, if you've earned a position alongside the captain-general himself. Tell me,' he went on with a sly grin, 'is it true that the Duke of Marlborough is as miserly as they say?'

'His Grace is the most generous-hearted man I know.'

'I speak not of his heart but of his purse. The rumour is that he keeps it shut tight. While our generals maintain their quarters in some style, the duke's, I gather, are unbefitting a man of his standing. It's the reason he tries to dine elsewhere instead of inviting guests to his own table.' He gave a chuckle. 'Why deny it? Everyone has heard about his reputation for meanness.'

'Then everyone has heard a foul calumny,' said Daniel, loyally. 'I've had the privilege of dining in His Grace's quarters on more than one occasion and he is an unstinting host.'

It was not entirely true but he said it with sufficient conviction to wipe the smirk off his companion's face. In fact, Daniel knew that the idle gossip about Marlborough's parsimony was not without foundation. By comparison with those of generals in allied armies, Marlborough's quarters were remarkably modest and he did dine in more comfortable surroundings whenever an invitation came. Daniel would never admit that to the lieutenant. He revered the captain-general as a man and as a soldier, believing that what he did with his money was his own business. Any criticism of his mentor would always be roundly contradicted by Daniel.

'What happens next?' asked the lieutenant.

'That remains to be decided.'

'Come now, Captain Rawson. You belong to the duke's staff. You know the way that his mind works and must have heard him discussing the possibilities that confront us. What course of action will he pursue?'

'I have no idea,' said Daniel, firmly.

'I find that hard to believe.'

'You can believe or disbelieve what you wish, Lieutenant. I have no knowledge of which way the wind blows, and even if I did, I'd never confide in someone who has such a distorted view of His Grace's character. One of his great virtues is his ability to keep secrets. Look in his face and you will have no idea what he is thinking. In short,' added Daniel, 'he is discretion personified.'

The lieutenant was peeved. 'I see that you take after him.'

'I can imagine nobody better on whom to pattern myself.'

'You're speaking as an Englishman now.'

'What do you mean?'

'With all respect, Captain Rawson,' said the other, sharply, 'I think that you ought to march under a Dutch flag from time to time. Then you'd realise that the duke is not the paragon you claim.'

'There's no better general on this earth,' affirmed Daniel.

'Oh, I agree, my friend. I just wish that he'd be as ready to spill British blood as he is to shed that of the Dutch. You only have to look at Blenheim. Yes, it was a famous victory but it came at a terrible price – and it was your fellow countrymen who paid most of it.'

'Casualties are inevitable in battle.'

'It just happens that we had more of them than the British.'

'Our regiments had their share of losses,' said Daniel, stoutly. 'I was there. I saw the carnage. Our soldiers fell all around me. Besides, if it's a question of counting the corpses, I think that you'll find the troops under Prince

Eugene sustained the highest number of casualties. Such figures, of course, were dwarfed by French losses. Some 20,000 Frenchmen were killed or wounded and many more deserted. You should be proud that so many Dutch regiments helped to achieve that victory.' Controlling his temper, he eyed the man coldly. 'Do you have any other ill-informed observations to make about His Grace?'

The lieutenant lapsed into a sullen silence. They rode on for another mile before he picked up the conversation again.

'My brother was killed at Blenheim,' said the man, sourly.

Daniel was sympathetic. 'I'm sorry to hear that.'

'He was shot during the first attack.'

'You can at least console yourself with the thought that he didn't sacrifice his life in vain. Your brother was part of an army that inflicted lasting humiliation on the French.'

The man was scornful. 'What bloody use is that?' he challenged. 'Humiliation didn't bring about surrender. We trounced the French at Blenheim, at Ramillies and now at Oudenarde but they still keep coming back at us. This damnable war drags on from year to year.'

'Granted,' said Daniel, 'but they fight with a debilitated army now. We have the upper hand and they know it. It's the reason their diplomats sue for peace so strenuously behind the scenes.'

'Then why is there no end to it all?'

'Because the terms they offer are unacceptable.'

'We have your precious Duke of Marlborough to thank for that,' alleged the other. 'Left to us, there'd have been an honourable peace treaty long before now.'

'There'd also be a Frenchman on the throne of Spain,' Daniel reminded him. 'That's what this war is all about. Do you really want King Louis to control the Spanish Empire and hold sway over the whole of Europe? Is that what you call an honourable peace? Or, to put it another way,' he added, 'did your brother, and the thousands like him, die for nothing?'

The man retreated into silence once more, cowed by Daniel's forthrightness but unconvinced by his argument. The lieutenant's desperation for peace was shared by many in the armies comprising the Grand Alliance. Wearied by fighting, shocked at the high death toll, frightened by the spiralling financial losses and robbed of any urge to press on, they were eager to negotiate a peace. Daniel knew full well that Marlborough was equally keen to see an end to the hostilities but neither he – nor the British government – could stomach the idea of leaving Louis XIV's grandson, Philip, Duke of Anjou, as the ruling Spanish monarch.

'No Peace Without Spain' – it had been the rallying cry from the start. As other voices grew faint, that of Marlborough – and that of Captain Daniel Rawson – remained as loud as ever. Until the French claim to the Spanish throne was renounced, there was no hope at all of peace. War would continue with undiminished ferocity. As the cavalcade rode on through the sunlit countryside, Daniel wondered how long it would be before the two sides would clash once more.

Travelling with the dragoons might give him companionship and ensure his safety but it also slowed Daniel down. On the last day, therefore, he bade farewell to the squadron and set off on his own. While the others kept to the main road, he was able to veer off it and cut miles off the journey. He was riding through familiar territory, passing towns and villages that the Confederate army had liberated, lost to the French, then recaptured once more. Vestigial signs of warfare were everywhere. He passed a windmill destroyed by fire, farms deprived of their livestock and fields churned up by the furious charges of cavalry regiments. All was tranquil now but it would not be long before further havoc was wreaked.

Daniel was skirting a wood when he heard the cry. It was a long, high-pitched scream of rage from the mouth of a woman in obvious distress. Kicking his horse into a gallop, Daniel came around the angle of the trees to be confronted by a strange sight. A man in the uniform of a Hessian officer was struggling to overpower a stout woman in rough clothing. Beside them were two horses and a donkey. No quarter was given in the fight. While the woman kicked, punched, bit and unleashed a torrent of expletives, the man pummelled away at her before managing to trip her up. As she fell to the ground, he dived on top of her, holding down both of her arms in an attempt to subdue her. Spitting in his face, she tried to throw him off but he was too strong and determined. When he punched her on the jaw, she was momentarily dazed and unable to stop him hauling up her skirt to reveal a pair of fleshy thighs. Before he could lower his breeches, however, he heard the approaching horse and looked up, snarling angrily when Daniel arrived and reined in his steed.

'Go on your way!' he ordered.

'It seems that I'm needed here,' said Daniel, dismounting.

'Stay out of this or you'll be sorry.'

'Leave the lady alone.'

Grabbing him by the scruff of his neck, Daniel yanked him clear of the woman then lifted him to his feet. The man swung a wild fist but Daniel parried it with an arm and replied with a relay of punches that made his adversary stagger back, blood cascading from his nose. Howling in pain, the man hurled himself at Daniel and they grappled for minutes, testing their strength, feeling for advantage, each trying to throw the other to the ground. Daniel slowly exerted pressure until he felt the Hessian weaken. Without warning, he suddenly brought his knee up into the man's groin, causing him to bend invitingly over and allow Daniel to fell him with a solid uppercut to the chin.

As the Hessian collapsed in a heap, the woman jumped up, pulled down her skirt and started to kick the fallen man as hard as she could. Taking her by the shoulders, Daniel eased her gently away.

'You saw what the bastard was trying to do to me!' she yelled.

'I want to know why,' said Daniel.

'He's a cheat and a liar. He promised to buy the horse off me then refused to pay. When I argued with him, he knocked me down and tried to rape me.' Realising that she hadn't even thanked him, she produced a warm smile. 'You came along at the right moment, sir. I'm very grateful to you. Where did you learn to speak German so well? There are not many British officers who can do that.'

'I speak Dutch, French and German,' he told her, 'and I sometimes act as an interpreter.'

'What about Welsh?'

He grinned. 'That's beyond me, I'm afraid.'

'It's a beautiful language. I could teach you, if you wish.'

'No, thank you.'

'May I know your name, please?'

'It's Captain Daniel Rawson.'

'I'm Rachel Rees,' she said with a lilt. 'I used to be Mrs Baggott, but my first husband – God bless the old fool! – got himself stabbed to death by a French bayonet. My second husband – I was Mrs Granger when I was married to him – was trampled to death at Ramillies. By the time I found the poor dab afterwards, his head had been smashed to a pulp. I only recognised him because of the wedding ring he wore in his ear. Ah well!' she sighed. 'Such are the fortunes of war.' Her brave smile was tinged with resignation. 'Since then, I've used my maiden name. I've been plain Rachel Rees and had to shift for myself.'

She was a woman of generous proportions and middle height, with a chubby prettiness not entirely obliterated by the ravages of an outdoor life and the imprint of marital tragedy. Daniel put her in her late thirties. He didn't need to be told what she did. Rachel Rees was a camp follower, one of the many females who trailed behind an army, acting as cooks, seamstresses, washerwomen and – in the wake of any fighting – as nurses. Clearly, she was also a scavenger, combing the battlefield after the slaughter had ceased and stripping the corpses of anything of value. Among her recent acquisitions, it appeared, was the horse now cropping the grass behind them. Daniel noted the quality of the saddle and the elaborate housing.

'This is a French officer's horse,' he observed.

'I found it looking for a new owner,' she said, airily, 'so I took care of it until I could sell it. This man offered me the best price,' she went on, indicating the Hessian who was now sitting up and rubbing his sore chin, 'and I was stupid enough to trust him. Well, you saw how he honours a bargain.'

'She's a horse thief!' said the man as he hauled himself gingerly to his feet. 'She deserves to be hanged from the nearest tree – if you can find one strong enough to support her.'

'What's that villain saying about me?' demanded Rachel.

'The lady deserves to be treated with respect,' said Daniel in fluent German. 'An apology would not come amiss.'

'Apologise to that big, fat, ugly tub of lard?' sneered the man. 'Nothing would make me do that!'

'Then you'll have to die unrepentant.'

Stepping back, Daniel drew his sword with a flourish and held the point against the man's throat, jabbing lightly to draw blood. The Hessian put a hand up to the scratch and swore volubly.

'Hold your tongue!' roared Rachel. 'There's no need for foul language. I know enough German to understand those vile words.'

'That means you have *two* things for which to apologise,' said Daniel, calmly. 'You must say sorry for assaulting the lady and ask her pardon for inadvertently swearing in her presence. Well?' He held out his sword. 'Which is it to be? You can either behave like a gentleman for once or be killed like the cheating rogue you are.'

The man hesitated, weighing up his chances. His sword lay on the ground. Daniel gestured towards it, encouraging him to pick it up. If he was to kill the man, he'd do so in a fair fight. But the Hessian had grave doubts that he could get the better of his opponent if they fought on equal terms. Daniel was fit, confident and had already demonstrated his superior strength and agility. The Hessian's one chance of winning was to shoot him with the pistol holstered beside the saddle of his horse. Pretending to bend down to retrieve his weapon, therefore, the man made a sudden dash for his horse. He was far too slow. Daniel had read his mind and stuck out a foot to send him tumbling to the ground. When the man rolled over on his back, he looked up at the sword that was poised to strike him.

'No, no!' he begged, losing his nerve completely. 'Don't kill me. I'm sorry that I attacked the lady and sorry that I swore in front of her. I apologise unreservedly. Look,' he went on, piteously, 'I'll pay her twice the price she asked for the horse and we'll part as friends.' He turned to her. 'What do you say to that?'

Rachel was unimpressed. 'I wouldn't sell it to you if you were the last man on earth,' she said, curling a derisive lip. She held out her hand. 'Give me the sword, Captain Rawson and let *me* kill him.'

'Don't let her touch me!' wailed the man.

'She won't need to now that the apology has been made,' said Daniel, lowering his weapon. 'Get up and go back to your regiment in disgrace.'

'He should pay for what he did to me!' shouted Rachel.

'Oh, he will – have no fear of that. The tables have been turned. He came to get a horse but will instead give one away.'

'You can't take my horse,' pleaded the man, scrambling to his feet. 'How will I get back to camp? It's miles away.'

'Then you'd better start walking.'

'I'm a cavalry officer. I must have a horse.'

'Buy one honestly,' said Daniel, using the flat of his sword to smack the man's buttocks. 'Off you go!'

With a yelp of pain, the Hessian scurried away, flinging abuse over his shoulder and vowing revenge. Daniel didn't even bother to listen. Instead, he sheathed his sword and indicated the man's horse.

'It's small recompense for the way he treated you,' he said, 'but it's yours to sell along with the other now. They're both fine animals and will each cost a pretty penny.'

'I can't thank you enough, sir,' said Rachel. 'When I've sold the pair of them, I'll have enough money to pay off all my debts and eat properly for a while.' She nodded at her donkey's huge saddlebags. 'And I'll be able to buy more stock. That's how I make ends meet, you see. I'm a sutler. I sell all sorts of things to the army.' Her face clouded for a moment. 'Don't think too harshly of me, Captain Rawson.'

'Why should I do that?' he asked. 'I admire you. When I came along, you were putting up a good fight against that man.'

'I know what people think about looters. They despise us for picking the pockets of the dead. But that's not what I do. I search for the living, not the deceased. I got to Will Baggott in time to hold him in my arms for a few minutes before he passed away. It was such a comfort to him. And I've done it to so many other brave boys,' she said, wistfully. 'They've been given up as dead and I nurse them back to life for a while so that they can have a woman's arms around them as they slip away. I'm there to give succour. I'm not like the others, Captain,' she went on, earnestly. 'I never take their money – not if they're British soldiers.' Her voice hardened. 'When it comes to the French, of course, it's a different matter. It was them who killed my two husbands and left me to fend for myself. They *owe* me something in return. I'm entitled to take whatever I can from them. After the battle at Oudenarde, it just happened to be that horse.'

'Be more careful when you sell it next time,' he advised. 'And try one of our own regiments. At least you'll be able to haggle in your own language then.'

'You don't disapprove of me, then?' she asked, hopefully.

'Of course not, Rachel – I'm sure that you deserve everything you find, especially as it comes with the compliments of the enemy.' They shared a laugh. 'I'm just grateful that I was riding this way at the right time.'

'I'm more than grateful,' she said, standing on her toes so that she could plant a wet kiss on his lips. 'Thank you, sir. I'll never forget this. You have a lifelong friend in Rachel Rees.'

'I'm glad to hear it,' he said, taken aback by her unexpected surge of affection. 'In times of war, a soldier can never have too many friends. But a new friendship was not all I forged today, I fancy.' He turned to look at the receding figure of the Hessian officer. 'I think I may have made a sworn enemy as well.'

Chapter Two

It was a brilliant plan. Conceived with care and explained in detail, it had the boldness, simplicity and originality characteristic of him. As he addressed the council of war, the Duke of Marlborough was given a respectful hearing. Daniel was there to act as an interpreter and he could see the looks of surprise – not to say amazement – on the faces of some of the Allied generals.

'In essence,' said Marlborough, indicating the map on the table before them, 'we strike where they least expect us, and that is deep into France itself. We should ignore their frontier fortresses, enter the heartland and move eventually towards Paris itself. Just imagine the panic an attack on the French capital would cause. Yes,' he went on, raising a palm to quell protests, 'I know what the objection is. How will we maintain supplies? The answer, gentlemen, is this. A seaborne force already assembled will seize the port of

Abbeville and that will be the base for our supply line.' He saw the doubt in their faces. 'We are masters of marching where we please. Why ignore such a huge advantage?'

'We may march where we please,' argued a Dutch general, 'but we'll not reduce French strongholds as we please, because we have no siege train. Nor are we able to transport one to the frontier by means of canals and rivers. The French still hold Ghent at the junction of the Lys and the Schelde. Vendôme and his army are skulking there and will block any attempts we make to move artillery by water.'

'Then we bring the siege train overland,' said Marlborough. 'We are not unprepared, gentlemen. I've already sent cavalry into northern France to gather supplies and seize cattle and horses. The British navy stands by to await orders. I hardly need remind you that my brother, Admiral George Churchill, is in charge of naval operations, so we may expect complete cooperation. Well,' he continued, spreading his arms, 'what do you think? There are dangers, I grant you, but they are substantially lessened if we strike while the iron is hot and catch the French off guard.' He turned to Prince Eugene of Savoy, sitting close to him. 'What comments would *you* make, Your Highness?'

Pursing his lips, Eugene weighed his words before replying.

'I congratulate you, Your Grace,' he said, politely. 'It is a clever and courageous plan and nobody but you could have devised it. However, I fear that it is too impracticable. We cannot venture into France until we have Lille as a *place d'armes* and magazine. Once that is secure, we will be in a far stronger position. Exciting as it may be, your plan involves too big a risk.'

'I disagree,' said Marlborough. 'On the surface, it may look wild and overambitious but that's all part of the deception. The French will never dream that we'd commit ourselves to an invasion on such a scale, so they will have taken no steps to counter it.'

'I think perhaps that you should call to mind the Swedish army. They showed great daring when they took on a foe like Russia. And what has happened?'

'They are worn out by hunger and fatigue.'

'And hindered by constant ambushes,' said Eugene. 'As a result, King Charles and his army are struggling.'

'We don't face a parallel situation,' contended Marlborough. 'There are similarities, I confess, but they are few in number. We can learn from the mistakes that King Charles made. I visited him last year and saw for myself his army's shortcomings.'

'It had no hospitals, no magazines, no food supplies and no reinforcements close at hand. It is an army that lives on what it finds, fighting a war of *chicane* that is bound to end in defeat. The Russians will use delay and evasion to frustrate them,' said Eugene, 'and that is the strategy the French would employ against us.'

'Not if we disable them by the suddenness of our attack.'

'I am sorry, Your Grace, but I lack your confidence in the reliability of supplies by sea. We might seize Abbeville or any other port, but think of the problems the vessels would encounter during winter. Some would surely founder and others would be uncertain to reach us during the gales they are bound to encounter.' Eugene placed a finger on the map. 'This is where we must start,' he said, collecting murmurs of approval and nods of affirmation from around the table. 'We must lay siege to Lille.'

'But that's precisely what they expect,' said Marlborough. 'According to our latest reports, Marshal Boufflers will be sent there with a sizeable force, and nobody is more experienced at defending a town than the marshal. If we invest Lille, we are in for a long, bitter siege that will be fiendishly expensive and cost us thousands of lives we can ill afford to lose.'

'Nevertheless, I believe it to be our next logical step.'

'I concur with His Highness,' said a Dutch voice. 'Lille is second in importance only to Paris. It's a pearl among fortresses. Take that and we'll send a shiver down the spine of King Louis himself. No matter how long it takes, we must invest Lille.'

There was general agreement around the table. When Daniel had finished translating from the Dutch for Marlborough's benefit, he caught the eye of Adam Cardonnel, secretary to the captain-general. Cardonnel was as disappointed as Daniel. Both of them thought the plan was an example of tactical genius yet it had been rejected out of hand. It was galling. Daniel accepted that the project was a gamble but, if it succeeded, it would surely hasten the end of the war. He'd been fired by the idea of invading France itself, sweeping all resistance aside and forcing Louis XIV to accept peace on Allied terms. It was not to be. While Daniel and Cardonnel concealed their resentment at the way the plan had been discarded, Marlborough started eagerly to discuss the siege of Lille as if that had been his intention all along. As always, he remained unfailingly courteous to those who'd wrecked yet another of his brilliant schemes.

It was only after the council of war ended, and its members had dispersed, that he let his true feelings show. Snatching up the map, he folded it angrily then slapped it back down on the table.

'Hell and damnation!' he exclaimed. 'Don't they *want* us to win this confounded war? Abide by my counsel and we at least have a chance of doing that. Follow their advice and we prolong the hostilities indefinitely. Laying siege to Lille could take us well into winter.'

'It was ever thus, Your Grace,' said Cardonnel, wearily. 'Every time you advocate real enterprise, they retreat into their shells like so many tortoises. It's exasperating.' He glanced apologetically at Daniel. 'Forgive me for casting aspersions on your fellow countrymen, but the Dutch are the real thorn in our sides.'

'I know it only too well,' said Daniel. 'They are far too cautious. I expected them to take fright at such an audacious scheme but I hoped it might win support from Prince Eugene.'

'So did I,' resumed Marlborough, running a hand across a worried brow. 'I have to admit that I was counting on his support. He commands great influence and is an intrepid commander. I thought my plan might appeal to his sense of adventure.'

'Unfortunately,' said Cardonnel, 'he found it *too* adventurous.'

'You can never be too adventurous in war, Adam.'

'After all this time, they should trust your instincts, Your Grace. You presented them with triumphs at Blenheim,

Ramillies and, only weeks ago, at Oudenarde. What more proof do they require of your unrivalled abilities in conducting a campaign?'

Marlborough heaved a sigh. 'I wish I knew!'

'I think I can explain Prince Eugene's position,' suggested Daniel. 'Alone of those present, he recognised the virtues of striking into France. What worried him was the role of the navy. He's accustomed to fighting land battles and has a natural distrust of amphibious warfare. The prince has some justification for his scepticism,' he said. 'Our sailors haven't had an unblemished record of success so far. Look at the way we failed to take the naval base at Toulon last year, for instance. That was a serious setback.'

'I still believe the project would have been feasible,' said Marlborough, sadly. 'Our cavalry met with little resistance in France. They briefly occupied towns like La Bassée, Lens, St-Quentin and Péronne and even raided the suburbs of Arras.'

'We come back to the same old problem,' noted Cardonnel. 'You are hampered by the constraints of leading a coalition army.'

'Had I been commanding a force made up entirely of British regiments, we'd now be surging through France instead of committing all our resources to Lille. As for the navy, I feel sure that they'd provide more than adequate support during summer and autumn. Even as we speak, Major General Erle is moored off the Isle of Wight with eleven embarked battalions. I accept that Abbeville would not be ideal for our purposes in winter,' admitted Marlborough, 'but – with luck and God's blessing – the war might not last that long. We stand a chance of bringing France to its knees before then.'

Cardonnel nodded. 'Instead of which we must brace ourselves for yet another campaign season next year.'

'Where on earth will I find the strength to continue?'

Marlborough emitted another long sigh. Daniel was alarmed to see him looking so tired and forlorn. At a time when he should have been exploiting the tactical initiative gained at Oudenarde, he was unable to carry his allies with him. There was no sign of his famed resilience now. He seemed old, listless and disillusioned. Daniel sought to raise his spirits.

'There is one ray of hope, Your Grace,' he opined.

'I fail to see it,' said Marlborough.

'The French prize Lille above all their fortresses. If they see it under threat, it might provoke them into battle.'

'I think that unlikely, Daniel.'

'Yet it's still a possibility.'

'A very faint one, alas,' said Cardonnel.

'Adam is right,' agreed Marlborough. 'Bringing the French to battle is like chasing moonbeams. Well, can you blame them? Every time they step onto a battlefield, we beat them. They're still smarting from their disaster at Oudenarde. We'll not lure Vendôme into action and Burgundy will not wish to lose even more men. No, Daniel, we are in for yet another protracted siege. However,' he said, trying to shake off his cares, 'let's not get too downhearted. Our course is set and we must follow it.' He straightened his shoulders. 'Let's turn to a more pleasant subject, shall we? I take it that you found time to pay a visit to Amsterdam.'

Daniel smiled fondly. 'I did, Your Grace.'

'And how did you find the dear lady?'

'Amalia was far happier to be in her home than imprisoned in the French camp. She'll not let herself be kidnapped again.'

'Unless the kidnapper happens to be a certain Captain Rawson, that is,' said Cardonnel with a grin. 'I'm afraid that Miss Janssen may not be seeing you again for some time.'

'She understands that,' said Daniel.

'What about my tapestry?' asked Marlborough. 'Her father must have started working on it by now.'

'It will take some time yet, Your Grace. It's intricate work that can't be rushed. Emanuel Janssen and his assistants each have a separate loom so that they can weave individual sections,' explained Daniel. 'Eventually, they'll sew all the different pieces together. Having fought in the battle, I was privileged to help with the design. I vow that you'll be delighted with it. Ramillies has been depicted with uncanny accuracy. It's going to be a masterpiece.'

Emanuel Janssen was a small, skinny, stooping man with silver hair and a beard. Long years of dedication to his craft had rounded his shoulders and dimmed his eyes, obliging him to wear spectacles. Peering through them as he worked from the back of the tapestry, he studied the mirror that showed him the front. Three other looms were in action, so the workshop at the rear of his house reverberated with rhythmical clatter. Two of his assistants had to raise their voices over the noise. The third, Kees Dopff, more of an adopted son than an assistant, had been dumb from birth, but his face was so expressive that he and his employer were able to conduct conversations without resorting to words. Janssen was still sewing meticulously away when he caught sight of his daughter out of the corner of his eye. He broke off immediately, knowing that Amalia would not have interrupted him on a whim. Something of significance must have happened. He could see the glow of excitement in her cheeks

'Let's step outside where it's a little quieter,' he suggested, guiding her back into the house. 'Now, then,' he said when they were out of earshot of the clamour, 'what's going on?'

'A letter has come for you,' she replied, holding it out.

'There's nothing unusual in that, Amalia. I get letters all the time. Couldn't this one have waited?'

'No, Father – it's from England.'

He took it from her. 'Really?'

'Look at the seal. It's from someone of consequence.'

'Then let's see what someone of consequence has to say, shall we?' Breaking the seal, he unfolded the letter then blinked in surprise. 'It's from Her Grace, the Duchess of Marlborough.'

'I could tell by the feel of it that it was important.'

'Then you can read it to me,' he said. 'My eyes are always a trifle blurred after hours at the loom and your command of English is far better than mine.'

'You must thank Daniel for that. He's encouraged me to become fluent. He's helped me with French as well.' She took the missive back and held it to her breast. 'Oh, if only this had come from him!'

Short, slight and fair-headed, Amalia had an elfin beauty that had enchanted Daniel Rawson from the start. Lost momentarily in her thoughts, she forgot that her father was even there.

'Well?' he asked with an amused smile. 'Do I get to

hear the contents or must I read it myself?'

Amalia giggled. 'I'm sorry, Father.' Glancing at the opening sentence, she let out a cry of joy. 'It's an invitation. Since your tapestry of Ramillies is to hang in Blenheim Palace, the duchess has invited you to England to see it being built.'

'What a wonderful treat!'

'She warns you that the palace is far from complete but thinks you'll find it interesting.'

'Then I must accept the invitation,' he decided, 'as long as it's extended to you as well.'

'Oh, yes,' said Amalia, reading on. 'I'm mentioned by name.'

'Let me see.'

Taking it from her for the second time, Janssen perused it with care. Amalia, meanwhile, was many days ahead of him, boarding a ship, sailing across the North Sea, setting foot in England and being driven to Oxfordshire to view the magnificent edifice awarded to the Duke of Marlborough in commemoration of his victory at the battle of Blenheim. She was enraptured. Doubts then began to creep in.

'What will I wear?' she asked with sudden anxiety. 'I've nothing suitable in my wardrobe. And how do I behave in front of a duchess? I'll make all sorts of terrible mistakes and say all the wrong things. I'm so afraid that I'll let you down, Father.'

'You could never do that, Amalia.'

'I'm trembling with nerves already.'

'That will soon pass. We've been invited to see the progress made on the palace, not summoned there so that the duchess can criticise your apparel and click her tongue at your manners. Besides,' he went on, 'you've met her husband a number of times and the duke has always been very gracious to you.'

'His wife may be much more censorious,' she said with concern. 'Daniel has told me a little about her. She's a determined lady with a mind of her own and she doesn't suffer fools gladly.'

He chuckled. 'Since when have you been a fool?'

'The duchess is so close to Her Majesty, the Queen, that they are virtually sisters. Do you see what I mean, Father? It's so daunting. When we get to England, our hostess will be a person who rubs shoulders with royalty.'

'There's nothing remarkable in that,' he riposted with a twinkle in his eye. 'I, too, have consorted with royalty. I lost count of the number of times I saw the king when I was at Versailles. He often spared me a few words – until he learnt that I was not simply there to weave a tapestry for him. We have that consolation,' he added with a laugh. 'Whatever happens, the duchess will not have us thrown into prison.' He put a comforting arm around her. 'Put away all fear, Amalia. You have nothing to be worried about. The duchess will find you as charming and lovely as everyone else does.'

She was uncertain. 'Do you think so, Father?'

He gave a shrug. 'If it causes you such distress, I can see that I'll have to go to England myself.'

'No, no,' she cried, 'I won't be left behind. Give me the letter so that I can read it again.' She snatched it from him. 'It's marvellous news. I can't wait to tell Daniel about it when I next write to him.'

Though he was now attached to Marlborough's staff, Daniel always made time whenever he could to visit his own regiment and see his friends. Chief among them was Sergeant Henry Welbeck, a man who'd known him since the time when Daniel himself had served in the ranks. Lacking the money to purchase a commission, Daniel owed his promotion to repeated acts of heroism in the face of enemy fire. His advancement had thus been strictly on merit. Nothing would induce Welbeck to join the officer class. In his view, they were an odious breed. He retained a barely concealed contempt for those above him, having seen too many of his men killed because of foolish decisions taken in battle by people with no business to be in command. Daniel was the only officer who'd earned his respect and affection.

They met outside Welbeck's tent.

'What news, Dan?' asked Welbeck, puffing on his pipe.

'We are to lay siege to Lille.'

'Even I'd worked that out.'

'What you don't yet know,' said Daniel, 'is that Prince Eugene will be in command with fifty battalions and ninety squadrons, mostly of Dutch and imperial troops.'

'Go on.'

'They are to be supported by a brigade of five British regiments, one of which will be our own dear 24th.'

Welbeck's nose wrinkled with displeasure. 'So we'll be taking orders from a foreigner, will we?'

'Prince Eugene is a gallant soldier.'

'He's far too gallant, in my opinion,' said Welbeck. 'He likes to lead his men into battle and expose himself to unnecessary danger. I'd rather serve under a man like the duke who's sensible enough to conduct affairs from a position of relative safety.'

'His Grace doesn't always hold back,' Daniel reminded

him. 'I was there when he led a charge at Ramillies.'

'It's just as well you *were* there, Dan. My spies tell me that our beloved captain-general was thrown from his horse. If you hadn't been on hand to rescue him, the Grand Alliance would now be under the control of some stupid, half-blind, weak-willed Dutch general with no idea of military strategy.' He bared his teeth in a hostile grin. 'The only thing the Dutch ever do with enthusiasm is to turn tail.'

Smiling tolerantly, Daniel refused to rise to the bait. Welbeck was a stocky man of middle height, with an ugly face given a sinister aspect by the long scar down one cheek. The sergeant's body, as his friend knew, bore even more livid reminders of a soldier's life. In the course of various skirmishes and battles, Welbeck had been shot, stabbed by a bayonet and slashed in several places by a sabre. He bore his injuries without complaint.

'So,' he said, eyeing Daniel up and down, 'while I'm undertaking the siege of Lille with the rest of the regiment, what will Captain Rawson be doing?'

'I'm awaiting orders from on high.'

Welbeck looked up at the sky. 'I didn't realise that you were in touch with the Almighty. You'll be telling me next that you hear voices – just like Joan of Arc.'

'The only difference is that she heard them in French,' said Daniel with a laugh. 'No, Henry, my orders come from closer to the earth. His Grace always dreams up something interesting for me.'

'When is he going to dream up a peace treaty?'

'When – and only when – we've finally won this war.'

Before he could reply, Welbeck noticed someone coming towards them. Daniel recognised the newcomer at once.

It was Rachel Rees, riding a horse and pulling her donkey behind her on a lead rein. She wore the same rough clothing as before but now sported a wide-brimmed hat with feathers stuck in it. When she waved familiarly at them, Welbeck was unwelcoming.

'What, in the sacred name of Satan, have we got here?'

'She's a lady I met on my travels,' said Daniel.

'Then you must travel to some strange places, Dan. Look at her, will you? She didn't get that fat on army food, and what is the woman wearing? I've seen better dressed beggars.'

'Her name is Rachel Rees and she's Welsh.'

'That's even worse!' snorted Welbeck, pulling his pipe from his mouth and tapping it on the sole of his boot to dislodge the tobacco. 'I know we're desperate for recruits, but we're surely not taking on roly-poly ragamuffins like her.'

'Keep your voice down, Henry, and show her some respect.'

'Respect? How can anyone respect a vagabond?'

'Rachel is no vagabond, as you'll find out.'

When she finally reached them, she hopped off the horse and exchanged greetings with Daniel before smiling at Welbeck.

'This is Sergeant Welbeck,' introduced Daniel, 'and I'd better warn you that he's a confirmed misogynist.'

She was baffled. 'What on earth is that?'

'I don't like women,' said Welbeck, bluntly.

'That's only because you haven't met the right one yet,' said Rachel, cheerfully. 'Will Baggott was the same. He was my first husband and a more defiant woman-hater you couldn't wish to meet. Then I came into his life and his eyes were suddenly opened.' She gave a throaty cackle. 'He made up for lost time. Will was a corporal in the Grenadiers until he was killed in action.'

'Did you manage to sell the horses?' asked Daniel.

'Yes, Captain Rawson, and I got a fair price for both of them.'

Welbeck frowned. 'What's this about selling horses?'

'I should explain,' said Daniel. 'Rachel and I met when she was having an argument with a Hessian cavalry officer who'd promised to buy a horse from her. He decided to steal it instead.'

'He tried to steal more than the horse,' she recalled with a grimace. 'If the captain hadn't arrived in time, I'd have been violated. Instead of that, I finished up owning the fellow's horse as well.'

'It was his own fault, Rachel. The long walk back to his regiment would have taught him to behave more honourably in future.'

'He's probably still nursing his wounds.' She turned to Welbeck. 'The captain beat him soundly, then knocked him senseless. He had to stop me from kicking the scoundrel's head in. Anyway,' she continued, putting a hand under the folds of her dress, 'I came to show you my appreciation by bringing you a gift.' She pulled out a dagger. 'This is for you, Captain Rawson.'

The two men were astounded. The dagger had an ornate handle and there were tiny jewels set into the leather sheath. When she drew out the long, razor-sharp blade, it glinted in the sun. Welbeck struck an accusatory note.

'Where did you steal that from?' he demanded.

'I took it from the French major who tried to stab me

with it,' she told him. 'It was after the battle of Ramillies. He was lying on the ground near to death and decided to take me with him. I'd already lost my second husband that day so I was throbbing with anger. I took the dagger from his hand and used it to finish him off.' She smiled grimly. 'That Frenchie had no use for the weapon so I kept it.'

'That's not stealing,' said Daniel. 'It's serendipity.'

'It sounds like thieving to me,' asserted Welbeck.

'And how many things have you picked up on a battlefield?' she challenged. 'If you'd seen a dagger like this, would you have left it lying there for someone else to claim? No, Sergeant Welbeck, you wouldn't. In the wake of a battle, all of you grab whatever souvenirs you can. That's what Ned Granger did – he was my second husband – and he built up quite a collection. Ned was a sergeant as well. He served in the 16th Regiment of Foot.' Sheathing the dagger, she offered it to Daniel. 'Please accept this small token of my undying gratitude.'

'Thank you, Rachel,' said Daniel, taking the weapon and examining it. 'It's a fine piece of work and I'll treasure it.'

'I'd rather you used it to kill more Frenchies. And don't forget what I said,' she added, wagging a finger. 'Whenever you need any help, call on Rachel Rees.' Her eyes flitted to Welbeck. 'The same goes for you, Sergeant. It's clear to me that you're more in need of help than the captain.'

Welbeck bristled. 'Why should I need help?'

'Someone has to change your warped view of women.'

'I don't like them, that's all.'

'Does that mean you despised your mother?'

'Well, no – of course not. She was different.'

'What about your grandmother?'

'What about her?' asked Welbeck.

'I can't believe you hated her as well.'

'She was family – it doesn't count.'

'Ah, I see,' said Rachel, 'you like all the women who belonged to your family and loathe the rest of us. What about religion? If you're a Christian, it must mean you love the Virgin Mary, not to mention all those other good ladies in the Bible. The tally is mounting all the time, isn't it? You don't hate *all* women. There are quite a few you like.'

'It's a fair point, Henry,' said Daniel, enjoying the exchange.

'Do you know what I think?' said Rachel.

'No,' retorted Welbeck, 'and I don't care.'

'You're hiding behind this so-called hatred. The only reason you pretend to detest women is that you're afraid of us.'

Welbeck exploded. 'I detest them because they always get in the way – just as you're doing right now. Women are a distraction in the army. They turn men's heads and make them lose concentration. They lie, they cosset, they badger, they deceive, they demand and they talk a man's ear off. Afraid of women?' said Welbeck with disgust. 'The only thing that scares me is that their tongues never stop wagging.'

'Oh, is that all?' asked Rachel, shaking with mirth.

'Keep away from me,' he warned.

'You talk just like Will Baggott, though his language was much coarser. It took me a long time to win him over but I managed it in the end.' She moved in closer to scrutinise his face. 'You even look a bit like old Will with that same nasty, unfriendly expression. You only ever see it on the faces of poor, cold-hearted men who've never been properly warmed through by a woman.'

Welbeck was pulsing with fury. 'Can you see now why I hate them so much, Dan?' he said, rancorously. 'They're harridans – all of them. I'll speak to you later when we're able to get a word in.' Turning on his heel, he plunged into his tent. 'Goodbye.'

'I think you frightened him off,' said Daniel. 'There are not many people who can make Henry take a backward step.'

'I didn't mean to do that, Captain Rawson. It's just that he did remind me so of my first husband. The only difference is that the sergeant is much better looking than Will Baggott.'

Daniel gasped. 'Henry is *better looking*?'

'Oh, yes,' she said. 'Put a smile on him and he'd look almost handsome in an ugly sort of way. My instincts about men are never wrong. Yes,' she went on, gazing pensively at the tent, 'I might have offered my help to *you*, but Sergeant Welbeck is the one who really deserves it. He needs the magic of a woman's touch in his life.'

CHAPTER THREE

Marshal James FitzJames, Duke of Berwick, arrived in the camp with his entourage and went straight to the quarters of its commander. He was dismayed to find the Duke of Vendôme reclining indolently on a couch with a glass of wine in his hand while attended by a handsome officer whose uniform was unbuttoned. Vendôme, who was as usual scruffily dressed, did not even rise to his feet to greet his visitor. His one concession to the newcomer was to dismiss his companion with a lordly wave of his hand. Buttoning up his uniform and putting down his glass, the man mumbled his apologies to Berwick and left swiftly. Berwick looked after him.

'He's rather young to be a captain,' he observed.

'Raoul Valeran is worthy of his promotion,' said Vendôme, sitting up. 'He's proved himself on the battlefield and is a man on whom I can rely completely. But do sit down, Your Grace,' he went on, indicating a chair. 'May I offer you wine?'

Berwick was brusque. 'No, thank you.'

'Would you care for some other refreshment?'

'I merely came to discuss military matters,' said the other, lowering himself into a chair. 'I expected to find you finalising your strategy, not entertaining a guest.'

'Captain Valeran is a valued friend.'

Berwick understood what that meant. Now in his fifties, Vendôme was notorious for his sexual appetite and would often travel with his latest mistress in tow. When no woman was available, he would take equal pleasure in the company of a man. Evidently, Captain Valeran was his current favourite. Berwick wondered how the smart young officer could bear to get so close to a man whose filthy clothing, spattered with food and wine stains, gave off a noisome smell. Vendôme might be a veteran soldier but his personal habits were offensive to someone as neat and fastidious as Berwick.

'Well,' said Vendôme, lazily, 'I can see that you're upset about something. Speak your mind, I pray.'

'Since I came to Flanders,' declared Berwick, 'I've been appalled at what I found. I first went post-haste to Tournai and gathered up thousands of stragglers from the battle. What they told me was difficult to believe.'

'Do not lay it at my door,' warned Vendôme. 'Had I been in command at Oudenarde, it would not have ended in a rout. In a moment of misguided affection for his grandson, His Majesty saw fit to saddle me with the Duke of Burgundy, a man whose high opinion of himself is not matched by deeds of valour in the field.'

'I served under him and thought him a competent general.'

'One needs more than competence to defeat Marlborough.'

'Yet we outnumbered his army and had choice of ground.'

'Oh, the ground was well chosen, I'll give the duke that. The problem was that he refused to leave it. While some of us fought hand-to-hand with the enemy, the king's grandson observed it all from a distance as if watching from a box at the opera.' Vendôme fiddled with his cravat. 'It is both wrong and dangerous to appoint someone in command simply because he has royal blood in his veins. Oh,' he said with a gesture of apology, 'that was not meant as a jibe at you.'

Berwick nevertheless took it as such. He was very conscious of being the illegitimate son of the Duke of York, later to become King James II of England. His mother had been Arabella Churchill, sister to the very man against whom he was now fighting. He knew that he could expect no avuncular indulgence from the Duke of Marlborough on the battlefield nor would he, in turn, show a nephew's respect for his esteemed relative. Educated in France, he was content to serve in its army and, though still in his early thirties, had risen to the coveted rank of marshal. He was annoyed to be reminded that he was born on the wrong side of the blanket.

'Your achievements in Spain have added to an already sparkling reputation,' said Vendôme, trying to mollify him.

'Thank you,' said Berwick, stiffly.

'You secured a crucial victory at Almanza last year and followed it up by taking Lerida. I've heard it said that you saved the Bourbon dynasty in Spain.'

'That's an exaggeration.'

'In effect, you kept King Philip on the throne there and deserve plaudits for that.' His face was split by a wicked grin. 'I'm tempted to say you need make no such effort to save another of the king's grandsons but that would be too unkind. Now that his shortcomings have been exposed, the Duke of Burgundy may come to his senses.'

Berwick grew impatient. 'I'm here to discuss your plans.'

'My immediate plans involve presenting a true account of the battle of Oudenarde to King Louis. I've already sent some despatches but my version of events – as you will imagine – has been questioned by the duke. Clarification is sought in Versailles.'

'You cannot waste time talking about a battle that's over when more fighting is at hand,' said Berwick, irritably. 'When we first arrived, I'd hoped to pose a threat to the flank and rear of Marlborough's army, but Prince Eugene reached Brussels with his troops and was able to provide cover. Their interest has now shifted to Lille.'

'It must not be allowed to fall,' said Vendôme, seriously. 'That would be a real calamity.'

'The Duke of Boufflers is to oversee its defence.'

'But what sort of force can he muster? Our army is desperately short of men. We lack the numbers to cover every eventuality.'

'Marlborough cannot take Lille without a siege train. Our main task must be to stop it reaching him.'

'It will not be transported by water, that's for certain. As long as we're camped here, we control the rivers and canals. That means it will go by land. A siege train of the requisite size will be several miles long.'

'That will stretch their resources to the limit,' said Berwick. 'Marlborough will not be able to protect it adequately. If we intercept it, we may stop it ever reaching its destination.'

'If we intercept it,' argued Vendôme, 'we must do more than simply stop it. We must capture as many cannon as we can. Our artillery was gravely depleted at Oudenarde.' He rolled his eyes. 'I leave you to guess whose fault that was. My ambition, I tell you now, is to make amends for the fatal errors made by the Duke of Burgundy.'

'France looks to us for a victory. We are in sore need of one.'

'I held Marlborough at bay in Flanders last year and you beat the Allied forces at Almanza. Between us, we have more than enough skill and experience to match the enemy.'

'But not in a pitched battle, I fear,' said Berwick.

'There are other ways to win wars. I would dearly love to accept surrender from Marlborough,' said Vendôme through gritted teeth, 'and there's another delight I'd seek. I'd like to ride back to Paris with the head of a certain Captain Daniel Rawson on a pole.'

Daniel handed over the dagger so that his friend could inspect it.

'It's magnificent!' said Jonathan Ainley.

'Apparently, it belonged to a French major.'

'He must have been blessed with wealth. A weapon like this must have cost a high price. I envy you, Daniel.'

'It was a present from an admirer.'

'Then he must admire you a great deal.'

'The admirer was a lady,' said Daniel, 'and she used the dagger to kill the man who owned it.' Ainley gulped. 'I make her sound more bloodthirsty than she really is. She found the major dying after the battle of Oudenarde and took exception to the fact that he tried to stab her.' Taking the dagger back, he sheathed it. 'His loss was my gain. However, I came here to cross swords with you, not to talk about daggers. Are you ready, Jonathan?'

'Yes,' said Ainley, 'I'm ready for my ritual humiliation.'

The lieutenant was a tall, spindly, pallid man with a beaky nose that attracted all manner of unflattering nicknames. Known for his affability, he was an efficient and dedicated officer who sought to emulate Daniel Rawson, a man he'd elevated to the status of a god. Swordplay was a vital part of their armoury and they both sought to keep their skills in good repair. While he was an able fencer, Ainley lacked Daniel's strength and flair. The longer any bout went on, the more decisively it swung in the captain's favour. Drawing his sword, Ainley prepared himself for defeat.

'You're far too quick and dexterous for me, Daniel.'

'The advantage may be yours this time.'

'Why?' asked Ainley with a hollow laugh. 'Are you going to fight with that dagger instead?'

'I'm not that foolhardy,' said Daniel. 'No, Jonathan, I'm going to hold the sword in my left hand.'

'You'll still be too good for me.'

'It's important to maintain my proficiency with both hands. If my right arm is wounded, I need to be able to defend myself.'

'Then do so now,' invited Ainley, brandishing his sword.

But the practice ended before it had even begun. A

messenger arrived to summon Daniel to the captain-general's quarters and the sword fight had to be abandoned. Daniel shrugged his shoulders.

'I'm sorry about this, Jonathan,' he said.

'Don't be – I'm sighing with relief.'

'I'll be back at the earliest opportunity.'

Ainley sheathed his sword. 'I'll hold you to that.'

As the lieutenant waved his friend off, Daniel followed the messenger on a twisting course through the ranks of tents until he came to Marlborough's quarters. When they came into sight, he recalled what the Dutch dragoon had said about him on the ride through Flanders. Someone in command of a vast coalition force might be expected to maintain palatial quarters, but that was not the case with Marlborough. It was left to people like Prince Eugene to occupy stately accommodation that proclaimed their importance and set them apart from the soldiers they led. Daniel chose to believe that the relative simplicity of Marlborough's quarters could be put down to the fact that he didn't wish to distance himself from those around him. Indeed, he sought to keep in touch as much with the ranks as with his officers, frequently touring the camp and engaging in conversation with the humblest privates. It had earned him the affectionate name of 'Corporal John'. Few commanders in any army were revered as much by their troops.

When he was admitted, Daniel found the captain-general talking to his secretary. Both gave him a cordial welcome. Offered a glass of wine, Daniel took it gratefully and sat down with the others.

'We have work for you,' said Marlborough.

'I had a feeling that you might have, Your Grace.'

'How much do you know about Lille?'

'I know that it's the best fortified town in French Flanders,' said Daniel. 'They call it Vauban's masterpiece because he devised the most ingenious series of defences. He tried to make it invincible.'

'No town is invincible if it is besieged correctly,' said Cardonnel. 'Look at the career of Richard the Lionheart.'

'Yes,' agreed Marlborough. 'He was a master of siege warfare. They said that Taillebourg was impregnable yet it fell to him, as did other strongholds. Though it took all of two years, the siege of Acre in the Holy Land was another triumph.'

'The strange paradox,' Daniel pointed out, 'is that a king who excelled in siege tactics should himself die during one. He expired from a crossbow wound while besieging a castle near Limoges.'

'I see that you know your history, Daniel.'

'I also like to feel that we've made some progress since the time of the Lionheart. Siege trains are vastly more effective now.'

'If one can be brought here intact,' said Marlborough. 'However, that's another problem. The one that confronts us now is that we can see the fortifications around Lille without quite understanding their exact design. To be more exact, we'd like to see them from *inside* the town as well as from outside.'

'Ideally,' said Cardonnel, 'we want Vauban's original plan. It must be somewhere inside Lille. Someone has to find it.'

'Finding it will be difficult enough,' said Daniel, warily, 'but we can't expect them to oblige us by handing it over.

Besides, it must be forty years since Vauban built the defences and the arsenal there. Later additions will have been made. You will surely want details of those as well.'

'We want everything you can get us, Daniel,' said Marlborough, 'including information about their troop numbers and how they intend to repel our attacks. It's going to be the most difficult siege we've ever undertaken. Lille already has natural protection from those unhealthy marshes around the Rivers Deûle and Marque. On three sides out of four, it's within striking distance of the French-held towns of Ypres, Tournai, Douai and Béthune, all of which could send operational support. We are in for an epic struggle.'

'That's nothing new, Your Grace,' said Cardonnel, waspishly. 'You have an epic struggle every time you hold a council of war.' The three of them laughed. 'The assignment may not be as intimidating as it might seem at first glance, Daniel.'

'No,' said Marlborough, taking over. 'Lille has not yet closed its gates for good, and it will be weeks before the peripheral lines of circumvallation are constructed. If you have a plausible reason for getting in, the French will not stop you, and our soldiers will not prevent you from getting out alive.'

Daniel grinned. 'That's reassuring to know.'

'We'll provide you with any forged documents you require.'

'Thank you, Your Grace.'

'All you have to decide is how you intend to proceed.'

'I think I'll start by drinking this,' said Daniel, taking a long sip of wine. 'I need fortifying just as much as Lille.'

'You managed to get into the Bastille,' remembered Cardonnel. 'Gaining access to a town should be far less taxing.'

'That's not my concern. Tracking down the information you want is the real test. Is there nobody inside Lille who could help?'

'Yes,' said Marlborough. 'His name is Guillaume Lizier. He runs a tavern there and will give you food and shelter. Adam will tell you how to find him.' Daniel lapsed into a reverie. It was a full minute before Marlborough interrupted him. 'I can see that you're already wondering in what guise to enter the town. Will it be as Marcel Daron, the wine merchant? That role has served you well in the past, and who is more likely to seek out a tavern keeper than a wine merchant? Are you to become Marcel Daron once more?'

A slow smile spread across Daniel's face. 'Who knows?' he said as an image began to form in his mind. 'When do I have to leave?'

'Go in your own time,' said Marlborough.

'Then I'll wait a day or two, Your Grace. And I'll not be travelling as a wine merchant this time. I fancy that another occupation will serve me better.' He finished his drink and stood up. 'I'll be grateful for those details about Monsieur Lizier.'

'I have them right here,' said Cardonnel, handing him a piece of paper. 'Commit everything to memory then burn it.'

'I will.'

Daniel glanced at the name and the address, wondering how a mere tavern keeper would be able to assist him in such a testing assignment. On the other hand, he'd taken on harder tasks without help from anyone. That gave him confidence, and the notion that he might somehow be able to gain an advantage for the besieging army brought out his sense of duty. The more he considered it, the more he began to look forward to the adventure.

He was about to take his leave when Marlborough picked up a letter that lay on the table amid a pile of documents. He unfolded it.

'This came today from my wife,' he said, 'and contains news that may be of interest to you, Daniel. It seems that Emanuel Janssen and his beautiful daughter are to sail to England. They've been invited to view progress on the building of Blenheim Palace. Janssen's tapestry of Ramillies will hang there one day.'

Daniel needed a few seconds to assimilate the news. He was sad that Amalia would be moving further away from him but his sadness was tempered by the thought of how much she would relish the visit. He rejoiced in her good fortune, hoping that some time in the country where he'd been brought up would give her a better understanding of him. His only regret was that he would not be there to act as her guide. When he imagined how she must have reacted to the invitation, he had to suppress a chuckle. Back in Amsterdam, inside the house he'd been to little more than a week ago, Amalia Janssen would be caught up in a positive whirl of anticipatory delight.

'I'm sorry, Miss Amalia, but it's impossible. I just *couldn't* go.'

'But you must, Beatrix. Your passage is booked.'

'Take one of the other servants.'

'You're far more than a servant to me,' said Amalia, 'and you know it. I couldn't conceive of going all that way without you.'

'My mind is made up. I'll not stir from here.'

'But a great honour has been bestowed on us.'

'On you, perhaps,' said Beatrix, 'but not on me.'

'We'll have the privilege of meeting a duchess and seeing one of the grandest houses in the whole of England. Well,' Amalia corrected herself, 'what there is of it, anyway.'

'Tell me all about it when you get back.'

'Don't be so stubborn, you're coming with us.'

'I can't, I won't, I mustn't. Please don't keep on at me.'

'At least tell me *why* you're so afraid to go.'

'You'll only laugh at me, if I do, Miss Amalia.'

'That's ridiculous. I never mock you. Now – what is it, Beatrix?'

Beatrix Udderzook was a plump, flabby-faced woman in her thirties, with a look of solid reliability that belied her nervousness. She was both maidservant and best friend to Amalia, sharing the joys and disappointments of many years with her. Though there was no great distance between their ages, Beatrix also acted as surrogate mother, guarding and guiding Amalia through life. The maidservant had still not forgiven herself for allowing Amalia to be abducted right under her nose. Beatrix was still tortured by guilt over the incident.

'I had a dream last night,' she said, fearfully.

'There's nothing unusual in that.'

'I dreamt that I was about to drown in the sea.'

'We all have dreams like that,' said Amalia.

'This was so *real*, Miss Amalia,' said Beatrix. 'In fact,

I don't think it was a dream at all. It was a premonition. That's why I daren't leave dry land.'

'And were you the only person to drown?'

'Yes.'

'What about the rest of us?'

'I don't understand what you mean.'

'Well,' said Amalia, teasingly, 'if *you* are to drown when you sail to England, so are the rest of us. The only way you could perish is if the ship went down with all its crew and passengers. Yet *I* didn't have a premonition that that would happen and nor did Father, as far as I know. Neither did anyone else who'll be boarding that vessel or none of them would dare to go to sea.' She took Beatrix by the shoulders. 'It was just a silly dream, that's all.'

Beatrix trembled. 'It scared me so much.'

'I'm often frightened by bad dreams. Then I wake up and realise that I haven't been harmed in any way so I dismiss them as nightmares.' She kissed the maidservant on the cheek. 'I *need* you to come with us, Beatrix. Don't you want to see England? Don't you want to be able to boast to the others that you met the Duchess of Marlborough?'

'Yes, I do,' conceded Beatrix.

'Who will look after me if you're not there?'

'The master will do that.'

'Father will be too busy to act as my chaperone all the time. I need the company of a woman. Oh,' said Amalia, earnestly, '*please* tell me you'll come with us.'

Beatrix was undecided. Torn between duty to Amalia and fear of the consequences, she chewed her lip and pondered. For her part, Amalia was deeply upset at the idea of travelling without her. None of the other servants had endured as many hardships with her as Beatrix, and none deserved to enjoy the privilege now being offered. Since the invitation had arrived, Amalia had been transported with delight. She always moved about the house with the grace of a dancer but now she seemed to be floating on air. She'd blithely assumed that Beatrix would be as thrilled as she and her father. Instead, the maidservant was refusing to step aboard a ship.

'That's it, then,' said Amalia, changing tack. 'I'll tell Father that we must decline the invitation. It will upset the duchess but that can't be helped. She, of course, will inform her husband of our decision and the duke will surely pass on the news to Captain Rawson.' She shook her head in mock desolation. 'He'll be very hurt by the tidings. He made me promise that, if ever I went to England, I should visit the farm where he was brought up. That is now out of the question, for we'll never get a second invitation. Father must write today,' she added, as if about to leave. 'He must explain that it's impossible for any of us to go because one of the servants had a bad dream.'

'That would be terrible,' wailed Beatrix, close to tears. 'It's an honour for you and your father. You *must* go, Miss Amalia. I can't spoil your visit. It would be on my conscience for the rest of my life.'

'And supposing *we* drown while you sit safely here?'

'What a dreadful thought!'

'It's one that would never enter my head because I have more faith in our sailors than you. We're a trading nation, Beatrix. Ships come and go every day without sinking. The Dutch are amongst the finest mariners in the world.'

'I know that.'

'Then put your trust in them. It's summer, the best possible time to go on a voyage. There's nothing whatsoever to stop us arriving safely in England.'

'What about sailing back?'

Amalia laughed. 'You're determined to drown one way or another, aren't you?' she said. 'But it's simply not going to happen. Don't take my word for it. Go down to the harbour and talk to the sailors. They'll reassure you. Or sail up and down the canal a few times to get over your fears.'

Beatrix was still reluctant to go. At the same time, she didn't wish to be responsible for the whole venture being abandoned. The mention of Daniel Rawson had weighed with her. When Amalia and her father had been rescued from France, Beatrix had been with them. She was eternally grateful to Daniel for saving their lives and had grown very fond of him. Wanting to keep his friendship, she feared that she might lose it if he heard that she was to blame for the failure to get to England. Pressure on her was steadily growing until she could resist it no longer.

'Very well,' she consented. 'I'll go, after all.'

'That's marvellous!' said Amalia, embracing her.

'As long as I don't have that same dream again.'

'Dream instead about riding through England. Have some happy dreams for a change. Oh, Beatrix, we're going to have the most wonderful time of our lives!'

New recruits were needed all the time in the British army to replace those who'd been killed or wounded so badly that they were effectively discharged. Few men actually volunteered for service so they had to be forced to risk their lives in a war against the French by a combination of money, bullying, trickery and false promises. Magistrates were useful recruiting sergeants, sending criminals off to the army instead of letting them fill up the prisons back in England. What people like Henry Welbeck often ended up with, therefore, were thieves, forgers, drunks and other highly unsuitable new recruits. His task was to transform them into part of a disciplined fighting force. As he surveyed the latest batch, he could see that he would have to work exceptionally hard this time. Eight ragged individuals stood resentfully before him.

'I'm Sergeant Welbeck,' he barked, 'and I'm the only person who can save you from being killed by the French. You must obey me or I'll tear you apart limb by limb and feed your carcasses to the crows. Is that understood?'

Most of them were already afraid of him, avoiding his gaze as he ran his eyes along the line. He was met by only one challenging stare. It came from a tall, gangly man in his thirties with unkempt hair, a tufted beard and a broken nose. Welbeck stepped up to him.

'Did you want to say something?' he asked.

'Yes, Sergeant – where are the women?'

'Silence!' bawled Welbeck as the others burst out laughing. He stood very close to the man who'd just spoken. 'What's your name?'

'Ben Plummer, Sergeant.'

'Then let me tell you something, Ben Plummer. This is the British army. There *are* no women. You're here to fight for glory not to dip your wick in some pox-ridden trull.'

'I only choose the ones without pox,' said Plummer, gaining another laugh from the others. 'I have standards, Sergeant.'

'So do I,' said Welbeck, warningly, 'and something tells

me that you are going to fall well below them. Why did you join the army?'

'It was the only way to stay out of prison.'

'And why would you have been sent there?'

'I was charged with running a disorderly house, Sergeant.'

Welbeck's eyes blazed. 'Well, lads,' he said, 'do you see what we have here? Ben Plummer was a pimp, an ugly scab on society, a man who made his odious living by leading poor women astray. You can bid farewell to all that, Benjamin. The army is no disorderly house. Order reigns supreme here. Remember that. When I give an order, you obey it. Is that clear, you lousy, rotten pimp? Speak up, man – is it?'

Plummer was bold. Folding his arms, he gave Welbeck a smile that comprised insolence, defiance and disrespect in equal measure. It did not stay on his face for long. Welbeck hit him with a fearful punch that dislodged his front teeth and sent him sprawling to the ground. Blood oozed from his mouth. The sergeant indicated two of the men.

'Pick him up!' he yelled. 'Pick up that pimp so that I can hit him harder this time.' They dragged Plummer to his feet but all the fight had gone out of him. Welbeck grabbed him by the throat. 'Are you ready to obey orders now?' he barked. Plummer nodded and brought up a hand to stem the flow of blood from his mouth. 'That's better.' He stood back to look along the line. 'Would anyone else like my services as a dentist? I remove teeth free.' There were some nervous grins. 'Good. I think we're making progress. At the moment, you look like the sweepings of the vilest slums in England but that will change. I'm going to turn you into soldiers.' He raised his voice. 'Private Hain!'

A soldier marched out from behind a nearby tent. Dressed as an infantryman, he was wearing a tricorned hat, leather shoes, white breeches and gaiters, and a red coat embellished with the linings and facings of the 24th Regiment of Foot. On his back were a knapsack, cooking pot and cloak. He stood to attention in front of the men, looking immaculate beside him.

'Believe it or not,' said Welbeck, 'Private Hain was just like you when he first came to me. He was caught stealing horses and decided that army life was preferable to being hanged from the nearest tree. He had even more to say for himself than Ben Plummer here. Isn't that true, Private Hain?'

'Yes, it is, Sergeant.'

'You were rowdy and disobedient.'

'Yes, I was, Sergeant.'

'And what are you now?'

'I like to think that I'm a good soldier, sir.'

'Thanks to me, you're a very good soldier. Look at him, all of you. That's what you'll all strive to be. I'll wave my magic wand and turn you all into good soldiers just like Private Hain. Note him well. He wears cross-belts and carries a flintlock and a bayonet. He also has twenty-four cartridges, giving him two dozen chances to kill a Frenchie. In all, he is carrying fifty pounds and that requires him to be fit. How did you come to be so fit, Private Hain?'

'You drilled us every day, Sergeant.'

'And what did I teach you?'

'You taught us how to march properly and how to conduct ourselves bravely in battle. You instructed us in how to fire two shots a minute, Sergeant.'

'I taught you how to kill the enemy before they kill you. That's what the rest of you, including Plummer, must learn. Let me give you three words to remember – listen, learn, obey. What are they?'

'Listen, learn, obey, Sergeant,' mumbled the others.

'I want to hear our pimp say it on his own.'

Plummer was still in pain. 'Listen, learn, obey,' he said.

'Forget all about women – especially the kind *you* employed. They don't exist here. I, on the other hand, do exist and I'll take very good care of you. Oh, and before you even think of running away,' he said with a grin, 'I should warn you that deserters are always caught and hanged. Oddly enough, they never try to desert us after that.'

After putting the fear of death into them, Welbeck spent hours working on basic drills. Hopeless at first, they slowly improved and his cold sarcasm eventually eased off. By the time they were dismissed, the men realised that their lives had changed irremediably for the worse. Welbeck reserved a final word for Ben Plummer.

'Are you still thinking about women?' he asked.

'No, I'm not, Sergeant,' said Plummer, mouth still on fire.

'The army has saved you from their clutches.'

'I see that now, Sergeant.'

'Women are worse enemies than the French. They'll sap your strength and take your mind off this great enterprise of winning a war. They destroy and corrupt. They steal a man's soul. You may not think it now, Ben Plummer, but the day will come when you thank me for keeping you away from women of all kinds.'

Plummer was not convinced. 'Yes, Sergeant,' he murmured.

'What were those three words again?'

'Listen, learn, obey.'

'Good man,' said Welbeck, patting him on the cheek and producing a groan of pain. 'You've still got plenty of teeth left to eat our delicious army food. Now go off and join the others. Corporal Jenner will look after you.'

Hand over his sore mouth, Plummer scampered gratefully off. Welbeck watched him go, satisfied that he'd stamped his authority on the latest sorry group of recruits. There'd be little time to turn them into fighting soldiers before they were involved in action but he was used to that. All the shouting had left Welbeck with a dry throat. He decided to have a drink before smoking his pipe. When he got back to his tent, a surprise lay in store. Not only was there a fresh flagon of beer awaiting him, there was a pouch of tobacco that he'd never seen before. Welbeck had no idea who had put them there and racked his brain in search of potential benefactors. None came easily to mind. The beer was very welcome and he took a long swig of it but it was the tobacco that intrigued him. Opening the pouch, he sniffed inside. The aroma made him sigh with pleasure. It was his favourite brand.

CHAPTER FOUR

Lieutenant Erich Schlager, the Hessian cavalry officer, was not a man to let any wrongs inflicted upon him go unanswered. Vengeful by nature, he always struck back hard at real or imagined slights. His confrontation with a British officer had involved far more than a slight and the memory of it was a constant flame inside his head. Schlager had not only lost a fine horse he'd intended to steal from the woman trying to sell it, he'd been prevented from taking his pleasure by force. Beaten and shamed in front of her, he'd been robbed of his own horse and compelled to walk several miles back to his camp where he'd had to endure the jeers of his fellow officers. Instead of coming back with two battle-trained horses, he had none at all, a severe handicap for someone in a cavalry regiment.

Bent on retribution, all that Schlager had was a name that the woman had mentioned – Captain Rawson. It was, however, a start and it gave him hope. Somewhere in one of the many British regiments forming part of the Allied army was the person he was after. All that Schlager had to do was to track him down before hostilities broke out again. To that end, he instructed a man to conduct a search on his behalf and he waited impatiently for tidings. Meanwhile, even though he'd acquired a new mount, he had to put up with continued mockery in the camp. Captain Rawson had turned him into a figure of fun and that was unforgivable.

At length the news finally came. It was brought to him by a short, whiskery, weasel-faced man with eyes unusually close to each other. He was licking his lips at the thought of his reward.

'Did you have any luck?' demanded Schlager.

'Yes, I did, Lieutenant.'

'Go on.'

'I tracked down Captain Daniel Rawson.'

'Where will I find him?'

'He's in the 24th Regiment of Foot,' said the man, 'and he's well spoken of by everybody.'

Schlager scowled. 'Not by me.'

'There's something else you should know, sir. Captain Rawson is part of the Duke of Marlborough's staff.' Schlager's eyebrows shot up in astonishment. 'By all accounts, he's something of a hero.'

'I don't care who he is – I want him.'

'Have I done well, sir?' asked the man.

'Find out where he is.'

'But I've just done that, Lieutenant. You promised me payment.'

'All that you've told me so far is the name of his regiment.'

'There's more,' said the man. 'Five British regiments have been assigned to Prince Eugene, who'll be your own commander during the siege. The 24th is one of them.'

'What use is that if Captain Rawson is not there?'

'But he may be.'

'Find out for definite.'

'It won't be easy, sir. I'm only a civilian. What I've learnt so far came from chatting to soldiers off duty. I had to buy more than a drink or two to get the information,' he went on, extending a palm. 'I'm out of pocket. I need the money I'm owed.'

Schlager was curt. 'You'll get nothing at all until you tell me how I can reach this heroic captain. Get me details. When you do that,' he said, dangling a bribe, 'I'll pay you twice the amount I offered before. Will that content you?'

'Yes, sir,' replied the man, obsequiously.

'If he's part of Marlborough's staff, he'll have quarters nearby. Tell me exactly where they are and your work is done.'

'Thank you, Lieutenant.'

'Well,' snapped Schlager, 'don't just stand there. Be quick about it, man. We could be moved from here at any moment. I need to locate Captain Rawson *now*. Go and discover where he is.'

'Yes, sir, I will.'

The man scurried off as if his heels had been set alight.

'Have you ever thought of getting married again, Rachel?' he asked.

'Oh, no,' she said, 'that would be tempting fate. I've

already buried two husbands. I couldn't bear the pain of seeing another one being lowered to the ground.'

'Supposing you only *pretended* to be married?'

She chortled merrily. 'I've done that a number of times, Captain Rawson – especially in cold weather when a woman needs company. They've been husbands for one night or maybe two, if I've taken a fancy to them.' Her grin became a frown. 'Don't look down on me for it, sir. It goes against my nature to be a nun. I'm a true Christian but I'm also a warm-blooded woman. I have needs.'

'How would you like to pretend to be married once more?' When he saw her features glow with delight, he hastened to explain. 'Don't misunderstand me, Rachel. That was not a proposal from me. I'm already spoken for. I'd only pretend to be your husband.'

'But that's what the others did.'

'There's only so far the pretence must go.'

Her face fell. 'I knew that it was too good an offer to believe.'

'How do you feel about the French?'

She growled. 'I hate them. They widowed me twice in a row.'

'What would you do to get back at them?'

'Anything at all,' she declared, bunching her fists. 'Give me a musket and I'll march in the front line.'

'I had something rather more subtle in mind,' he said. 'We are, as you're undoubtedly aware, besieging Lille. For reasons I can't divulge, I need to get inside the town for a while. You might help me do that.'

Rachel blinked. 'How?'

'If I approach the place on my own, I have to concoct

a story to get me through the gates. Whereas, if the two of us ride up with a load of wares, everyone will see what our purpose is.'

'I don't want to sell anything to the French unless it's poison.'

'You won't have to, Rachel,' he said. 'Once inside, you can stay quietly out of the way while I go about my business.'

'And what business is that, Captain Rawson?'

'I'm not at liberty to tell you.'

'Will it be dangerous?'

He was impassive. 'It could be.'

'Does that mean it will be dangerous for me as well?'

'There is a risk involved,' he admitted, 'but it's one I hoped you were brave enough to take. This is important work and it might help to shorten the length of the siege. Besides, I thought you might be interested to see the inside of Lille. I certainly am.'

Rachel had grave misgivings. She knew how well fortified the town was and she feared that, once inside, she might be trapped there indefinitely while the Allies pounded away with their cannon. The last thing she wished to do was to present an inadvertent target to her own soldiers. Her instinct was to decline the offer but she didn't wish to let Daniel down. There were obligations to fulfil. He'd saved her from a violent assault and given her the Hessian officer's horse to sell. It had brought a very good price, as did the horse already in her possession. Without Daniel's assistance, she'd have ended up with nothing but bruises and a sense of shame. Both horses would now be encamped with the Hessian cavalry and Rachel would have no means of redress.

Her debt to the British captain was enormous and it could not be discharged by the gift of a French dagger, however costly it might be.

Riding into an enemy stronghold would be hazardous but she'd coped with many hazards as she scoured a battlefield, climbing over mounds of dead soldiers and horses, trying to ignore the hideous sights and the overwhelming stench, avoiding the desperate lunges from dying Frenchmen and warding off scavengers who thought she was after their booty. Every time she'd gone to show some tenderness to a British casualty, she'd put herself in jeopardy yet always come through unharmed. This time, at least, she wouldn't be alone. She'd have someone to shield her and had been given vivid proof of Daniel's ability to do that. And even though she might not share his bed, Rachel would nevertheless savour the thrill, if only for a short time, of pretending to be his wife. A visit to Lille was not as forbidding as it had first appeared to her.

'What must I do, Captain Rawson?' she wondered.

'The first thing is to forget my name,' he told her. 'From now on, I am Alain Borrel and you are Madame Borrel. You married me when I left the French army as an invalid. We scratch a living as sutlers.'

'Rachel Borrel,' she mused. 'I like the sound of that.'

'How much French can you speak?'

'Enough to get by,' she said. 'It's easier to learn than German. Some of the French words are very similar to those in Welsh. Look at 'window', for instance. In French, it's *fenêtre* and in Welsh it's *ffenestr*.'

'I don't expect you to pretend to be a French matron. You're the Welsh wife of Alain Borrel, citizen of Paris and former soldier. If anything should happen to me, however, I wanted to be sure that you have enough command of the language to hold a conversation.'

'I do, Captain Rawson… Oops!' She gave a laugh. 'I should have called you Alain.'

'Does that mean you agree to come?'

'Yes – when do we go?'

'I'll let my beard grow for a couple of days first.'

'But I prefer you clean-shaven.'

'You have no choice in the matter,' he said. 'I have to look very different. Captain Daniel Rawson is not exactly unknown to the French. There's always a faint chance that someone will recognise me. The less I look like him, therefore, the better.' He kissed her gently on the cheek. 'Thank you so much for doing this, Rachel. You could be performing a very valuable service for us.'

'I'm always at your beck and call, Alain.'

'I'll hold you to that, Madame Borell. Now then, when it's time to go, where will I find you?'

She chortled again. 'I'll be waiting for my husband.'

It was Amalia Janssen who began to have cold feet about the voyage. When she reached the harbour with her father and her maidservant, she was taken aback by the tumult. The quays and the vessels were swarming with people, making as much noise as they possibly could, the hullabaloo intensified by the unrelenting cries of the gulls as they floated on the wind or swooped low over the water. Every dog in Amsterdam also seemed to have turned up to swell the cacophony. Emanuel Janssen was one of Europe's leading tapestry-makers but he was just another passenger now. His status had vanished completely. Amalia was shocked by the lack of respect he got as they were herded onto the ship by a rough-looking member of the crew. Even while moored, they were bobbing up and down. The stiffening breeze was blowing the curls that peeped out from under Amalia's bonnet and a sharp tang invaded her nostrils.

Ironically, Beatrix seemed to be unperturbed by it all.

'Oh, I'm so glad that I decided to come,' she said.

Amalia winced. 'I thought it would be more romantic than this.'

'There's no romance in sailing over the sea,' said Janssen with a grin. 'Wait until we are hit by a squall.'

'I thought the weather would be fine at this time of year, Father.'

'Summer storms can come when least expected.'

'Don't worry, Miss Amalia,' said Beatrix. 'I'll take care of you.'

It was a complete reversal of their positions. Amalia had anticipated looking after Beatrix, giving her affection and reassurance throughout a voyage that would unnerve her from start to finish. Yet the many things upsetting Amalia seemed to have no effect on the maidservant. Unlike her mistress, she was not worried by the tilting deck, continual din, or the lecherous grins and knowing nudges of the crew. To be surrounded by so many crudely inquisitive sailors unsettled Amalia. She felt as if she were being stripped naked by their burning eyes. It brought a blush to her cheeks.

When the ship finally set sail, however, everything changed. The sun blazed down, the prow cut cleanly through the water and the crew were too busy hoisting the sails to notice any of the passengers. While Beatrix and her father began to feel a trifle queasy, Amalia had no discomfort. As the three of them watched Amsterdam receding slowly behind them, she adjusted quickly to the motion of the deck. Timbers creaked, the sea swished by and a flock of gulls bade them farewell. She was embarking on an adventure and was determined to relish every second of it. They were well clear of land before her companions felt ready for conversation.

'How are you, Amalia?' asked Janssen.

'I'm fine,' she replied. 'What about you, Father?'

'My stomach is rather unsettled at the moment.'

'So is mine,' complained Beatrix. 'I feel sick.'

She was not the only one. Two other passengers had already vomited into the sea and a third was about to do so. As the waves splashed against the hull, spray came up to drench their faces. Beatrix decided to go below deck, working her way carefully along the bulwark before descending the steps. Janssen turned to his daughter.

'What are you most looking forward to, Amalia?'

'The sheer excitement of being in England,' she said. 'Daniel has told me so much about it.'

'We'll make sure we visit Somerset while we're there.'

'I know how to find the farm where he grew up and I'd like to lay some flowers on his father's grave. It's what Daniel always does whenever he returns to England.'

'That's very thoughtful of you.'

'What about you, Father? What do you intend to do?'

'Well,' he said, 'first and foremost, we must call on the Duchess of Marlborough so that I can show her the design for the tapestry, then get some idea of where it will hang. It's not the first commission I've had from England. Some of my work is already on show there and I'd like to visit one or two of the houses where it is. We'll have a carriage at our disposal so must make best use of it.'

'Beatrix wants to see London.'

Janssen laughed. 'With respect to Beatrix, this trip has not been arranged primarily for her benefit. On the other hand, we couldn't possible go to England without visiting its capital city, so her wish will be granted.'

'I'm longing to write to Daniel about our exploits. There'll be so much to tell him.'

'Don't get ahead of yourself, my dear. We haven't even crossed the North Sea yet.' He put a hand to his stomach. 'I can't say that I'm enjoying this stage of the journey so far.'

'Hopefully, the discomfort will soon wear off,' she said. 'I think you're better off on deck in the fresh air. It's very bracing.'

He pulled a face. 'I'll take your word for it.'

Janssen turned to gaze at the tiny sails of a ship that had just appeared on the horizon, leaving Amalia alone with her thoughts. It was not long before Daniel came into her mind and she felt sad that her first visit to England could not be with him beside her to act as a guide. She wondered where he was at that moment, what he was doing and how much danger he was courting. Looking back at her, Janssen saw her faraway expression.

'Daniel is a good soldier,' he said. 'Don't worry about him.'

'There are lots of good soldiers and many of them get killed.'

'He has something very special to live for, Amalia.'

She squeezed his hand. 'Thank you, Father.'

'Would you rather he was a tapestry-maker?'

'Oh, no,' she cried. 'It's a worthy occupation, as you know better than anyone, but it's not as thrilling as being a soldier. I wouldn't change Daniel in any particular. I love him just the way that he is.'

It was unlikely that Amalia Janssen would even have recognised him at that point in time, still less have approved of his face besmirched with grime, his prickly stubble, his crumpled hat and his tattered clothing. Had she seen him hobbling along with the aid of a walking stick, she'd have taken him for someone much older. The disguise fooled Henry Welbeck as well. When he spotted the two figures coming slowly towards him in the camp, he spared the man only a cursory glance. It was the portly woman beside him who caught the sergeant's attention and ignited his ire. He held up a decisive hand to stop her.

'Come no further,' he ordered. 'You don't belong here.'

'I only came to bid you adieu,' she said, amiably. 'You can spare me a moment, can't you, Sergeant?'

'No, I can't. Now take yourself off.'

'I thought that you and I were friends.'

'Then you thought wrong,' he said, sticking out his jaw. 'I have no female friends. I've told you why.'

'But I had the feeling that you liked me.'

'I abhor all women, especially your kind.'

'And what exactly *is* my kind, Henry Welbeck?' she said, hands on hips. 'Go on. Swear, if you must. My two husbands were soldiers, remember. There are no curses I haven't heard before.'

'Disappear!' he yelled, pointing a finger. 'And take this miserable vagrant with you.'

'That's a very unkind thing to say of Captain Rawson.'

Welbeck was bewildered. 'Is that *you*, Dan?' he asked, peering at him. 'What on earth are you dressed like that for?'

'I wanted to put you to the test,' said Daniel. 'If I can deceive my best friend, I can deceive anyone.'

'I just can't believe that it's you.'

Rachel beamed. 'Yet you recognised me.'

'Only too well,' said Welbeck. 'Why did you have to bring her, Dan? You know my opinion of women.'

'This is no ordinary woman, Henry. You're speaking of my wife.'

'That's me,' said Rachel with a curtsey. 'Madame Borrel.'

Knowing that he could trust Welbeck implicitly, Daniel told him of his assignment and explained the purpose of the disguises. It made the sergeant regard Rachel with a measure of respect. If she was willing to enter an enemy stronghold, he could see that she must have courage. He just wished that she wouldn't keep smiling at him in such a warm and familiar way.

'How long will you be away, Dan?' he asked.

'For as long as it takes,' replied Daniel.

'What if they find out who you really are?'

'I'll make sure that never happens.'

'But even if it does, you'll have an advantage. Being an officer, you'll fetch a tidy sum.'

'I don't understand,' said Rachel.

'That's because you've never seen a cartel for the exchange of prisoners of war,' said Welbeck. 'It lists the amount of money each rank is worth. As a captain, Dan would need a sizeable ransom. For lower orders like me,' he added with asperity, 'the enemy will probably pay to get rid of us.'

'I won't rely on any exchange of prisoners,' said Daniel. 'In the unlikely event that I'm captured, I'll expect you to come and rescue me, Henry.'

Welbeck snorted. 'You're out of luck, Dan!'

'You saved me once before from French hands.'

'That was much easier because you were travelling along a road in a waggon. How, in the name of all that's holy, could I get inside Lille to bring you out?'

'I'm sure you'd think of something, Henry.'

'Don't forget me,' said Rachel. 'I'd want to be rescued as well, Sergeant, or do you object to saving women in distress?' Welbeck was temporarily lost for words and it made her cackle. 'There you are,' she continued, 'you don't hate us as much after all, or you'd have told me you'd leave me there to rot.'

'I daren't put into words what I really think,' he said, crisply.

'We'll have to make sure that the situation doesn't arise,' decided Daniel. 'My aim is to get in and out of the town as quickly as we can. These clothes are starting to stink. I'll want to get back in uniform immediately.'

'Let me know how you get on, Dan.'

'We will,' said Rachel, chirpily.

'I wasn't talking to you.'

'I heard you all the same, Henry.'

'And you've no right to call me by my first name.'

'As a friend, I think I have every right.'

'That's a fair point,' noted Daniel.

'But this woman is no friend of mine.'

'You're only saying that,' she purred, patting him on the arm. 'Will Baggott said exactly the same words to me except that he added a few nastier ones as well. Yet, in the end, he came to see me for what I was and we had a very happy marriage. You ought to try being happily married, Henry. It's the greatest pleasure known to man.'

'Then it's one that Henry will have to forego,' said Daniel, seeing the glint in his friend's eye and wishing to prevent an argument from developing. 'We must be on our way, Madame Borrel. I want to be out of Lille well before the bombardment begins. Goodbye, Henry.'

'Good luck, Dan!' said Welbeck.

'I hope that goes for me as well,' said Rachel but she got no answer. 'No? That's a pity because I fancy I'll need all the luck I can get. Goodbye, Henry. Enjoy your pipe.'

She and Daniel turned round and headed off together. Rachel bustled along in her usual purposeful manner while Daniel limped beside her on his walking stick. Welbeck watched them go before returning to his tent and absent-mindedly reaching for his pipe. He was about to open the tobacco pouch when he heard once again the last words that Rachel had said to him. He recoiled slightly as if from a blow. The pouch suddenly felt hot in his hands. Tossing it onto the camp bed, he lurched out of the tent in a state of confusion.

The Duke of Marlborough had removed his periwig so that he could put both hands close to his pounding head. He always suffered from migraines after a battle but they seemed to be coming with more regularity now. It was worrying.

He was ill, hurt and dejected. Only his secretary and his physician were ever allowed to see him in such a state. For everyone else, the mask of capability was kept firmly in place. Nobody saw even a glimpse of his weakness, his doubts and his periods of despair. Marlborough was resting in his quarters while Adam Cardonnel worked quietly at the table, reading and answering correspondence and doing his best to take the weight off the captain-general's shoulders. Marlborough looked across at him.

'You work too hard, Adam,' he said.

'I got that habit from you, Your Grace.'

'Then it's a bad one. Look where it's got me. I've still two years to go before I reach sixty yet I already have one foot in the grave. I should have become a gentleman farmer and lived a life of ease.'

'You won't find many farmers calling it a life of ease,' said Cardonnel. 'They're at the mercy of the weather and that can be a cruel master. The French have had a dreadful harvest this year – on and off the battlefield. You made the right decision, Your Grace.'

'Did I?'

'You were born to be a soldier.'

'I actually thought that was a blessing at one time,' confided Marlborough, 'but I'm beginning to view it in its true light as a curse. My life has been a series of manoeuvres, counter-manoeuvres, councils of war, sudden offensives, sieges, skirmishes, battles, advances, retreats and betrayals by conniving politicians back home in England. What do I have to show for all those years in combat? It's insufferable. I am under siege just as surely as Lille is, surrounded by generals who resent my being in command or who are too timid to accept any of the daring strategies I put forward. There's no respite. Fresh responsibilities are loaded onto me every day and enemy forces threaten at every turn. It's no wonder my head is splitting as if it's been struck by a cannonball.'

'The pain will ease off in time, Your Grace.'

'That only means I have to climb back on the treadmill.'

'As a rule, you leap willingly onto it.'

'What clearer sign of madness could there be?'

A voice called from outside, making Cardonnel rise to his feet.

'Wait a moment,' he said, giving Marlborough ample time to replace his wig and adjust his clothing. 'Very well – you may come in.'

A courier entered, took a despatch from a leather pouch and handed it over to the secretary. A nod sent him out again. Opening the despatch, Cardonnel read its contents.

'What does it say?' asked Marlborough.

'Wait until you are ready for the treadmill again.'

'If it's important news, I want to hear it this minute. Does it concern the convoy?'

'It does, Your Grace.'

'Where is it?'

Cardonnel passed the despatch to him. 'It's reached Menin without the least annoyance.'

'God be praised!'

'How is your headache now, Your Grace?'

'It's starting to fade already, Adam.' He read the despatch and slapped his thigh. 'William Cadogan is a genius. I knew that he'd get that siege train through.'

'There's still some way to go,' Cardonnel reminded him,

'and it's moving slowly. You can't transport artillery of that size at speed.'

It was the first of two convoys coming from Brussels and hoping to travel the seventy miles to Lille without being intercepted. Vast and cumbersome, it required the services of a multitude of horses and mules. It stretched over such a long distance that, even with its protective army, it was vulnerable to attack. Somehow the French had failed to seize the initiative. Marlborough sought to explain the fact.

'Vendôme is too lazy and Burgundy too slow. They spend so much time bickering that they cannot reach a prompt decision. As for my nephew,' he went on, 'Marshal Berwick must be still trying to find his way around Flanders. We've been very fortunate, Adam.'

'I think it appropriate that they should pause in Menin, another town that was fortified by Vauban.'

'And fortified extremely well,' complimented Marlborough, 'until we invested it two years ago. The garrison fought bravely but their task was hopeless. We prevailed in the end. I spent some time in the trenches myself and it was so gratifying to see a white flag planted on the breach. This augurs well, Adam. It lifts my spirits.'

'There's plenty of room on the treadmill, Your Grace.'

'Then move aside while I step back on.' He waved the despatch. 'These are glad tidings indeed. We can now rely on having at least part of our siege train. All we require now are precise details of what we are up against and we must trust that Captain Rawson will acquire them.'

'I have every confidence in him,' said Cardonnel. 'You

could not have chosen an abler man for the assignment. My guess is that Daniel is already inside the town, taking stock of its defences.'

It had been more difficult to get into Lille than Daniel had anticipated. Security at the gates had been tightened and he was interrogated for several minutes before he and Rachel were admitted. The soldiers on duty had been sceptical about his claims to having served in the army until he gave them detailed accounts of some of the battles in which he'd fought. What Daniel did not tell them, of course, was that he was wearing a British uniform at the time. Once inside the town, they made their way through a maze of streets and alleys until they reached the *Coq d'Or*, a tavern near the heart of Lille. Judging by the sounds of merriment coming from inside, it was a popular place. Riding a horse apiece, they'd pulled the donkey behind them. Daniel tethered the animals and went into the tavern, leaving Rachel outside to guard her wares.

The bar was quite full, wine was flowing and there was an atmosphere of jollity. Clouds of tobacco curled under the low ceiling. A man lay in a drunken stupor across a table. Daniel was interested to note that some of the customers were in uniform. It made him more circumspect. He walked to the counter, ordered some wine from the barmaid, then sipped it before leaning in to speak to her.

'I'm looking for Guillaume Lizier,' he said.

She was suspicious. 'Who are you?'

'I'm a friend of his.'

'We've never seen you in here before.'

'I'm an *old* friend,' said Daniel. 'Guillaume will remember me.'

'What's your name?'

'Alain Borrel. My wife and I need a room here.'

'We've none to spare.'

'Guillaume told me he'd always find somewhere for a friend.'

The woman's face was expressionless but she exuded a sense of distrust. Thin, angular, dark-haired and of middle years, she had black eyes and a swarthy complexion. She glanced around to make sure that she was not overheard by anyone else.

'What was the name again?'

'I am Alain Borrel,' said Daniel.

'Wait here while I speak to Madame Lizier.'

'It's her husband I came to see.'

'Wait here.'

The barmaid let herself out and was away for a couple of minutes. Daniel, meanwhile, sampled more of the wine and gazed around the bar. The man asleep on the table gradually slumped to the floor but nobody else seemed to notice or care. Putting his wine and walking stick aside, Daniel picked him up and sat him more securely in a chair. He earned a grunt of thanks from the man. Daniel went back to the counter. He was still appraising the customers when the barmaid returned.

'Monsieur Borrel?' she called.

He swung round. 'Yes?'

'Madame Lizier will see you in the back room.'

'Is Guillaume in there as well?'

'Talk to his wife first.'

She pointed to the door in the corner and Daniel walked across to it. Wine in one hand, he used his stick to tap on the stout timber before opening the door. It gave access to a large, stone-floored, well-stocked storeroom. Seated behind a table at the far end was a lean woman with such a close resemblance to the barmaid that they had to be sisters. She indicated a chair.

'Come in and sit down, Monsieur,' she invited.

'Thank you,' he said.

Daniel turned to close the door but it was slammed shut by the young man who'd been hiding behind it and the newcomer found himself staring at the barrel of a pistol. The weapon was thrust hard against Daniel's forehead by the young man, who looked as if he was desperate for an excuse to pull the trigger. The situation was crystal clear to Daniel. One false move and his mission would come to a sudden end. He tried to remain calm. Eyes smouldering, the young man spat his questions at Daniel.

'Who are you?' he demanded. 'And what are you doing here?'

CHAPTER FIVE

Daniel showed no fear. Though the weapon felt as if it were trying to bore into his skull, he didn't flinch or beg for mercy. Instead he met the young man's gaze and spoke with quiet assurance.

'My name is Alain Borell and I wish to see Guillaume Lizier.'

'Why?' snapped the other.

'I am an old friend of his.'

'You're a liar. My father often talks about his friends and I've never heard any mention of you. I think you're an impostor.'

'There's a simple way to prove who I am,' said Daniel, 'and that's to bring your father here. I'm sure he'll vouch for me.'

'What do you want from him?'

'I'm hoping that he'll be able to help me.'

'So that's it,' sneered the young man. 'You've fallen on hard times and you've come to wheedle some money out of us.'

'I want no money.'

'Then what are you after?'

As the pistol was pressed ever harder against his forehead, Daniel held his ground. He looked deep into the young man's eyes. Behind the anger and the bravado, he detected a flicker of doubt. His captor was not really sure what to do.

'There's no need to stand so close, Raymond,' said the woman. 'You can kill him just as easily from a yard away. Move back.' Her son took a reluctant step backwards. 'That's better.'

'Don't worry, Madame Lizier,' said Daniel, glancing over his shoulder. 'Raymond is not going to shoot me. He's far too sensible to do that. There are soldiers in the bar. If they hear gunfire, they'll rush in here at once. How will you explain the fact that I'm lying dead on the floor? And there's another thing,' he went on, turning back to Raymond again. 'I don't think your son is used to handling that weapon. Do you see? His hand is shaking slightly.'

'Be quiet!' yelled Raymond. 'Or I'll shoot.'

'Now he's starting to lose his nerve.'

'That's not true.'

'Then pull the trigger,' urged Daniel. 'Go on. Bring those soldiers charging in here. Is that what you want to do?'

Raymond was beginning to tremble. Incensed that Daniel was obviously unafraid of him, he turned the pistol over so that he could use the butt as a club. Daniel moved swiftly. Hurling his wine into Raymond's eyes, he dodged the blow then cracked his attacker on the wrist with his walking stick, making him drop the pistol with a yelp. While Raymond was still blinded, Daniel snatched it deftly up from the ground and – when Raymond could see properly again – he used it to motion him across the room so that he was standing near his mother. Now that he was no longer in danger, Daniel let the weapon hang by his side.

'Let *me* ask some questions now,' he began. 'Why are you so suspicious of me?'

'Because we've been deceived before,' replied Bette Lizier.

'Where is your husband?'

'They took him away.'

'Who did?'

'My father's in police custody,' said Raymond, resenting the way he'd been so easily disarmed and looking for a chance to strike back. 'Someone just like you came here and claimed to be his friend. The next thing we knew, Father had been hauled off.'

'What was the charge against him?'

'They say he's a spy for the British.'

'Is that true?'

Raymond glanced uneasily at his mother but her face gave nothing away. Conscious that the young man was waiting to pounce on him, Daniel tried to win his confidence. He held out the pistol.

'Go on – take it.'

Raymond was wary. 'It's a trick.'

'I'm trying to prove that I came here in the spirit of friendship. Let's be honest,' said Daniel, pulling himself up to his full height, 'you're no match for me. I've been a soldier for many years and learnt everything there is to learn about fighting. But that's not why I came.' He put the pistol on the table then stepped back with his arms outspread. Raymond grabbed the weapon. 'You won't need that. I mean no harm.'

'Put it down, Raymond,' said his mother, getting to her feet.

'I don't trust him,' asserted Raymond.

'Put it down.'

The steel in her voice made him obey. When the pistol was on the table, she conducted a long scrutiny of Daniel before coming to stand in front of him. She looked at the walking stick.

'You don't really need that, do you?' she said.

'Only when Raymond tries to knock me out,' he replied with a smile. 'I'm sorry that I had to hit your son but I had no option.'

'Who are you?'

'I've told you. My name is Alain Borrel.'

'And what's your real name?'

'You've just heard it,' said Daniel. 'If you don't believe me, go outside and speak to my wife, Rachel. She's keeping an eye on our wares. We've brought things to sell in the market.'

'Why did you come to the *Coq d'Or*?'

'I hoped that your husband could assist us.'

'In what way?'

'Well, to begin with, we need somewhere to stay.'

'Is that *all* you came after, Monsieur Borrel?'

He searched her eyes, wondering how much she knew about her husband's activities on behalf of the British army, uncertain if she was his accomplice or had deliberately been kept ignorant. Bette Lizier, meanwhile, was trying in turn to fathom him out. He was patently not the disabled man who'd first hobbled into the room.

'No, Madame,' said Daniel at length, 'I came for something else as well but it's clear that you and your son are unable to give it to me. I'll simply apologise for intruding and go my way.'

'Wait!' she said as he made to leave. 'Stay a moment.'

She had a long, whispered conversation with her son. Whatever feelings she might have about Daniel, it was evident that Raymond still regarded him as an enemy that had to be destroyed. He was annoyed when his mother took the contrary view.

'Perhaps we *can* offer you and your wife accommodation,' she said to Daniel. 'What else will you need?'

'I'll need someone to show me around the town,' he said.

'Raymond can do that.'

'I fancied that your husband would be a better guide, Madame. He's more likely to know the place I'm after.'

'I've lived here all my life,' said Raymond, affronted. 'There's nowhere in Lille I haven't been.'

'I'll need your father's word on that,' said Daniel. 'I assume that he's allowed visitors. To be quite frank, I'd rather speak directly to Guillaume before I go any further.'

'I think you're lying,' said Raymond.

'No, he's not,' countered Bette. 'I trust him. Monsieur Borrel is not like the man who came last week.'

Daniel's ears pricked up. 'What man was that?'

'He came asking for Guillaume when all the time he knew that my husband was already behind bars. He was pretending to be a British agent in order to draw out some sort of confession that would be used as evidence against both me and my husband.'

'We *knew* he was an impostor,' boasted Raymond.

'So we gave nothing away.'

'I hope Raymond didn't wave a pistol in his face as well,' said Daniel. 'That would have been evidence of something to hide.'

'We gave him none,' she said, proudly. 'We know where our loyalties lie, Monsieur – as do you. Well,' she added, 'now that we've become properly acquainted, perhaps you should bring your wife in. It must be very tedious standing out there. Raymond will show you where to stable the animals.'

'Thank you, Madame. You are very kind.' He offered his hand to Raymond. 'We are on the same side, I promise you.'

After a moment's hesitation, Raymond shook his hand. Daniel was in. He was dismayed to hear that Guillaume Lizier was under arrest and knew that that would make his task more difficult, but he could not turn back now. He clapped a hand on Raymond's shoulder.

'Come and meet my wife,' he said, 'but leave the pistol here.'

A soldier since he was a boy, Erich Schlager had always considered the Hessians to be better than any other army and he felt that a cavalry officer was far superior to an infantryman. The fact that Daniel Rawson belonged to a regiment of foot was an additional insult to him. It served to put a sharper edge on his lust for revenge. He pictured himself, galloping straight at the British soldier and hacking him to pieces with his sabre. After that, he'd find the woman who'd taken his horse and reclaim it without ceremony. She had to be punished as well. If circumstances were propitious, he'd tear off her clothes and violate her at will before stealing everything she had of value. Rachel Rees would not be saved by her champion a second time. Rawson would already have been killed.

Schlager was impatient, keen to strike soon, before the siege of Lille was really under way and before his target might be moved out of range. He was still subjected to ridicule by other officers and that served to keep his anger simmering away. It could only be appeased by the death of a man and the humiliation of a woman. He'd still not decided if he'd kill Rachel Rees or simply mutilate her. It would depend on his mood at the time. At all events, she would suffer. She'd pay dearly for being a witness to Schlager's mortification at the hands of a British officer.

He was still mulling over the finer details of his revenge when the man came looking for him. Schlager grabbed him by the lapel.

'Well?' he said. 'I hope you haven't come empty-handed.'

'No, Lieutenant. I found out what you wanted.'

'Tell me where he is.'

'Let go of me for a moment,' said the man, 'and I'll show you.' Released by Schlager, he pulled a grubby piece of paper from his pocket and handed it over. 'This is a very rough map of the camp,' he explained. 'That cross is the Duke of Marlborough's quarters and, only walking distance away,' he went on, pointing to a crude circle, 'is where you'll find Captain Rawson.'

'Is he there now?'

'I'm afraid not, sir.'

'Then where is he?'

'Nobody seemed to know.'

'How hard have you looked?'

'I've spoken to dozens of people,' said the man, defensively, 'and they all told me the same. Captain Rawson has left the camp.'

'Go back until he returns.'

'That might be days away, Lieutenant.'

'I don't care how long it takes,' said Schlager, taking out a small purse and dropping it into his hand. 'That's to encourage you. There'll be lots more when I know where they both are.'

After weighing the purse in his hand, the man put it away in his pocket. 'I thought I was only searching for one person,' he said. 'Who else am I supposed to find?'

'Her name is Rachel Rees and she's a camp follower.'

'There are hundreds of those with the British regiments. How can I pick out one of them in particular?'

'This woman is quite distinctive. She's big, fat and Welsh. Oh,' he said as he recalled something, 'and she drives a hard bargain. She tried to make me pay twice as much as a horse was worth. That's why I chose to take it for nothing.'

The man smirked. 'But I heard you'd actually *lost* a horse, sir, not bought one.'

'Shut your filthy mouth!'

Schlager's fist hit him so hard on the side of the head that he rolled over in the grass. To be taunted by his fellow officers was one thing, but he would not stomach any derision from a civilian. The very fact that the man had even somehow heard the news was infuriating. He wondered how many other people like him were whispering the name of Erich Schlager and sniggering at his expense. He stood menacingly over the body.

'Don't you ever say that again!' he cautioned.

'No, no, sir,' promised the other, rubbing the side of his head. 'I'm sorry. I didn't mean to offend you. Forget what I said.' Schlager stood back so that he could clamber to his feet. 'I'll find the woman for you. Big, fat and Welsh – that's what you told me. If she's in the camp, I'll ferret her out. Should I say that you're looking for her?'

'Of course not, you idiot,' cried Schlager. 'I just want to know where the old sow is. Now, disappear before I hit you again.'

Daniel wasted no time. When Rachel was safely bestowed at the tavern, he went off for a first look at the defences. He was guided by Raymond, now coming to accept him and wishing to make amends for his earlier hostility. Daniel found him a useful guide. What he lacked in intelligence, he made up for with low cunning and that was a quality more suited to the occasion. They had to take a mental inventory without appearing to do so and Raymond was adept at doing that. They chatted casually to guards, took note of the cannonballs, stones and supplies of oil being hoisted up to the ramparts, and watched as yet another column of soldiers marched in through the main gate. Lille was preparing for a long and bitter siege. Daniel felt sorry for those from his own regiment who'd be crushed by boulders or scalded by boiling oil as it gushed down on them.

Guillaume Lizier's wife was the only person allowed to

visit her husband, so Daniel had told her the questions he wanted put to the prisoner. Whether or not Lizier could provide all the answers was debatable but Daniel wanted to make contact with him, if only by proxy. Having often worked as a spy himself, Daniel had intense fellow feeling for a British agent. He appreciated the great risks that Lizier had taken and admired his wife and son for continuing the work in his absence.

'What do you want to see next?' asked Raymond.

'Show me some of the churches.'

His companion was surprised. 'You wish to pray?'

'No,' said Daniel, 'I just wish to see them.'

He was moved neither by any spiritual urge nor by an interest in ecclesiastical architecture. Daniel had found from experience that churches were excellent places in which to hide. The time might come when he and Rachel had to seek refuge for a while. It was important to know where the bolt-holes were. One thing still puzzled Daniel.

'Why does your father choose to help the British?' he asked.

'We've been treated badly by the French,' said Raymond with a scowl. 'We used to own one of the largest taverns in the city but they took it away from us and gave us very little compensation. The *Coq d'Or* is tiny compared to the place we used to have. Also,' he added as if repeating something he'd heard his father say, 'we want an end to this war and the French will never win it. All the battles are won by the Duke of Marlborough.'

'He's an absolute master of strategy.'

'When he gets what he wants – and what his Allies want – the war will be over. We can live in peace instead of cowering behind the walls under siege.'

'I can see why your father might wish to help the British but why are you so eager to do so as well, Raymond?'

'I have my own reason, Monsieur Borrel.'

'And what's that?'

'The woman I am going to marry is English.'

It was the first time that Daniel had ever seen him smile. Until then Raymond had been a rather tense, watchful, humourless individual with an aggressive streak. Evidently, there was a softer side to him. As they explored some of the city's churches, Daniel got him talking about his forthcoming marriage and about his hopes for the future. Raymond began to sound like any other young man in love and bursting with optimism. A shadow then fell across his face.

'We have only one fear,' he confessed. 'When the siege is over, we're afraid that there will be very little of the town left to live in. Is that Marlborough's plan?' he asked in consternation. 'Does he want to reduce Lille to rubble?'

'No, Raymond. He wants to take Lille by inflicting as little damage as possible. He always respects the rights of a civilian population and will not destroy any homes, if it can be avoided.'

'And *can* it be avoided, Monsieur?'

Daniel was honest. 'In this case,' he said, 'I think it unlikely.'

It had taken a full day for Emanuel Janssen and Beatrix Udderzook to get their sea legs. Once they became accustomed to the constant roll of the ship, the thunderous flapping of the sails and the feel of spray on their cheeks, they found the voyage less of a trial. Everything was relative. What they thought was a choppy sea was described by the sailors as an unusually calm one. What they called a howling gale was no more than a strong wind to the crew. Amalia had suffered no ill effects since coming aboard and, unlike the others, slept well at night. Her affliction was boredom. After the initial exhilaration of ploughing majestically through the waves, she grew tired of seeing nothing but apparently limitless expanses of water on all sides of her. As well as finding it monotonous, she was filled with a sense of insignificance. In the midst of the North Sea, all her high ambitions appeared incredibly petty and selfish now.

'How much longer will it be?' asked Beatrix.

'I don't know,' replied Amalia, scanning the horizon for a sight of land. 'It seems like an age since we set off.'

'Did you ask your father about going to London?'

'Yes, Beatrix, and we will spend time there at the end of our stay. You'll get a brief glimpse of the city when we land there, but we have to drive straight off to Oxfordshire then. I'll be so interested to see what the fashions are in England,' she said. 'I'm afraid they'll make me look so dowdy and provincial.'

'You could never do that, Miss Amalia,' said the ever-faithful Beatrix. 'Even in Paris, you outshone all those grand ladies with their silken dresses and ridiculous wigs.'

Amalia remembered it otherwise. Beside the flamboyance of the French aristocracy, she'd always felt invisible. It had made her take more interest in fashion for its own sake. Beatrix, however, would hear no criticism of her mistress. As ever, Amalia was touched by her maidservant's unswerving loyalty.

'What do you think of your dream?' she asked. 'According to that, we should all have drowned by now.'

Beatrix laughed. 'They were silly fears.'

'Do you feel safe and sound?'

'Yes, I do – now that we're actually at sea. I'm enjoying it, Miss Amalia. It's not at all as I'd imagined.'

'I hadn't realised it would be quite so noisy.'

'You get used to that,' said Beatrix. She inhaled deeply. 'If only the other servants could see me now. They were very jealous when I told them we'd be staying at a palace.'

'That's not strictly true,' explained Amalia. 'It will be years before Blenheim is actually finished. The duchess has kindly found us some accommodation in Woodstock. It's a village nearby.'

'What do they eat in England?'

'Much the same as we do, I suppose.'

'Didn't Captain Rawson tell you what to expect?'

'He had no idea that we were going there.'

'I thought that you wrote to tell him.'

'I did, Beatrix, but my letters take a long time to reach him. I can't even be sure where he is. The army is always on the move. The chances are that he hasn't even read my letter.'

'What will he think when he *does* read it, Miss Amalia?'

'He'll be very pleased. He wanted me to see England.'

'Would you ever think of living there?'

'Hold on,' said Amalia with a laugh. 'We haven't got that far yet.'

'I don't think it would appeal to me.'

'Why is that?'

'To start with, I hate the sound of their language.'

'That works both ways. They're not enamoured of Dutch.'

'Well, they ought to be,' said Beatrix. 'It has a nicer ring to it. No, the truth is that I could never feel at home anywhere else than Amsterdam. But I want you to know that my feelings don't come into it,' she went on. 'I'd follow you wherever you wanted to go, whether it was England, Italy, Turkey or even Russia. I'll always be at your side, Miss Amalia – except that you might be Mrs Daniel Rawson by then.'

Amalia suddenly felt bashful and unsure how to respond. She was spared the effort of doing so by a shout from the man in the crow's nest. He'd seen a speck in the far distance.

'Land ho!'

Everyone rushed to the bulwark. It was England at last.

Rachel Rees settled into the tavern very quickly. Though she couldn't understand every word that was spoken, she could sense moods instantly. There was an underlying tension in the place. With her husband in custody, Madame Lizier was clearly under great strain and her fears were shared by her son and her sister. Rachel sought to relieve the pressure of work on the others by making the beds in the guest rooms, helping with the cooking and, most notably, taking a turn as a serving wench that evening when the place really filled up. Her vivacity made her immediately popular and she enjoyed the lively banter. The customers cheered to the echo when they discovered that she had a beautiful singing voice.

Daniel was grateful for the way she threw herself into

the work even though she had no real idea of why they were there. With her natural affability and bustling competence, she made Estelle, the unmarried sister of Madame Lizier, look slow and dull beside her. Rachel was good for business. Wanting a chance to speak to her, the customers – soldiers, in particular – called her over and ordered more wine than they would normally do so. The more they drank, the less discreet they became. Seated among them, Daniel was able to tease out many crucial details of the reinforcement of Lille. His decision to take Rachel Rees with him had been vindicated.

There was only one problem and it arose during a slight lull.

'You're doing wonders, Rachel,' he said, taking her aside. 'Go on like this and they'll want to keep you here for ever.'

'One thing I can do, Alain, is to sell. It's my living.'

'Madame Lizier is very pleased with what you've done.'

'It's the least I can do in return for the accommodation. By the way,' she said with a playful nudge, 'we'll have to be careful tonight.'

'Why is that?'

'The bed creaks like anything. There'll be no secrets in the dark tonight. Everyone will know what we get up to.'

Before Daniel could tell her that he wouldn't be sharing the bed with her, another customer came up. He was a big, paunchy soldier in his forties with a waxed moustache that he fingered with one hand. His eyes gleamed familiarly. When he whispered something in Rachel's ears, she gave a loud cackle of pleasure. Daniel slipped away and left them to it. He found Bette Lizier alone in the kitchen. It was the first chance he'd had to speak to her since she'd returned from visiting her husband.

'How did you find Guillaume?' he asked.

'He's very annoyed at being kept there.'

'Do they have any real evidence against him?'

'No,' she said. 'He was arrested on the strength of idle gossip.'

'Then they must release him in time. How is he being treated?'

'The food is poor but at least they are leaving him alone. They no longer question him every day. Guillaume says that they are more interested in the siege than in him.'

'So you were able to talk to him freely?'

'Yes, Monsieur Borrel,' she replied. 'I told him about you and he agreed that you could be trusted.'

'Did you put those questions of mine to him?'

'I did.'

'Was he able to help me in any way?'

'I'm not sure. Guillaume says that only old documents are likely to be in the town hall. There's a room where the archives are kept. It's on the first floor at the back of the building.'

'That sounds promising,' said Daniel. 'What else did he tell you?'

'The only time you could get in there is after dark. Guillaume said that the best way would be through one of the attic rooms but you'd have to be able to climb.'

'I've had plenty of practice at that.'

'Be careful, Monsieur. There are guards outside the main

door and a nightwatchman is on patrol inside the building until dawn.'

'Thanks for the warning.'

'As for the other things you wanted to know,' she continued, 'Guillaume was not really able to help. He has no idea where plans of any new fortifications are kept. But he did have one suggestion.'

'What was that?'

'Talk to the men who are building them. Guillaume says that it's not being left only to soldiers. They're getting people from the town to do the digging as well. My husband is the only person still kept under lock and key. The others were all released to work on the defences.'

'Thank you,' said Daniel. 'That's worth knowing.'

Bette Lizier stepped back and studied him quizzically.

'May I ask *you* a question now?' she said.

'Please do.'

'How long have you been married?'

'Not very long,' he said, evasively.

'I rather think it is not at all.'

Daniel was curious. 'Why do you say that?'

'Rachel is a good woman and she's been a wonderful help to me but she's not the wife you'd choose, Monsieur. She looks as if she's married to you but you don't look as if you're married to her.'

'We're travelling as man and wife, that's all I can say.'

'Forgive me for being so nosy.'

'Not at all, Madame,' said Daniel. 'You have sharp eyes. And so, I should tell you, does Raymond. During our tour of the town, he was very useful. He obviously takes after you.'

'He thought you were an impostor. I sensed that you were not.'

'What else did you sense?'

She gave a quiet smile. 'That would be telling, Monsieur.' She heard raucous laughter from the bar. 'Rachel has been in there far too long. Perhaps it's time for me to relieve your wife.'

'Leave her be,' said Daniel. 'She's enjoying every moment.'

It was late when the customers finally left the conviviality of the *Coq d'Or* and rolled off to their homes or their billets. Daniel and Raymond helped the women to clear up in the bar. It was extraordinary how much debris a few dozen people could create. The first thing that Daniel did was to open the windows to get rid of the smell of tobacco and cooked food. The fug gradually cleared. When everything had been put away in readiness for the morrow, the candles were snuffed out and they all retired upstairs.

Having had several drinks bought for her by customers, Rachel was in high spirits. She tripped up the stairs with the eagerness of a young bride on the first night of her honeymoon. Daniel lingered in the passageway outside their bedroom so that she would have ample time to change into her nightdress. Before he entered the room, he first tapped politely on the door.

'There's no need for you to knock,' said Rachel, sitting up in bed. 'We're husband and wife, after all.'

'Not when we're alone like this,' he corrected.

'Do I look so hideous to you?'

'No, no, you're a very attractive woman, Rachel.'

'Those soldiers seemed to think so. It's just as well I didn't understand everything they said.' She giggled. 'They were making some very rude remarks.' She patted the bed beside her. 'Come and join me, Monsieur Borrel.'

'I'll sleep on the floor, if you don't mind.'

'I *do* mind. I want some company.'

'You heard what I said. I'm already spoken for.'

'Why not come to bed and tell me all about her?' said Rachel, beckoning him to her. 'We'll simply talk, I promise you.'

Daniel knew that it was a promise she had no intention of keeping. By the light of the single candle, she was doing her best to look seductive, pulling her nightdress down to expose both shoulders and beaming at him. Resisting temptation, Daniel took one of the blankets from the bed and placed it on the floor.

She was piqued. 'Don't I even get a kiss?'

Daniel got up and placed a kiss on her forehead.

'Good night, Madame Borell,' he said, blowing out the candle.

'You know where I am, if you change your mind.'

But Daniel had no urge whatsoever to do so. After taking off his clothes, he settled down on the blanket in his nightshirt, trying to adjust his body to the undulations in the oak flooring. As he lay there in the dark, he reviewed what he'd so far learnt and what he needed to do on the following day. He was soon interrupted by loud snores from the bed. Rachel had given up all hope of enticing him into it. While she was deeply asleep, Daniel remained awake. Instincts sharpened by years of being on continual guard against attack made him listen intently. The floorboards in the passageway were creaking gently. Somebody was on the move.

The only weapon he'd brought with him was the dagger that Rachel had given him as a gift. Reaching for it, he kept it concealed beneath the blanket. His ears hadn't deceived him. The footsteps stopped outside the door and someone tentatively lifted the latch. A moment later, the door swung open and Daniel saw a figure enter in the gloom. The newcomer groped his way to the bed.

'Rachel, Rachel,' he said, drunkenly, 'where are you, my love?'

She woke with a start. 'Is that you, Alain?'

'No, it's me, Sergeant Furneaux.'

He dived on top of her and groped her breast. Rachel was horrified. Apart from anything else, the Frenchman was stark naked.

'Get off me!' she cried, pushing him away.

'I want you,' he insisted, silencing her protests with a kiss.

It was as far as his courtship was allowed to go. Leaping up from the floor, Daniel dragged him from the bed and knocked him out with a single punch. Covering the interloper with a blanket, he put him over his shoulder and took him out of the room. Too drunk to know what he was doing, Sergeant Furneaux was now too dazed to know what was happening. Daniel carried him down the stairs and out into the yard, removing the blanket before dropping him in the horse trough. He left Furneaux spluttering in the water.

When he got back to the bedroom, Daniel saw that

Rachel had lit the candle again. She was shocked and frightened.

'What have you done to him?' she asked.

'The same thing I'd do to any man who tries to molest my wife,' he said with a grin. 'Don't worry about him. By morning, he won't remember a thing about it.'

Chapter Six

Renowned for the roar of his voice and the strictness of his discipline, Henry Welbeck was not the ogre he always appeared to those under him. He really cared for his men and hated the thought of losing some of them every time an engagement with the enemy took place. Though nobody would have guessed it, he took an almost paternal interest in his charges, striving to turn uncouth recruits into responsible human beings and schooling them to be capable soldiers in order to give them a better chance of survival. Nothing upset him more than to lead a burial detail over a battlefield. After all these years, the pain of losing his men in such large numbers was still intense. It was even more intolerable if the deaths had been as a result of horrendous mistakes by a senior officer. He was scathing in his denunciation of those above him.

After drilling his new recruits, he stood them in a line

before him. It was a very hot day and they were dripping with sweat. Ben Plummer looked as if he was about to collapse from exhaustion.

'I am your salvation,' Welbeck told them. 'Don't look to the officers to act in your best interest. Many of them will not even be there. It's soldiers like us who face enemy fire time and again. There are officers in every regiment who never even leave the comforts of their home in England. Once they've bought their commissions, they stay as far away from danger as possible. They leave that to us.' He glared at Plummer. 'What do they leave to us, Ben?'

'Danger, Sergeant,' said Plummer.

'The only danger you ever met before, I daresay, was from a diseased whore.' The other men sniggered. 'Well, you'll get more than a burning prick when French muskets start to aim at you. The first thing you'll do is to fill your breeches in sheer terror. Unless,' he emphasised, tapping his chest, 'unless, that is, you listen to, learn from and obey your dear Sergeant Welbeck. In other words, I'm the only thing standing between you and a hideous death. I'm your true saviour. Now, do you have any questions?'

'Are we dismissed, Sergeant?' gasped Plummer.

'No, you're not. We've barely started.'

'When do we eat?' asked another man.

'You eat when I say, you hungry little turd.'

A third voice piped up. 'When do we have muskets?'

'Well done,' said Welbeck without sarcasm. 'Someone's asked a sensible question at last. The answer is that you have muskets when I can trust you not to shoot me with them.' They laughed. 'Oh, it has happened in the past, believe me. I've had two people who tried to blow me to pieces and one who did his best to run me through with a bayonet. They lived to regret it. We flog people who show that kind of disrespect to a sergeant. We flay them alive.' He walked along the line. 'Is there anyone here who'd like to find out what two hundred lashes feel like on your bare back?' There was long silence. 'No? I thought not. We've got no idiots here. We've got no heroes either, by the look of you. It's up to me to put some heroism into you. I'll not take cowards into battle under my command. I only want men with backbone. Be warned. I have a reputation to keep.'

They were all too aware of it. Having talked to other soldiers in the regiment, they'd learnt about Sergeant Welbeck's reputation as a merciless taskmaster. Everyone had suffered under him. At the same time, however, there were those who spoke up for him. He might be hard, they conceded, but he was scrupulously fair. There was no favouritism shown. He was also courageous under fire, leading his men into battle with exemplary commitment and risking his life along with theirs. Even among those who hated him, most had a grudging admiration for Henry Welbeck.

He drilled them for another two blistering hours before he dismissed them. Ben Plummer was detained for a final word.

'How do you like army life, Benjamin?' he asked.

Plummer grimaced. 'I'd sooner have gone to prison.'

'You'll learn to love it in time.'

'Do *you* love it, Sergeant?'

'I do my duty, lad.'

'That's not the same thing,' said Plummer. 'Do you like

being a soldier and having someone trying to kill you all the time?'

Welbeck grinned. 'The trick is to kill them first.'

'Is that what you enjoy doing, Sergeant?'

'I enjoy staying alive, Plummer, and meeting people like you.'

'This is a living hell to me.'

'Wait until the firing starts. What's happened so far will seem like heaven then.'

'How can you have a heaven with no women here?'

'Curb your fleshly desires, man. Cleanse your soul.'

'Even you must want a woman *sometimes*, Sergeant.'

'That's none of your business.'

'Have you never been married?'

'The army is my life,' said Welbeck, briskly.

Plummer smirked. 'You don't know what you're missing.'

Welbeck shoved him backwards. 'Do you want another visit to the dentist, Ben Plummer?' he threatened, holding up a fist. 'I can knock out every one of your ugly teeth, if you wish.'

'No, no, Sergeant – please don't hit me again.'

'Join the others before I lose my temper.'

'I will,' said Plummer, stepping out of range before delivering his parting shot. 'But I still feel sorry for you, not knowing what it's like.'

'Don't say another word!'

Welbeck's howl of rage made Plummer turn tail and scuttle away like a frightened rabbit. He'd caught the sergeant on a raw spot and would pay for his impudence. The truth was that, even in his youth, Welbeck had never been at ease with the opposite sex. There had been friendships with young women but they'd never matured into anything else because he had no inclination for them to do so. The rough-and-ready world of the army was much more appealing to him, a natural milieu for a man with great physical attributes and a love of danger. Nothing else mattered to him. While he was eager for the war to come to an end, it wouldn't mark his departure from the army. He was a soldier to his fingertips. Even in peace time, that is what he'd continue to be. Others managed to combine marriage with service to their country but Welbeck didn't believe such a thing was really possible. A woman was bound to influence emotions. Even someone as single-minded as Daniel Rawson could be distracted.

Welbeck took comfort from the fact that such a thing would never happen to him. He could concentrate all his efforts on his duties and ignore the taunts of people like Ben Plummer. When the muskets starting popping and the artillery booming, there was no place in a man's heart for a woman. Those who went into battle worrying about wives and children were bad soldiers. Welbeck made certain that he never suffered from their affliction.

As he entered his tent, he congratulated himself on the way that his recruits were responding to his instruction. Only one of them, Ben Plummer, hadn't yet been quelled into instant obedience. That would soon change. Reaching for his pipe, Welbeck filled it with tobacco and tamped it down with a finger. After setting it alight, he inhaled deeply and felt a surge of satisfaction run through his body. The aroma of the tobacco was itself a delight to him. It was only after a few minutes that he remembered who'd given him the pouch. This time, however, he didn't toss it away. Rachel Rees's tobacco was good. Smoking it laid no obligation on him. Adjusting the pipe in his mouth, he took another long, pleasing pull on it.

The market in Lille opened early and Rachel Rees was there not long after the first customers began to drift in. Wanting to see more of the town, Daniel accompanied her and helped her to unload some of the items from the saddlebags and pouches on the back of her donkey. Rachel was in her element, haggling, laughing and joking her way through hour after hour. Much of what she had was sold at a profit and she promptly bought more wares from other stallholders in order to sell it again at a higher price. Daniel was impressed at the effortless way she drew people in by chatting to them before even trying to interest them in what she had to offer. In the busy market, few were as relentlessly busy as Rachel Rees.

'I'll leave you to it now,' said Daniel.

'Where are you going?' she asked.

'I need to make some enquiries.'

She folded her arms in mock disapproval. 'Well, I hope you don't make them of other women. You're a married man, Alain Borrel. Bear that in mind.'

'I will,' he said with a conspiratorial smile, 'though you're the one who should be mindful of her marriage vows, Rachel. Who was it who enticed a French soldier into her bed last night?'

'I did nothing of the kind. He came unbidden.'

'He also came with no clothing on. Madame Lizier found his uniform under the stairs. He'd have had a lot of explaining to do when he got back to his regiment.'

'You saved my virtue,' she said, kissing him, fondly.

'That's what husbands are for, Rachel.'

Leaving her to cope with fresh customers, Daniel began his second tour of Lille, looking at all the landmarks pointed out by Raymond Lizier and paying particular attention to the town hall. It was an imposing structure with decorative architecture and a steep roof pierced by a series of dormer windows. In order to get inside the building, Daniel somehow had to mountaineer to its very top. A daunting task in daylight, it would be even more difficult at night. He walked slowly around it four times before he decided which approach to take. There was no certainty that the plans were there but Daniel felt that he nevertheless had to investigate the archives.

He switched his attention from past fortifications to those that were now being constructed. Additional defences were being hastily thrown up around the perimeter of Lille and Daniel needed to know their nature and extent. He walked to a tavern near the main gate, reasoning that it was likely to be frequented by soldiers from the garrison. He'd guessed right. When he went into the bar, there were blue uniforms on every side. Talk was exclusively of the impending siege and he listened intently to various conversations. He eventually fell in with a group sitting near the window.

'I think we should surrender,' said one soldier, dolefully.

'Never!' retorted another.

'We lack the numbers to hold out long. Marlborough will starve us to death. What happens when our ammunition runs out? All we can do then is to hide behind the walls until he smashes them down.'

'We fight back. Nobody has ever taken this town and nobody ever will. Vauban saw to that.'

'I agree,' said Daniel, easing his way into the discussion. 'The walls will hold. We'll never be forced into surrender. However, we'll suffer a terrible bombardment from the enemy.'

'We'll give as good as we get,' said the second man. 'You should be ashamed to talk of surrender, Martin!'

'I want to save bloodshed,' said Martin.

'It sounds like cowardice to me.'

'It's plain common sense, Bernard. Unless you've forgotten, we haven't been paid for a long time. How can we fight on with empty pockets? How can we support our families without any money?'

'That is a problem,' agreed Bernard.

'But it's no reason to hand over Lille,' argued Daniel. 'I was a soldier myself for many years and I fought under commanders who wouldn't yield one square yard of ground without a fight. We mustn't make it easy for Marlborough.'

'Well said, my friend!'

'The enemy not only have to contend with Vauban's brilliance: there are fresh ditches and barricades being added all the time. It will take the Allied army weeks to surround us properly.'

'Yes,' said Martin, 'then they'll crack us open like an egg.'

'I very much doubt that.'

'So do I,' said Bernard. 'The siege will last for months.'

'And then we'll be forced to give in,' insisted Martin.

'Or *they'll* be forced to withdraw.'

'It's more likely to be the latter,' said Daniel, aligning

himself with Bernard. 'The longer the siege goes on, the more difficult it will be to sustain. It will be bad enough moving troops and supplies in autumn. In winter, it will be well nigh impossible.'

'We'll never hold out that long,' said Martin.

'You will if you get reinforcements.'

'It's not reinforcements I need, it's my pay!'

Some of the others shared his sentiments. Like soldiers everywhere, they were full of complaints but most of them were prepared to fight on in defence of the town. Daniel worked the conversation around to the subject of the additional fortifications being erected and he gained a lot of useful information from them. Bernard offered him more than a description.

'If you come up on the ramparts,' he said, affably, 'you'll see exactly what they're doing.'

'Thank you,' said Daniel, 'I'd appreciate that.'

'I'll take you there when we go back on duty.'

'That's very kind of you.'

Martin was adamant. 'I still think we should talk of surrender.'

'You're being defeatist,' chided Daniel.

'Marlborough is a gentleman. He'll offer us good terms. There's no dishonour in saving a beautiful city from ruin. Do you want Lille to be running with blood?'

'It won't come to that, I'm sure.'

'So am I,' said Bernard. 'You're getting soft, Martin.'

Martin stiffened. 'I've never walked away from a fight.'

'Then why do you want to do so now?'

'Because I don't want to see Lille turned into a pile of stones.'

'That will never happen,' said Daniel. 'They'd first have to make a breach in the walls and you'd never let them get close enough.'

'Listen to him,' urged Bernard. 'What's your name, friend?'

'Alain Borrel.'

'You talk like a true soldier, Alain – unlike some people.'

Martin was enraged. 'Do you mean me?' he demanded. 'I'm as true a soldier as anyone here and you should know it, Bernard. If we decide to withstand the siege, I'll be ready to fight until I drop.'

'Then no more talk of surrender,' said Daniel. 'Let us drink to victory instead.'

When he bought a round of drinks for them, they had a toast to success. Daniel mixed easily with the group, convincing them that he'd fought in the French army by being able to talk on their level. By the time they tumbled out of the tavern, he was looked upon as a friend. It was Bernard who took care of him. They went up onto the ramparts near the main gate and Daniel was given a privileged view of the defences from above. He gazed down on what was a geometrical work of art, sculpted in stone.

Lille was the most complex of all of Vauban's fortress cities. It consisted of zigzagging outer ramparts studded with massive jutting bastions that enclosed a broad moat drawing its water from the River Deûle. Within the moat itself were triangular island defences, from which defenders could fire at any attackers who'd managed to breach the outer walls. On the far side of the moat was another towering wall of ashlar, flanked at regular intervals by more bastions. From high and well-defended positions, the garrison could shoot at the enemy, treat them to an avalanche of stone or drench them in a waterfall of boiling oil. Daniel's mind was like a sponge as he surveyed the scene. Every detail was sucked in.

Beyond the existing defences others were being constructed. To ensure a good view of any attackers, trees and copses within half a mile of the town were being cut down. Even from that distance Daniel could hear the thud of axes and the crash of timber. Once felled, the trunks were hauled off to form fresh palisades. Nothing was left to offer the enemy even the semblance of protection.

'There you are,' said Bernard, proudly. 'We are completely safe.'

'You could hold out for ever,' said Daniel.

'We can now.' He gestured excitedly towards the horizon where clouds of dust were billowing. 'Do you see them, Alain? They're here at last. Marshal Boufflers is bringing reinforcements. With luck, he'll bring enough money to pay the arrears of our troops as well. Even Martin will not be able to complain then. We are saved, my friend,' he went on, slapping Daniel on the back. 'The marshal has defended many towns that have been invested. He's reckoned to be a genius at it. All at once the balance of power has shifted in our favour.'

Daniel was afraid that the man's optimism was justified.

England was so dramatically different to Holland that the visitors gaped at it in wonder. They had never seen so many hills and woods and vast expanses of fertile land. Coming from a relatively flat and featureless country, they were amazed at the varying contours of the areas through which they travelled. It took them two days to reach Oxfordshire, another verdant county fed by sparkling rivers and containing quaint villages, fields of crops or livestock and occasional houses so grand that they took the newcomers' breath away.

'There's another one,' said Amalia, pointing.

'It makes our own home seem so absurdly small,' opined her father. 'The estate must be huge.'

'How many servants would a house like that need?' asked Beatrix, counting the windows. 'And how ever do they find their way around a place that big?'

Amalia giggled. 'The only way to find out is to work there.'

'No, thank you. I'm very happy where I am, Miss Amalia.'

'That's good because we'd never think of letting you go.'

Having marvelled at so many sights, they still had enough open-mouthed awe left to be completely overwhelmed by Blenheim Palace itself. The scale of it was immense. As their carriage rolled up the long, arrow-straight drive, they got some idea of the size and design of the place. Even in its still unfinished state it was truly inspiring, a home of baroque magnificence that was fit for royalty. A veritable army of stonemasons, carpenters and other tradesmen were crawling over what seemed to be miles of wooden scaffolding. Carts were bringing in fresh materials that were swiftly unloaded and stacked ready for use. There was a general sense of urgency. In the grounds, too, there was great activity as a host of gardeners worked manfully away to transform the landscape into a model of scenic beauty.

'In some ways,' said Janssen, 'it's even better than Versailles.'

Amalia was nervous. 'I can't believe that we're guests here.'

'I don't belong in a place like this,' said Beatrix, trembling.

'It is rather daunting, I agree.'

'I think it's wonderful,' said Janssen, studying it with the eye of an artist. 'There's a perfect blend of ornamentation and symmetry. The effect is astonishing.'

When they got close enough to see the architectural detail, they were deprived of speech. Janssen could create superlative designs on his tapestry but he lacked the vision to conjure a whole palace into being. Wherever they looked, there was something else to praise. It was only when they rolled into the Great Court with its view of the north front that they regained their voices.

'I feel so *privileged,*' said Amalia, eyes shining with delight.

'How do you think *I* feel?' asked her father. 'My work is actually going to be on display here. What greater blessing could there be?'

Amalia could think of one and it involved Daniel Rawson. Before she could put her thoughts into words, however, she was diverted by an argument on the other side of the courtyard. A middle-aged man in fashionable attire and a periwig was being berated by a strikingly handsome woman in her late forties. When he indicated something on the plan he was holding, she shook her head decisively and continued her rant. Admitting defeat, the man eventually gave a polite bow and withdrew. Her gaze swept across the courtyard until it alighted on the three figures descending from the carriage. She crooked her finger to beckon them over to her.

Beatrix stayed beside the carriage while Amalia and her father set off on the long walk. Standing in the terrace above them, Sarah, Duchess of Marlborough, was a commanding figure, poised, dignified, potent and immaculately dressed. Amalia felt that she was in the presence of a queen. After bowing to the duchess, Janssen performed the introductions.

'I've brought the design of the tapestry with me, Your Grace,' he said. 'You may see it whenever you wish.'

'Well, it won't be for some time,' said Sarah, tartly. 'My attention is needed here. The moment I turn my back, they start to change things without my permission. I've just had to put that irritating architect in his place,' she went on. 'Mr Vanbrugh doesn't seem to realise that we will have the palace we choose and not one that he foists upon us.'

'Work seems to be proceeding apace,' observed Janssen.

'That's only because I'm here. In fact, we're months behind and everyone is trying to charge too much for their services.' She fixed Janssen with a stare. 'I hope that you don't mean to exploit us, sir. We'll pay a reasonable price for the tapestry, not an exorbitant one.'

'As a matter of fact, Your Grace…'

'Not now,' she said, rudely interrupting him. 'I'm far too busy here. I suggest that you drive to your accommodation in Woodstock while I go off and bang a few heads together. I'll be in touch in due course. Good day to you both.'

Before they could open their mouths, she swept off.

Amalia was deeply disappointed and her father was frankly insulted. Having come all that way to show his design to the Duchess of Marlborough, he was treated almost with disdain and made to feel like a fraudulent tradesman bent on making an undeserved profit from his work.

It was a bad omen.

Heavy rain on two successive nights forced Daniel to postpone his attempt. On the third night, it was completely dry and there was enough moonlight to aid him in what was going to be a hazardous undertaking. Having borrowed a rope from the *Coq d'Or*, he pressed Raymond Lizier into service. They padded through the town in the small hours.

Raymond was sceptical. 'You'll never climb up onto the roof of the town hall,' he said. 'It's far too high.'

'We shall see,' said Daniel, confidently.

'What am I to do, Monsieur?'

'You'll act as my lookout.'

'There should be nobody abroad at this time of night.'

'Just in case there is,' said Daniel, 'we must devise a signal. If you see someone coming, you must whistle three times.'

'Will you hear me all the way up there?'

'Oh, I think so. Sound carries.'

On their way to the town hall, they saw nobody at all, though they disturbed a cat that was sleeping in a doorway. After a screech of protest, it went off in search of another billet.

'Why did you need such a long rope?' asked Raymond.

'It must span the distance I estimated.'

'Are you going to toss it up to the roof?'

'My arm is not strong enough for that,' said Daniel, 'so I'm going to need some help from the Almighty.'

'Do you mean that you're going to pray for a miracle?'

'No, Raymond, I simply intend to go to church.'

The town hall was a looming silhouette against the sky. Guards were posted outside its main door. Daniel therefore led his accomplice to the rear of the building which was adjacent to a church. Raymond was still perplexed.

'How will you get in?' he said. 'It's locked at night.'

'That's why I took the precaution of acquiring a key,' explained Daniel, taking it from his pocket. 'Your mother was good enough to provide me with some wax so I slipped in here yesterday, made an impression of the key and had a duplicate made by a locksmith. It opens the door at the side.'

'Do I come in there with you?'

'No, Raymond. Stay here and keep watch.'

'What about my signal?'

'I'm hoping it won't be necessary.'

Rope over his shoulder, Daniel went off round the side of the church, leaving Raymond mystified as to how entry to the town hall could be gained. Reaching the small side door, Daniel let himself in with the key and left the door unlocked. A dank smell greeted him. As a further precaution, he'd taken the trouble on his earlier visit to memorise the disposition of the seating in the nave so that he could move about in the dark without blundering into anything. He made his way to the bell tower and felt his way up the circular staircase. It was an odd sensation, groping the cold stone as he climbed upwards for minute after minute. It was like stumbling blindfold through a labyrinth. He eventually reached the bells themselves and collided heavily with one of them, embracing it immediately to stop it from moving, highly aware that there was no surer way to advertise his presence than by making a church bell ring out.

Taking out one of the candles he'd brought with him, Daniel used a tinder box to light it, then held the candle up so that he could carry out an inspection. There were five bells in all, each a different size and weight. Spiders and other insects had made the place their home and Daniel had to brush away cobwebs as he moved to the narrow door in the corner. It opened onto a wooden staircase that was almost vertical. Daniel shifted the rope to the other shoulder and began the ascent. At the very top of the staircase was a door bolted from the inside. Releasing the bolt, he went through the door and out onto the stone balcony at the base of the spire.

A sudden rush of air blew out the candle but he no longer needed it. He could see well enough in the moonlight to pick out his target with ease. His estimate had been sound. He was virtually level with the roof beams of the town hall. That meant the dormer windows were above him. Selecting the one directly opposite, he began to uncoil the rope. During his years as a boy on the farm, he'd often had to use a rope to catch a wayward animal and was proficient at making a noose. On this occasion, he had an advantage. His target was no elusive horse or recalcitrant bullock. It was a stationary object. All that he had to do was to throw the noose over it and pull the rope tight. It should be a fairly easy task.

Yet his first attempt failed miserably, falling well short. The second was only marginally better. What he hadn't allowed for was the weight of the rope. It was much thicker and heavier than anything he'd used on the farm. As he reeled it in again, he resolved to throw it higher and harder. No matter how long it took him, he was determined to hit his target, a stone finial near a dormer window.

After his long wait in the gloom, Raymond Lizier was alerted by the sound of a noise high above his head. He looked up to see a rope slithering off the roof of the town hall before being hauled up to balcony at the base of the church spire. He couldn't believe his eyes. When he realised what Daniel was trying to do, he thought it an act of madness that was doomed to fail. How could anyone secure a rope between church and town hall then climb across it? His fear now was not that anyone would come along to disturb them but that his friend would fall to a grotesque death. He tried to raise the alarm in order to stop Daniel from going ahead but his lips were too dry to produce a whistle. In any case, after a succession of failures, the rope finally looped itself around the finial and was pulled tight.

There was now a bridge between the two buildings, albeit a perilous one. Raymond's stomach heaved. Having no head for heights, he wouldn't have dared to go out on the balcony, let alone consider climbing across several yards of open space on a rope. Yet that was exactly what Daniel was proposing to do. Raymond wanted to call out and beg him not to take the risk but he was too late. To his utter amazement, a figure suddenly appeared above him.

The trick, Daniel knew, was not to look down. Since the rope was secured around solid stone at both ends, he was confident that it would bear his weight. He just wished that it had remained as tight as he'd tried to make it. Legs around the rope, he used both hands to move slowly backwards across the chasm. Because of the strain put on it, the tension of the rope eased slightly. Feeling it give at one point, Daniel had to stop and simply cling on for a moment. When he continued his snail's pace climb, he reflected on what he was doing. Was it a case of bravery or lunacy? Why was he risking his life to get to something that might not even be there? What would Amalia think if he plunged to his death on a forlorn mission? Who could explain to her the irresistible urge that made him attempt such a dangerous exercise? And even if he did get safely to the other side, how would he return? Because of the angle of the rope, he was climbing upwards towards the dormer. Did he really want to put himself into such jeopardy for a second time?

The rope slackened again and his feet were almost dislodged. Clinging on desperately, he put in a last, urgent, muscle-aching effort and, to his relief, felt his hand touch a roof tile. Daniel was there. As he pulled himself to safety, he understood how a drowning man must feel when hauled out of the water just in time. He lay on the roof for some while in order to get his breath back and to let his legs and arms lose their stabbing pain. Then he used the rope once more to clamber up to the dormer window. The shutters were locked but he was able to force the latch by inserting the end of his dagger. Turning the weapon around, he smashed the window with the handle, then reached inside to undo the catch. Within seconds, he was inside the attic room.

There was no time for self-congratulation. He still had far too much to do. Lighting another candle, he held it up to discover that he was in a cluttered storeroom. A scampering noise told him that some mice had also taken up residence. It had a musty atmosphere and, from the number of cobwebs, he could see that it hadn't been visited for some time. Fortunately, the door was unlocked. Letting himself out and holding the candle up, he stepped into a narrow passageway that ran the length of the building. There was a nightwatchman on duty but Daniel doubted if the man bothered to come up to the attic rooms. The visitor could move about with impunity. On the next floor down, Daniel was more cautious, shielding the candle with a hand as he went from room to room.

It was on the floor below that he eventually found the place he was after. A sign on the door told him that the municipal archives were kept there. There was only one problem. The door was securely locked. He first tried to unlock it with the point of his dagger but to no avail. Since the weapon was a treasured gift, he didn't want to risk damaging it by using it as a lever to prise open the door so he fell back on brute force. Taking a few steps back, he flung himself hard at the door. His right shoulder hit the timber with such impetus that the lock snapped open and the door was flung back on its hinges. In the cavernous emptiness of the town hall, the noise was amplified ten-fold. It reverberated for seconds.

From somewhere far below, an angry yell arose.

'Who's up there?'

Daniel had company.

CHAPTER SEVEN

There was no apparent escape. Daniel couldn't risk leaving by means of the rope and, in any case, he refused to run away without even trying to find Vauban's plan. Since the nightwatchman would have to conduct a systematic search of a large building, Daniel would at least have some time on his side. What he needed to do, he decided, was to create some kind of diversion. Candle in hand, he went along the corridor and tried all the doors until he found one that was unlocked. He darted inside, pulled out a wastepaper basket and swept all the letters and documents on the desk into it. Then he set the paper alight with his candle and put it where the flames would catch the edge of a chair. He rushed out and closed the door behind him.

As he ran back to the other room, he heard worrying sounds from below. The nightwatchman had opened the main door and was asking for help from the guards outside.

Daniel counted three pairs of footsteps pounding up the stairs. He moved like lightning. Entering the room with the archives, he closed the door and propped a chair against it. Then he began as thorough a search as he could manage by the light of the candle, opening drawers in sequence and taking out armfuls of charters, muniments and other documents. What he was given was a fleeting history of Lille and, under other circumstances, would have found it quite fascinating. Now, however, everything was hastily discarded onto the floor as he scrambled to find the details of the fortifications.

There was no sign of them and he began to wonder if the plan had been commandeered by someone in charge of extending the defences at present. It was conceivable that it wasn't in Lille at all but was being kept in Versailles as an example of how best to fortify a town. It might even be in the possession of Vauban's nephew, an engineer in the French army travelling with Marshal Boufflers. Daniel searched on with growing desperation, ever more conscious of the heavy footsteps working their way along the corridor outside. Each door was unlocked so that the guards and the nightwatchman could look inside. Their voices were getting closer and closer. Evidently, one of the men was losing patience.

'Are you sure you heard a noise?' he demanded.

'I heard it loud and clear,' said the nightwatchman.

'It could have been a dream. We know you sleep in here most of the night.'

'That's unfair. I never close my eyes. I patrol the building with great care. What I heard was the sound of a door bursting open.'

'I think you farted in your sleep and that woke you up.'

They opened another door and Daniel could hear them clearly, stamping around inside. It was only a question of time before they reached him. Opening the last drawer, he scooped up everything in it and dropped it on the desk before going through it. There was no shortage of plans but they all related to buildings or churches. There was an edge of desperation in his search now. A glance was all he bestowed on each document before tossing it away. Daniel felt cheated. After risking death and capture, he'd hoped for more than details about the architecture of the town and the wills of some of its richest inhabitants. He was just about to give up when he flicked another document onto the floor and glanced at the next one. At first, he wasn't quite sure what he was looking at. Then he saw a name that set his blood racing – Sébastien Vauban, Marshal of France. It was there after all.

Without even bothering to scrutinise the plan, he folded it up and stuffed it inside his shirt, blowing out his candle as he did so. Moving the chair from behind the door, he put his back to the timber and listened. The voices seemed to be directly outside.

'We're wasting our time,' said one of the guards.

'No,' said the nightwatchman. 'We must check every room.'

'How could anyone have possibly got in?'

'I don't know but someone did. Perhaps he came in during the day and hid in here. Perhaps he climbed in through a window.'

The guard was contemptuous. 'There are bars on all the windows except those in the attic. Only an imbecile would try to clamber up onto the roof. I think you made a mistake.'

Daniel heard a key being put in the lock and saw a glimmer of light from a lantern peeping under the door. He braced himself for action, taking out his dagger in readiness and hoping that the element of surprise would aid his escape. His body was tense, his nerves tingling. A second away from discovery, he crouched in the darkness and steeled himself. Now that he'd found it, he wasn't going to yield up Vauban's plan without a fight.

But nobody came in. Instead the three men were distracted.

'I can smell something,' said the nightwatchman.

'You must have farted again,' said one of the guards, laughing.

'It's smoke, I tell you. Take a deep sniff.'

'He's right,' said the other guard. 'Something's on fire.'

'It must be coming from further down the corridor,' decided the nightwatchman. 'Hold up that lantern. We don't want the place to burn down around our ears.'

They rushed off until they came to the room where the fire had been started. When they saw smoke issuing from under the door, they flung it open and went in. The chair was alight now and the fire was spreading. They cried out in panic. Daniel didn't wait to see how they'd cope with the emergency. As soon as he heard them dash off, he opened the door, waited until the coast was clear, then fled down the stairs, holding the banister all the way to make sure he didn't miss his footing in the dark. Candles were alight in the entrance hall so he was able to sprint across it and let himself out into the night. The guards who would have stopped him were too busy trying to put out the fire upstairs. Daniel went round to the rear of the building and saw Raymond craning his neck to look upwards. Creeping up behind him, Daniel tapped him on the shoulder.

'Time to leave,' he said. 'I came back the easy way.'

Raymond gulped. 'You made me jump,' he admitted, hand on his heart. He pointed to a window in the town hall. Flames were dancing in it. 'Did you know that there's a fire up there, Monsieur?'

'Is there?' said Daniel, feigning surprise. 'People should be more careful with their candles.'

The man with the close-set eyes had been there day after day without success. Everyone in the regiment knew who Captain Daniel Rawson was but nobody could tell him where he could be found. When he saw another officer strolling near the edge of the camp, he sidled over to him and spoke with a guttural accent.

'Good afternoon, Lieutenant,' he said, politely.

'How did you recognise my rank?' asked Jonathan Ainley. 'Most civilians can't tell the difference between one uniform and another.'

'I once served in the Hessian army, sir.'

'Ah, I see.'

'If I wasn't so old, I'd still be bearing arms now.'

'We all have to retire some day. Even our esteemed captain-general will leave the army in due course, though I suspect that he has a few years left in him yet.'

'Soldiers mature with age,' said the man with an ingratiating smile. 'Look at Marshal Boufflers. He must be in his sixties yet the French still think he's the best man to send to Lille.'

'You seem well-informed, my friend.'

'I like to know what's going on.'

As they chatted casually, Ainley was weighing the man up and was careful to give no information about the role that his regiment was playing. Though the fellow had an unprepossessing appearance, he had an engaging manner and slowly won Ainley's confidence. The man chose his moment to broach the topic that had brought him there.

'You belong to a fine regiment, Lieutenant,' he said.

'I like to think so.'

'Even someone like me knows about the 24th Foot.'

'All our infantry regiments have high standards.'

'But this is the only one that has such an outstanding officer.'

Ainley laughed self-effacingly. 'You flatter me, my friend.'

'Oh, I wasn't talking about you, sir,' said the man, touching his arm. 'The person I had in mind was Captain Rawson.'

'You've *heard* of him?'

'His fame is widespread.'

'Then it's deservedly so,' said Ainley with enthusiasm. 'He's truly earned his renown. Daniel – Captain Rawson – is the very epitome of gallantry. I'm proud to be a fellow officer of his.'

'You're not the only one, sir. I was in a tavern some days ago when officers from this regiment came in. I heard the name of Captain Rawson spoken with reverence.'

'That's as it should be.'

'I hope to get a sighting of him one day. If the reports of his escapades are true, we've nobody like him in the Hessian army.'

Ainley laughed again. 'Nor in any other army, I fancy. I'd go so far as to say that Captain Rawson is unique. I can tell you one thing: I'm grateful that he belongs to us. I'd hate to fight against a soldier of that calibre.'

'So would I, Lieutenant.'

'One can learn so much from watching a man like that.'

'When will he be returning to camp?'

'How did you know he'd left it?' asked Ainley with suspicion.

'I overheard one of the officers say so in the tavern.'

Ainley's tone sharpened. 'Is that why you were hanging around in there – to listen to the gossip?'

'No, no,' said the man, annoyed with himself for having aroused distrust. 'I was there to visit an old friend of mine who's the landlord there.' The lie tripped easily off his tongue. 'It was difficult *not* to hear mention of Captain Rawson. But I can see that I've offended you in some way,' he went on, obsequiously, 'and I didn't mean to do that, sir. I thank you for sparing the time to talk to me and will bid you farewell.'

'I'm not offended,' said Ainley, soothed by what he thought was a genuine apology. 'And there's no reason why you shouldn't hear the name of Captain Rawson on people's tongues. He's off on his latest adventure at the moment and I'm already missing him. Not to worry,' he added. 'The captain is certain to be back in a day or two.'

The man nodded in gratitude. He had what he wanted.

* * *

'Why do we have to leave?' protested Rachel. 'I like it here.'

'You *like* being in an enemy stronghold?'

'I feel at home in the *Coq d'Or*. Both of my husbands talked about leaving the army and running an inn. Neither of them lived to do that, alas, but the idea always appealed to me. I think that I'd make a good landlady.'

'There's no doubting that,' said Daniel. 'You've served behind the bar every day since we've been here and the customers love you. Madame Lizier has been delighted to have your help.'

'I've never had so many drinks bought for me before.'

They were in their room at the tavern. Rachel had taken to life as a barmaid. Gregarious by nature, she revelled in the hustle and bustle of the *Coq d'Or*. Given the choice, customers all preferred to be served by her rather than by anyone else. She had only one complaint. While she enjoyed being Daniel's wife by day, she wished that their marriage could have continued throughout the night. To a woman as sensual as Rachel Rees, sleeping alone while a highly desirable man slumbered on the floor beside her bed was more than frustrating. It was almost agonising. But she abided by their verbal contract and made no attempt to seduce him away from it.

'It's far too dangerous to stay,' Daniel explained.

'I don't feel under threat in any way.'

'That's because you haven't been out yet. The streets are full of soldiers. There was an incident at the town hall last night and security has been tightened as a result.'

She turned a roguish eye on him. 'I don't suppose that Alain Borrel had anything to do with the incident, did he?'

Daniel was stone-faced. 'I really don't know what you mean.'

'Why did you borrow that rope from Madame Lizier? And where did you and Raymond go in the middle of the night?'

'We went in search of wild horses.'

'There are no wild horses in a town.'

'That's why we came back empty-handed.'

Rachel cackled. 'You give nothing away, do you?'

'Silence is golden,' he said, a finger to his lips. 'Now gather up your things and we'll take our leave.'

'Can't we stay just one more night?' she begged.

'What if Sergeant Furneaux comes looking for you after dark? And if it isn't him, it will be some other over-amorous Frenchman. I've seen the way they look at you, Rachel. Do you really want to give yourself to an enemy soldier?'

'That would be a terrible betrayal of our army,' she said, vehemently. 'I'd never do such a thing. If any of them tried to climb into my bed with nothing on, I'd cut off his *Coq d'Or*.'

When they'd packed everything up, they went to see their friends. Bette Lizier was sad to see them go but she recognised that it would be foolish for them to stay any longer. With the garrison swelled by the arrival of fresh troops, work on the defences had been sped up. It would soon be difficult to get in and out of the town. Raymond was patently upset by their sudden departure, astounded by Daniel's daredevil antics the previous night and hoping to emulate him one day. He embraced Daniel with tears in his eyes.

It was Estelle who caused the real surprise. During their

stay there, she'd been a quiet, undemonstrative barmaid who fulfilled her duties with great efficiency. While she might lack Rachel's outgoing nature, she was no shrinking violet, coping well with boisterous customers and bringing a dry humour to any badinage. When she was not at work, Daniel had noticed, she seemed a rather lonely person. Yet here she was, squeezing his hands as he kissed her on the cheeks and shooting him a strange look.

'I hope that Guillaume is soon released,' he observed.

'It can only be a matter of time,' said Bette Lizier.

'Thank him for his excellent advice.'

Rachel was curious. 'What advice was that?'

'Nothing that need concern you,' said Daniel.

'I'd just like to know what's going on, Alain.'

'I'll tell you when we get back.'

After a final round of farewells, they went out to the stables and collected their horses. After helping Rachel into the saddle, Daniel handed her the lead rein of the donkey. She kicked her mount into action and trotted out through the gate. Daniel was a few yards behind her. As he turned back to the tavern, he saw Raymond and his mother waving vigorously, but it was the face at the window that he would remember most clearly. Estelle was staring blankly at him, her hand raised in a forlorn wave.

The streets were teeming and Daniel had difficulty keeping up with Rachel as she threaded carefully through the jostling hordes. Soldiers were everywhere. The arrival of Marshal Boufflers with the reinforcements had lifted the spirits of the whole town. What Daniel didn't know at that time was that the marshal had wisely brought bags of gold coin with him to pay the arrears of the garrison. At a stroke, he'd removed the main cause of discontent. When they got in sight of the main gate, Daniel saw that there would be a long delay. Soldiers were stopping everyone who wanted to leave, questioning them at length and searching their belongings.

Two of them spotted Rachel and both reached the same conclusion. Making their way across to her, they asked her to dismount from her horse. Upset by their curt manner, she glared at them as she descended to the ground. Daniel nudged his horse across to her and spoke as if he'd never met her before.

'Is something wrong, Madame?' he asked.

'Go your way, Monsieur,' she advised. 'These dolts have mistaken me for someone else. They say that I'm under arrest.'

He turned to the soldiers. 'What's her offence?'

'Mind your own business!' one of them snapped.

'You can't arrest an innocent person.'

'We can do as we wish, Monsieur, as you'll see if you don't get out of our way. Would you like to be locked up as well?'

Since he was carrying the stolen plan, the last thing that Daniel wanted was a spell behind bars. He'd certainly be searched and his guilt would be exposed. Looking at Rachel, he tried to explain his dilemma without using any words. She understood how important it was for him to get out of the town.

'Don't bother about me,' she told him. 'It's very kind of you to take an interest but there's no need. Once this matter is sorted out, they'll have to release me. I bid you goodbye – and thank you.'

There was no more to be said. Rachel was led off by one of the soldiers while the other tugged the two animals behind him. Daniel joined the queue at the gate, wondering what could possibly have happened. Had they known what he was carrying, the soldiers would have arrested him, yet it was Rachel – blithely ignorant of his activities in Lille – who'd been taken into custody. It was alarming. His turn at the gate eventually came and he dismounted to answer a barrage of questions. He submitted readily to a search, doffing his hat and holding his arms out wide so that he could be patted down. Finding nothing suspicious on him, they sent him on his way. Daniel waited until he was outside the town before he put on the hat in which his dagger was cunningly hidden. Vauban's plan was concealed in one of his boots and he'd not been asked to remove those.

In the sense that he'd obtained the plan, his mission had been a success but the unexpected loss of his accomplice removed any feeling of achievement. One thing was uppermost in his mind. He owed a profound debt to Rachel. She'd trusted him enough to enter an enemy town with him even though he was unable to tell her why they were there. What she'd offered him was a means of disguise. He couldn't abandon her now. His priority was to deliver Vauban's plan to the Duke of Marlborough but, the moment that was done, something else would take precedence.

He had to return to Lille to rescue Rachel Rees.

Amalia Janssen and her father had been jangled as they were driven away from Blenheim Palace. The Duchess of Marlborough's attitude towards them had been wounding. They'd been treated less like honoured guests than unwelcome interlopers. They nursed their hurt feelings all the way to Woodstock. When they saw the accommodation, however, the clouds over their visit dispersed instantly. A rambling house awaited them, complete with two servants and a cook. Occupying a corner of a large estate, it had sizeable gardens at the front and rear. It was utterly charming and picturesque. What added to their pleasure was that the owner arrived on horseback to greet them in person.

'Welcome, welcome,' he said, effusively. 'As long as you're here, be bold to call on me for anything you require – Sir John Rievers at your service.'

'Thank you, Sir John,' said Janssen before introducing his daughter. 'Your kindness is much appreciated.'

'Oh, it's not kindness, dear sir. It's an act of homage. Your reputation comes before you. I have a friend who owns a tapestry woven by Emanuel Janssen and I'm consumed with envy whenever I behold it.' He smiled at Amalia. 'Your father is an exquisite artist.'

'I know of none finer,' she said, loyally.

'Nor do I, nor do I.'

Remaining in the saddle, Sir John swept off his hat and beamed at his visitors. He was a fleshy man of medium height with impeccable attire cut by an expensive tailor to diminish the bulge of his paunch. Well into his forties, he had an unforced air of distinction that could only have come from good breeding. Framed by a periwig that rested on his shoulders, his face had a flabby openness that endeared them to him immediately.

'By Jove!' he cried. 'It's a joy to entertain you.'

'The pleasure is ours, Sir John,' said Janssen.

'Have you met Her Grace yet?' When their faces

darkened, he burst out laughing. 'Yes, I can see that you have. Blenheim Palace is not the ideal venue for a first encounter. Whenever she's there, Sarah spends all her time battling with the architect or the builders.'

'The duchess did seem rather preoccupied,' said Amalia.

'Take no notice of it. That's just her way.'

'I'm glad to hear it, Sir John.'

'When she sees you tomorrow, she'll be full of apologies, I'm sure. Oh, in my urge to meet you, I almost forgot. You're invited to dine with me at the Hall. Sarah – Her Grace, I should say – will be joining us for an hour or so.'

'That sounds encouraging,' said Janssen.

'It's a very informal gathering. My dear wife will be there, of course, though I should warn you that Lady Rievers is not in the best of health. A malady has been dogging her in recent years. Barbara has stoic endurance but she tires easily. However,' he went on, 'she was as insistent as I am that you dine with us tomorrow and tell us how we can best be of use to you.'

'We've no wish to put you out, Sir John.'

'You could never do that, Mr Janssen.'

'Your cordiality is a tonic in itself.'

'Then I'll not give you an overdose of it,' said Sir John, putting his hat back on at a rakish angle, 'for I know how weary you must be after all that travelling. Rest is the order of the day. Servants are at your disposal and you must eat your fill.'

'We cannot thank you enough.'

'No,' said Amalia, overcome by his generosity. 'We are in your debt, Sir John.' She glanced round. 'Is the Hall nearby?'

'It's on the other side of the estate,' explained Sir John, 'less than a half a mile away. Rievers Hall is nowhere near as sumptuous as Blenheim Palace but it's a comfortable home and has been for generations of my family. I guarantee that you and your father will find your visit there – indeed, your whole stay with us – a memorable event.' He shared a smile between them. 'That's a promise.'

Wheeling his horse, he rode off across the estate at a canter. Amalia watched him go, grateful for the way he'd obliterated the memory of their discourteous reception at Blenheim Palace. Sir John Rievers had been genial and reassuring. He'd clearly gone to great trouble for their sake. Sarah, Duchess of Marlborough had been less approachable but in Sir John, Amalia sensed, they had a real friend.

As he rode out of Lille, Daniel went past the teams of men working on the outer defences and he made a mental note of their progress. Some of them were waist-deep in a ditch, shovelling out earth to form a rampart. With the aid of horses, others were trying to manoeuvre massive tree trunks into place. Before the Allies got anywhere near to the town walls, there'd be many obstacles in their way. They, in turn, had not been idle. When he was some distance from the town, Daniel saw other groups toiling in the morning sunshine, sturdy peasants who'd been recruited from the surrounding countryside, helping to build fortifications that would eventually encircle Lille and cut off all access to it. British and Dutch engineers were in charge but it was local labour providing much of the workforce. Having seen what was happening in and immediately outside the town,

Daniel was certain of one thing. Lille would not capitulate easily.

'Saints preserve us!' exclaimed Marlborough, rising from his chair. 'Is that you, Captain Rawson?'

'It is, Your Grace, and I apologise for presenting myself in this state. I just felt that you'd want to see this as soon as I got back.' He handed the plan to him. 'Otherwise, I'd have taken the trouble to wash, shave and put on my uniform.'

'You found it?' said Cardonnel. 'Well done, Daniel!'

'Well done, indeed,' echoed Marlborough, unfolding the plan and placing it on the table. 'This will be invaluable. When we sent you off to Lille, I wasn't even sure that this would be there.'

'I, too, had grave doubts, Your Grace.'

Cardonnel was excited. 'Do tell us how you came by it,' he encouraged. 'Where was it and how did you manage to steal it?'

Daniel smiled. 'It's a long story.'

'We insist on hearing every bit of it.'

'And don't couch it in any false modesty,' said Marlborough. 'Give us the full details. You're entitled to boast.'

'My visit was not entirely successful, Your Grace,' said Daniel, thinking of Rachel Rees. 'Let me explain.'

They were upset to hear that Guillaume Lizier was in custody but impressed by the way that his family had sheltered the visitors. What amazed them was how Daniel had used a rope to cross from the church to the town hall. It had been a remarkable feat. Since the rope had been left in place and since the archives had been scattered everywhere, the guards had quickly worked out that enemy agents had been in the town. Measures had been taken to stop them escaping. Only one of them had managed to leave.

'Why should they arrest your accomplice?' said Cardonnel.

Daniel shrugged. 'I wish I knew.'

'Was she carrying anything that gave her away?'

'Not as far as I know. Rachel had sold most of her wares in the market. There was very little left in her saddlebags.'

'At least they didn't connect the two of you,' said Marlborough. 'It would have been a catastrophe if you'd been arrested as well.'

'I agree, Your Grace,' said Daniel. 'Had they found that plan on me, I'd have been hanged with the rope I used to get into the town hall. I'd look for no mercy from them.'

'How will you get back into the town?'

'I'll have to devise a different method next time.'

'Will you go alone?'

'No, I'll take someone with me, Your Grace. Before I do that,' said Daniel, 'I'd like to get out of these clothes and have a good wash. I'm not sure that a beard suits me.'

'It changes your appearance completely,' said Cardonnel.

'Well, it's not going to stay.'

After exchanging a few pleasantries, Daniel went out and headed for his own quarters. He was intercepted by Jonathan Ainley who had to look twice before being able to identify him.

'You're back with us, then,' he noted.

'It's only for a short time, Jonathan.'

'May I ask where you've been?'

'You may ask,' said Daniel, 'but I'm not able to tell you. Suffice it to say that I've been busy behind enemy lines.'

'Better you than me, Daniel. I wouldn't have the bravado for that kind of work. I could never pass myself off as a Frenchman or as anyone else for that matter. As soon as people look at me and listen to my voice, they know that I couldn't be anything other than a British officer.' Pursing his lips, he shook his head. 'It's a shame, really. I'd love to do something really venturesome.'

'Isn't fighting a battle venturesome enough for you?' They traded a laugh. 'You'll have to excuse me while I clean myself off.'

'Of course,' said Ainley. 'By the way, there was someone asking after you the other day.'

'Oh – who was that?'

'I didn't get his name. He's one of the camp followers, I think. He fought in the Hessian army earlier in his life. But he was very keen to talk about you.'

'Why was that, I wonder?'

'He'd heard about some of your exploits.'

'Have you seen this man since?' asked Daniel.

'Yes,' replied Ainley. 'He was hanging around this morning, as it happens. He seemed a friendly sort of fellow.'

Daniel thanked him for the information and went off. Now that he was back in camp, he was keen to shed his disguise. When he was shaving, however, he decided that the beard would not vanish in its entirety. He kept a neat moustache and trimmed it with care. As he admired the effect in the mirror, an idea slowly blossomed. It made him smile. Donning his uniform, he rode off to the other camp in search of Henry Welbeck. As expected, he met with refusal.

'No, no, no, Dan!' said Welbeck, jabbing his pipe in the air.

'All I ask is that you think it over.'

'The answer will remain the same.'

'A lady is in distress. Doesn't that mean anything to you?'

'Yes,' said the other with a glint. 'It means that the blessed woman won't be able to pester me here in camp.'

'That's very ungrateful of you,' said Daniel. 'You're talking about someone who gave you a pouch of tobacco out of the kindness of her heart. Rachel told me about it on the way to Lille. It was your favourite brand as well, wasn't it? You're enjoying it this very moment.'

Snatching the pipe from his mouth, Welbeck banged it on his heel to empty its contents before stuffing it into his pocket. He spoke with a resentful curiosity.

'How on earth did she know it was my favourite?'

'She has a way of finding out these things.'

'Well, she can stop finding out things about me because I don't like anyone poking their nose into my business – especially if it's a woman like her.'

'Rachel is a courageous lady. When I asked her to go into Lille with me, she didn't hesitate to come.'

'And where did it get her? Locked up.'

'That's not her fault, Henry.'

'The woman is a menace. Leave her there, I say.'

'Don't be so unkind,' scolded Daniel. 'You may not like

Rachel Rees but she made lots of friends at the tavern where we stayed. A sergeant – looking rather like you, now I come to think of it – was so smitten that he tried to jump into bed with her. I had to dump him in the horse trough to cool his ardour.'

'Well, you won't have to do that with me,' said Welbeck with asperity. 'I've no ardour to cool.' He took a deep breath. 'Listen, Dan, I'm sorry that you have this problem but I'm not the person who can help you solve it. Take someone else – Lieutenant Ainley, for instance.'

Daniel grinned. 'He's the *last* person I'd choose.'

'You wouldn't need to ask him twice.'

'I wouldn't even bother to do it once. Jonathan knows the reason why. In fact, he admitted as much to me earlier. No matter what sort of disguise he had, he'd look and sound exactly what he is. He'd never convince anyone that he was a French soldier.'

'French soldier?' repeated Welbeck, incredulously.

'Well, we can hardly ride up to Lille in *these* uniforms.'

'I'm not going in any uniform, Dan. Whatever hare-brained scheme you have this time, keep me out of it. My work is here, trying to turn the latest useless recruits into something akin to soldiers. It's like making bricks without straw.'

'Other sergeants could do that job. Only you can help me.'

'You're a liar, Dan Rawson.'

'You are, Henry. I know that I can trust you. Besides, you have a personal interest. You know Rachel.'

Welbeck was puce. 'I have no personal interest in *any* woman,' he asserted, 'least of all that particular harpy! I'm certainly not going to risk my life so that she can come back here to be a nuisance.'

'You may have second thoughts. Yes,' Daniel went on, quickly, 'I know that it seems unlikely, but I ask you to remember this. Think how much you enjoyed that visit you and I made to the French camp before the battle of Oudenarde. I could see that you were thrilled by it. And when I was held captive, you didn't turn your back on me. You used cunning and bravery to rescue me.' He took a step closer. 'It was reckless of us to go there but you loved every second of it, Henry.'

Leaving his friend to consider his request, Daniel mounted his horse and rode back to Marlborough's quarters in the main camp to give a fuller account of the new defences he'd seen being built in Lille and to describe the inspirational effect of Marshal Boufflers' arrival in the town.

'It's hardly surprising,' said Cardonnel. 'Boufflers used to be governor of French Flanders and of Lille itself. They adore him.'

'He's had a distinguished career,' conceded Marlborough, 'and, even at his advanced age, he has the energy for a fight. Pray God that *I'm* not still in uniform when I'm in my sixties. King Louis has sent the right man. He'll be a worthy opponent.'

'I agree, Your Grace. Marshal Boufflers is well versed in military engineering and no French commander has withstood so many sieges. It's no wonder they cheered him to the echo.'

'I was on the ramparts when it happened,' recalled Daniel. 'He was welcomed like a deliverer. However, he's not always been the victor,' he reminded them. 'I fought with King William when we besieged Namur in 1695. The marshal was forced to surrender after losing two-thirds of his 13,000 men.'

'Let's hope we don't have to kill quite so many before he gives in this time,' said Marlborough, solemnly. 'There'll come a point when he realises it's senseless to go on. To reach that point, of course, we have to maintain a constant bombardment of the town and have a ready supply of food and ammunition. It's going to be a tricky exercise,' he confessed, gazing down at the plan of Vauban's defences. 'We could be here until Christmas.'

The discussion went on for a long time and Daniel felt privileged to be taken into the captain-general's confidence. The plan that he'd retrieved from Lille would be sent to Prince Eugene who was in charge of siege operations. It would help him to decide on the best mode of attack. Knowing exactly what they were up against was a real bonus. Because he didn't intend to set out until evening, Daniel was going to dine with Ainley and some of the other officers. After all his exertions, it would be good to have a respite. Before that, however, he needed to return to his quarters. On the way there, he caught a glimpse of someone dodging between the tents. When he stopped to look more closely, the figure had disappeared. Deciding that he'd been mistaken, Daniel walked briskly on.

His mind was still grappling with the problem of how to rescue Rachel Rees and with the more difficult task of persuading Henry Welbeck to join him in the venture. Preoccupied and off guard, he wasn't ready for the attack.

For as soon as he entered his quarters, he was tripped up and sent head first to the ground. Rolling quickly over, he saw that the point of a sword was being held inches from his neck.

'Remember me?' asked a voice.

CHAPTER EIGHT

Since the man was not in uniform, Daniel didn't recognise him at first. His attacker was dressed in civilian clothing and wore a hat that came low over his forehead. It was the voice that told Daniel who his unwelcome visitor was. The Hessian cavalry officer whom he'd beaten and shamed had come for revenge. Poised for a fatal thrust, Erich Schlager stood over him and grinned malevolently.

'Where is she?' he demanded.

'Who are you talking about?'

'That fat sow who owes me two horses.'

'Her name is Rachel Rees,' said Daniel, calmly, 'and she owes you nothing whatsoever.'

'Tell me where she is. I came here for both of you.'

'The horses have both been sold.'

'That's not what I asked,' said Schlager, prodding Daniel's chest with the point of his sword. 'Where will I find her?'

'You wouldn't believe me if I told you.'

'If she's in this camp, my man will sniff her out. He found you for me in the end. Where should he start looking for Rachel Rees?'

'In the town of Lille,' replied Daniel.

'Don't jest with me, Captain Rawson,' warned the man, jabbing him again. 'Be kind to yourself. Tell me what I want to know and I'll make it a quick death. Lie to me and I'll cut off your ears, your nose and your balls before digging out your heart.'

'I swear to you that I'm telling the truth. Rachel is in Lille.'

'And what could she possibly be doing there?'

Faint hope stirred. Daniel's survival rested on his being able to keep the man talking for as long as he could. The Hessian could have killed him already but he needed information first. Daniel tried to turn that information to his advantage.

'I was sent to Lille on an assignment,' he explained. 'It was at the special request of His Grace, the Duke of Marlborough.'

'Yes, I know that you're attached to his staff.'

'To get into the town, I went in disguise, wearing those clothes over there.' Schlager turned his head to look at the items draped over the back of a chair. 'Rachel came with me, posing as my wife.'

Schlager goggled. 'Your *wife?*' he said with disgust. 'Who'd ever think of marrying that bloated whore?'

'She's not a whore,' said Daniel, stoutly. 'She's a brave woman who risked her life for a cause in which *you* ought to believe. Good heavens, man! We're fighting on the same side. Doesn't that mean anything to you?' Schlager's eyelids fluttered. It had obviously never entered his mind. 'As for husbands, Rachel has already buried two of them after they'd been killed in battle. Such is the lot of a soldier's wife. Since then she's struggled along as best she can.'

Schlager took a step backward. 'Why is she still in Lille?'

'I don't know. They arrested her as we left.'

'Why was that?'

'I wish I had the answer,' said Daniel, mind whirring as he sought a means of escape. 'I was the one carrying what we went there to steal but they stopped her at the main gate. If you don't believe me, the Duke of Marlborough will confirm every word I say. He'll also suggest to you that it's not the function of Allies to kill each other when we have a common enemy to defeat. Do you want to do the French army's work for them?' He tried to reason with the man. 'I can see why I made you so angry,' he continued, 'but you have to admit that it was a fair fight. I gave you far more chance than you're giving me.'

'You let that woman mock me,' said Schlager, wincing at the memory. 'When I got back to camp without a horse, I was a laughing stock. You and she must pay for that.'

'Rachel is miles away in Lille.'

'Then you must die first, Captain Rawson.'

'Wait!' said Daniel, sitting up and raising his palm. 'Honour is at stake here. You have every right to demand satisfaction. I accept that. Let me have my sword and we'll find somewhere quiet to fight a duel.'

Schlager sniggered. 'I'm not such a fool as that. The minute you have a weapon in your hand, you'll call out for help and your friends will come running. I'll be outnumbered.'

'I give you my word that I won't do that.'

'You won't get the opportunity.'

Daniel was in earnest. 'This is between you and me,' he urged. 'Let's settle it like soldiers and men of honour. You can choose the place right now.'

Schlager paused long enough to consider the suggestion. The brief distraction was his downfall. Noting the hesitation, Daniel leapt to his feet in an instant and grabbed the chair, shaking the items of apparel to the ground. The next moment he was using it to fend off the violent attack that was suddenly unleashed. Schlager came at him as if in a cavalry charge, his sword flailing away with brutal power. Pieces of wood were hacked viciously off the chair and went spinning in the air. When one of the legs was snapped clean off by the force of a blow, Daniel realised that he couldn't hold out for long. What his makeshift shield did, however, was to give him the opportunity to work his way to the corner where his own sword was hanging. Flinging the chair into the Hessian's face, he drew his sabre and squared up to his man.

'Now we can fight on equal terms,' said Daniel, breathlessly. 'Cowards like you only strike when they have all the advantages.'

'I'm no coward!' yelled Schlager, throwing his hat aside.

'Prove it.'

The Hessian launched another attack, lunging dementedly away in a bid to slaughter his man quickly. Daniel parried every thrust and ducked under every desperate swing. Even in the confined space of a tent, he used his superior footwork to effect, dodging, weaving and throwing his adversary off balance. Sparks went everywhere as the blades clashed. The noise was deafening. There was a loud tearing sound as the point of Schlager's sword ripped accidentally through the canvas. He was panting heavily and beginning to slow down. Sweat oozed out of every pore. His act of revenge had turned into a fight for his life. Cursing himself for not killing his prisoner when he had the chance, he hurled himself forward again and made one last, wild, murderous thrust. Daniel anticipated him and, as he parried the blade, stepped smartly to one side, bringing his own sword in a swift arc to cut clean through the Hessian's wrist. Erich Schlager howled in agony. He looked down with mingled horror and disbelief at his sword, now on the ground with his hand still clasped around it. Blood was pouring out of the wound. Crying in pain, he put the stump under his other arm in a bid to stem the bleeding.

It was at that moment that Jonathan Ainley opened the tent flap and pushed in the man with the close-set eyes.

'What's going on, Captain Rawson?' he asked, taking in the scene. 'I heard sounds of a fight and found this man lurking outside your quarters.'

Daniel took control. 'Fetch a surgeon, Lieutenant,' he ordered, grabbing the shirt from the ground to use as a tourniquet. 'We have to keep this devil alive to face a court martial.'

Rievers Hall was magnificent. Dating back to the reign of Henry VIII, it was a fortified manor house encircled by a deep moat. Amalia Janssen and her father were dazzled by its combination of architectural beauty and awesome solidity.

Such daunting battlements would allow the inhabitants of the house to withstand a siege for a long time. The carriage delivered them to the massive oak front door and a liveried servant let them in and conducted them to their hosts. Both of the visitors had taken immense care with their dress and with their appearance but they were made to feel embarrassingly commonplace in the presence of the Duchess of Marlborough, who was attired with regal splendour. Diamond rings and a gorgeous diamond necklace added to her grandeur. Her manner was condescending but she did show a genuine interest in Emanuel Janssen's design for the tapestry.

'This is very stirring,' she complimented. 'My husband tells me that you had the help of someone who actually fought at Ramillies.'

'That's true, Your Grace,' he said. 'His name is Captain Daniel Rawson and he was beside your husband during the battle.'

'Yes, I've met Captain Rawson more than once. He's a most admirable soldier.'

Amalia was delighted to hear Daniel being praised. She'd hoped for an apology from the duchess for the offhand way the visitors had been treated at Blenheim Palace but it was not forthcoming. It soon became clear that Sarah never deigned to apologise. All that she was concerned about was the tardiness of the builders and what she perceived as their excessive costs. She railed against everyone, from the architect to the lowliest stonemason. Sir John Rievers tried to jolly her out of her obsession with the house and her interest shifted to the war. Another string of complaints followed, many of them directed against scheming politicians whom she accused of working behind Marlborough's back to weaken his position as the overall commander. When she'd vented her fury, she rose to her feet, made a few gracious remarks to each of them and withdrew.

'I thought Her Grace was dining with us,' said Janssen.

'No,' replied Sir John. 'She had a prior invitation but was kind enough to show her face here for your benefit. As you saw, she is in essence a delightful lady. Sarah's bark is far worse than her bite.'

'That's a dreadful expression,' complained his wife.

He gave a ripe chuckle. 'But nevertheless apt, I think.'

'I couldn't disagree with you more.'

'I'm sorry if the expression offended your sensibilities, my love,' he said, penitently. 'I'll amend it. A better way of putting it is that Sarah may have a reputation for being combative but she has a softer side that can transform her into the semblance of an angel.'

Lady Rievers smiled. 'That's going too far, my dear.'

Amalia had taken to her hostess at once. Lady Rievers was a stately woman with a ravished beauty. Arthritis had crippled her joints and something was eating her slowly away. There was an almost deathly pallor on her cheeks. She bore her afflictions with remarkable dignity and without even a trace of self-pity. What struck Amalia was the way in which her husband treated her. Sir John was patient and attentive, helping her to her feet when they adjourned to the dining room and lowering her gently into her chair. It was noticeable that she could only use one hand. Throughout the meal, therefore, he sat beside her so that he could cut up some of the food on her plate. All the time, he kept the conversation flowing.

'What is your next commission?' he asked Janssen. 'You'll be weaving a tapestry of the battle of Oudenarde, I daresay.'

'His Grace has not approached me yet,' said Janssen. 'Nor will he do so until he's seen the Ramillies tapestry. What happens next depends on how pleased he is with my work.'

'He'll be thrilled, Mr Janssen.'

'I endorse that,' said Lady Rievers, sweetly. 'I've seen one of your tapestries and thought it superb.'

'Thank you, Lady Rievers.'

'Listen to my wife,' advised Sir John. 'Barbara has excellent taste. It's the reason she chose to marry me.'

His guests joined in the laughter. Amalia could see how little Lady Rievers ate of the meal but she herself was unable to match the appetite shown by the two men. The quantity and quality of the food was way beyond what she customarily had. The first course comprised a leg of mutton with cauliflower, a steak pie, a shoulder of lamb and a dish of peas. This was followed by a sweetbread pie, a capon, a gooseberry tart and a mixture of seasonal fruit. Wine was served at regular intervals but Amalia was abstemious.

'How do you go about it, Mr Janssen?' said Lady Rievers. 'With a tapestry like your latest one, for instance, where did you start?'

'You can't expect him to give away the tricks of the trade, my love,' joked Sir John. 'He's too afraid that we might pick his brains and set up as weavers ourselves.'

'Not at all,' said Janssen. 'I'll be happy to explain. In the case of a battle, it's important to combine drama with verisimilitude. If it's to hang in Blenheim Palace, it will be seen over the years by a large number of people, some of whom might well have fought at Ramillies.'

'Captain Rawson will be one of them,' said Amalia, involuntarily.

'The first thing I was shown was the order of battle.'

'Let me explain,' said Sir John to his wife. 'That's the order of battle drawn up by the quartermaster-generals so that everyone knows his exact position in the field.'

'At Ramillies,' resumed Janssen, 'the dragoons were on the wings, the cavalry were on the flanks and the infantry were in the centre. His Grace was on a hill overlooking the battlefield, so I was able to show it from his perspective. He will thus be on horseback in the foreground with the fighting taking place below him.'

'And what of this fellow who offered expert advice?'

'Captain Rawson was of immense help to me.'

'What's his regiment?'

'It's the 24th Regiment of Foot, Sir John.'

'I was a major in the dragoons.'

'Don't remind me,' said Lady Rievers, raising a skeletal hand to her brow. 'I worried so much when you were in the army. Appalling things can happen in warfare. I wanted my husband here with me where he was safe and sound.'

He gave her arm an affectionate squeeze. 'That's where I'm content to be, my love – at home in the bosom of my family. Not that we see anything of the twins these days. They've both flown the coop. But tell us more about this Captain Rawson,' he went on. 'He sounds like an interesting character.'

'Oh, he is,' said Amalia, face radiant.

'My daughter is the best person to talk about him,' said

Janssen with a smile. 'Captain Rawson rescued her from perilous situations on two separate occasions. I doubt if anyone is as well qualified to speak about him as Amalia.'

'How ever did he get into the camp in the first place?'

'That's what I want to know,' said Daniel, angrily. 'I've asked Lieutenant Ainley to look into it while I'm away. What were the piquets doing letting unauthorised civilians walk around at will?'

'Someone should be punished for this,' said Welbeck, grimly. 'Supposing you hadn't been alone when you went into your quarters?'

'That thought crossed my mind, Henry. If His Grace had stepped into that tent ahead of me, he might have been killed and we'd be looking for a new captain-general.'

'Who was the man?'

'His name is Lieutenant Erich Schlager. He's the Hessian cavalry officer I told you about, the one who assaulted Rachel.'

'Yes,' said Welbeck under his breath, 'well, I don't blame him for that. The woman can be very provocative. What surprises me,' he went on raising his voice, 'is that he knew when and where to find you.'

'Apparently, he hired a man to keep watch for me. Jonathan Ainley caught the wretch. He was an ugly little creature who'd been asking all sorts of people about me.'

'Didn't that arouse the lieutenant's suspicion?'

'It did eventually.'

'Herr Schlager came for revenge, did he?'

'It was not only me he was after, Henry. He wanted to hunt Rachel down as well. Both of us were meant to die.

Luckily,' said Daniel, 'he got more than he bargained for. He not only lost a hand; he'll lose far more when he faces a court martial.'

'What about his accomplice?'

'He'll be charged with being party to a conspiracy to murder.'

'You should have wrung his neck there and then.'

'I was too busy trying to stop Schlager from bleeding to death.'

It was late evening and the two of them were riding towards Lille in the gathering gloom. Both were wearing French uniforms salvaged from the battlefield at Oudenarde because their owners no longer had any use for them. They were posing as couriers and carried forged despatches, ostensibly for Marshal Boufflers. Against his better judgement, Welbeck had agreed to join Daniel in his quest to release Rachel from gaol. A mediocre horseman, he was already complaining about being saddle-sore. At the same time he felt a surge of excitement running through his body. Taking part in a dangerous enterprise was more exhilarating than drilling new recruits. Since he was far from fluent in French, he decided to leave all the talking to Daniel.

'What if they don't let us in, Dan?'

'They have to let us in. We carry important despatches.'

'Why are we travelling at night?'

'We don't want to be too visible. The guards will only see our faces by their torches and not in broad daylight.'

'How will we get Rachel Rees out of gaol?'

'To be honest, I really don't know.'

'Then why are we going to all this trouble?'

'There'll be a way, Henry,' soothed Daniel. 'All we have to do is to work out what it is.'

Guards had been posted at the outer defences of the town but the visitors had no problem getting past them. When they reached the main gates, however, they were asked to dismount before being questioned closely. Daniel was so plausible that all Welbeck was required to do was to nod from time to time. They were given directions to Marshal Boufflers' quarters, then let in through the gates. Conscious that they were being watched by the guards, Daniel followed their directions. As soon as he was out of sight, however, he veered off towards the *Coq d'Or*. He and Welbeck were soon stabling their horses at the tavern. When they entered the building, they found Bette Lizier in the kitchen. Seeing the uniforms, she stiffened at once.

'Don't you recognise me, Madame?' teased Daniel.

'Is that you, Alain?' she said, holding his face in her hands. 'What's happened to your beard?'

'I had to shave it off. I needed a different disguise.'

'I like your moustache.'

Daniel introduced Welbeck and she shook his hand warmly.

'There's no need to tell me why you're here,' she said.

'I've come to rescue my wife,' said Daniel, ignoring the sardonic glance from Welbeck. 'Rachel was arrested at the gates.'

'I know. Guillaume told me about it when I visited him today. He said that she was bellowing like mad when they locked her up.'

Daniel grinned. 'That sounds like Rachel.'

Bette Lizier offered her help without being asked. She

would provide accommodation even though it consisted of two small rooms. Since they'd ridden some way, she decided that they needed some refreshments. Welbeck warmed to her as she set out a repast on the table. Though he preferred beer, he found the wine very drinkable. They were still eating their impromptu meal when Estelle walked in. At the sight of the uniforms, she came to a dead halt.

'Have you forgotten me so soon?' asked Daniel.

'Alain?' she gasped, running to grasp his hands. 'Is it you?'

'It is – and this is my friend, Henri.'

Staring at his face, she didn't even notice Welbeck. Estelle was amazed at how handsome Daniel was now that he'd shaved off his beard and put on a smart uniform. She couldn't take her eyes off him.

'Is anyone left in the bar, Estelle?' asked Bette.

'Only a few stragglers – Raymond can serve them.'

'Then you must sit down and join us.' Estelle pulled up a chair beside Daniel. 'Now, Alain, what can we do for you?'

'There's one obvious thing,' he explained. 'You've visited your husband many times in the gaol. We need you to draw a rough plan of the building. Will you be going there again tomorrow?' She nodded. 'Could you find out exactly where Rachel is being held?'

'Guillaume has already told me – and yes, I can draw a sketch of the gaol for you. '

'That's good,' said Welbeck, unused to seeing women involved in a dangerous scheme and impressed by her readiness to help. 'And so is this food, Madame. We must thank you.'

'It's the least we can do, Henri. By the way, Estelle,' she

went on, turning to her sister, 'our friends will be staying the night here in the two attic rooms.'

Estelle stood up. 'I'll make the beds at once.'

'Don't make any effort for us,' said Daniel. 'We're soldiers.'

'We're used to sleeping on the bare earth,' added Welbeck.

'We can do better than that, Monsieur,' said Estelle. 'Excuse me. I won't be long.'

She rushed out and left them to finish their meal. Bette could still not get used to the sight of Daniel without his beard and rough attire. In their short time together, she'd grown fond of him. Instinct told her that it would be more difficult to become fond of his friend.

'Wait until Raymond sees you,' she said. 'He hasn't stopped talking about the wonderful Alain Borrel since you left. He was so proud to have helped you last night.'

'There may be more work for your son,' Daniel warned. 'He's a brave young man and we may well have to call on him.'

'Please do so – Raymond won't let you down. It's not just my husband who is at your service, Alain. Everyone at the *Coq d'Or* is only too pleased to assist you. Just tell us what to do.'

'There is one thing, Madame.'

'Yes?'

'When you visit tomorrow, can you find out why Rachel is being held there? We need to know what charges are being levelled at her. Oh,' he continued, 'and if you can get a message to her, let her know that we're thinking about her.'

* * *

In the course of an eventful life, Rachel Rees had slept in all kinds of uncomfortable places. Necessity had made her spend the night in a barn, a cart, a stable, a field, a haystack, a garden, a doorway, a cellar, a barge, on a canal bank or even up a tree. But she'd never suffered as many aches and pains as she did on the plank of bare wood that was chained to the wall of her cell. It was too hard, too uneven, too narrow and, with its abiding stink, too redolent of its previous occupants. Whichever way she twisted, she found herself in pain. The worst of it was that she still had no firm idea of why she was being held. Without explanation, she'd been placed under arrest. Her horse and donkey had been taken along with the contents of their saddlebags. She had nothing.

The contrast could not have been more dramatic. The stay in Lille had been unexpectedly pleasurable and she'd made herself well liked at the tavern. The whole experience had been like a holiday that was taken in the company of a good-looking man who pretended to be her husband. She'd felt no sense of threat. Indeed, as they rode towards the main gate, she was reflecting on how much enjoyment she'd had in Lille. Snatched from her, that enjoyment had been turned into a physical and mental torment. The cell was dirty, the food was inedible and the water brackish. To answer the call of nature, she had a wooden bucket. Most infuriating of all was that nobody would talk to her. When she demanded to know why she was there, she was warned of severe punishment if she continued to harangue the gaolers. Being a woman would not excuse her.

Cowed into silence during the day, she had another fear at night. His name was Pons and he was a big, slovenly man in his thirties, with a repulsive face made even more unlovely by its expression of barely controlled carnal lust. He constantly visited her cell, peering through the bars with eyes ablaze, roving her body with such intensity that she could feel the heat of his stare. His lopsided grin was unsettling and she was revolted by the spittle that dribbled out of the side of his mouth. Whenever he came to look at her, Rachel turned her back on him so that she wouldn't have to read the message in those eyes anymore. Pons eventually withdrew to the outer room but he hadn't done with her. He left the door slightly ajar so that he could sit at the table and watch her through the crack.

Rachel had spent the night before sleeping in the same room as a decent, well-mannered British officer. She was now at the mercy of an oafish gaoler who'd come to work after drinking heavily at a nearby tavern. Nobody was there to protect her. Daniel couldn't come to her rescue this time.

The attic room was small, cluttered with rough-hewn rafters, but Daniel found it serviceable. He stayed awake for a long time, laying there with his hands behind his head as he tried to work out a plan for the morrow. To begin with, he and Welbeck would change into the civilian clothing they'd brought with them in their saddlebags. Asking his friend to sustain the guise of a French officer for any length of time would be inviting trouble. Welbeck would soon be exposed. Both of them needed to be able to merge with the general population. The first place they'd visit was the gaol in order to assess their chances of a rescue. They had to get Rachel Rees out of the town somehow. When he finally drifted off, he forgot all about the prisoner.

It was Amalia Janssen who filled his mind now, walking familiarly into his dream and telling him how much she'd missed him. At first, they were in Amsterdam, strolling along the canal. The scene then shifted seamlessly to England where he was acting as her guide, pointing out the landmarks of his youth and taking her to the churchyard where his father, Nathan Rawson, was buried. Just as swiftly, Daniel was transported back to a tavern in Lille and found himself climbing into bed in an attic room with rough-hewn rafters above his head. No sooner had he snuffed out the candle than he felt Amalia slip in under the blanket to caress him with uncharacteristic boldness, her soft, supple, naked body pressed warmly against his, her urgent lips giving him the sort of kiss that meant she was ready to surrender to him completely.

The sheer impossibility of the dream brought him instantly awake. It took him a moment to realise what was happening. He was indeed being kissed and caressed but it was not by Amalia Janssen. The frantic woman beside him was Estelle and she tried to kiss him again. He drew quickly away from her.

'Don't be angry with me, Alain,' she begged. 'All I ask for is this one night. I know you can't be mine for more than that.'

'Estelle,' he said, restraining her, 'you can't stay here.'

'I wouldn't have done this if you'd really been married but I could see that you weren't. That was only pretence. I watched Rachel in the bar, talking to the customers. No married woman would behave like that. You didn't even sleep in the same bed with her.'

Daniel sat up. 'That's enough,' he said. 'Go back to your

room and we'll talk about this in the morning.'

'I want you.'

'Estelle…'

'Every night you stayed here, I peeped in and saw you asleep on the floor. I longed to take you off to my own bed.'

'That can never happen.'

She was hurt. 'Do you find me so ugly?'

'No, no – you're an attractive woman.'

'Is my body so revolting to you?'

'That's irrelevant,' he said, easing her away. 'Now, please, put your nightdress on again and go back to your room.'

She began to sob. 'You're annoyed at me, aren't you?'

'No – I'm very…surprised, that's all.'

'You never noticed me when you were here but I noticed you. That's why I did it, Alain. I *had* to see you again. It was the only way to make you come back. Don't blame me. I want you so much.'

She flung herself at him and held him with a desperation that was unnerving. Gently, but firmly, he disentangled himself from her. Unaware of the passion she'd been nursing for him, Daniel had been shocked by her arrival in his bed. It did, however, answer a question that had been buzzing incessantly inside his head.

'It was *you*, wasn't it?' he said. 'Because you wanted to see me again, you made sure that Rachel was kept here.'

'Rachel didn't need you – *I* did.'

He shook her hard. 'What did you *do*, Estelle?'

There seemed to be no limit to the effort Sir John Rievers was prepared to make for his guests. He was determined

that they would thoroughly enjoy their first visit to England.
When Emanuel Janssen expressed an interest in meeting the
architect of Blenheim Palace, their host promptly arranged
it, assuring Janssen that – with his Flemish ancestry –
Vanbrugh would have much in common with him. Amalia's
need for diversion was not ignored. Having discovered that
she was a keen horsewoman, Sir John took her out riding
that afternoon to show her his estate and something of the
countryside beyond. It was many years since his wife had
been able to ride out with him and that caused him profound
regret. Mounted on a bay mare, Amalia made use of the
beautiful side-saddle given as a present to Lady Rievers by
her husband. It had the family crest on it.

'Father was so grateful to you for the opportunity to
meet Mr Vanbrugh,' she said, as they trotted together across
unspoilt parkland. 'He'll be enthralled.'

'I didn't want to ruin the surprise by warning him,'
said Sir John, 'but he'll find that he and Vanbrugh have an
unusual bond.'

'Oh?'

'Both have seen the inside of the Bastille.'

'But for different reasons, surely,' she said. 'Father was
held there because he was suspected of spying for the
enemy.'

'John Vanbrugh was also alleged to be a spy.'

She was taken aback. 'Is that why he was imprisoned
there?'

'Yes, Miss Janssen,' said Sir John. 'Unfortunately for
Vanbrugh, he had no Captain Rawson to rescue him. He
was kept behind bars for a long time. Being a man with a
lively mind, Vanbrugh didn't simply languish in his cell.

He whiled away the time by writing plays.'

'Father could never have done that.'

Sir John smiled. 'Even if he *had* been a dramatist, I don't think your dear father would have produced anything as robust and highly seasoned as Vanbrugh did. Dutch taste is a little more conservative, I fancy. Plays like *The Relapse* and *The Provok'd Wife* would cause a scandal in Amsterdam. They made Vanbrugh famous and set London laughing for many a month.'

'So he's both playwright *and* architect,' she said, impressed.

'Oh, he's far more than that. At one time, for instance, he held a captaincy in the army. Vanbrugh has also been a theatre manager and he dabbles in politics. His position as Comptroller of Works makes him influential, so people flock to gain his acquaintance.'

'And yet he found time in his busy life to see Father. That's very gracious of so celebrated a man.'

'Vanbrugh and I are old friends,' said Sir John, easily. 'He wouldn't refuse a request from me. But enough of your father's interest in architecture,' he continued. 'One of the reasons I wanted time with you alone was to hear more about this splendid Captain Rawson of yours. Where is he at the moment?'

'I'm not sure,' she said. 'I haven't heard from Daniel since he left Amsterdam. He rarely has time to write.'

'Then I may know more than you, Miss Janssen. According to reports, the Allies are besieging Lille. Captain Rawson's regiment is certain to be involved. I can find out more, if you wish.'

'Oh – yes, please, Sir John!'

'It pays to have friends in the right places. And as an old army man, I like to follow the conduct of the war. Indeed, left to myself, I'd probably be taking part in it but, as you saw, my wife needs me here.'

'Lady Rievers is an example to us all,' said Amalia. 'She bears her ill health without any complaint.'

'Yes,' he agreed with a sigh. 'Unfortunately, her malady gets worse by the day. Her physician is unable to alleviate her suffering, still less to cure its root cause. We're both resigned to the fact that our time together may be limited.'

Amalia was upset. 'I feel so guilty for taking you away from her.'

'No, Amalia, don't vex yourself over that. My wife spends most of the afternoon asleep. Besides, there's a sense in which I *am* spending time with Barbara.'

'I don't follow you, Sir John.'

There was a long pause. 'Let's ride down to the lake.'

Kicking their horses into a gentle canter, they rode on until they came around the edge of a copse and saw the water shimmering ahead of them. Oval in shape, the lake was dotted with tiny islands that each had their own inhabitants. Ducks, swans, geese and other waterfowl waddled among the reeds. Squawking conversations were held about territorial rights and there was an occasional flurry of wings and an angry extended neck.

'It's beautiful,' said Amalia, enchanted by the scene.

She gazed at it for a long time, watching the swans moving serenely through the water and the ducklings swimming uncertainly behind their mothers. Five geese flew overhead together before coming in to land on the bank. After watching them for a long while, Amalia became aware that Sir John was staring at her.

'I'm sorry,' he said with an apologetic smile. 'It's just that you remind me so much of my wife when she was your age. That's why I brought you to this particular spot, Miss Janssen. I proposed to Barbara under this very tree.' He touched her shoulder. 'Thank you so much for helping me to revive that memory if only for a fleeting moment. I appreciate it. However,' he added, 'you still haven't told me all there is to tell about Captain Rawson. Do you fret when he's involved in a campaign? When do you expect to see him again? Have you and he made any plans for the future? Come on,' he urged. 'I want to know *everything*.'

CHAPTER NINE

Knowing the inevitable response from his friend, Daniel was too embarrassed to recount what had happened in his room during the night. It would only have served to confirm Welbeck's prejudices against women and give him an excuse to deliver his well-worn lecture on their essential wickedness. Daniel was keen to avoid creating any tension in the *Coq d'Or.* When he confided his news over breakfast next morning, therefore, he made no mention whatsoever of Estelle or of her troubling infatuation with him.

'It seems that someone informed against Rachel,' he said. 'They claimed to have seen her leaving the town hall through the main door at the very time when the guards were dealing with the fire.'

Welbeck was incredulous. 'That's absurd,' he protested. 'Who'd ever believe that it was Rachel Rees who climbed onto the roof? With a dead weight like that on it, the rope would have snapped in two and she'd have fallen to her death.'

'Don't be unkind, Henry.'

'Do *you* believe she could have done what you did?'

'Of course not,' said Daniel.

'Then why treat her as a suspect?'

'The person who sent the anonymous letter claimed that Rachel was in the company of a man. They'd have assumed that he'd actually broken into the place and that she was acting as a lookout for him. There was only a shadowy description of him, apparently, but Rachel was described in some detail. She is unmistakable. How many women like her *are* there in Lille?'

'None at all,' replied Welbeck, sourly. 'No wonder they picked her out so easily. Rachel would stick out from a million women. She's frighteningly unique.' He reached for some more bread. 'Yet the odd thing is that she had nothing to do with the theft at the town hall.'

'*We* know that, Henry, but they don't. When I was breaking into the place, she was here in the tavern. However,' said Daniel, thinking it over, 'strictly speaking, she *is* my accomplice so they've arrested the right person without realising it.'

'Who informed on her?'

'I wish I knew!'

'It has to be someone from here, surely,' said Welbeck through a mouthful of bread. 'From what you've told me, Rachel spent most of her time at the tavern, and I know from personal experience that she has a gift for upsetting people.'

'She may have upset you, Henry, but every woman does

that simply by virtue of her existence. As it happens, when she worked here in the bar, Rachel made lots of friends. You ask Madame Lizier,' suggested Daniel. 'She thought Rachel was a wonderful serving wench because of her vitality.'

'That's one thing I do admit. She's full of life. Rachel has ten times the energy of someone like Madame Lizier's sister – what's her name again?'

'Estelle.'

'She strikes me as a rather cold, miserable creature.'

Daniel thought about the fervour shown by Estelle when she joined him in bed. She'd been neither cold nor miserable then. But he said nothing to Welbeck. She, too, had resolved to keep silent about the events of the night. Overcome with remorse at what she'd done, she told Daniel that she'd been in the grip of a wild hope that she now realised could never be fulfilled. That's what had driven her to take such extreme and damaging action. She chastised herself for using Rachel as a means of luring Daniel back to the town but it was the only way she could think of doing it. Rueful and contrite, she'd sobbed in his attic room for the best part of an hour until he managed to calm her down. When she left, Estelle had been sobered. Daniel knew that she'd never dare to jump into his bed again.

'What about that French soldier, Dan?' asked Welbeck.

'Which one?'

'The one you dropped in the horse trough.'

'Oh, that was Sergeant Furneaux.'

'He must have been upset when Rachel rejected him. Perhaps *he* was the one who had her arrested.'

'It could well be,' said Daniel, concealing the truth.

'What happens now?'

'We have to wait until Madame Lizier gets back from the gaol. She likes to visit her husband every morning and take in food for him. I'm hoping that she may have news of Rachel.'

Welbeck was mordant. 'Then it's sure to be *bad* news.'

'Why do you say that?'

'It's all she's ever brought you, Dan. Because of her, you came close to being killed by that Hessian officer and now you have to risk your life again to release her from gaol.'

'It's not Rachel's fault that she was arrested.'

'*Everything* is her damned fault.'

Daniel laughed derisively. 'So if we have a thunderstorm today, *that's* her fault as well, is it?'

'It probably is.'

Accepting that his claim was ludicrous, Welbeck grinned sheepishly. He also remembered the seductive aroma of his favourite tobacco and that stopped him from making any more tart remarks about her. He and Daniel finished their breakfast. They were about to get up when Estelle came into the room. It was the first time she'd seen Daniel since their nocturnal encounter and she found it difficult to look him in the eye.

'My sister has just come back from the gaol,' she told them.

Daniel was on his feet at once. 'And?'

'She wasn't even admitted.'

'Why was that?'

'Guillaume is no longer there.'

'Where has he gone?'

'They've taken him off to join the men at work on the outer defences. That's where he'll be every day from now on.'

'I must speak to her,' said Daniel.

Followed by Welbeck and Estelle, he left the room and went straight to the kitchen where Bette Lizier was perched on a stool, staring ahead of her, lost in thought. When the others entered, she needed time to come out of her reverie. She looked forlorn and Daniel sensed that she'd been crying.

'We hear that you were turned away from the gaol,' he said.

'That's right, Alain,' she replied, sadly. 'Guillaume is not there.'

'Is there a time when you *can* see your husband?'

'No – they told me not to come back.'

'That's going to make things more difficult.'

Welbeck was dejected. 'It's made our task impossible.'

'Not necessarily.'

'What earthly chance do we have?'

'I don't know,' confessed Daniel, 'but we mustn't give up. It's a setback, I grant you, but that's all it is. Madame Lizier has at least been able to give us a sketch of the gaol.'

'What use is that?'

'It may prove to be a great deal of use.'

'I don't see how,' said Welbeck. 'If you ask me, we may as well abandon the whole project right now.'

'Oh no!' cried Estelle, 'you mustn't do that.'

'No,' said Bette. 'It would be so unfair on Rachel.'

'We won't give up,' Daniel assured her. 'We came for her and we won't leave Lille without her.'

'Thank you, Alain. She and Guillaume are two of a kind. They've both been arrested on the word of some anonymous informer.'

'Yes,' said Welbeck, vengefully. 'I'd like to get my hands on the man responsible for putting Rachel in that gaol. I'd throttle him until his eyes popped out.'

Estelle reddened guiltily but neither he nor Bette noticed. Her reaction wasn't lost on Daniel, however. Seeing how much she was suffering, he began to feel sorry for her. Acting on impulse, she'd caused an immense amount of trouble without really intending to do so. She simply hadn't considered the full consequences of what she was doing. Estelle was now tormented by her impetuous action and Bette was on the verge of despair. To rally them, Daniel tried to sound confident.

'We'll devise a plan to get her out of there somehow,' he told Welbeck. 'Escape is always possible.'

'What did you have in mind?' asked his friend, cynically. 'A trumpet that blows down the gaol like the walls of Jericho – or do you happen to have a magic carpet to whisk us over the walls?'

'There's no need to be so sarcastic.'

'I'm simply facing facts. The streets of Lille are crawling with French soldiers. You saw that when we first arrived. How can two of us outwit a garrison of that size?'

'It's not just the two of us,' Daniel argued. 'There's Raymond as well. He helped me last time.'

'You can also rely on me, remember,' affirmed Bette.

'Then there's me,' said Estelle with conviction. 'Please, *please* call on me, Alain. There's nothing I wouldn't do to get Rachel out of there. If it were possible, I'd willingly change places with her. It must be terrible for her inside that gaol. Rachel will be distraught.'

* * *

When she finally managed to fall asleep, it seemed like minutes before Rachel Rees was awake again, roused by the sustained clamour of cell doors being opened and clanged shut. There was a loud clatter as the prisoners were marched off at dawn to start work on the fortifications. Unknown to her, Guillaume Lizier was one of them. After the tumult of their departure, there was a long silence and the gaol felt strangely empty. Rachel took the opportunity to make use of the wooden bucket while she was not under surveillance by Pons. It was a rare moment of privacy. When breakfast eventually came, it was so unappetising that she tipped it into the bucket with the beaker of foul water she was offered. Starvation was a more appealing option.

An hour later, she was taken out for questioning. Relieved to be out of her cell, she was grateful to be able to sit on a chair in the far more comfortable surroundings of a large room. The interrogation was conducted by a short, trim individual in a smart uniform. Captain Aumonier had a handsome face disfigured by an unsightly rash on both cheeks. He introduced himself with politeness. His voice was low, his manner unthreatening.

'I hope that this will not take long,' he began.

'You're not the only one,' said Rachel with feeling. 'I want to be released immediately. You've no reason to hold me.'

'We'll come to that in a moment. Can you first confirm that you are Madame Rachel Borrel?'

'Yes, I can.'

'What are you doing in Lille?'

'I came to sell my goods in the market.' A memory

nudged her. 'By the way, what's happened to my horse and donkey? They're my livelihood.'

'Did you come to the town alone?'

'Yes,' she lied, determined to make no reference to Daniel.

'What about your husband?'

'Which husband do you mean?'

He was amused. 'How many have you had?'

'Three so far,' she said. 'The first two were soldiers and both were killed in battle. My third husband, Alain, died of a fever last year. I'll not marry again.'

'Where were you two nights ago, Madame?' he asked, eyelids narrowing as he concentrated his gaze. 'Think back.'

'I was fast asleep in bed.'

'And where was that?'

Rachel paused to consider her answer. In the event of arrest, Daniel had warned her, she was to say as little as possible. Whatever happened, she was not to reveal where she'd been staying or the *Coq d'Or* would come under suspicion. Since its landlord was already in custody, his family might well join him. Bette Lizier, her son and her sister had been unfailingly kind to Rachel and she was anxious not to incriminate them in any way. Captain Aumonier was impatient.

'Well, Madame, have you forgotten already?' he pressed.

'No, no, that's not the problem.'

'Then what is, pray?'

'I don't wish you to think ill of me, Captain.'

'Now why should I do that?'

She gave a guilty smile. 'I wasn't alone that night.'

'Ah, I see. You shared a bed with someone else. And

would the gentleman in question be prepared to vouch for that? Give me his address and I'll have him sent for at once.'

'That would be pointless, I fear. He'll deny even knowing me because he has a wife. He forgot all about her when he was with me, of course, but that's the way with married men.'

He continued to stare at her through half-closed lids. Not wanting to meet his gaze, she looked at the rash on his face and wondered if it was giving him any pain. Rachel felt increasingly uneasy. Captain Aumonier didn't believe her. She could tell.

'Does this fellow have a name?' he asked.

'I'd rather not say what it is, Captain.'

'And was he the same person you accompanied to the town hall that night? While you kept watch, was your friend – this married man you entertained – climbing on a rope that stretched from a church tower to the roof of the building?'

She was flustered. 'I don't know what you're talking about.'

'We suspect that you were involved in the theft of something from the town hall that night, Madame Borrel. Information has come into our hands, suggesting that you were an accomplice. A woman answering your description – and it fits you exactly – was seen leaving the scene of the crime with a man.' His smile was icy. 'No doubt the pair of you celebrated your success by retiring to bed together.'

'That's not true!' she exclaimed.

'Indeed, that may have been the reward for your assistance.'

'Don't insult me.'

'Tell me the truth, Madame Borrel.'

'You've mistaken me for someone else.'

'Nobody would do that,' he said with a grin.

'Listen,' she said, trying to work it out in her head, 'I think I can see what happened. Someone has laid false accusations against me and I think I know who it is. It must be the wife of the man I spent the night with. She's done this out of spite. It's obvious, isn't it? Well,' she said with a forced laugh, 'I'm glad we've cleared that up. Set me free and I'll be on my way. But before I go, Captain,' she added, 'I have some ointment in my saddlebag that will cure that rash for you.'

Her offer enraged him. 'I want none of your fake remedies,' he snarled. 'What I want is the truth and I haven't heard even a whisper of it so far. Two nights ago, you claim, you had a lover – but you won't give his name. His wife informed against you yet she too, it seems, is nameless. The reason for that, of course, is that she doesn't exist.'

'But she *does*, Captain – I swear it!'

'Then tell me where I can find her and she'll be summoned. If this lady really *has* laid a false accusation against you, then she'll take your place in here and you'll be free to go.' He stood over her. 'Well, Madame, don't you *want* to get out of here?'

Rachel was trapped. Captain Aumonier was far too shrewd to be hoodwinked. At least she now knew why she'd been put in gaol but it brought her little comfort. It was ironic. In acting as Daniel's wife, she'd been aiding and abetting an enemy agent. That couldn't be denied. Yet she'd been arrested for something that she hadn't actually done. At a time when Daniel Rawson was slipping out of the town hall with a stolen map, Rachel had been snoring happily in bed.

'We take this matter seriously, Madame,' resumed Aumonier. 'You and I both know what was stolen that night. As a result, we can only conclude that you were working for the enemy. I'll give you the opportunity to reflect on the situation. When we next meet, I hope that you'll have come to your senses and be prepared to tell the truth. If not,' he said, calmly, 'I'll order your execution.'

Rachel felt as if she'd just been hit by a runaway horse.

Daniel's first task that morning was to take a close look at the gaol. He had a hazy idea of its internal structure from the sketch drawn by Bette Lizier but that would be useless if he could find no way to get inside the building. Welbeck had expected to go with him but was instead sent off with Raymond to familiarise himself with the town and to inspect each of its gates. Daniel wanted to know through which of them they could most easily escape. Wearing the nondescript clothing into which he'd changed, he now ambled along with his hands in his pockets and his cap pulled down. In the crowded main streets, nobody gave him a second glance.

There was one consolation. Rachel Rees was being held in the old town gaol. Had she been incarcerated in the citadel, Lille's giant keep, the chances of rescuing her would have been virtually non-existent. It was so well defended that Daniel would never have been able to get anywhere near the prisoner. As it was, his problems were significant enough. The gaol was an ugly, square, stone building of three storeys, with armed guards outside the double doors at the front. Daniel could see no obvious way of gaining illegal access. When he circled it for the first time, there was no conveniently adjacent church from which he could string a rope across to the roof of the gaol. Indeed, any attempt to climb to the top of the building would be hazardous. The smooth stone offered no footholds.

He withdrew to a tavern from which he could study the gaol through a window. As he sipped his wine, he let his gaze run up and down its full length. He saw some visitors arrive at the main gate. After a short discussion with the guards, they were turned away. The incident took less than a minute but it implanted a seed in Daniel's mind. He sat there long enough for it to grow into a vague plan. When he finished his drink, he stepped back out into the street to make another circuit of the gaol. Bette Lizier had told him that Rachel's cell was on the first floor at the rear of the building. When he walked to the street at the back, Daniel was looking up at a line of identical barred windows. He couldn't be certain which of the cells was occupied by Rachel Rees. That was a handicap. Until he knew exactly where she was being held, he couldn't hope to get to her.

Not wishing to draw attention to himself, he sauntered the length of the street, then waited several minutes before going back in the opposite direction. On this occasion, he couldn't have timed his arrival better. As he reached the midway point, he heard a familiar cry of fury, then saw something being poured through the bars of a cell on the first floor. It cascaded down yards ahead of him and he had to step back to avoid being splashed. Daniel didn't realise that Rachel had just tipped the contents of her bucket out of the window and he didn't care. His visit to the gaol had brought a positive reward.

He knew exactly where she was being held.

Amalia Janssen was constantly delighted by the novelty of England. Wherever she went, she marvelled at the architecture, took a close interest in what people were wearing and listened with amusement to the rustic accents of Oxfordshire. Late morning found her sitting on the terrace outside the house with her father. With two servants and a cook already provided, there was little for Beatrix Udderzook to do so she hovered nearby and wiped the dirt from one of the wooden tables. Bright sunshine turned the roof to pure gold and gave the whole property a magical glow. Summer birdsong delighted the ear.

'I love it here,' said Amalia, beaming.

'My first impressions have been good as well,' said her father. 'If we overlook our meeting with Her Grace, that is.'

'Sir John says that she can be prickly at times.'

'She *invited* us here, Amalia. She seems to have forgotten that.'

'Her Grace has found able deputies. Sir John and Lady Rievers have been perfect hosts. They seem to look on me like a long-lost daughter. I'm going out riding again this afternoon.'

'What about me?' muttered Beatrix. 'I'm your chaperone.'

'You could always go for a drive in the carriage with Father. It must be rather boring for you to be left here on your own.'

'It's the other servants, Miss Amalia,' complained Beatrix. 'I can't get on with them. They've all worked for lords and ladies in grand houses and look down on me because I have a humbler station. I've heard them laughing behind my back at my voice.'

'There's nothing wrong with your voice,' said Janssen.

'It's Dutch, sir. They seem to find that very funny.'

'I find the English language rather comical at times.'

'I don't,' said Amalia. 'I like it. I just wish that I could speak it as beautifully as someone like Sir John.'

Janssen smiled. 'Or someone like Captain Rawson, perhaps?'

'Oh, I could listen to Daniel speaking English all day.'

'He sounds better in Dutch to me,' said Beatrix, bluntly.

She moved away, scouring the terrace in search of another chore. Unlike the others, she hadn't adjusted to life in a foreign country and was extremely homesick. In their short time at the cottage, Beatrix had lacked a real function. Back in Amsterdam, Amalia would never venture out without taking her maidservant as a chaperone. Yet she'd already gone out riding alone with a man and was preparing to do so for the second time. Janssen understood why Beatrix was so tetchy.

'I think she's jealous,' he suggested.

'She's no reason to be, Father.'

'Beatrix likes to be involved. At the moment, she's just twiddling her thumbs out of boredom. You and I are having a splendid time here and that makes her envious.'

'Well, I can hardly take her riding with me,' said Amalia.

'And I'm afraid that I can't invite her to join me for

a drive this afternoon. Thanks to Sir John, I've had an invitation to visit one of his neighbours who, it transpires, is an avid collector of tapestries. If I take Beatrix,' he went on, 'she'd only be in the way.'

'What she really wants to do is to see more of London.'

'Then she'll have to wait, Amalia. We have lots of other places to visit first.'

'Yes,' she said, 'one of them has to be Daniel's farm.'

Janssen frowned. 'I'd never take him for a farmer somehow. He always looks as if he's been a soldier from birth. It's in his blood.'

'His father was a soldier *and* a farmer.'

'Is that what Daniel wants to do when he retires – go back to farming? Not that I can ever imagine him hanging up his weapons,' he said. 'As long as there's a war, he'll want to fight in it.'

Her face darkened. 'That's what worries me. He loves the thrill of battle. But, then, so did Sir John. He was Daniel's age when he left the army. He told me that he misses it a great deal but he couldn't stay abroad when his wife was taken ill.'

'No, the poor lady is clearly fading.'

Amalia reached out to clasp his hand. What she and her father had recognised in Lady Rievers were the signs that they'd seen in Amalia's mother. After being struck down with a disease, she'd simply wasted away in front of them. The helplessness they'd both felt had been intense. All that they could do – as Sir John was doing to his wife – was to nurse her with love until the time came. They sat there without speaking for a long time, sharing silent memories of the last fatal days. What the tragedy had done was to draw Amalia and her father much closer together. United in grief, they'd forged a new life that slowly brought joy back into their world.

It was an odd coincidence, Amalia thought. Their time on the estate had conjured two beloved faces out of the past. When she met Lady Rievers and saw how bad her condition was, she was reminded of her own mother's decline. For his part, Sir John had looked at Amalia and been struck by the resemblance she showed to his wife in her younger days. In both cases, past and present had overlapped for a moment.

'Oh, I meant to tell you,' said Amalia as she remembered the promise. 'Sir John is going to find out about Daniel.'

'What do you mean?'

'He knows people who have continuous reports of the progress of the campaign. If Daniel is mentioned in despatches, Sir John will get to hear about it. Isn't that wonderful?'

'If he's able to pass on *good* news,' said Janssen, guardedly.

Amalia giggled. 'Any news about Daniel is bound to be good.'

The anger which had made Rachel Rees hurl the contents of her wooden bucket through the window had been born of dread. It was her gesture of defiance at the sentence hanging over her. Once she'd made it, however, she lapsed into torpor, sitting on the floor of her cell and speculating on how the execution would be carried out. Would she be lined up in front of a firing squad or must she suffer the greater humiliation of being hanged in public? Her only hope of mercy, as she perceived it, was to tell the truth: to describe how she'd been persuaded to act as the accomplice of a British army officer and to reveal the assistance they'd been given at the *Coq d'Or*. Such a course of action would, unfortunately, result in the instant arrest of Bette Lizier, her son and her sister. What Rachel would receive in return for her confession, she could only guess. In admitting to being an enemy agent, she'd be courting death. On the other hand, Captain Aumonier might feel lenient towards her if she handed over three conspirators to him and confirmed that Guillaume Lizier had been in the pay of the Allied army.

She found it impossible to reach a decision. Rachel tried to tell herself that she owed no loyalty to anyone. She had to think solely of herself. Locked in her cell, she felt lonely, abandoned, doomed. If she could buy her survival by sending other people to their deaths, then it was tempting to do so. Why should she be the scapegoat? Yet even as she considered a full confession, something told her that she could never make it. The people at the tavern were friends. They'd formed a bond with her. Rachel couldn't betray them. All that she could do when she was next interrogated was to maintain a dignified silence. Aumonier would get no names out of her.

The stink of the cell invaded her nostrils and made her retch. Rachel got to her feet and pressed her face to the bars, inhaling the fresh air to cleanse her lungs. She looked down with envy at the people walking past the gaol, enjoying a freedom that she'd never have again. None of them even bothered to lift up their heads towards her. None of them realised her terrifying predicament. None of them cared. While Captain Aumonier had used no violence against her, there'd been murder in his voice. If she continued to lie to him, he'd have no compunction about sending her to her fate. That thought made her heart pound like a drum. Her throat went dry. Beads of sweat broke out on her brow and her eyes misted over. When they eventually cleared, she gazed down at the street once more and was suddenly jolted out of her misery.

Someone did look up at her this time. He even took off his cap so that she could see him more distinctly. Using her knuckles to wipe her eyes, Rachel took a second look at the man. He was moving away now but she was certain of his identity.

It was Daniel Rawson. He'd come back for her.

'I've carried out a full reconnaissance,' said Prince Eugene, 'and I've decided to attack the northern sector of Lille.'

'I applaud that decision, Your Highness,' said Marlborough.

'The ground is firmer there and the River Marque will offer us a measure of protection to the rear.'

'That was our feeling. From whom did you take advice?'

'I consulted two of the chief engineers, Des Roques and Du Muy. They agreed wholeheartedly with me.'

'You chose the best men, Your Highness,' said Cardonnel, proudly. 'Both of them are Huguenots. I come from Huguenot stock myself. We all have a very special reason to hate the French.'

Marlborough's secretary was referring to the Revocation of the Edict of Nantes, an act conferring religious and civil liberties on Huguenot subjects in France. When the edict was revoked without warning, it led to appalling slaughter. To escape death, Huguenots fled from a Roman

Catholic populace that despised them. Though the crisis had occurred over twenty years earlier, it was still fresh in the minds of people like Adam Cardonnel, whose family had been among the thousands of refugees. Nobody had such strong motivation to fight the armies of Louis XIV as Huguenots.

'There is another obvious advantage,' added Cardonnel. 'By assaulting the northern sector, you'll be in much closer proximity to our own camp.'

'Quite so,' said Marlborough. 'If there's an attack on you from Vendôme or Berwick or even Burgundy, we'll be able to provide cover. In all respects, it's a good decision.'

They were in the captain-general's quarters. Prince Eugene of Savoy had ridden to the main camp with some of the Dutch generals under his command. The council of war was, for once, not marked by any disagreement. Marlborough was grateful for that. He'd been forced to compromise on too many occasions in the past. Now that the siege had been undertaken, it was important that they all favoured the same strategy. On the table in front of them was the plan that Daniel had stolen from Lille.

'These are our two targets,' said Eugene, tapping it with his finger. 'We'll attack the gates of Magdalen and St Andrew. As you can see, there are solid hornworks close by but I still feel that we can batter a way through.'

'How long do you estimate it will take?' asked Marlborough.

Eugene laughed mirthlessly. 'Only a fool would even try to answer that question, Your Grace,' he admitted. 'It will certainly take many weeks to bring Lille to its knees. It may even be a matter of months. Marshal Boufflers will hold out to the bitter end.'

'The conditions are hardly propitious. This sweltering heat is no help to us. Digging the peripheral lines of circumvallation must be like working in the seventh circle of hell. Then there's the problem of the marshes. Insects breed like mad in this weather,' noted Marlborough. 'We'll have men collapsing from disease before long.'

'That can't be helped, Your Grace.'

'Alas, no – we must press on.'

'What will decide the issue is the maintenance of supplies.'

'That's always the case with a siege,' said Marlborough. 'The first convoy reached us without undue hindrance but we can't rely on the French to let the next one slip past them unobserved. It's a much bigger siege train than the other one.' He turned to his secretary. 'Remind us what it contains, Adam.'

Cardonnel knew the details by heart. 'It has eighty siege pieces, each requiring twenty horses to haul it and twenty siege mortars that will each need almost as many horses. There'll be no less than thirty thousand munition waggons, pulled by four horses apiece. All in all,' he concluded, 'it will stretch for several miles.'

'It will make a very tempting target,' said Eugene.

'That's why you must guard it every inch of the way, Your Highness,' said Marlborough. 'There are reports that Burgundy is moving forward from Bruges towards Alost with thirty thousand men. We must hope that he doesn't try to intercept the convoy.'

'If he does, we'll fight him off.'

Marlborough was anxious. 'At all events, the cannon must be saved,' he insisted. 'Lose that and we are toothless.'

His brittle smile hid his concern. 'But I have every faith in our ability to bring the convoy here without any substantial damage to it. Once our artillery is in place, we can bombard Lille with full force.'

Eugene's eyes gleamed in anticipation. 'I look forward to that.'

'We can also turn our attention to *their* supplies,' said Marlborough. 'If the siege lasts for any length of time – as it assuredly will – they'll begin to run out of food and ammunition. We must ensure that none gets through to them from outside. That's our strategy, gentlemen,' he said, indicating the plan.

'We put a ring of steel around Lille,' declared Eugene.

'Exactly.'

'Nobody will be allowed to get out.'

'And, by the same token,' emphasised Marlborough, glancing around the faces, 'nobody must be able to get in. Cut off his supplies and even Boufflers will think twice about holding out indefinitely.'

While the rescue of Rachel Rees took priority, there was still a tavern to run. Bette Lizier and Estelle were thus kept busy serving drinks and providing food. It was only towards the end of the afternoon that there was a sufficient lull for them to be able to take a break. After handing over to the two hired members of staff, they adjourned to the kitchen. Henry Welbeck and Raymond were already there, disputing the best way to escape from Lille. Shortly after the women arrived, Daniel returned from his scouting expedition.

'What took you so long?' asked Welbeck, peevishly.

'I had a lot to do.'

'So did we – Raymond and I rode over every inch of Lille.'

'I'll be interested to hear your findings,' said Daniel. 'First, however, I must tell you my news. I've established exactly where Rachel is being held.'

'Do you have a plan?' asked Raymond, excitedly. 'Can you climb in through the roof again, Alain?'

'Not this time, I fear.'

'Then how will you break into the gaol?'

Daniel shrugged. 'I don't think that it can be done.'

'We can't leave Rachel there,' wailed Estelle. 'It's a terrible place. You ask my sister. She's seen what it's like inside.'

'It's really dreadful,' Bette confirmed. 'The gaol is filthy and the stench is disgusting. Guillaume's cell was foul. But that's not what worries me. When he first went there, they tried to beat the truth out of him. He told them nothing. What if they torture Rachel?'

'She's a woman,' said Raymond, 'surely, she'd be spared.'

'That's not what Guillaume told me. He heard the cries of men being beaten but he also heard screams from women. If they think Rachel can tell them something, they won't hold back.'

'That means she may give them *our* names,' said Raymond.

Estelle blanched. 'We could all finish up in gaol.'

'Don't desert her, Alain. She must be rescued.'

'Calm down,' said Daniel. 'I'm not going to desert her at all. And I agree that we must try to get her out of there before she comes to any harm.'

'Hold on,' suggested Welbeck. 'A moment ago, you told us that it was impossible to break into the gaol.'

'That's true.'

'Then there's nothing at all that you can do.'

'I think that there is.'

'You're talking in riddles,' complained Raymond. 'If you can't break in there, how can you possibly help Rachel?'

'I'll do so from the inside,' said Daniel, cheerfully. 'Since I can't break *into* the gaol, I'll do my best to break *out* of it. All I have to do is to get myself arrested and I'll be thrown in there straight away. That's when I can put my plan into action.'

Welbeck was agog. 'You'll be taking the most terrible risk.'

'That's what husbands do for their wives.'

Chapter Ten

Raymond Lizier was thrilled to be involved. Having seen vivid proof of Daniel's bravery at first hand, he had no doubt that the man he thought of as Alain Borrel would succeed once again with an audacious plan. Raymond had only one reservation.

'If you can rescue *one* person from gaol, Alain,' he said, 'then you should be able to bring out two at the same time.'

'You're thinking of your father,' guessed Daniel.

'We'd dearly love to get him out of there.'

'I'm sure that you would, Raymond. He's patently suffering in gaol but his is a very different case.'

'I don't see why. He and Rachel face the same charge.'

'Look ahead for a moment,' advised Daniel. 'If we manage to rescue Rachel, then we'll disappear from Lille as soon as we can. There'll be no trace of us. That's not what would happen to your father. If he escaped, he'd go straight back to the *Coq d'Or* and that would be the first place they'd search for him.'

'We'd hide him,' asserted Raymond.

'How long could you do that?'

'For as long as we needed.'

'That might mean for ever,' said Welbeck. 'You'd spend your whole lives looking over your shoulder. And there's another thing to consider. If your father tries to escape, it will be seen as a proof of guilt. He'd never be able to show his face in Lille again.'

'Henri is right,' said Daniel. 'This tavern is your home and your livelihood. You can't just abandon it and flee over the wall. I'm sure that your father will be released in time. If they had proper evidence against him,' he pointed out, 'then he'd have been sent to trial weeks ago. That hasn't happened.'

'What if Lille is captured by the Allies?'

'That might make a difference, I agree. But the siege could go on for months and your father would be on the run as long as it lasted. I'm sorry, Raymond,' he continued, a hand on his arm, 'the truth of the matter is that I'm hoping to reach Rachel when your father won't even *be* in the gaol. He'll have been marched off to work with the other prisoners.'

Though he was visibly disappointed, Raymond accepted that his father would have to wait to be released. He missed him badly. It placed a greater responsibility on him. As the only man in the house, he had to take on additional duties. He consoled himself with the thought that his father would be very proud of the way that his son was helping two soldiers from the British army. Raymond had no qualms about what he had to do. He drew strength from the long experience of his two companions. With such men at his side, he felt capable of anything.

'When do we go, Alain?' he asked.

'Not for an hour at least,' replied Daniel. 'We must let night draw in first.'

'Yes,' said Welbeck, 'the darker it is, the better.'

The three of them were in the tavern that Daniel had visited earlier. Seated in the window, they could keep an eye on the gaol. Having rehearsed their roles many times, they were confident that they could give a convincing performance. Welbeck sipped his drink and voiced a lingering doubt.

'What if you can't get out of there?' he wondered.

'I'll manage it somehow,' said Daniel.

'They might put you in chains. Have you thought of that?'

'I won't be fettered for my crime, Henri. They must lock up drunks like me all the time – except that I'll be quite sober, of course. My guess is that they'll simply throw me into a cell to sleep off my stupor. In due course, I'd have to pay a fine.'

'Do you have enough money?'

'I won't need it. I'll be long gone by then.'

'What if Rachel is in no condition to travel?'

'Nothing will stop her getting out of there,' said Daniel, 'even if she has to crawl out. Rachel is indomitable.'

'That's not the word *I'd* use,' murmured Welbeck.

They stayed in the window for another hour, searching the sky like three astronomers as the last specks of light were wiped out of it. At length, Daniel slapped his thigh.

'Time to go, my friends,' he said. 'You know what to do.'

Raymond was first on his feet. 'I can't wait.'

'There's no rush,' cautioned Welbeck, getting up slowly. He shook Daniel's hand. 'Good luck!'

'Do you have a message for Rachel?' teased Daniel.

By way of reply, he got a hostile glare. Welbeck and Raymond left the tavern first. Daniel gave them plenty of time to get into position before he went out after them. The night was dark and a capricious breeze was blowing rubbish along the ground. Dogs were sniffing in corners. There were several people walking past but Daniel was only interested in two of them. As soon as he got within sight of the guards outside the gaol, his leisurely gait became a drunken roll. Holding a flagon of wine in one hand, he took a long swig from it, then pretended to lose his footing and tumble to the ground. He got up with difficulty and staggered on, singing a French song hopelessly out of tune.

When two people came towards him, he grabbed one of them by the collar and demanded money. Welbeck tried to push him away but Daniel clung on, cursing him for his meanness. It was left to Raymond to pull Daniel away so that he and Welbeck could continue on past the gaol. Barely managing to keep his balance, Daniel yelled abuse after them, then appeared to take another swig from his flagon. He wobbled uncertainly in the direction of the guards.

'Would anyone like a drink?' he asked, slurring his words.

As he reached out to offer it, he deliberately dropped the flagon and it smashed on the cobbles, sending the remains of the wine over the boots of the two men.

'You idiot!' yelled one of the guards, punching him in the chest. Daniel rocked back on his heels. 'Look what you've done.'

'Don't you touch me,' gabbled Daniel, raising his fists.

'You're drunk. Get home to your wife.'

'I want an apology first. I'll knock it out of you.'

Lunging towards the guard, he took a wild swing at him but only managed to dislodge his hat. When the man grabbed him, Daniel kicked him on the shin and rid himself of a torrent of expletives. It was too much for the guard. He slapped Daniel's face, then used the butt of his musket to hit him in the stomach. Doubling up in pain, Daniel fell to the ground and moaned. His attacker took him by the scruff of the neck.

'Let's get him inside before he spews all over us,' he said.

The two of them picked Daniel up and carried him off.

Rachel Rees had not been looking forward to another night in the company of Pons, the turnkey with the lecherous eyes. When he came on duty, she was the first prisoner he visited and he leered at her through the bars. Eventually, he went off on his rounds and Rachel was left alone to reflect that she would actually live to see another day. She'd spent most of the previous one, twitching nervously at the sound of each footstep, fearing that Captain Aumonier had returned to question her again. The sight of Daniel Rawson in the street outside had raised her morale at first but she couldn't believe that he'd reach her soon enough to rescue her. Time was rapidly running out.

When Pons returned, he leant against the bars and used

the back of his hand to wipe away the moisture on his lips. His sly grin exposed a row of ugly, black teeth. The stink of his breath made her turn her head away.

'Would you like some company, Madame?' he asked.

'No, I wouldn't,' she said, forcefully.

'I could make your stay in here a lot easier.'

'You could only do that by going away.'

He guffawed. 'I like a woman with spirit.'

'Leave me alone.'

'You're a prisoner,' he reminded her, tone hardening. 'That means *I* give the orders. You have no rights at all, Madame Borrel. I can do whatever I like with you.'

'If you touch me,' she warned, 'I'll scream the place down.'

'That would be very silly of you. If any of the other guards came running, they'd want a turn as well. Now we wouldn't want that to happen, would we?' He bared his teeth again. 'You're all *mine*.' He put a hand through the bars. 'What about a first kiss?'

She stepped out of reach. 'Keep away from me.'

'You're not helping yourself,' he said, softly. 'I can bring you proper food and good wine. All you have to do is to be nice to me. Is that too much to ask?'

He unhooked the ring of keys that dangled from his belt and selected one of them. Watching it being inserted into the lock, Rachel was horrified. She felt like a caged animal. As the key was turned, she flattened herself against the wall. The door swung open and Pons gave a triumphant grin. It froze immediately as Rachel was given an unexpected reprieve.

'Pons!' shouted a voice in the distance. 'Where are you?'

Stamping his foot in exasperation, Pons locked the door of the cell again and attached the keys to his belt. He looked Rachel up and down once again, then chuckled.

'I'll wait until dawn,' he decided, 'when the other prisoners go off to work. We'll be all alone then – just you and me. Scream as much as you like. Nobody will come to save you. Besides,' he said, ogling her, 'I've got something much better for your tongue to do than scream.'

'Pons!' called the voice, angrily.

'I'll have to go, my darling. Think of me until I come back.'

Rachel could think of nothing else. As the turnkey went out, she slumped to the wooden board and brought both hands to her face. Pons had her at his mercy. A grotesque image of what was in store for her came into her mind and it made her shudder. The man was a monster. He'd take her by force. Rachel even found herself wishing that she'd been executed instead. Instant death in front of a firing squad would be preferable to the protracted ordeal that lay ahead. Her hands began to shake uncontrollably and her stomach churned. Glancing through the window, she wondered how long it would be before dawn broke through the smothering blackness of night.

She'd forgotten all about her glimpse of Daniel Rawson. The man in the street had been a phantom. The turnkey, on the other hand, was real. Pons would be back to claim his prize.

Bruised and aching, Daniel sat with his back to the wall of the cell. The turnkey who'd taken charge of him hadn't stood on ceremony. He'd simply unlocked the door and dumped the prisoner inside. The stench of stale urine and vomit was so powerful that Daniel kept a hand over his nose and mouth. Though he'd taken some punishment, he'd achieved his objective. He was inside the gaol. Because he was viewed as a harmless drunk, the search had been perfunctory. Only the few coins in his pocket had been confiscated. The various items that he'd carefully concealed under his clothing hadn't been discovered.

Henry Welbeck and Raymond Lizier had helped him to get into the gaol but their work wasn't finished. Daniel hoped that they'd be waiting outside when he and Rachel emerged. For that to happen, everything must go to plan. There was no chance of sleep. Heavy feet pounded up and down the corridor all night and doors clanged. A fight broke out in a nearby cell and he heard raised voices. Turnkeys made no attempt to intervene. The hours passed by with painful slowness. One eye on the window, he wondered how Rachel was coping with imprisonment and hoped that she'd not been mistreated in any way. Daniel blamed himself for her dilemma. Had he not persuaded her to come to Lille in the first place, she'd be free, sleeping in the British camp before rising next morning to ply her trade. Yet his rescue attempt had not only been prompted by guilt. He was fond of Rachel Rees, admiring her tenacity in overcoming the setbacks in her life. Daniel wanted to hear that throaty cackle again and see that broad smile. Most of all, he wanted to watch her reaction to Henry Welbeck when she realised that he'd been involved in her rescue.

When the first gesture of dawn finally arrived, the gaol suddenly exploded with noise. Voices yelled, doors opened, feet marched and dozens of prisoners were driven past his cell. He peered out, trying to decide which of them might be Guillaume Lizier and wishing that he could pass him a message from his wife. The pandemonium lasted a long time before it gradually faded away into a cold silence. A sense of alarm brought Daniel to his feet. Held behind bars, he was helpless. He had no control over his own fate. That had passed to someone else and it made him feel uneasy. All that he could do was to watch, wait and pray that nothing went wrong. Daniel had found a way into the gaol. His deliverer now had to do the same thing.

'You're too late,' said the guard. 'The prisoners have all left.'

'My husband isn't one of them,' she said. 'He was arrested for being drunk and is probably lying in there with a terrible headache. A friend of mine saw him having a fight with someone. I'm so sorry if it was you, Monsieur.'

'It was,' he grunted.

'Alain is not a violent man. It's only when he has too much to drink that he's aggressive. It preys on his mind, you see.' She bit her lip and tears welled up in her eyes. 'We lost our eldest son at the battle of Oudenarde. I told Alain that we should be proud that he died fighting for France but all that my husband can do is to try to block it out of his mind by getting drunk. He's been in gaol before so I know how awful the food is in there.' She held up her basket. 'That's why I've brought a few things for him.'

Estelle spoke with great feeling. In referring to Daniel as her husband, she was indulging in a fantasy she'd nursed during his stay at the tavern. To win the sympathy of the guards, he'd told her to invent a son who'd died in the recent battle. The two men hesitated, unsure whether to admit her or send her on her way. Estelle put her hand into the basket.

'If you've been out here all night,' she said, offering them a pie, 'you must be very hungry. Why don't you share this between you?'

'Thank you, Madame,' said one of them, taking the pie and having a first bite of it. He nodded. 'It's very tasty.' Chewing happily, he passed it to his company. 'You try it.'

'All I ask is the chance to give the food to Alain,' she went on. 'And there is something else as well.' Estelle lifted a small bottle out of the basket. 'It's Alain's medicine. He has to take it every day.'

'Then he should drink more of that and less of the wine,' said the first guard, nudging the other. 'He's lucky that I didn't crack open his skull last night.'

Estelle apologised profusely for the trouble caused and begged for a moment with her wayward husband. The guards explained that it would not be their decision. Agreeing to let her into the gaol, they told her that she'd have to persuade the duty sergeant to allow a visit to her husband's cell. When they unlocked the door for her, she was so overwhelmed with gratitude that she kissed each one of them. They went off to finish their pie.

The duty sergeant presented more of a challenge. He was a narrow-faced man of medium height, with bushy, black eyebrows complementing his full beard. When Estelle told her tale, he was watchful and suspicious, demanding the name, address, age and occupation of the prisoner. She invented the details and waited as they were written down in a ledger. He tried to catch her out with some searching questions but she always contrived to give plausible answers.

Fearing that she might be turned away, Estelle was relieved when he sniffed her basket.

'Something in there smells good,' he said.

'It's fresh bread, Sergeant,' she replied, setting the basket on the counter. 'Have some of it, if you wish.'

'I will, Madame.' He broke off a large hunk then pulled out the other pie. 'This is too good for the likes of him.'

'May I see Alain?' she pleaded.

'Two minutes – that's all you get.'

Estelle fought hard to conceal the elation she felt. She watched the duty sergeant take a ring of keys from a wooden peg, then followed him along a gloomy corridor. When he opened a door, he locked it behind them. Estelle noticed that the three doors they went through in the main corridor could all be opened by the same key. Stopping outside a cell, he called in.

'You don't deserve it but your wife's brought you some food.'

Daniel lay motionless on the floor, face buried in matted straw.

'Can I give it to Alain myself?' she asked.

'No, I'll do that.' After unlocking the door, he snatched the basket from her and stepped into the cell. 'Wake up, you drunken fool.' He kicked Daniel's thigh. 'Wake up, damn you!'

When the prisoner remained quite still, the sergeant bent down to shake him vigorously by the shoulders. Daniel came to life in a flash, rolling over and pulling the sergeant to the floor. Before the man could even begin to protect himself, he was hit by a succession of hard punches to the face and body. All the wind was knocked out of him and he lapsed into unconsciousness. Without even pausing to thank or congratulate Estelle, Daniel pulled out the stout cord he'd tied around his body and used the knife he'd also smuggled in to cut it into pieces. When the sergeant was trussed up hand and foot, a piece of cloth was thrust into his mouth and held in place by some cord. Only then did Daniel turn to his accomplice.

'Thank you, Estelle,' he said, embracing her.

'I owed it to you.' As he picked up the ring of keys, she retrieved the basket. 'The same key opens all the doors in the corridor,' she recalled.

'Rachel is on the first floor. Did you pass a staircase?'

'Yes, I can show you.'

After locking the cell door, Daniel set off with Estelle at his side. They moved furtively, listening for footsteps and hoping that only a skeleton staff was on duty now that all the prisoners had left. They had to go through two doors before they came to a flight of stone steps. Daniel led the way, using the same key to open the door at the top. They didn't need to be told which cell belonged to Rachel because she emitted a cry of absolute terror.

Pons had bided his time until everyone else had left and he used the interval to speculate on what he'd do to the prisoner when he made his move. Rachel tried everything to stop him. She pleaded, she swore, she showed defiance and she even threatened to scratch his eyes out if he came anywhere near her. But she knew she was no match for a man of such brutish strength. Pons had been in no hurry. Inviting her to watch, he undressed slowly and left his uniform on the chair. Trembling with fear, Rachel couldn't bear to look but she could hear his hoarse breathing and his vile taunts. He reached for his keys and selected the one that would admit him to paradise. Licking his lips, he unlocked the door and pushed it wide open.

Unable to escape, Rachel flung herself at him and began to beat his chest. He overpowered her with ease and stole a first kiss from her. Fondling her breast, he pushed her against the wall and began to tear at her clothes. It was when his hand explored her thighs that she let out her scream. He clapped a hand over her mouth.

'You'll be screaming with pleasure soon,' he told her. 'You'll be begging for more.'

Rachel sank her teeth into his hand and drew blood. Pulling it away, he howled in pain then slapped her vengefully across the face before flinging her roughly on to the floor. The next moment, he heard footsteps running along the corridor and turned to see a man hurtling towards him. Daniel didn't wait for introductions. Diving at Pons with all his might, he pushed him so hard against the wall that the man's head was split open by the rough stone. The turnkey was completely dazed, swaying about with a hand against the wound. Daniel seized the opportunity to help Rachel up and pass her to Estelle.

'Take her down the corridor, Estelle,' he said.

Rachel was amazed. 'Where did you come from?'

'I'll explain,' said Estelle, leading her away.

As his head cleared, Pons was ready to fight. He'd been deprived of his pleasure and violently attacked. He wanted retribution. Lunging at Daniel, he tried to grip him by the throat but he was too slow and clumsy. Daniel evaded his grasp and pummelled him with both fists, drawing gasps of pain and gouts of blood. It was no time for a long fight. Every second was vital. Set on murder, Pons grappled wildly with him, forcing him against the bars and trying to break his back in a bear hug. Daniel responded instinctively. With a surge of strength, he swung his opponent round, banged his forehead time after time against the iron bars and, before the turnkey could recover, slit his throat from behind. There was still work to do. Hand over the man's mouth, Daniel held him tight as Pons struggled desperately to get free, bucking, twisting, clutching at his throat and whimpering like a child as his lifeblood gushed away down his bare chest. When the turnkey was finally released, he slumped to the floor with a thud.

Raymond Lizier was beginning to lose hope. As he sat on the cart with the reins in his hands, he became increasingly dejected.

'They're not coming.'

'Give them time,' said Welbeck.

'They should have been out by now.'

'Calm down, Raymond.'

'Something's gone wrong. Estelle has been caught.'

'We saw her being let into the gaol by those two guards.'

'Yes,' said Raymond, 'but we don't know what happened once she was inside. Suppose they didn't believe her?'

'Suppose they locked her up. Suppose they tortured the truth out of Rachel. If you're determined to fear the worst,' said Welbeck, 'suppose that neither they nor Alain will come out alive.' He clicked his tongue. 'You'd never make a soldier, my friend.'

'Why do you say that?'

'Patience is everything. You need to keep your nerve as you wait for the enemy to come. You're like a hunter, stalking a prey. One false move and you lose your chance. Take heart, Raymond. Have trust.'

'But so many things could go wrong.'

'Try not to think about them.'

Raymond looked up at the sky. 'If we wait much longer,' he said, anxiously, 'then it will be daylight.'

It was not long after dawn and there was sufficient gloom to give them a degree of anonymity as they waited at the rear of the prison. Lille was already wide awake and early customers were making their way to market. A cart trundled past. Raymond tensed as two mounted soldiers rode towards them. His fears were unfounded. After tossing them a glance, the soldiers rode on. While Raymond continued to fret, Welbeck kept his eyes fixed firmly on the back door of the gaol. When he saw it open, he gave Raymond a sharp nudge.

'Now!' he ordered.

Snapping the reins, Raymond set the horse in motion. As they got nearer, he was able to see the figure standing beside the door and he felt that his worst fears had been realised.

'That's one of the turnkeys!' he said in alarm.

'No,' said Welbeck. 'Look at his face – it's Alain.'

To conduct the two women to the rear exit, Daniel had put on the uniform discarded by Pons. It was too large for him but nobody would notice that from a distance. He waited until the cart drew level with him before he opened the door and ushered the two women out. Daniel locked the door behind them. Overjoyed to be free at last, Rachel needed a moment to adjust to her freedom. Her gaze then alighted on Welbeck.

'Henry!' she cried, grabbing his hand. 'You came for me!'

The visit to Oxford was an unexpected treat for Amalia Janssen and her father. Sir John Rievers insisted on acting as their guide and taking them there in his own carriage. It was far more ornate and comfortable than the one they'd been given as a courtesy. He apologised that his wife was unable to join them but such an outing would place far too great a strain on her. Amalia was struck yet again by his unassailable buoyancy. In spite of his domestic concerns, he was jovial and light-hearted.

'Oxford is unparalleled,' he told them. 'I know that you have universities in Holland but they are nothing at all like Oxford.'

'Why is that, Sir John?' asked Amalia.

'You must decide for yourselves.'

'I'm told that it has fine buildings,' said Janssen.

'Fine buildings, tall spires and delightful parks,' said Sir John. 'It has such an atmosphere of learning that you forget it's also the home of ordinary people.'

'How do they feel about having so many students there?'

'To tell the truth, they're not very pleased about it. Indeed, over the years, there've been some mighty battles between town and gown. Go back two or three centuries and you'd find something like open warfare in the streets.' He chortled merrily. 'Things are much calmer now. I doubt very much if we'll see any blood on the cobblestones.'

Oxford enraptured them. Amalia and her father were so impressed by what they found that their mouths were agape for the first hour. The town was utterly entrancing. Imposing enough on their own, the various colleges were awe-inspiring when seen in concert. Churches, civic buildings, fine houses and coaching inns added to the architectural charm. Amalia particularly loved the winding streets, lined with their quaint shops, and the narrow lanes with their rows of tiny cottages. Their tour began with a gentle drive up the High Street then down St Aldates but they abandoned their carriage outside Christ Church and continued on foot. After a fascinating look at the interior of the college, they strolled across the meadows to the river. On such a bright, cloudless day, it was an idyllic scene and Amalia gazed her fill.

Punts glided past with the unhurried gracefulness of swans, their occupants reclining on cushions and shielding themselves from the sun with parasols. Perched on a branch, a kingfisher suddenly swooped down over the water, caught its prey and made off with it wriggling in its beak. Some people had spread a blanket on the grass so that they could eat a picnic. Amalia was bound to compare the serenity of it all with the hurly-burly of war on the Continent. Places like Blenheim, Ramillies and Oudenarde seemed a million miles away now. Out of the corner of her eye, she became conscious that Sir John was watching her intently and deduced that he'd seen once again the clear resemblance she bore to the lovely young woman who'd become his bride. When she turned to him, his smile was radiant.

After a bracing walk along the river, they dined at an inn

before resuming their tour. There was something of interest at every turn. As well as having a detailed knowledge of the history of Oxford, Sir John had a fund of anecdotes that kept his guests laughing and took their minds off the fact that they'd been walking so long.

'Why are there bars on the windows?' asked Amalia, looking up at one of the colleges.

'I should imagine that it's to stop the students from falling out,' said her father. 'Is that not so, Sir John?'

'It has a double function, Mr Janssen,' replied the other. 'It stops the undergraduates from accidentally falling out and it prevents them from smuggling young ladies into their rooms.'

Amalia coloured. 'I never thought of that.'

'You have a pure mind, Amalia. Though they are here to study, young gentlemen can be very frolicsome. Drink and female company are their twin delights. The story is told – I hope you won't find this too indecorous – of a tutor who was very unpopular with his students. His room was on the first floor. When he heard a banging noise at his window one day, he saw, to his revulsion, that someone in the room above was dangling a chamber pot on the end of a rope. He opened the window, thrust his hand through the bars and grabbed hold of the handle, whereupon the mischievous young fellow in the room above let go of the rope.' Sir John burst out laughing. 'You can imagine how it must have looked. He could neither pull the pot in through the bars nor drop it for fear of hitting someone below. There was a further piece of tomfoolery, too crude to mention. Suffice it to say, that the chamber pot became heavier as a result.' He put an arm around Amalia's shoulders. 'I hope that I haven't offended you, Miss Janssen.'

'No, Sir John,' she said. 'It must have been very amusing.'

'A small crowd formed outside to watch it all.'

'The young will always tease their elders,' said Janssen. 'I've had one or two tricks played on me by my apprentices but nothing as malicious as that.'

They walked on until they came to the window of a shop. A gilt-framed painting of the Sheldonian Theatre was on display and it intrigued Janssen. He scrutinised it for a long time, allowing the others some minutes alone.

'We can't thank you enough, Sir John,' said Amalia.

'You've already done so simply by being here,' he told her. 'It's I who should be thanking you for reviving some golden memories for me. It must be all of twenty years ago that I brought Barbara here for the first time. Thank you for being *her*, Miss Janssen.'

His smile had an element of calculation this time and his gaze was more searching. For a reason she couldn't understand, Amalia felt a momentary unease.

No sooner had they met outside the gaol than they dispersed by prior arrangement in different directions. Daniel was afraid that they'd attract attention if they stayed together. Welbeck therefore set off on foot to walk back to the *Coq d'Or*. Basket over her arm, Estelle made for the market where she could lose herself in the throng. Since there were so many soldiers at the tavern, it was deemed unsafe to take Rachel Rees there. She'd be a hunted woman with her description widely circulated. Raymond instead drove her off in the cart to the house of a trusted friend who could offer her refuge. Daniel, meanwhile, ducked into the nearest alleyway to divest himself of the uniform that he'd put on over his own clothing. He stuffed it in a doorway along with the keys he'd taken from the duty sergeant. Then he lengthened his stride to get well away from the area before the dead body of Pons was discovered. There'd be a great commotion. A thorough search of the immediate environs of the gaol was bound to follow.

When he felt that he was clear of danger, Daniel found his way to the address where Rachel was hiding. She was shuttling between fear and exultation.

'What if they catch me?' she asked, querulously. 'They won't even bother to question me. They'll just skin me alive.'

'Forget about that,' counselled Daniel. 'You're free and that's the only thing that need concern you.'

Her face ignited. 'Yes, I'm free. Thanks to you, I've got out of that unspeakable place. You didn't come a moment too soon. That beast would have ravished me.' She kissed him on the lips and clung gratefully to his body. 'That's the third time you've saved me from being molested. The turnkey was an animal.'

He laughed. 'You do seem to attract the wrong sort of men, Rachel. First, there was that Hessian cavalry officer, and then Sergeant Furneaux decided that you were the woman of his dreams.'

'This last one was worse than the other two put together. He was a pig. And I shouldn't really count Sergeant Furneaux,' she said, thinking back to the enjoyable chat she'd had with him in the bar. 'If he'd been Welsh instead of French, I might have asked him to stay.'

'What – even with your husband in the room?'

They were in a small house not far from a tannery. Rachel felt that the pungent smell in the air would keep inquisitive people away and thereby guarantee her safety. Nobody had seen her slip into the house and her head had, in any case, been covered by a shawl. What she really wanted to know was how Daniel and Estelle had managed to rescue her. When he explained, she was full of admiration for both of them. Rachel gave an account of what had happened to her during her stay in gaol and Daniel was relieved to hear that she'd given nothing away. Now that she was free, there was only one thing on her mind.

'When do we leave?'

'Not for a few days,' he said.

Rachel was distressed. 'A few days – I don't want to spend another hour in this place! I was hoping you'd have a plan to get me out of Lille almost immediately.'

'It's too dangerous, Rachel.'

'It can't be any more dangerous than climbing on the roof of the town hall or tricking your way inside the gaol.'

'I couldn't do either of those things now,' he admitted. 'A prisoner has been rescued and a turnkey was killed in the process. The alarm has been well and truly raised by that. A hue and cry has been set up for you. It's not just the soldiers who'll be scouring the streets for you– there's sure to be a reward offered. Anybody who recognises you will want to collect it.'

'A reward?' she said, tickled by the notion. 'How much am I worth?'

'You're worth far more to us than they could ever pay,'

he said, courteously, 'but that's beside the point. You must stay hidden until the commotion starts to die down and they begin to wonder if you've already fled from Lille.'

'Will you be staying with me?'

'I'll be here some of the time.'

'I'll get very bored on my own, you know.'

'Would you like me to send Sergeant Furneaux around?'

She shook with mirth. 'I've had enough eager suitors for a while, thank you. If I had to live in France, I might even think of taking the veil. It would give me an opportunity to repent of my sins.' Something popped into her mind. 'If *you* can't be here with me, is there any chance that you could send Henry in your place?'

'I'm afraid not, Rachel.'

'Why not – he obviously likes me.'

'That would be overstating the case a little.'

'Oh,' she said, flicking a hand, 'I know that he keeps up this pose of hating anything in skirts but I'm not deceived by that. It's a shell he's built around him like a giant snail.'

Daniel grinned. 'Don't ever call him a snail in his hearing,' he warned, 'or he'll wish he never got caught up in the rescue attempt.'

'I was so surprised to see him.'

'He took some persuading to come to Lille with me.'

'Was it the tobacco that won him over?'

'I don't think any blandishments of that kind would ever weigh with Henry Welbeck. He and I are old friends,' said Daniel. 'That's the real reason I felt able to call on him. I needed someone to guard my back and he's an expert at doing that.'

'When can I see him?' she asked, enthusiastically.

'Not until it's time for us to leave.'

'But I must see Henry before then. I need to thank him.'

'I can tell him how grateful you are.'

'Let me do so in person.'

'You'll have to wait,' he said. 'Henry is busy at the moment.'

'Why – where is he?'

'He's practising his old trade, Rachel.'

'And what was that?'

'Carpentry,' said Daniel. 'Before he joined the army, he was apprenticed to a carpenter.'

The noise upset the horses at first but they soon got accustomed to it. Welbeck had set up two trestles in the stables at the *Coq d'Or* and had rested the timber across them. He was working with borrowed tools and taking time to get used to them. When Raymond joined him, the young Frenchman was wearing a leather apron. Welbeck straightened up and put his battered plane aside.

'How are you getting on?' asked Raymond.

'It's slow work. I've forgotten all I ever learnt.'

'These wood shavings will make good fuel when we have a fire in the bar again.' He looked at the timber. 'Is that the base?'

'Yes, it is but it needs to be shaped properly first.'

'Do you think that it will be big enough for Rachel?'

'I hope so,' said Welbeck, standing back to appraise his work. 'This is the best I can do. The truth is that I've never made a coffin before.' He thought of Rachel Rees and grunted with satisfaction. 'Though, to be frank, I must say that I'm enjoying making this one.'

CHAPTER ELEVEN

Louis François, Duke of Boufflers and Marshal of France, had had a long and distinguished military career that began at the siege of Marsal in 1663. Respected for his experience and renowned for his gallantry, he'd been an obvious choice to conduct the defence of Lille. Though well into his sixties, he'd retained all the skills he'd developed over the years and was still impelled by a will to win at all costs. He was seated in his quarters that morning, bristling with annoyance at what he was hearing. It had fallen to Captain Aumonier to pass on the bad news.

'The woman *escaped*?' said Boufflers in disbelief.

'To be more exact,' explained Aumonier, 'she was rescued by a man who inveigled his way into the gaol by posing as a drunk.'

'Are there no locks on the cell doors?'

'Of course, Your Grace.'

'Then how does a prisoner get out of his cell, kill one of the turnkeys and walk free from the gaol with this female?'

'They had an accomplice.'

Boufflers was even more displeased by the full details. Two people had bamboozled their way into the gaol in order to rescue a third person. The only man who'd tried to stop them had had his throat cut and his uniform stolen. Aumonier made a vain attempt to wrest some consolation from the incident.

'It proves one thing,' he said. 'We were right to arrest Madame Borrel. During my interrogation of her, I sensed that she was lying.'

Boufflers banged the table. 'Then why didn't you ensure that she was guarded night and day? I'm disappointed in you, Captain. Had you done that, she'd never have been whisked away with such ease. I deplore what's happened,' said Boufflers, 'but I'm bound to admire the daring behind this rescue. Only a bold man could have conceived and executed it.'

'That brings me to the earlier outrage. You've been told, I'm sure, about the theft of Vauban's plan of the fortifications.'

'Yes – it was another unpardonable lapse.'

'I believe that the man responsible for it was the same one who got himself arrested for being drunk and disorderly in order to worm his way into gaol.'

Aumonier smiled hopefully, expecting to be congratulated on his feat of deduction. Boufflers was scathing.

'That's as plain as the rash on your face, Captain,' he said. 'Why else would the woman need to be released from gaol unless she was a party to the earlier theft? And who else

would have the nerve and invention to effect that release
but the man who gained entry to the town hall by means
of a rope attached to a nearby church tower? On both
regrettable events, I perceive the same signature.'

'That's very astute of you, Your Grace,' said Aumonier,
face burning with embarrassment. 'But there's something
that you've not been able to divine.'

'What I divine is a catalogue of folly and ineptitude.'

'We may know who the fellow is.'

'May, may, *may*,' said Boufflers, irritably. 'Give me no
may and might and possibly, Captain Aumonier. I want
incontrovertible fact. I want the name of this impudent
rogue.'

'Then I believe it to be Daniel Rawson.'

'And on what is this belief based, may I ask?'

'On a letter from my elder brother, Your Grace.'

Boufflers rolled his eyes in dismay. Adjusting his periwig,
he sat back in his chair and studied his visitor with a blend of
dislike and distrust. He gnashed his teeth before speaking.

'Is your brother stationed here in Lille?'

'No, he's not.'

'Is he aware of the details of these two incidents?'

'Not yet, Your Grace.'

'Then how can his correspondence enlighten us?'

'Pascal – my brother – is a major in an infantry regiment
under the command of the Duke of Vendôme. He told
me of a British officer who not only penetrated the French
camp in order to rescue a young woman, he came back a
second time to retrieve a sword. In fact,' said Aumonier,
'he was captured on the second occasion but rescued on his
way to Paris.' Boufflers looked unconvinced. 'There's more,

Your Grace, and it's very relevant to the matter before us. Two years ago, it transpires, the very same man somehow got into no less a place than the Bastille and spirited away a prisoner held on a charge of spying for the enemy. Do you detect a pattern here, Your Grace?'

'I do,' said Boufflers, interested at last. 'Even the British army cannot have many men capable of such intrepidity.'

'His name, as I said, is Daniel Rawson.'

'What's his rank?'

'He's a captain in the 24th Foot.'

'Their captains seem to be far more enterprising than ours.'

'He's also attached to the Duke of Marlborough's staff,' said Aumonier, smarting at the rebuke. 'Since he's been chosen for dangerous missions before, it's highly likely that he would have been called upon again.'

'That's a reasonable supposition,' admitted Boufflers. 'So – we have a name, but do we have a face?'

'Yes, we do. Three people have described it. We also know the face of his female accomplice, Your Grace, and it's quite unforgettable. I'd recognise her anywhere.'

'I thought there were *two* female accomplices.'

'The guards on duty that night have given a good description of the other woman,' said Aumonier, 'as has the duty sergeant.'

Boufflers raised a cynical eyebrow. 'Was this before or after the duty sergeant was let out of one of his own cells? I must say that if I'd found him bound and gagged like that, I'd have been tempted to leave him behind bars for a week.'

'He *has* been disciplined, Your Grace.'

'What of the search?'

'It's still going on but – so far – without success.'

'Then they must already have left Lille.'

'I think that unlikely, Your Grace. The moment the escape was discovered, word was sent post-haste to every gate. Madame Borrel is so distinctive that it would be virtually impossible to disguise her. Nobody answering her description departed from Lille today. The guards were absolutely certain of that. She and her rescuers are still here, Your Grace.'

'Find them.'

'We'll endeavour to do so.'

'Find them quickly before they do any more damage.'

'We will, Your Grace.'

'And one last thing,' said Boufflers, his voice softening. 'Next time you write to your elder brother, thank him for telling you about Captain Daniel Rawson.'

The search was so intense and sustained that Daniel didn't even consider trying to get out of Lille. At every single gate, people were thoroughly searched and questioned before being allowed to leave. Posters had been put up, offering handsome rewards for information leading to the capture of the fugitives. Descriptions of all three of them were given. More disturbing was the fact that Daniel's real name and rank were printed on the poster. The only crumb of comfort was that the search was limited to a man and two women. The authorities were clearly unaware that Henry Welbeck and Raymond Lizier had also been involved in the escape.

'So there's nothing to stop me leaving today,' said Welbeck.

'Not if you can talk your way past the guards at the gate,'

said Daniel. 'I wouldn't suggest you don a French uniform when you do that. It's never wise to use the same deception twice.'

'Do you think I *should* go now, Dan?'

'It's your decision.'

'I'd hate to leave you in the lurch.'

'We're relatively safe if we keep our heads down.'

'Only as long as Rachel stays hidden,' said Welbeck, ruefully. 'The minute that mad Welsh hag steps out into the street, someone will recognise her from the description on the poster and want to collect that reward. How is she?'

'Rachel is bored and lonely.'

'She's been shut away for days now.'

'That's an unfortunate necessity.'

'Have you told her how she's going to be smuggled out?'

'Not yet,' said Daniel. 'I thought you might like that pleasure.'

Welbeck laughed. 'I had the pleasure of making that coffin,' he confessed, 'and imagining it being lowered into the ground with her in it. Explaining to Rachel what's going to happen is another matter altogether. She's bound to object strongly.'

'She might not object when she hears that you made the coffin especially for her, Henry. She holds you in high regard. Rachel would do anything for you.'

'That's why I'm thinking of leaving.'

'Every time I go there, she begs me to bring you as well.'

'Tell her that I'm not available.'

'She looks upon you as a hero who helped to save her life.'

'You and Estelle did that.'

'We don't have quite the same appeal as you,' said Daniel. 'It wouldn't hurt you to sneak across to the house after dark to pay a visit to Rachel.'

Welbeck was adamant. 'No, Dan – there's only so much a man can be expected to do for a pouch of tobacco and I've already done it.'

The two men were in the stables at the *Coq d'Or*, standing beside the finished coffin which had now been covered by a tarpaulin. When they heard footsteps coming across the yard, they both took a precautionary grip on their daggers. They were relieved to see that it was only Estelle. A chevron of concern was stamped on her brow.

'What's happened?' said Daniel.

'Someone just came in to ask after Rachel,' she replied. 'He said that he'd heard of a woman who worked here as a serving wench for a few days, and that she sounded very much like the person for whom they were searching.'

'What did you tell them?'

'I left it to my sister to do the talking. There was no point in denying that Rachel was here – many of our customers remember her. So Bette simply said that she'd worked here briefly, then had vanished into thin air. We had no idea where she was now.'

'Do you think Madame Lizier was believed?'

'It was difficult to tell, Alain.' She stifled a smile. 'I suppose that I should call you Daniel in private now.'

'I'd prefer to remain Alain Borrel for the time being.'

'As you wish,' she said. 'I came to warn you. The man went away but we fear that he might come back with other soldiers and ask to search the premises. Since your description is on the posters, it might be better if you weren't here.'

'That goes for me as well,' said Welbeck. 'I'm ready to leave.'

'We have to stay a little longer until things quieten down,' said Daniel. 'There are too many soldiers in the streets for my liking. But thank you, Estelle,' he went on, gently touching her arm. 'It's a timely warning. I'll move out later on.'

She was saddened. 'I'll be sorry to see you go.'

'It's for your safety as much as mine. If I was to be caught here, they'd realise there was a link between me and the tavern, and that I must have been working in harness with Rachel.'

'If that happened, we'd *all* be caught,' said Welbeck, gloomily.

'I'll go – tell that to your sister, Estelle.'

'What about me, Dan?'

'You could always come with me to the house by the tannery.'

'Not if Rachel is still there.'

'Then you can either stay here or take your chance of getting out of Lille by relying on your wits.'

'They're not as sharp as yours.'

'In that case, you wait until we're ready.'

'Yes,' said Estelle, 'stay as long as you wish. It's not you they're looking for – it's Alain and Rachel Borrel.' She gave Daniel a long stare before making for the door. 'Excuse me.'

Welbeck was curious. 'And what was all that about, Dan?'

'What do you mean?'

'I saw the look on Estelle's face. You've made a conquest.'

'Then it's an unintentional one.'

'I wondered why Estelle always made an excuse to come out here when the two of us were together.'

'Don't jump to conclusions, Henry,' said Daniel, quickly. 'Estelle has had no encouragement from me. Nor would she ever do so. I'm just grateful for the way she helped us during the rescue.'

He was more than grateful. Daniel had been discomfited by her unheralded appearance in his bed and since then there'd been some awkward moments between the two of them. To make amends, she'd more or less insisted on being part of the rescue team. It had been a risk to involve her but Daniel had taken it. Estelle had shown such courage and resourcefulness that he felt she'd redeemed herself. As far as he was concerned, it had wiped the slate clean.

It was Welbeck's turn to mock. 'Don't you dare tease me about Rachel Rees again,' he said, 'or I'll remind you of your admirer.'

'Estelle is not my admirer.'

'I've seen women look at you like that before, Dan.'

'There's no harm in their looking.'

'Is that what you're going to say in your next letter?'

'What next letter?'

'The one you write to Amalia Janssen,' said Welbeck, grinning. 'Are you going to tell her that you've not only been married to Rachel Rees while you were in Lille but that you've beguiled a Frenchwoman as well? How is Amalia going to react to that news?'

* * *

The first gift had thrilled Amalia. It was a huge basket of flowers that filled the whole house with their fragrance. On the second day, a leather-bound history of Oxford was sent to her, complete with some enchanting illustrations. While out riding with Sir John Rievers on the third day, Amalia received an expensive silver brooch in the shape of a horse. When more gifts arrived on subsequent days, she began to get worried. Sir John was not merely expressing his affection for her. She had the feeling that she was being courted and it was unnerving. Given the situation, Amalia was glad that she and her father were leaving the cottage for a few days to visit someone in Cirencester who owned one of Janssen's tapestries and who'd invited him to stay if ever he should be in England. Beatrix helped to load the baggage. They were about to depart in the carriage when Sir John cantered up on his horse. He doffed his hat to Amalia.

'Good day to you!' he said, sharing a smile between her and her father. 'I hope you have a pleasant journey.'

'Thank you, Sir John,' said Janssen.

'Who knows? Another commission may arise out of it.'

'Father is not short of commissions,' Amalia pointed out. 'He has a whole host of customers waiting to buy his work.'

'I'm sure he does, Miss Janssen. Genius of that kind is always in demand. As for customers, I bring a message from one of the most illustrious. Her Grace, the Duchess of Marlborough is sad that she's been able to see so little of you so far and invites you to dine with her when you return from the Cotswolds.'

'That's very obliging of her,' said Janssen, pleased.

'Yes,' agreed Amalia, 'it is. We'll look forward to it.'

'I'll tell her that you accept,' said Sir John, affably. 'You'll have to endure my company again, alas, because the meal will be served at Rievers Hall. Our humble abode can never rival Blenheim Palace but, unlike that incomparable edifice, we do have a dining room.'

'There's a magnificent dining room at Blenheim Palace,' joked Janssen, 'but, unfortunately, it hasn't been built yet. The architect was kind enough to show me the plan.'

'I knew that that you and Vanbrugh would get along.'

'I admire his work enormously, Sir John – and that of Mr Hawksmoor, who's worked for him on Blenheim. Of course, the English architect I revere most is Sir Christopher Wren.'

'I had a feeling you'd say that.'

'We intend to see St Paul's Cathedral when we go to London,' said Amalia. 'We've heard so much about his masterpiece.'

'You'll not be disappointed, Miss Janssen. As it happens,' said Sir John, 'I'll be in London myself tomorrow. I'll see if I can find any glowing reports about Captain Rawson for you.'

'Oh, he isn't often mentioned in despatches.'

'If what you tell me is true, he ought to be.' He replaced his hat. 'When you come back to Woodstock, I hope to have glad tidings for you. I know how much you miss the good captain.'

'I do, Sir John,' confessed Amalia.

'That's as it should be.'

He gazed at her with such undisguised fondness that she could feel a blush coming. Seeing his daughter's uneasiness, Janssen tried to turn attention away from her.

'How is Lady Rievers, may I ask?'

'She's bearing up as usual,' said Sir John. 'Unhappily, my dear wife views Her Grace's visit with some misgiving. Much as she adores Sarah, she does find her company rather exhausting. Oh,' he added, slapping his boot with a riding crop, 'that's the other thing I meant to tell you. I found out why you had such a poor reception when you first arrived at Blenheim.'

'You explained it to us,' recalled Amalia. 'You told us that Her Grace doesn't see eye to eye with the builders or with the architect.'

'It's true with regard to Mr Vanbrugh,' said Janssen, meekly. 'He admitted as much to me. There have been some fierce exchanges between them.'

'Not only on matters of design,' confided Sir John. 'Her Grace has been kind enough to lend Vanbrugh some money to pay off the debts he incurred when running his theatre. That's led to friction. But something else has been upsetting her.'

'May we know what it is?'

'You may indeed, Mr Janssen. It concerns the thanksgiving service for the victory at Oudenarde. It's to be held in the place that you just mentioned – St Paul's Cathedral. Her Grace, the Duchess of Marlborough, simply must be present.'

'It's only natural – her husband was responsible for the victory.'

'There's another reason,' said Sir John. 'She holds some high offices at Court and will therefore travel to the service in the carriage belonging to Her Majesty, the Queen.'

'What a signal honour!'

Sir John pursed his lips. 'In this instance, it may be more of an ordeal. That's why it's been preying on Her Grace's mind and making her seem aloof and offhand. Ten years ago, she and Her Majesty were the very best of friends. Sisters could not have been closer. They were always in each other's company both in private and in public. For some reason,' he went on, lowering his voice to a discreet whisper, 'the frost seems to have affected that close friendship. As a result, the service at St Paul's may turn out to be something of a trial for both of them.'

Sarah, Duchess of Marlborough, had many fine qualities but tact was not one of them. When she felt affronted, she tended to strike back without first considering the effect of her barbs. Relations between her and Queen Anne had been deteriorating steadily ever since Sarah had been replaced as her favourite by Abigail Masham. What rankled with Sarah was the fact that she'd actually secured for Abigail the post of Woman of the Bedchamber, not realising that she was helping the very woman by whom she'd be supplanted. Never one to forgive an injury, Sarah wanted revenge and she listened to the advice of a new friend, Arthur Maynwaring. A Whig barrister with a malicious streak, Maynwaring wrote a scurrilous ballad about the relationship between the Queen and Abigail, implying that the two were lesbian lovers. The unsigned ballad was sold throughout the city and sung to the tune of *Fair Rosamund*.

Other women might have felt that the sheer existence of the ballad was revenge enough, but Sarah insisted on showing it to the queen by way of an indictment. Anne, a sick, overweight woman, was deeply shocked by the grotesque charge and outraged by the wicked verses:

> When as Queene Anne of Great Renown
> Great Britain's sceptre sway'd
> Beside the Church she dearly lov'd
> A dirty Chambermaid.
>
> O! Abigail that was her name
> She stiched and starched full well
> But how she pierc'd this Royal Heart
> No mortal man can tell.

Most explicit and hurtful was a reference to the 'Dark Deeds at Night'. Being shown the defamatory ballad by Sarah hardly endeared her to the queen. It made the rift between them widen irreparably. There was nobody Anne would less like to invite to the service than her former friend, but protocol had to be followed. As Groom of the Stole and Mistress of the Robes, Sarah had to be there to perform her state duties. One of them was to lay out the queen's clothing and her jewels. She would never yield this prerogative to anyone else. On the day itself, Sarah discharged her duty with care and attention. She was therefore mortified when Anne stepped into her carriage wearing no jewellery at all. The ride to St Paul's was marked by dissension. Sarah was pulsing with fury.

'I vow, Your Majesty,' she said, 'it will seem strange to any onlooker that you celebrate so great a victory in so mean a manner.'

'I will celebrate it as I wish,' declared Anne, maintaining a smile for the crowds who cheered her as they passed. 'If I do not choose to wear any jewellery, that's my affair.'

'This is no simple whim of yours. It's a deliberate insult.'

'Against whom, I pray?'

'Against *me*, Your Majesty,' said Sarah, spitting out the words. 'Because I was responsible for laying out the jewels, you refused to wear them. And we both know why,' she added. 'It was at the behest of that venomous creature, Abigail, the chambermaid.'

'I deny that.'

'Deny it all you will. The truth is self-evident. Oh, the black ingratitude of that beastly woman whom I took out of a garret and saved from starvation!'

'Please moderate your language,' said Anne, sharply. 'These cheers will drown out most of what you say, but stray words may still be heard from an open carriage.'

'Deeds speak louder than words, Your Majesty,' said Sarah, bitterly. 'As we enter St Paul's, everyone will be aware of your foul deed. In dispensing with your jewels, you offend both me and my beloved husband. Have you so soon forgotten that he delivered at Oudenarde a victory in the largest battle so far waged in the war? Is that not something to celebrate with full pomp?'

'Yes, it is,' conceded Anne, wearily, 'though I do long for a time when all this bloodshed will cease.' She made an effort to smooth ruffled feathers. 'No insult was intended to you or to your husband. Let that be clear. Nor was my decision influenced by anyone else, least of all the person to whom you referred in so cruel a manner.'

'All of London has taken her true measure,' said Sarah, nastily.

'I simply did not wish to wear any jewels today. With

this robe and the regalia, I have enough weight to bear as it is. As you well know, Sarah, I'm not in rude health and find these occasions trying. If I can lighten my load even a little, then it's a blessed relief.'

Sarah pounced. 'The best way to lighten the load would be to dismiss that she-devil who has suborned you.'

'That's a monstrous suggestion!'

'It's one that's made throughout the city.'

'Really?' rejoined Anne, indicating the enthusiastic crowds on both sides of the road. 'There's no hint of malice in what I can hear. That sounds like acclamation to me.'

Sarah was provoked into even wilder comments. Certain that the jewels had been disregarded in order to humiliate her, she kept upbraiding the queen all the way to their destination. As they stepped down from the carriage, Anne tried to answer the criticism but it was the strident voice of the Duchess of Marlborough that was heard by those standing nearby.

'Be quiet!' snapped Sarah.

Rachel Rees had spent over a week cooped up in a small house and surviving on a mean diet. It had made her tetchy and impatient. When she was offered even smaller accommodation, she was incensed.

'A coffin!' she cried. 'You wish to put me in a coffin?'

'It's only for a short time,' said Daniel.

'One minute would be too long. I may have to inhabit a coffin one day but I hope that it will be later rather than sooner. I was better off in the gaol,' she argued. 'At least I could walk around in that cell. Being locked in a coffin is like being buried alive.' She gurgled and shivered simultaneously. 'I refuse to do it.'

'Then you must stay in Lille indefinitely.'

'What about you and Henry?'

'We'll bid you farewell.'

'You can't go without me,' she yelled.

'We can't go *with* you unless you're disguised in some way,' said Daniel. 'You were arrested at the gate once before. Do you wish that to happen again?'

'No, I do not.'

'Then you must abide by our device.'

'It's unthinkable.'

'In that case, you stay in hiding and inhale the stink of leather.'

Daniel nodded in the direction of the tannery. Rachel bit her lip as she meditated. Anxious to escape from Lille, she'd been horrified to hear that she might have to do so by posing as a dead body. The more she thought about it, the more disturbing it became. In her febrile state, she could already hear the nails being hammered in.

'Henry made it especially for you,' said Daniel.

'A coffin is a coffin,' she retorted, 'whoever makes it. When you told me that he'd been apprenticed to a carpenter, I thought he might be making us a ladder so that we could climb over the walls. Yet all the time he was seeking to bury me.'

'The coffin will stay above ground, Rachel.'

'Not if we're caught, it won't. They'll either bury me there and then or set fire to me. I'll be helpless. And that's another thing,' she went on, wagging her head. 'How can I breathe inside it? By the time you let me out, I'll have suffocated.'

'Henry allowed for that,' said Daniel. 'He's made a series of holes in the timber to allow the free passage of air. You'll be able to breathe properly and – because we'll line it with cushions – you'll be quite snug in there.'

'Snug!' she howled. 'That's very reassuring. I may expire in there but at least I'll die in comfort – is that what you're saying?'

Daniel sighed. 'You know quite well that it isn't.'

It took him another hour to persuade her. Word was sent to the tavern and the coffin arrived on the back of a cart driven by Welbeck. Pleased to see the sergeant again, Rachel was aghast when she clapped eyes on his handiwork.

'I'll never get in there!' she protested.

'It's bigger than it looks,' said Welbeck.

'Even if I did manage to squeeze in, how on earth would you get me out again? I could be stuck in there for life.'

Welbeck had to bite back his approval of that eventuality.

'Let's get it inside the house,' said Daniel.

He and Welbeck carried the coffin into the living room and set it down on the floor. When the lid was removed, Rachel was upset to realise that she'd have company in there. Two daggers and a pistol would also share the cushions.

'What are they for?' she asked, testily. 'Am I supposed to commit suicide if things go awry?'

'We'll be searched at the gate,' said Welbeck. 'We can't let them find weapons on us – especially the dagger you gave to Dan. The one place they won't look is inside the coffin.'

'Try it for size,' urged Daniel. 'After all, you're a unique corpse. Every other one has to die before they're put into a wooden box.'

'I've come close enough to death,' she grumbled. 'Why I agreed to come to Lille, I shall never know. Since we arrived, I've been molested in my bed by a naked man, arrested, thrown into prison and assaulted by that disgusting turnkey. On top of all that, I had my worldly goods confiscated. If we get out of here alive, I'll be a pauper.'

Daniel hugged her. 'No, you won't,' he promised, soothingly. 'I had to buy the horse and cart to get us out of here. When we get back to camp, you can have them by way of compensation for your loss.'

'Yes,' said Welbeck, 'and you can keep the coffin as well. I paid for the timber out of my own purse.'

'What use is it to me?' she demanded.

'A sutler like you is sure to find one.'

Rachel laughed. She then took Welbeck's arm so that he could help her into the coffin. Lowering herself gingerly, she sat upright and ran her palms along the edges.

'There are no splinters,' he said. 'I used a plane on it.'

'Well,' she observed, 'I have to admit that it's bigger than it looks. Let's see what happens when I lie down.'

Welbeck supported her shoulders as she eased herself gently backward. Having guessed at her dimensions, he was pleased to see that he had overestimated them. There was ample room for Rachel. She'd be able to move her limbs quite freely. Before it was nailed down, the lid was put loosely in place so that she could move it away if she began to panic. Rachel found that the holes cut in the timber let in plenty of air. The cushions were soft and the whole interior had been sweetened with herbs. Wishing to get the experience over as quickly as possible, she moved the lid and sat up.

'Nail me in and let's be away,' she ordered.

'There'll only be two proper nails,' explained Welbeck, holding them up. 'They'll keep the lid in place. The others will be there for appearance only. They're too short to penetrate the lid.'

'That was Henry's idea,' said Daniel. 'In a crisis – if anything should happen to us, for instance – you can prise the lid off by forcing it up with your hands. This is a very special coffin, Rachel. It's the only one ever built with an escape hatch.'

Without a word, she lay down obediently so that the nails could be hammered into place. Being carried out of the house was rather unsettling because she was jiggled from side to side. Once the coffin was put on the cart, however, it was more stable. Rachel was grateful for the cushions. Without them, she'd have felt every cobblestone over which the wheels rumbled. Secure in her box, she could hear almost nothing and lost all sense of where she was.

While Daniel drove the cart, Welbeck adopted the posture of a grieving son. Both wore the rough apparel of tradesmen. Daniel's neat moustache had now been subsumed into his full beard. A patch over one eye helped to transform his appearance.

'Why did you choose St Andrew's Gate?' asked Welbeck.

'It's in the northern sector,' replied Daniel, 'and is therefore closer to our camp. It's also the part of Lille that Prince Eugene is most likely to attack, I believe, so we must pray that he's not yet ready to unleash the power of his siege guns.'

'The signal for attack can't be far away, Dan.'

'That's a chance we'll have to take. Ideally, we'd have left days ago but there were too many search parties in action. They seem to have died away now.'

'They must think we've already escaped.'

'I doubt that, Henry. They'll still be on the alert.'

'What was her name?'

'Who?'

'My mother,' said Welbeck. 'If I'm bewailing her death, I'd like to know what she was called when she was alive.'

'Invent a name,' said Daniel, 'as long as it's not Rachel.'

'I've got *her* just where I want her.'

'Don't be so heartless. I sympathise with her. It must be quite frightening to be in that coffin.'

Welbeck was unmoved. 'At least it will keep her quiet for a bit.'

As the ring around Lille was tightened, very few people wanted to come in through its gates. There were still those, however, keen to escape before the bombardment began, anxious people going off to stay with family members or friends elsewhere until the issue was resolved one way or the other. The cart had to wait in the queue until its turn came. It was surrounded by four guards. One of them banged the side of the coffin with the butt of his musket.

'Respect for the dead, please!' admonished Daniel. 'That's his mother in there.'

'What did she die of?' asked the guard.

'Old age.'

'Where are you taking her?'

'Back home to St Andrew. She was born in the village and her son promised to bury her there when the time came. It's a vow that he has to keep.'

'It is,' said Welbeck, tearfully.

They were questioned at length by the four suspicious soldiers, each one trying to find an excuse to refuse them the right to leave. Daniel and Welbeck were made to remove their coats so that they could be searched. The soldiers even looked under the cart to see if anything was hidden there. One of them tapped the coffin.

'Open it up!' he said.

'No!' begged Welbeck. 'Leave my mother in peace.'

'Let's show them, Henri,' offered Daniel, climbing onto the back of the cart. 'But you'll need to stand well off, gentlemen. The lady has been dead for a week. When this lid is opened, you won't like what you smell.' He reached out a hand to one of the men. 'Lend me your musket and I'll open the lid with the bayonet.'

'There's no need,' said the man.

'Come, sir – we'll show you we've nothing to hide.'

Daniel's apparent readiness to cooperate convinced them that they would indeed find the corpse of an old woman inside the coffin. After a further bout of questioning, they waved the cart on. As they went through St Andrew's Gate, Daniel hoped that he wouldn't have to return to Lille a third time. He'd made some good friends there and was sad to leave Raymond and Bette Lizier. About Estelle, his feelings were more ambiguous. His one hope was that Guillaume Lizier would soon be returned to the bosom of his family.

The village of St Andrew was barely a mile north. After rattling along past ditches, ramparts and other defences, they were relieved to reach somewhere with a semblance of normality. It was a small community, with houses and shops clustered around the village square and with a church sitting on a hill and attesting its presence with a tall spire.

Driving round to the rear of the building, Daniel found a quiet spot beneath the boughs of a tree. Taking the lid off the coffin was the work of seconds. Rachel was lifted out of her tomb.

'Where are we?' she gasped, blinking in the daylight.

'Next to the churchyard,' said Welbeck, gesturing towards the headstones. 'This is where we're going to bury you.'

'I wouldn't get back in that coffin if you paid me.'

'Put the lid back on, Henry,' said Daniel as he took out the weapons. 'It can't be seen like that. You sit with me, Rachel. After all that time in there, I daresay you want some fresh air.'

'All I want is to get far away from Lille,' she said, grimly.

When the lid had been hammered back into place, they left St Andrew and followed a track that led them in the direction of the Allied camp. It was a fine day with a cool breeze fanning the leaves of the trees. After the hustle and bustle of Lille, it was wonderfully calm and peaceful. They let the sun play on their faces. The tranquillity did not hold. It was suddenly shattered by a series of loud explosions, and cannonballs went whistling over their heads. Their ears were soon deafened by the full thunder of an attack.

'*Iesu Mawr!*' shouted Rachel, lapsing into her native language. 'Now that we've escaped the enemy, we're going to be killed by our own bleeding cannon. Stop it!' she yelled, cupping her hands around her mouth. 'We're on your side, you blind fools!'

The visit to Cirencester had been an unqualified success. They stayed at the home of a wealthy wool merchant and had been given unstinting hospitality. Since their host wanted to talk endlessly to Emanuel Janssen about weaving, Amalia was free to investigate the town with Beatrix. They discovered that it had many souvenirs of its time as an important regional centre during the Roman occupation. Amalia loved its magnificent church and its meandering streets, but Beatrix was drawn more to its thriving market. Poking happily about among the stalls, she felt that she was back in Amsterdam again, accompanying her mistress on one of their regular shopping expeditions. For her it was the best moment so far of the entire trip to England.

All three of them were sad to leave the town but they didn't wish to outstay their welcome. When they finally got back to Woodstock, it was Janssen who received a gift from Sir John Rievers this time.

'I couldn't possibly accept it,' said Janssen.

'Don't you like it?'

'I adore it, Sir John.'

'That's what I realised when I saw you staring at it in Oxford. While you were away,' said Sir John, 'I sent someone back to that shop to purchase it.'

'At the very least, let me give you the money.'

'I'll not hear of it, Mr Janssen. The painting is yours as, I hope, a treasured memento of a wonderful day we shared in Oxford. You did say that you revered Sir Christopher Wren and I remember how much you admired his Sheldonian Theatre when we stood before it. Now that you have this version of it,' he said, pointing to the gift, 'you may gaze upon it whenever you wish.'

'You're too kind, Sir John,' said Janssen, transfixed.

'We can't thank you enough,' added Amalia.

Sir John's smile faded and he took her by the arm to

guide her into the adjoining room. While her father was distracted, he took the opportunity to speak to her in private. His face was solemn, his voice tinged with sorrow. He reached out to take her hands in his.

'I only wish I had a gift for you, Miss Janssen,' he said, 'but all that I can offer you is sad news. I refused to believe it at first but my source is very reliable. Captain Daniel Rawson has been commended for his bravery yet again but is unable to enjoy the praise.' He swallowed hard. 'It's my duty to inform you that he was killed in action at the siege of Lille.'

Amalia felt as if something had just exploded inside her head. Daniel was dead? It was unthinkable. Her whole future crumbled before her eyes. How could she live without him? Unable to cope with the searing horror of the news, Amalia lost all control of her body. As her eyes closed and her legs collapsed under her, Sir John reached out quickly to catch her. He held her in his arms and pulled her close, inhaling her fragrance, then brushing her lips with a kiss. Gazing at her face as if it were on a pillow beside him, he savoured every second of his unlicensed intimacy. Amalia was warm, delicate and wholly defenceless. Only when she began to recover did he call for her father.

CHAPTER TWELVE

With nothing but bad tidings to report, Captain Aumonier approached the marshal's quarters with some trepidation. A meeting had just taken place in the room and five senior officers hurried out through the door to implement their orders. Aumonier waited nervously, listening to the fierce bombardment by the enemy and to the booming replies of their own cannon. It was like hearing the approach of a thunderstorm. When the captain was finally summoned into the room, he found Boufflers seated at his desk with a series of maps and documents spread out before him on the table.

'It's started,' he said, calmly.

'I'd hoped we'd have more time to prepare, Your Grace.'

'We must make the most of what we have.'

'The appeal obviously fell on deaf ears.'

'I knew that it would,' said Boufflers, 'but the people of Lille had the right to ask for mercy. They sought clemency from Prince Eugene, begging him to spare the town the full rigours of a siege. I have a copy of the prince's response,' he went on, picking up a piece of paper. 'It's fairly uncompromising.'

'What does it say, Your Grace?'

Boufflers read it out. 'A besieged town ought to be kept very close. But when he should be master of the place, the burghers might be assured of his protection, provided he should be satisfied that they had deserved it, by their impartial carriage during the siege.'

'That's a rather pointless proviso,' said Aumonier. 'Since the citizens are lawful subjects of the French crown, the prince must know that they could never show impartiality. We may have a large Flemish population but this is essentially a French town.'

'I know that better than anyone – I was governor here.'

'The local militia are fighting beside us at this very moment.'

'I'm grateful for their help. We have few enough men, as it is.'

'Is there no hope of relief, Your Grace?'

'The Duke of Vendôme has been ordered to come to our rescue but he seems to be dragging his heels. The latest information I have is that he's still encamped near Ghent.'

'Is the Duke of Berwick any closer?'

'His army has joined forces with Vendôme.'

'Why do they delay when they're needed here?'

'If you would care to ask them,' said Boufflers, dryly, 'I'd be interested in their reply. There's an army of thirty-five thousand men out there, bent on reducing Lille to ashes. We need assistance.' He stood up and appraised his visitor. 'But let's forget the enemies outside the walls for a moment, shall we? Tell me about the enemies within.'

Aumonier cleared his throat. 'They're still at liberty.'

'How can they be after all this time?'

'They must have escaped, Your Grace.'

'You assured me that that was impossible.'

'I know,' admitted Aumonier, 'but I reckoned without Captain Rawson's guile. It seems that he can find a way out of anywhere. Though how he contrived to take someone like Madame Borrel with him is beyond me. From the description on the posters, anyone would recognise her instantly.'

'Perhaps the captain has left and she remains here.'

'I incline to the view that both have fled. Our diligence cannot be faulted, Your Grace,' he added, defensively. 'We've knocked on almost every door in Lille. We searched high and low but we've never so much as had a sniff of either of them.'

'Call off the search.'

'I've already done so.'

'Good – that's the first bit of enterprise you've shown.'

'The men are needed on the ramparts, Your Grace,' said the other, pleased that his decision had been ratified. 'We can't have them wasting their time in a futile search.'

'You've taken the words out of my mouth, Captain Aumonier. For the time being, we can forget all about this Daniel Rawson and his female companions. If – by the grace of God – Vendôme does manage to relieve us, I'll make a point of discussing this infuriating British officer with him. He, too, has a score to settle with Captain Rawson.'

'According to my brother, the fellow was the talk of the camp.'

'He's made a name for himself in Lille as well.'

'There is one hope for us, Your Grace.'

'Oh?' asked Boufflers. 'What's that?'

'Rawson and the others may have escaped this very day.'

'That would be too great a blessing.'

'Just imagine,' said Aumonier, smirking. 'The very moment they escape from Lille, the bombardment begins. It's a perfect case of jumping out of the frying pan and into the fire.'

Boufflers smiled. 'What a pleasing thought,' he said, waving a hand in the direction of the window. 'Listen to those cannon firing at each other. It's an inferno out there. If Rawson and the woman are caught in the middle of it, they won't get a hundred yards before they're blown to pieces.' His smile broadened into a grin. 'Even the gallant Captain Rawson won't be able to escape from that.'

Daniel had been under fire many times but he'd never before been the target for his own artillery. Equally seasoned in battle, Welbeck had learnt how to cope with the noise, carnage and chaos of warfare. Like his friend, however, he was in a novel and hazardous situation, caught in the crossfire between the two sides. For Rachel Rees, it was the stuff of nightmares. While she'd seen the horrors of combat at close quarters, she'd never ventured onto a battlefield until the fighting was over and she could pick her way through the debris.

'We're going to need that coffin, after all,' she cried.

'Keep your head down,' warned Daniel.

'I'm sorry. I can't hear a word you're saying in this din.'

'Stay down,' said Welbeck, pulling her down beside him on the back of the cart. 'Hold tight and pray hard.'

As they fled from St Andrew after the opening salvoes, they saw frightened villagers running to the church for sanctuary. Daniel was on the driving seat, crouching low and using all his strength to stop the terrified horse from bolting. The siege guns continued to pound the fortifications and French cannon gave an ear-shattering response. In the momentary pauses between firing, the fugitives could hear the piteous cries of wounded and dying men. The siege had claimed its first casualties. Holding to his belief that the object of the attack would be the gates on the northern side of Lille, Daniel tried to drive due west in the hope of finding uncontested terrain. It was a spine-tingling ride through a hail of cannonballs and round shot. Some of the Allied fire fell short of its target but much of it smashed into the defensive lines and sent chunks of masonry hurtling through the air.

The desperate dash to safety seemed likely to end in disaster any minute but Daniel never lost heart. Indeed, as the concerted attack began to ease off slightly, he even dared to hope that they were nearing the extremity of the Allied gun emplacements. Once out of their range, they could afford to laugh with relief at the jeopardy they'd been in. It was not to be. As they rattled across the plain, a massive cannonball landed directly ahead of them and gouged a hole in the ground. There was no way to avoid it. Though the horse missed the gaping cavity, one cartwheel went straight into it, causing the whole vehicle to tip over and shed its occupants. Strapped between the shafts, the horse was thrown violently sideways, snapping its hind leg in the process and rolling in agony on the ground.

Daniel was the first to recover. After checking to see that

the others were not injured, he took pity on the animal that was now threshing wildly and neighing in agony. Taking the pistol from his belt, Daniel put a bullet through its brain.

Rachel was fuming. 'What did you do that for?'

'I had to put him out of his misery,' said Daniel.

'You told me I could have the horse and cart as compensation for my losses. What use are they now?'

'The coffin is undamaged,' noted Welbeck, brushing the dust off his breeches. 'Take that instead.'

He ducked as another cannonball explored the ground nearby and sent up a shower of earth over them. Daniel remained sanguine.

'It's getting better,' he claimed.

'This is *better*?' yelled Rachel, incredulously.

'Follow me and stay low.'

'Are you sure you know where you're going, Dan?' shouted Welbeck, trotting after his friend. 'What if there's another line of attack further west?'

'That would mean an assault on the citadel,' said Daniel, 'and Prince Eugene needs to get much closer to Lille to do that. No, I fancy that the citadel will be the *last* target.'

'How much farther must we go?' asked Rachel, panting.

'We don't go any farther!' replied Welbeck, throwing an arm around her as he dived to the ground to evade the cannonball he'd seen coming. 'I'm sorry I had to do that,' he said when the danger had passed. 'Are you hurt?'

'Who minds a few bruises when a man saves your life?' she said with a grin. 'Thank you, Henry. I knew that you cared.'

He released her immediately. Daniel had also flattened himself on the ground. Getting up again, he led them on, heading for a copse in the middle distance. It looked impossibly far away to Rachel but she struggled gamely on. Welbeck made a point of keeping ahead of her so that he wouldn't be called upon to wrestle her to the ground again. When she began to lag behind, Daniel slowed down and offered her his arm. Rachel had no breath left with which to thank him.

The onslaught continued with undiminished fury but they were no longer at the centre of the action. The pandemonium slowly began to fade and there were no stray cannonballs to dodge. Instead of lurching along at speed, they were able to walk side by side. The trees ahead held promise of protection. It looked as if they might reach them, after all.

'What will become of me?' asked Rachel with a sigh.

'There's one thing I can promise,' said Daniel. 'I won't be inviting you to go to Lille again. The same applies to you, Henry.'

'Nothing would get me inside that place again,' said Welbeck.

Rachel giggled. 'What if I was held prisoner there?'

'I'd cheer.'

'That's not very courteous,' chided Daniel.

'It's an honest answer.'

'He's only teasing,' said Rachel, patting Welbeck's arm.

'Let go of me, woman.'

She and the sergeant bickered away until they got within forty yards of the copse. Exhaustion then made Rachel stumble. As she was about to fall on the ground, Welbeck moved instinctively and grabbed her just in time. He helped her to stand upright. Realising what he'd done, he let go of her as if she was on fire.

'I'm in your debt once again, Henry,' she said.

'You owe me nothing except the promise to keep away from me.'

'But I feel that we've been drawn together.'

'That wasn't by choice,' said Welbeck, grumpily.

'Then why did you come to Lille to rescue me?'

'I was only there to support Captain Rawson.'

Before Rachel could reply, a warning shot was fired above their heads and they came to an abrupt halt. Several muskets poked out from the trees and a Dutch voice issued the command.

'Don't move an inch or we'll shoot!'

Amalia Janssen was still shaken by the enormity of the shock. As she sat in the chair, her mind was racing wildly as she tried to consider the implications of what she'd been told. Her father stood one side of her and Beatrix knelt solicitously on the other, holding Amalia's hand. Sir John Rievers looked down at her with sympathy and attempted to take some of the sting out of his news.

'It could well be a mistake,' he said. 'They do occur in reports.'

'But what if it's not?' asked Amalia, lower lip trembling.

'We must remain optimistic.'

'How can we be optimistic in the face of such terrible tidings, Sir John?' asked Janssen. 'You told us that your sources were usually reliable. Is that not so?'

'Yes,' said Sir John, 'they are reliable as a rule.'

'Then we have no hope. Captain Rawson is dead.'

'Don't say that, Father!' begged Amalia.

'I'm sorry, my dear.'

'I must have some hope to cling to or I'll die.'

Beatrix tightened her grip. 'I'll not let that happen, Miss Amalia,' she said with almost maternal concern. 'Whatever's happened, I'll be here to help you through the pain.'

'Thank you, Beatrix.'

'I will promise no less,' said Sir John, softly. 'You're in a house on my property and that gives me responsibilities. Be bold enough to lean on me. I'll nurse you through this terrible time. The first thing I'll do is to verify this information, of course.'

'How soon can you do that?' asked Janssen.

'It may take a little time.'

'The wait will be an agony.'

'Try to stay brave, Mr Janssen.'

'That's asking too much, Sir John,' said Amalia, sobbing. 'How can we stay brave in the face of such a tragedy? If it's true – and I pray to God that it's not – then I've lost *everything*. My life would simply not be worth living.'

'That's a frightful thing to say, Miss Amalia,' said Beatrix. 'You'll still have your father. You'll still have me and Kees and all the others. Do we count for nothing?'

'No, of course you don't, Beatrix.'

'We're not going anywhere,' affirmed Janssen, bending over to plant a kiss on the top of her head. 'We *need* you, Amalia.'

She squeezed his arm. 'I know, Father.'

Sir John watched the tender moment between them and smiled.

'At the moment, I might suggest, it's *you* who need your father, Miss Janssen. The best thing for you to do is to retire to bed. Rest is the only way to cope with these grim tidings,' he said. 'The news may seem a trifle less distressing after a few hours' sleep.'

Amalia shook her head. 'I couldn't sleep a wink, Sir John.'

'You may surprise yourself. Trust me – I'm something of an expert in these matters. When I see signs of stress in my wife, I put her to bed during the day and have done for years now. In fact, I daresay I'll do the same this very afternoon. Yes,' he added, 'I know that Lady Rievers is ill, but then grief is a form of disease as well. It invades the brain and makes the body helpless. Sleep is the best remedy, Miss Janssen. It will ease the burden of your anguish.'

'That's sound advice,' decided Janssen, helping his daughter to her feet. 'Take her upstairs, Beatrix.'

'Yes, Master,' said the maidservant.

'How can I sleep with so much on my mind?' asked Amalia as she was led out. 'I'll just lie there in torment.'

She and Beatrix left the room and ascended the stairs together.

'I'm sorry to bring such heavy news,' said Sir John, spreading his arms in apology. 'I could wish that it were anyone but Captain Rawson.'

'Amalia dotes on him, Sir John.'

'I established that the first time she spoke of him. Your daughter was not born to dissemble. She wears her heart on her sleeve.' He looked upward. 'Sleep would help to soothe her. The physician is coming to my wife today. Would you like me to send him here so that he can give your daughter a potion of some kind?'

'That won't be necessary,' said Janssen. 'Besides, you've already spoilt us. I haven't really thanked you properly for the gift of that painting. It's just that…well, the news about Captain Rawson has cast a shadow over everything else.'

'I understand. The time will come when you can allow yourself to enjoy the painting and savour its fine detail. You have an artist's eye, Mr Janssen. You appreciate quality.' He walked to the door before turning back. 'Please keep me informed about Miss Janssen's state of mind,' said Sir John. 'She's such a dear creature. I felt cruel passing on news that turned that beautiful face into a mask of suffering. To make amends, I'll do everything in my power to restore her happiness.'

'How can you possibly do that, Sir John?'

'By finding out that Captain Rawson is, in fact, still alive.'

The Duke of Marlborough and his secretary were no strangers to tales of heroism. A long, bloody war like the one in which they were fighting spawned them on a regular basis. Daring and danger were everyday events. Extraordinary feats took place routinely on the battlefield. Yet they'd never heard anything quite as bizarre as the story that Daniel now told them. Because of his modesty, it was a tale of heroism without a hero. Playing down his own part in the rescue of Rachel Rees, he emphasised instead the roles taken by Henry Welbeck and Raymond Lizier. While he praised Estelle for her courage in wheedling her way into prison, he said nothing of the desire that had brought her into his bed at the tavern.

'Lille has clearly put you on your mettle,' said Marlborough. 'As usual, you rose to meet every challenge – though I do question your wisdom in getting arrested for drunkenness. How could you be sure that this woman,

Estelle – quite untried in such things – could help to get you out of your cell?'

'Estelle is by no means untried, Your Grace. She's been working with her brother-in-law and sister for a long time. Acting as an enemy agent calls for nerve and ingenuity. Estelle has both.'

'So it would appear,' observed Cardonnel.

They were in Marlborough's quarters and Daniel had just returned to the camp on a borrowed horse. Welbeck and Rachel Rees, meanwhile, had rejoined the 24th Foot which was involved in the siege. The Dutch soldiers who'd accosted them in the copse had also been under the command of Prince Eugene.

'The one thing that worries me,' said Marlborough, 'is the fate of Guillaume Lizier. He's been a valuable source of intelligence for us.'

'I'm sure,' said Daniel. 'His wife told me what a brave man he is. Madame Lizier will be relieved that her husband is no longer digging ditches in a work party. Now that the attack has begun, only an idiot would dare to stay out there in the crossfire.' He grinned. 'You're looking at one such idiot right now.'

'You weren't to know when the bombardment would start.'

'Forewarning would have been very helpful, Your Grace.'

'But the warning would have kept you inside Lille,' noted Cardonnel. 'Would you like to have spent the entire siege there?'

'No, thank you,' said Daniel. 'I love action. I'd hate having to sit out the siege inside the town.'

'What's the general feeling there?' asked Marlborough.

'The people are quaking, Your Grace. They've all heard how you destroyed the French army at Oudenarde. I listened to some of the customers at the *Coq d.Or*. They're desperately worried that their homes and places of work will be razed to the ground.'

'It may not come to that,' said Cardonnel. 'What of the army?'

'You've no need to ask that, Adam,' said Marlborough. 'They'll fight tooth and nail. Marshal Boufflers will expect no less of them.'

'He made an immediate difference,' said Daniel. 'Before he arrived, the soldiers were losing heart and talking of surrender. Once their arrears had been paid by the marshal, their attitude changed. He's instilled faith in them.'

'He's more than capable of doing that, Daniel.'

'You fought beside him once, didn't you, Your Grace?'

'Yes, he and I were comrades-in-arms. He's a charming man and a fine soldier. We can expect ferocious resistance from him.'

'Marshal Boufflers can't hold out for ever with a garrison of that size. He must be hoping for relief from outside.'

'It's not been forthcoming so far,' said Marlborough. 'As you must recall, besieging Lille was not my first priority. Now that it's in train, we must pursue it with all our might, but I never envisaged it to be an end in itself, Daniel. You will doubtless guess why.'

'Yes, Your Grace,' replied Daniel. 'Your real aim is to provoke the French army to attack. When they see Lille about to fall, they should come rushing to its defence.'

'They should – but, alas, they won't.'

'Why not?'

'Vendôme is too slothful and Burgundy too inexperienced. Both are still blaming each other for the defeat at Oudenarde.'

'What about the Duke of Berwick?'

'My nephew will not risk his army in a major engagement. I know the way his mind works. He's sent reinforcements to Lille but is resigned to its loss because he'd rather see it fall than have the whole French army cut to pieces. In his place,' said Marlborough, 'I'd think the same. A town can always be recaptured but not with a shattered army. James – the Duke of Berwick – is looking to the campaign season *next* year. I think his advice will be heeded in Versailles.'

'In short,' said Daniel, 'the siege will continue until the end.'

'Yes,' replied Marlborough, jadedly. 'There'll be skirmishes with the enemy, of course, that's inevitable, but it's foolish of us to expect another Oudenarde.'

Talk turned to the 'great convoy', making its unwieldy way south under the aegis of William Cadogan. Until the rest of their siege guns, ammunition and powder arrived, they'd not be able to put Lille under maximum pressure. So far, Daniel was pleased to hear, the convoy had not been harassed by the enemy. He knew how much the Allied army relied on its safe arrival. To lose any part of it would seriously damage their ability to continue the siege.

Before he left the quarters, he drew Marlborough's attentions to the sterling efforts made by Rachel Rees. Even though ignorant of their true purpose in going there, she'd agreed to accompany Daniel to Lille and provided him with some cover. He pointed out that Rachel had been given scant reward in return. Not only were her animals and her wares confiscated, she'd been imprisoned in the gaol and all but raped by a turnkey.

Marlborough stopped Daniel's recitation with a raised palm.

'No special pleading is required,' he said. 'The lady deserves tangible proof of our gratitude. Tell her that she'll be reimbursed for her losses.'

'Thank you, Your Grace.'

'It's heartening to hear that we have such people among our camp followers. Many of them are of dubious character but Rachel Rees has risen above the common herd.'

'She's a remarkable lady,' said Daniel.

'Aren't we forgetting Sergeant Welbeck?' asked Cardonnel. 'From what you told us, he should also earn our congratulations.'

'That's true.'

'I'll write to him,' volunteered Marlborough.

'The sergeant will appreciate that, Your Grace.'

'I'd be happy to promote him but, from what you've told us about him, I suspect that he'd refuse the offer.'

'I know for a fact that he would,' said Daniel. 'Henry Welbeck is too boneheaded to accept promotion. He could never feel at home as an officer. Why lose a first-rate sergeant in exchange for a disgruntled lieutenant?'

Marlborough chuckled. 'That's an interesting way of putting it.'

'I was trying to be practical, Your Grace.'

'He must settle for a letter from me, then.'

'Nothing would please him more,' Daniel assured him.

* * *

It was not the first letter of commendation Welbeck had received from the captain-general of the Allied army but it still produced a surge of pride in his breast. He resolved to cherish it. As a soldier who'd spent years on the move, he had very few treasured possessions. The new letter from Marlborough was one of them. After reading it for the fourth time, he was troubled by the thought that there was nobody to whom he could bequeath his property. No wife, no child, no member of his family existed who could inherit his minor trophies and take some pleasure from them. Once he passed away, a record of his deeds would perish with him. Nobody would mourn him and nobody would remember his military record. It was saddening.

Putting the letter safely away, he opened the flap and stepped out of the tent. The first thing he saw was a musket aimed straight at him. Welbeck came to a halt and tensed. The weapon was held by Ben Plummer who lowered it with a snigger.

'Don't worry, Sergeant,' he said. 'It's not loaded.'

'Never point a musket at someone unless you mean to use it.'

'That's what we've been told, sir.'

'Who's been looking after you while I was away?'

'Sergeant McGregor.'

'He's a good man.'

'He drilled us until we were ready to drop,' said Plummer. 'We preferred you, Sergeant. Where've you been?'

'I went behind enemy lines..'

The recruit was impressed. 'You went into Lille?'

'Yes, I did,' said Welbeck, 'for a time.'

Plummer's eyes sparkled. 'Were there any women there?'

'I didn't notice.'

'Why didn't you bring a couple back for us? It's not healthy for a man to be deprived of the feel of a woman. We have needs.'

'The only need you have,' warned Welbeck, 'is to mind your manners when you address a superior. And don't ever point a musket at anyone in fun or he's likely to take it from you and put it somewhere that will make your eyes water. Most of all, Ben Plummer, forget about women. Save all your manly marrow for combat. When you've been fighting the French night and day, you'll ache so much with fatigue that you won't have the strength to lift a finger, let alone any other part of your anatomy. Women won't exist for you.'

'What's that about women, Henry?' asked Rachel Rees, coming towards them. 'Are you taking our name in vain again?'

'He loathes the whole sex,' said Plummer.

'Disappear!' ordered Welbeck.

'It's a hatred based on ignorance, if you ask me.'

'Disappear!'

The order was supplemented by a punch that sent Plummer wobbling backwards. Regaining his balance, he vanished at speed. Welbeck turned an unwelcoming glare on Rachel.

'What do you want?' he said.

'I came to thank you.'

'The best way to do that is to keep out of my sight.'

She cackled. 'He's at it again – still pretending to dislike me.'

'Detest is the word I'd choose.'

'Come now, Henry, how can you expect me to believe

that? You took your life in your hands when you went to Lille. You took even greater risks when you rescued me from gaol. You put real love into the making of that coffin. Who else would have thought of lining it with cushions? And then, when you saw that cannonball ahead of us, you pulled me to the ground to save me.' She gave him a playful push. 'Are you claiming that you did all that because you detested me?'

'I was prompted by my friendship with Captain Rawson.'

'*I* was the one you saved – not him.'

'You don't understand.'

'I understand you only too well, Henry. However,' she went on, 'let me tell you the good news.'

Hope stirred. 'You're going away?'

'I'm going nowhere.'

'Oh.' His face fell.

'I'll be able to continue my work as a sutler because I'm going to be compensated for my losses. Isn't that wonderful?' said Rachel, clapping her hands. 'Captain Rawson spoke up on my behalf. Just think – His Grace, the Duke of Marlborough was actually talking about *me*. But wait a moment,' she went on, mistaking his misery for disappointment, 'you should be rewarded as well, Henry. You're a hero. At the very least, you should be given a promotion.'

'I'm happy serving in the ranks.'

'Don't you want to be an officer?'

'They're a loathsome species.'

'My first husband was the same. He never wanted to be an officer either and it was just as well because he didn't have the money to buy a commission. Will Baggott liked what he was, especially when he was married to me. I know how to keep a man contented.' She became serious. 'Is it going to be a long siege?'

'All the signs point that way.'

'After listening to that clamour, I still can't hear properly.'

'Then you need to rest,' he said, trying to move her away.

'Why don't you come and rest with me?'

'I've no time to talk, I'm afraid. I'm back in uniform now with men to lead. They rely on me.'

'So do I,' she said. 'You'll always be in my thoughts, Henry. I know you act like a flint-hearted curmudgeon but I've had a glimpse of the real Sergeant Welbeck and I was touched. When this is all over,' she continued, gesturing towards Lille, 'I'll be waiting for you.'

When she kissed him, he put a hand to his cheek as if he'd just been stung by a wasp. While he could subdue the most unruly recruit, Welbeck had no control at all over the irrepressible Rachel Rees. As he watched her go, he was filled with a compound of emotions. And the kiss still burnt on his cheek.

Relations between Vendôme and Berwick had never been harmonious. Meetings between them therefore tended to be conducted with a terse politeness. While Berwick was keen to act, Vendôme was all for delay. It needed a few tart despatches from Versailles to goad the older man out of his obsession with the failure of the French army at the battle of Oudenarde. Spurred into action at last, he issued orders, then stepped outside his quarters to review his troops. A few minutes later, Berwick rode up and dismounted.

'We are ready to move,' said Vendôme, complacently.

'Not before time,' observed Berwick. 'Our army should have been on the march long before now.'

'We had protective duties in this area.'

'Against whom or what, may I ask, were we supposed to be offering protection? Prince Eugene is committed to the siege of Lille and Marlborough is covering him. Neither of their armies is anywhere near Ghent.'

Vendôme was haughty. 'I'm well aware of their movements.'

'Then why have we not responded to them?'

'Patrols have been sent out day after day. Their orders were to search for and harass any siege train on its way to the enemy. What you call delay is a sensible pause to take full stock of the situation. With all due respect, Your Grace,' he said, brushing some crumbs off his sleeve, 'we'll achieve nothing with ill-directed action.'

'Our orders are to delay the fall of siege until winter comes to our aid. When cartwheels get stuck in the mud and frost starts to bite the fingers, even Marlborough will lose his urge to continue.'

'I know your uncle better than you.'

'I dispute that.'

'He'll fight on until Christmas, if need be.'

'His army will be in winter quarters by then.'

Vendôme grinned. 'Would you care to place a wager on that?'

'No, I would not,' said Berwick, bluntly. 'And, in any case, I will not be beside you to collect the wager. I've come to inform you that I've resigned my field command and will henceforth have only an advisory role under the Duke of Burgundy.'

Vendôme was both surprised and shocked by the news. While he'd never warmed to Berwick, he didn't like the thought that the other man was effectively displaying a lack of confidence in him. For his part, Berwick had no regrets. He'd found Vendôme an unsavoury and impossible colleague. Rather than continue to work alongside him, he was prepared to demote himself to a lesser role in the conflict. Vendôme was patently insulted by his decision but Berwick made no attempt to justify it. Instead, he produced a letter from his pocket.

'I received this from Marshal Boufflers,' he said, handing it over. 'I thought it might interest you.'

'Does it have any bearing on our orders?'

'None at all, but it contains a name you might recognise.'

Vendôme read the missive. 'Captain Rawson!' he growled.

'I remember your mentioning his name to me.'

'It looks as if he's been up to his old tricks again.'

'Judging by his success, he's obviously a brave and determined man. One has to salute such extraordinary nerve.'

'I don't salute it,' said Vendôme, thrusting the letter back at him. 'I condemn the garrison at Lille for letting Rawson make fools of them. I just hope the rogue crosses *my* path again.'

'I endorse that hope,' said Berwick, sardonically. 'Captain Daniel Rawson seems to be the only person who can instil into you an urge to fight. For that, at least, I'm eternally grateful to him.'

He mounted his horse and rode off. Vendôme seethed with rage.

In the course of his adventures in Lille, Daniel had had little time to luxuriate in thoughts of Amalia Janssen. Back in camp, he could now snatch a moment to dash off a brief letter to her. It would be taken to England by the courier in charge of the official correspondence sent by Marlborough. When Amalia finally read it, the news would be very much out of date but she'd be heartened by the fact that she was in his mind. As with all such letters, his problem was what to leave out rather than what to put in. A detailed description of his exploits would only alarm her and he had no intention of mentioning Rachel Rees at all. To do so would require too much explanation and he had no wish to arouse even the tiniest flicker of jealousy in Amalia. Recalling the jibe from Henry Welbeck, he also kept Estelle's name out of the letter.

Daniel tried to sound optimistic about the siege even though he knew – having seen the ingenuity of the fortifications – that there'd be no immediate capitulation. What Amalia really wanted to hear was that he was safe and well and looking forward to being reunited with her. That much he could write with great enthusiasm. Having sealed the letter, Daniel kissed it before taking it off to begin its long journey.

Amalia had kept her spirits up by refusing to believe that Daniel had been killed in action. She told herself that he was too experienced a soldier to die at French hands. It was the careless and the unwary who fell first. Emanuel Janssen sustained her by reminding her of Daniel's remarkable capacity for survival, demonstrated most clearly in his rescue bid at the Bastille and in the subsequent race to freedom. He'd saved their lives as well as his own. Amalia called to mind her later rescue from the French camp. Daniel's achievement on that occasion had bordered on the impossible.

'He's still alive,' she said, smiling. 'I feel it in my bones.'

'So do I, Amalia,' said her father.

'Yet you believed the news at first.'

'That was only because Sir John seemed so certain about it. But, as he pointed out, mistakes do creep in. We'd not be the first people to mourn a soldier who was still very much alive. Sir John was in a quandary,' he continued. 'He confided to me that he wasn't at all sure whether or not he should tell you what he'd found out. At first he'd wanted to keep it to himself and spare you the agony. But that would only have delayed the shock and he felt that he was cheating you by holding the information back.'

'I'd rather have known,' she said. 'He made the right decision. It was good of Sir John to take the trouble to find word of Daniel.'

'He's been a wonderful host in every way.'

'I know, Father. We've never enjoyed such hospitality. Sir John has been so considerate. He's treated us like members of his family.'

Janssen smiled. 'No member of my family would ever buy me such a splendid painting as that one of the Sheldonian Theatre.'

'I, too, have had lovely gifts from him.'

'He's very fond of you, Amalia.'

'It's his consideration that I appreciate. When he saw how badly shaken I was by the news, he wrote at once to Her Grace to postpone the dinner he'd arranged. I'm so relieved that he did that,' she said. 'In my present state of mind, I don't wish to see *anybody*.'

'Unless his name is Captain Rawson, that is.'

They shared a smile. They were in the living room at the house and, although Janssen sat beside her and held his daughter's hand, he kept flicking one eye at the painting given to him by Sir John Rievers. He'd already decided on which wall it would hang when they returned to their home in Amsterdam.

'How can we thank *him*, Amalia?' he wondered.

'Sir John?'

'I feel as if I should weave a tapestry for him.'

'He'd be delighted with that, Father.'

'First things first,' he said. 'Let's wait until this big, black cloud hanging over us has been lifted.'

'Daniel is alive, alive, alive,' she asserted.

'We'll soon know the truth of the matter.'

'It *has* to be a mistake.'

'I pray that it is, Amalia, and so does Sir John. That's why he's gone back to London to see if the earlier report was a false one. He's eager to bring you good news.'

Sir John Rievers stood on the quay and handed a purse over. The man felt its weight in his palm and nodded approvingly.

'There'll be twice as much as that if all goes to plan.'

'It will, Sir John,' said the man. 'I've never failed you before.'

'This will be your most difficult assignment.'

'Where's the difficulty? You forget that I know the region well. I fought there when I was in the army myself. I'm sailing on a fast ship,' he said, indicating the vessel beside him, 'and the weather could not be better for a voyage.'

'I only wish that I was able to take care of this myself.'

'Leave it to me, Sir John. It's the kind of work I enjoy.'

'Send me word as soon as it's done.'

'I will.'

Andrew Syme had a smirking confidence. He was a slim, sinewy individual in his thirties, with a military air about him. Sir John knew that he could be trusted to obey orders and to keep his mouth shut when he'd done so. The man's mission was simple. He had to turn a cruel lie into a truth. Only then, Sir John realised, would Amalia Janssen come within his reach.

'May good fortune attend you!' said Sir John.

'I need no luck for this enterprise.'

'Much is riding on your success.'

'You may take it as a foregone conclusion, Sir John.'

They shook hands. The man was about to move away when he was held by the shoulder. Sir John looked deep into his eyes.

'A word of warning,' he said. 'Don't come back until Captain Daniel Rawson is dead.'

Chapter Thirteen

While artillery was employed to great effect by both sides, there was abundant action for the Allied troops. Advancing from the north, they met with strong resistance, particularly at the chapel of St Magdalen where there was fierce hand-to-hand fighting. The booming of the cannon was interspersed with the popping of muskets and the clash of steel as bayonet met bayonet. But the attack was inconclusive and the Allies eventually withdrew. Their own defences weren't neglected. Towards the end of August, the nine-mile-long lines of circumvallation (facing outwards from the town) and contravallation (facing inwards) were completed, signalling to the enemy that they were endeavouring to put a stranglehold on Lille. In blistering sunshine, the digging of trenches continued apace with a reluctant local peasantry pressed into service. With August drawing to its close, Eugene's breaching bombardment became more intense. As the siege rolled on into its second month, hostilities reached a new pitch of ferocity.

Marlborough still felt partly under siege himself. Though he was satisfied with the progress made so far, he was dogged by ill health, depressed at the possibility of a long siege, worried by the appearance of a French army of one hundred and ten thousand men on the River Dender, irritated by reports of political machinations back in England and shaken by the letter he'd just received from his wife. After reading it through once more, he tossed it aside and brought a hand to his aching forehead. At a time when he needed to concentrate on the siege, he didn't wish to be distracted by Sarah's searing account of what had happened at the thanksgiving service. Until the missive had arrived, Marlborough had believed that relations between his wife and Queen Anne could not deteriorate even more. That misconception had now been shattered.

He was alone in his quarters, slumped in his chair with his periwig on the table in front of him. Marlborough's famed vigour was nowhere in evidence. His face was drawn, his eyes dull, his whole body slack. He seemed to lack energy and sense of purpose. Not for the first time, he began to wonder how long he could go on commanding a coalition army and bearing the concomitant responsibilities and frustrations. Yet when he glanced down at the letter, he couldn't envisage a return to domestic life in England as a source of real contentment. His wife's feud with the queen was set to bring further upheaval to the Marlborough household.

Hearing voices outside, he quickly replaced his periwig. Adam Cardonnel entered with Daniel Rawson at his heels.

Even though Marlborough had straightened his shoulders and tried to look alert, they both noticed an uncharacteristic listlessness about him. After an exchange of greetings, the newcomers took their seats. It was Cardonnel who recognised the handwriting on the letter that lay open on the table.

'You've had word from Her Grace, I see,' he noted.

Marlborough sighed. 'Indeed, I have.'

'Not bad news, I hope.'

'It could never be construed as *good* news, Adam.'

'Oh?'

Picking up the letter, Marlborough looked from one to the other.

'I know that I can rely on your discretion,' he said. 'What I tell you now must go no further.' They nodded obediently. 'Much as I love my dear wife, I have to admit that she can be rather bellicose at times and those times are not always well chosen. It transpires that she had a furious argument with Her Majesty on their way to the thanksgiving service in St Paul's. It concerned some jewels that were put out for Her Majesty and which she refused to wear.'

'Ah,' said Cardonnel, 'I can imagine how the quarrel began. Her Grace felt insulted that the jewels she chose were spurned.'

'It matters not what the argument was about, Adam. The fact that it took place at that particular time is what annoys me. They were on their way to celebrate our victory at Oudenarde.'

'And rightly so,' observed Daniel.

'It's maddening,' said Marlborough. 'We beat the French in a pitched battle yet again and are entitled to have a thanksgiving service in honour of it. Yet the event is notable less for a violent encounter between two armies than for a squabble – in public, alas – between two ladies who should know better. Do forgive me,' he added. 'I mean no disloyalty to my wife but there is an important point at issue here.'

'The continuance of the war depends on political support from the British government,' said Daniel. 'Now that Her Majesty is under the influence of the Tories, that support is starting to waver.'

'It's done so for some time, Daniel.'

'The queen ought to be wooed,' said Cardonnel, 'and not further estranged. If it's the latter, we stand to suffer the consequences.'

'I blame that damnable barrister,' complained Marlborough. He saw the look of bafflement on Daniel's face. 'Oh, I'm sorry. Let me explain. I was referring to Arthur Maynwaring, a so-called friend of my wife who's been giving her all manner of bad advice and making grotesque allegations about Her Majesty's private life. I won't regale you with the details. They're too distressing for me to repeat. Of far more interest to you is something in the letter that pertains to Captain Rawson.'

'What's that, Your Grace?' asked Daniel.

'Actually, it pertains to your inamorata. It appears that Miss Janssen and her father were due to dine with my wife in the company of Sir John and Lady Rievers but the dinner had to be postponed because Miss Janssen was indisposed.'

Daniel was alarmed. 'Indisposed – in what way?'

'There are no precise details,' said Marlborough, consulting the letter, 'but it's something to do with the death of a friend. When she heard the news, Miss Janssen was so upset that she felt unable to fulfil any social engagements.'

'A relative of hers must have passed away,' said Cardonnel.

'I think not, Adam. My wife describes the person as a close friend. Daniel can probably tell us who it is.'

'I wish that I could,' said Daniel, clearly disturbed. 'The obvious person would be Beatrix, her maidservant.'

'One *can* get attached to servants, I agree.'

'Then again, it might be Kees Dopff, one of the apprentices.'

'Would that be sufficient to make her withdraw into mourning?'

'Perhaps not,' said Daniel, running through the list of Amalia's friends in his mind. 'On the other hand, she might feel the loss more keenly because she was abroad when it happened.' He went off into a reverie, then quickly brought himself out of it. 'I do apologise, Your Grace,' he said. 'We're here to discuss the progress of the siege. I shouldn't let my personal concerns impinge upon that.'

Conversation switched to military matters but Daniel was only half-listening to the comments of his companions. The news about Amalia had upset him at a deep level. If she was bereaved, he wanted to be there to comfort her. Instead, he was trapped indefinitely in the vicinity of Lille. One question kept tapping remorselessly at his brain like the beak of a woodpecker.

Whose death had caused Amalia such pain?

By dint of repeating it to herself over and over again, Amalia had come to believe that a hideous error had been made and that Daniel was still alive. Janssen was less certain of that but he kept his doubts hidden and made sure that Beatrix did the same. In a crisis such as this, Amalia needed the full support of both of them. Had they been at home in Amsterdam, the news would have been dreadful but at least they'd have been in familiar surroundings. Marooned in England and staying in the property of a stranger, they'd felt the blow more keenly. Amalia's first thought had been to rush back to the Continent and make her way to the British camp in order to establish the truth or otherwise of the report. Her response was natural but unfeasible. It was only when she emerged from her initial despair that she spied a reason to hope. It took a firm grip on her mind.

'Daniel is alive,' she said for the fiftieth time that day. 'I'd *know* if anything had happened to him.'

'I'm sure that you would, Amalia,' said her father.

'He came through the battle of Oudenarde unscathed. You saw him when he visited us. A siege is very different from a battle. Daniel explained the sequence of events to me.'

'Soldiers do nevertheless get killed at sieges.'

She was dogmatic. 'Daniel is not one of them.'

'No, no, I'm certain that he isn't.'

'He always mixes daring with caution.'

They were taking a stroll through the estate and walking in the direction of the lake. While they found the parkland delightful, they were both wishing that they weren't there. Being in a foreign country made them feel strangely vulnerable.

'When will Sir John return?' she asked, impatiently.

'He'll come as soon as he has news, Amalia.'

'I pray that it will be soon.'

'It was kind of Lady Rievers to write to you,' he said. 'She has so many problems of her own to contend with yet she found the time to offer you good advice. Don't grieve until you are absolutely sure of the facts, she counselled. It's wrong to endure anguish that may turn out to be completely misplaced.'

'Her letter was very heartening. In fact...'

The sound of hoof beats made her voice trail away and she turned to see a figure riding towards them. When she realised that it was Sir John Rievers, a mingled hope and consternation whirled inside her head. She tried to discern from his demeanour what news he was bringing but his upright position in the saddle gave nothing away. As he drew nearer, her conviction that Daniel was alive started to weaken. If he had good tidings, she thought, Sir John would surely have given them a signal of some kind. He'd seen the effect that the news had had on her and knew the agony she must be suffering. Out of the affection he bore her, Sir John wouldn't hesitate to relieve her suffering if it was in his power to do so.

Yet no signal came. When they could see his face clearly, it had a grim expression that made Amalia's blood run cold. Anticipating bad news, Emanuel Janssen reached out to hold his daughter's hand. He braced himself to catch her in case she fainted again. Sir John rode up to them, brought his horse to a halt and dismounted. He removed his hat in a gesture of courtesy.

'Well?' asked Amalia, now on tenterhooks.

'What did you find out, Sir John?' pressed Jansen.

'Nothing,' replied Sir John, sorrowfully. 'I could neither confirm nor disprove what I'd learnt earlier. There was a report of his demise but that could well be an unfortunate error.'

Janssen grasped at straws. 'It may even be that the Captain Rawson who is listed may not be the one we know. It's not a common name,' he went on, 'yet neither is it uncommon. Could it not be that there is more than one Captain Rawson in the British ranks?'

'No, Father,' said Amalia. 'That's too big a coincidence.'

'I can't tell you how disappointed I am to come back empty-handed, so to speak,' said Sir John. 'I would love to have been the bearer of the news that we all desire – namely, that Captain Rawson is alive and is continuing to infuriate the enemy in his inimitable way. Given what I've heard about him, I find it hard to accept that such a remarkable soldier has fallen in action.'

'I *don't* accept it, Sir John,' she attested.

'Your attitude is wholly laudable, Miss Janssen.'

'I have complete faith in Daniel.'

'And it's obviously justified,' said Sir John, smiling benignly at her. 'I, too, am coming to share it. I remain sanguine.'

'So do we,' said Janssen, 'but this waiting is taking its toll on our nerves. Is there no way that the information can be verified?'

'Not in London,' answered Sir John, concealing the fact that he'd actually returned from Harwich rather than from the capital. 'That leaves us with only one avenue to explore.'

'And what's that?'

'Someone must be sent to Lille to unearth the truth.'

Amalia was impulsive. 'I'll go,' she said.

'I don't think that would be wise,' said her father.

'It's neither wise nor necessary,' explained Sir John. 'I know how much this affects your prospects of happiness, Miss Janssen, and I can't stand by and watch you in torment. To that end, I've instructed someone to sail to the Continent, then make his way with all haste to the place where the 24th Regiment of Foot is encamped. The fellow is to enquire after Captain Rawson and return with his findings as fast as is humanly possible.'

'Oh,' said Amalia, profoundly touched. 'Have you really done all this on our behalf?'

'To restore your happiness, Miss Janssen,' he said with apparent sincerity, 'I'd do much, much more.'

'Thank you, Sir John – I am ever in your debt.'

'No debt has been incurred. It's a pleasure to help you.'

'Coming back to this person you instructed,' said Janssen. 'Is he a man who can be entrusted with such a mission?'

'He is, Mr Janssen,' said Sir John, confidently. 'Andrew Syme has never let me down. You may rest easy on that score. Of one thing I can assure you – he will obey his orders to the letter.'

Syme was not a man to pass the day in idleness. The ship on which he'd embarked from Harwich was also carrying reinforcements for the Allies. As a former soldier, he found it easy to fall in with them and soon befriended a young lieutenant eager to join him in swordplay. When the two men had a practice bout, a crowd of soldiers gathered to watch them and to urge the lieutenant on. Their encouragement was wasted because their man was hopelessly outclassed. With a sword in his hand, Syme looked to be almost invincible. Indeed, so great was his superiority that he brought the practice to an end by forcing his opponent back against the bulwark, then disarming him with a sudden jab that produced a trickle of blood from the other's hand. As the lieutenant's sword clattered to the deck, he was jeered at by his fellows. Syme turned to confront them with a smile.

'Can anyone else do better?' he challenged.

Nobody was willing to accept the invitation. Having seen Syme in action, they decided that discretion was the better part of valour. One advantage of the bout was that he was now fully accepted by his fellow voyagers. Some of them even restored his former rank and referred to him as 'Major Syme'. He enjoyed their company and was happy to talk about his military experiences. It helped to while away the time afloat. When he returned to his cabin that night, he placed a row of weapons on the table so that he could examine them. Beside his sword were a dagger, two pistols and a short length of rope.

'Well, Captain Rawson,' he said, softly, 'how would you like to die? I can disembowel you, stab you through the heart, shoot you between the eyes or strangle you with the rope. If you'd prefer, of course, I can kill you with my bare hands.' He laughed quietly. 'Yes, I'd enjoy that.'

Throughout the ranks of the Allies, there was general optimism about the siege. The steady pounding of their heavy guns resulted in cracks, then major fissures, then complete breaches in the outer works of Lille. Enemy soldiers were being killed or wounded. A few positions were being abandoned. Amid the garrison, spirits were low. Fearing that further resistance was pointless, some deserted and reported that Boufflers was already pulling back part of his artillery inside the citadel. It was the spur needed by the encircling army. On the evening of 7th September, a major assault was launched on the outer works, involving thousands of grenadiers supported by a dozen battalions. Having made gaping holes in the defences, they fully expected to sweep through them and drive the enemy back to the town itself.

But the attack did not go to plan. Resistance was ferocious and it took over half an hour to dislodge the soldiers in the outer works. As they pulled back, they continued to inflict casualties on the Allies with sustained and accurate fire. They also set off four massive mines that killed, wounded or blinded those rushing headlong after them. Among those who fell were six engineers charged with the task of directing workmen to take over the ravelins and make them fit for use by the Allies. Such was the intensity of the fighting, however, that the workmen lost their nerve and ran away under cover of the dwindling light. The ravelins – two embankments built at a salient angle – were never properly secured.

Even with Vauban's plan of the fortifications at their disposal, the Allies were caught out by its geometrical complexity. It was a labyrinth of intersecting walls and re-entering angles. Breaking through one of the outer works, the attackers would find themselves at the mercy of punitive volleys from different directions. The outer fortifications had been designed to help the retreat of the defenders while allowing them to harry the enemy. The noise was ear-splitting, the light uncertain and the stench of smoke all-pervading. While many French soldiers perished, Allied losses were frighteningly high. Their attack had been premature and unsuccessful. Some ground had been taken but there was no cause for congratulation.

Henry Welbeck was even more contemptuous than usual.

'What lunatic devised that attack?' he asked, scornfully. 'I thought we had a plan of their defences.'

'We do,' replied Daniel. 'I'm the person who supplied it.'

'Well, I wish you'd supplied them with the intelligence to understand the plan. We were lured this way and that, Dan. Wherever we turned, we faced continuous fire. They seemed to be on all sides of us at the same time.'

'That was the beauty of Vauban's design.'

'Beauty!' Welbeck spat the word out like a hot coal. 'Where was the beauty in that? It was one of the ugliest assaults I've ever been involved in. I lost some of my best men, and many of those who survived will never be able to bear arms again. We set out to claim some glory, not to be let down by the idiocy of our officers.'

'You can't blame it all on our deficiencies, Henry,' said Daniel. 'Give Boufflers and his men their due. They anticipated the attack and were ready for you.'

Daniel had been sent to the camp with despatches for Prince Eugene. Having delivered them, he sought out his regiment and asked his friend what had occurred. Shot through with colourful language, Welbeck's account had ended with a gloomy warning. There was no longer any cause for optimism among the Allies. On the evidence of the recent engagement, the siege would take far longer than had been estimated. Lille was living up to its reputation of impregnability.

'It was like dancing in front of a firing squad,' complained Welbeck. 'If they'd been able to see straight, the Frenchies could have mowed down even more of us. It was purgatory out there, Dan.' He spat on the ground, then ran the back of his hand across his mouth. 'Yet I suppose it had one thing in its favour.'

'What was that?'

'I was safe from *her*.'

Daniel grinned. 'Are you talking about Rachel Rees?'

'She's the bane of my life.'

'It's your own fault for setting her heart aflame.'

'I wish I could set that huge body of hers aflame as well,' said Welbeck, darkly. 'That would get rid of her for good. I could tie her to a stake and pile logs around her.'

'Even you wouldn't be that cruel,' said Daniel, reproachfully. 'Rachel deserves better treatment than that. Did she tell you that she's had compensation for her losses?'

'Yes, she did.'

'It was well earned.'

Welbeck was enraged. 'Where's *my* compensation,' he yelled, 'that's what I want to know? I need compensation for the loss of my privacy. Rachel follows me around day and night. The woman pops up everywhere. Then there's the loss of my authority. When they see her badgering me, my men laugh out loud. I've had to hit so many of them that my knuckles are sore.'

'Rachel can't follow you into action, Henry.'

'Thank heaven for that!'

'And there'll be a lot more of it to come.'

Welbeck rolled his eyes. 'I hate sieges. Why can't we

resolve the whole thing with a decent battle then creep off to winter quarters?'

'His Grace has offered them battle twice,' said Daniel, 'but they declined on both occasions, even though they outnumbered us. It begins to look as if their policy is to starve us of supplies.'

'We can't carry on without food and ammunition.'

'The same goes for Marshal Boufflers. He may have repulsed the attack but it will have diminished his magazine. We have to make sure that no fresh supplies get through to him.'

'We will, Dan. Lille is surrounded now.' An idea put a smile on his face. 'Is there any chance of sending Rachel into the town again?'

Daniel laughed. 'Not a hope.'

'I'd much rather have her there than here.'

'Then why did you help to rescue her?'

Welbeck groaned. 'I've been asking myself that ever since.'

'Perhaps it's time you let a woman into your life.'

'I didn't *let* her in – she jumped over the barricades.'

'That's the surprising thing,' mused Daniel. 'You're as well defended as Lille. No other woman has ever got past your outer ramparts yet they don't appear to exist for Rachel. She's laid siege to you, Henry. She's fired gifts at you from her cannon. Rachel Rees has entrenched herself around you and will wait patiently until you agree to surrender.'

'Then she can wait for all bleeding eternity,' said Welbeck with a dismissive gesture. 'I wouldn't touch that harpy for a king's ransom. But tell me about the woman in *your* life,

Dan,' he added, keen to move away from the subject of Rachel Rees. 'Have you heard from Miss Janssen recently?'

Daniel's face clouded. 'Not *from* her,' he said, 'but I've heard *of* Amalia and, to be truthful, I was rather concerned.'

'Go on.'

'Well, her name was mentioned in a letter to His Grace.'

Daniel told him about the news concerning Amalia and how much it had upset him to hear that she was mourning a close friend. What puzzled him was that he couldn't decide who that friend might be.

'Was it a man or a woman?' asked Welbeck.

'The letter didn't say.'

'Is she still in England?'

'I believe so.'

'Does Miss Janssen have many close friends?'

'No, Henry,' said Daniel. 'That's the odd thing. She has a very small circle of friends and they're almost exclusively female.'

'That's not entirely true, Dan.'

'What do you mean?'

'Well. I'd say that her best friend was a certain Captain Rawson of the 24th.' Welbeck winked at him. 'Do you happen to know if that handsome devil is still alive?'

Amalia Janssen had no complaints about their hospitality. They were well fed and living in extreme comfort. Sir John Rievers had been attentive to their needs, calling on them every day to see how they were and what they wanted. While she held to the belief that Daniel was still alive, Amalia was troubled by fleeting doubts. In the hope of banishing them, she decided to honour a promise she'd made to him to visit Somerset. When Sir John offered to accompany them, she politely declined, not wishing to trespass even more on his kindness. Amalia was also looking forward to an escape from the place where she'd received such appalling news. As long as their host was with them, she'd be reminded of that terrible moment.

Persistent drizzle turned the first day of their journey into a sodden and miserable affair. Amalia, her father and her maidservant spent most of the time huddled up in the coach. By prior agreement, Janssen and Beatrix never introduced the name of Daniel Rawson into the conversation and tried instead to divert Amalia with prattle on a variety of topics. If she herself talked of Daniel, the others voiced their conviction that the report of his death was unquestionably mistaken. Their allotted task was to bolster her morale.

When they finally got to Somerset, they were greeted by warm sunshine. Amalia took the improvement in the weather as a hopeful portent. The first place they visited was the farm where Daniel had been born and brought up. It was exactly as he'd described it to her and she tried to envisage him as a small boy, tending the stock, helping in the fields and adapting to the changing seasons. Amalia recalled that it was from the farm that Daniel had waved off his father as Captain Nathan Rawson went to join the doomed rebellion that cost him his life. Imagining the effect that the public execution of his father must have had on Daniel, she shuddered.

They went on to the village and took rooms at the largest

of the three inns. While her father and Beatrix settled in, Amalia strolled up to the little church, its ancient walls sculpted by the passage of time and its graveyard filled with headstones that leant at different angles like petrified drunken revellers. She was shocked to remember that Daniel's father had been buried hurriedly under a hedge after being cut down from the gallows and carried away in secret at night. It was only years later that Daniel had prevailed upon the vicar to re-inter Nathan Rawson with full burial rites. A tall, grey, moss-covered headstone now marked the place, his name chiselled proudly into it. There was no mention of his humiliating death after the battle of Sedgemoor. He was simply referred to as 'Nathaniel Rawson – Soldier'.

Kneeling before the headstone, Amalia found tears coursing down her cheeks. At that moment, she realised something about Daniel. He lived in two parallel worlds. He was simultaneously English and Dutch. His father was buried in Somerset while his mother had been laid to rest in Amsterdam. From Nathan Rawson, he'd inherited an unquenchable desire to be a soldier that defied his mother's plea for him to pursue a peaceable occupation. Daniel had been driven by an ambition that his father would have recognised and which made his mother weep. Amalia, too, had known the desperation of waiting for news from a battlefield and struggling to cope with uncertainty. She was struggling to do so at that very moment. Was Daniel alive or dead? Had he survived yet again or gone to join his father as one more tragic victim of warfare? Amalia tried hard to keep fear at bay. With great tenderness, she placed some flowers on the grave then closed her eyes and prayed with fervour that she would never have to kneel at the final resting place of Daniel Rawson – Soldier.

'What did Henry have to say about me?' she asked.

'He said very little,' replied Daniel, tactfully. 'He's preoccupied with what happened yesterday in that assault.'

'Yes, I heard about that.'

'Henry had to watch some of his men die and he hates that.'

'I'm sure,' said Rachel. 'It shows what a dear man he is at heart.'

'I suggest that you leave him in peace for a while.'

'Yes, I will, Captain Rawson.'

Daniel had been about to leave the camp when he encountered Rachel Rees. Seated on her new cart, she was on her way to sell some of her wares. Daniel noticed how many provisions she had.

'Where did you buy all those things?' he said.

'It's only a question of knowing where to look.'

'You wouldn't have carried all that on the back of your donkey.'

'I know.'

'Are you pleased with your recompense?'

'I'm delighted,' she said. 'I'm getting too old to sit astride a horse for any length of time. A cart makes life much easier. Mind you,' she went on, 'nothing could recompense me for the horrors I went through in Lille. Well, you saw that brute of a turnkey. Heaven knows what would have happened if you and Estelle hadn't come along!'

'He won't ever bother a woman again,' Daniel reminded her.

'I know. But I'll never forget the stink of his breath. But what about you and Henry?' she went on. 'What sort of reward did the pair of you get? After all, you were the real heroes, finding a way into Lille like that. I think you both deserve a promotion.'

'I didn't ask for it and Henry wouldn't have accepted it. He has a very low opinion of officers. As for me, my reward is the honour of working as part of His Grace's personal staff.'

'Does that mean Henry got nothing at all?'

'He received a letter of commendation.'

'Really? Why did he never mention it to me?'

'He's too modest to do so.'

'But it's something to shout about from the rooftops. Was it written in the Duke of Marlborough's own hand?'

'Every word of it,' he told her.

Daniel was pleased to see her looking so well. The first time he'd met her, he'd been struck by her resilience and it was visible again. Rachel seemed to have shrugged off her horrific experiences in Lille. Even the flight from the town during a bombardment hadn't robbed her of her essential zest. Eyeing him up and down, she beamed.

'I thought I'd never marry another soldier,' she said, 'but I made an exception in your case. I enjoyed being Madame Borrel even though that marriage fell short of expectation.'

'It was a marriage in name only.'

'That was my complaint.' They laughed. 'Not that I could ever marry an officer. I'm like Henry Welbeck – I belong in the ranks. The secret of happiness is to know who you are and where you best fit in. Those with ridiculous ambitions always lead lives of disappointment.' She cackled.

'That sounds almost like wisdom, doesn't it?'

'You're a true philosopher.'

'No, I'm just plain Rachel Rees and happy to be so.'

'I must away, alas,' he said. 'I have to get back to His Grace.'

'Thank him for my horse and cart, won't you?'

'I'll make a point of doing so.'

She looked around. 'I'm going to miss all this, you know.'

'I don't understand.'

'Being with an army,' she explained. 'I've spent too many years at it. Ned Granger – he was my second husband – had a good way of putting it. He said that fighting in a war was mostly sheer boredom with a little bit of terror thrown in. I'm starting to get bored with the boredom and I had enough terror in Lille to last me a lifetime.'

'Where will you go, Rachel?'

'Back home to Wales, I expect.' She gave an almost girlish giggle. 'Unless, that is, Henry makes me an offer I can't refuse.'

It had been their first taste of battle and two of them hadn't lived to pass their judgement on the experience. One had been so badly wounded that he'd be a permanent invalid and another one had lost an eye. All who'd survived had been shaken up by their assault on the enemy. Henry Welbeck was sorry that his recruits had been hurled into action so soon, but that was in the nature of warfare. French soldiers couldn't be expected to wait until every member of a British regiment was fully trained. Having been taught to fire a musket, the recruits were deemed ready for battle.

When the sergeant visited the ragged band of survivors, they were sitting on the ground, comparing the bruises and scratches they'd picked up. There was a despondent air about them. Even the impudent Ben Plummer was subdued. Welbeck knelt down to speak to the soldier whose empty eye socket was covered in bandaging.

'How do you feel, lad?' he enquired.

'I want to go home, Sergeant,' said the other.

'We *all* want that but there's a war to win first.'

'I'm no use in the army with only one eye.'

'A one-eyed soldier is a lot more use than our blind, bleeding officers,' Welbeck argued, getting a muted laugh from the men. 'Our brainless superiors are the *other* enemy we're up against.' He patted the man's arm. 'You did well, lad. And the same goes for the rest of you,' he said, looking around them. 'None of you ran away. None of you spewed up your dinner. You fought bravely.'

'What's the use of that?' asked Plummer, sullenly.

Welbeck stood up. 'It's a matter of self-respect.'

'I've never had any.'

'That's because of the wicked life you led, Ben Plummer, but you have a chance to atone for that now. Giving of your best for queen and country should make you feel proud.'

'I don't feel proud, Sergeant,' said the one-eyed man.

'Neither do I,' said Plummer. 'I just feel bewildered. What are we doing here among all these Dutch and Austrians?'

'They're our Allies,' said Welbeck.

'Then let them do the fighting.'

'We're in this together, standing shoulder to shoulder.'

'None of them was shoulder to shoulder with me,' said Plummer, scornfully. 'I stood next to Dirk Megson and he was shot dead. On the other side of me was Harry Gaunt and they put his eye out, didn't they, Harry?'

'Send me home,' pleaded Gaunt.

'You're a real soldier now,' said Welbeck. 'You've been blooded.'

'I've had enough soldiering.'

'So have the rest of us,' said Plummer, eliciting a general murmur of consent. 'I'd rather be serving my sentence back in England. At least I wouldn't be shot at in gaol.' He grinned wearily. 'And I'd have pretty women coming to visit me.'

'Be grateful to the army,' said Welbeck, solemnly. 'It's saved you from temptations of the flesh.'

'It hasn't saved *you*, Sergeant.'

Welbeck bridled. 'What do you mean?'

'Well, you have that woman tempting you,' said Plummer. 'I'd never call her pretty but there's plenty of flesh there to lure you.'

'Yes,' said Gaunt over the sniggers, 'she's a big lady.'

'That's enough!' snapped Welbeck.

'It's unfair,' continued Plummer, warming to his theme. 'Why should you have pleasures denied the rest of us? We've seen her slipping into your tent.'

'It was not by invitation.'

'I'd be ready to invite her, I can tell you.'

'All that you're inviting, Plummer, is a punch on that ugly nose of yours. Now let's have no more of this nonsense or I may lose my temper. That could be dangerous for all of you.'

There was a long, uneasy silence. Having come to offer them sympathy, Welbeck had been thrown on the defensive. The fault lay with Rachel Rees. Unwanted and unbidden, she'd sneaked into his tent on more than one occasion to leave small gifts there. It was highly embarrassing and it served to undermine his control. Yet he could find no effective way of getting rid of her. Plummer read his mind.

'There's only one way to get rid of her, Sergeant,' he said, 'and that's to give her what she wants.'

'Even with only one eye, I can see what that is,' added Gaunt, mischievously.

'When you're done with her, you can send the lady over to us. That's the best way to get self-respect,' claimed Plummer, using an obscene gesture. 'It makes you feel like a real man.'

'Be quiet!' ordered Welbeck over the derisive laughter. It died instantly. 'Enjoy some rest while you can. You'll soon be getting ready for the next attack. It won't be long.'

'When will the siege end, Sergeant?' asked Gaunt.

'Not until we've reduced the walls to rubble.'

'We never got anywhere near the town itself.'

'We will,' said Welbeck. 'We'll wear them down slowly.'

'How many of our lives will that cost?' asked Plummer. 'They say we had well over a couple of thousand men killed or wounded last time. It could be our turn next.'

'Try not to think about that.'

'I'll be thinking of nothing else, Sergeant.'

'And do you imagine you're the only one whose knees are trembling?' asked Welbeck, pointing in the direction of Lille. 'They have a garrison of only fifteen thousand in the town – less than that, if you take their casualties into account. We have an army of thirty-five thousand men.'

'Less, if you take *our* casualties into account,' said Plummer.

'Look at it another way. Where would you rather be – out here or in there? Would you rather be the hunter or the prey? Prince Eugene is a fine soldier, for all that he's a foreigner. I trust him to conduct this siege well.'

'He hasn't done it so far,' protested Gaunt, pointing to his bandage. 'This is how I'll remember Prince Eugene.'

'What you'll remember is being part of a victorious army,' said Welbeck, slapping him on the back. 'You may not believe that now because you're still in pain. Just you wait until those French bastards surrender. You'll feel it was all worth it then, lad. You'll carry your scars with pride and spend the rest of your life boasting that you were present at the fall of Lille.'

There was another silence. It was broken at length by Plummer.

'Supposing that Lille *doesn't* fall, Sergeant – what then?'

It was uncanny. Sir John Rievers seemed to know the exact moment when they'd reach his property. As their carriage rolled in through the gates, he was there with a welcoming wave. Amalia mistook his elation as a sign that he'd received good news about Daniel but her hopes soon foundered. Riding along beside them, Sir John admitted that he'd heard nothing about Daniel's fate and didn't expect to do so for some time. It was a simple delight in their return that made him look so pleased and buoyant. When they reached the house they went inside while the luggage was unloaded. Sir John pressed for details of their trip to Somerset and, though Janssen took it upon himself to describe their adventures, he didn't hold Sir John's attention. Their host's eyes rarely left Amalia. Feeling self-conscious under his gaze she tried to divert his attention by asking after his wife.

'Lady Rievers is not well,' he explained. 'Her condition is such that she is caught up in the ebb and flow of the malady. At present, it's flowing rather too strongly and she's been obliged to spend the last couple of days in bed.'

'I'm sorry to hear that, Sir John,' said Amalia.

'So am I,' said Janssen. 'Is Lady Rievers able to receive visitors?'

'Not at the moment,' replied Sir John, sadly.

'When she is, we'd be happy to call on her.'

'Yes,' said Amalia. 'Lady Rievers may be glad of company.'

Sir John's cheeks dimpled. 'Any visit from you would be a source of gladness, Amalia,' he said. 'And the very fact that you offer to come brings me cheer because it shows me how much you've recovered from your earlier shock. You'd not even venture to show your lovely face outdoors then.'

'That was when I believed the news, Sir John. I now know that it wasn't true. That's the secret of my recovery.'

'You prefer to rely on instinct, then?'

'I do,' said Amalia.

'It's the same with me. No matter how far away I may be, I always know how my wife is faring. Indeed, there have been occasions when I've ridden back through the night because I sensed that she was in decline. I was never wrong.'

'Neither am I in this instance.'

'Your faith in Captain Rawson is very touching.'

'It's based on my knowledge of him,' said Amalia, fondly.

'He may court danger but he never does so recklessly. He's supremely able to take care of himself on a battlefield. No, Sir John,' she decided, 'he has not been killed in action. Instinct tells me that Captain Rawson is very much alive and that he's not in any jeopardy.'

The voyage to Ostend had been relatively free of discomfort. Andrew Syme had both made several new friends and secured a regiment of bodyguards for the journey south. Their task was to reinforce the Allied army, whereas Syme's assignment was enticingly simple. At most, it would take him a few minutes to earn a substantial reward. All that he had to do was to kill Captain Daniel Rawson.

Chapter Fourteen

The council of war was held in the main camp under the supervision of the Duke of Marlborough, visibly unwell yet still able to discharge his duties with aplomb. Along with others, Prince Eugene and General Overkirk, commander of the Dutch forces, had temporarily left the siege operations. Daniel Rawson was present at the meeting to act as an interpreter and Adam Cardonnel kept a record of the deliberations with his customary efficiency. It was mid September and the early confidence of the Allies had been whittled away. Though he was as disappointed as any of his generals, Marlborough tried to sound a positive note.

'The French have missed their chance,' he said. 'Even with their superior numbers, they didn't dare to mount an attack. Vendôme postured in front of us but, failing to draw us out of our entrenchments, he gave the signal to pull back. I have every reason to believe that they've struck their tents for good.'

'That's welcome news,' said Eugene. 'When you were under threat here, we had to send sizeable reinforcements. Those men are desperately needed at the siege.'

'They can be released to rejoin you, Your Highness.'

'Thank you.'

'In place of an attack,' said Marlborough, 'the French have adopted a new strategy. They mean to impose a blockade along the River Schelde in order to sever our links with Brussels.'

'If they succeed,' warned Overkirk, 'it could severely hamper us.'

'Then we'll have to ensure that they *don't* succeed.'

'You have a gift for frustrating French strategy, Your Grace. Because you always anticipate their next move, you can take steps to counter it.'

'At least they'll not be harrying us outside Lille,' said Eugene, gratefully. 'Instead of looking over our shoulders, we can concentrate our fire on Marshal Boufflers.'

'He must be running short of supplies by now,' said Overkirk.

'When they dwindle some more, the notion of surrender may finally enter his mind.'

'Not for some time yet,' declared Marlborough. 'I know him well, both as a comrade-in-arms and as an opponent. Lille will have to be tottering before Boufflers considers surrender.'

Daniel listened to the debate with interest, admiring the way that Marlborough gave everyone around the table a chance to voice an opinion. The discussion was even-tempered. It had not always been the case. During his time with the Allies, General Slangenburg had been an obstructive and disputatious presence. Daniel had marvelled at the way that Marlborough retained his composure in the face of such provocation. Fortunately, he was always supported by Overkirk, his loyal friend. Much of Slangenburg's disruptive behaviour had been seated in envy. The Dutch malcontent felt that he should be in overall command of the armies of the Grand Alliance. His departure from office had made councils of war less confrontational.

Respecting Overkirk as a man and as a warrior, Daniel was worried by the man's appearance. He looked old, tired and ailing. Helping to conduct a difficult siege imposed great physical and mental pressure on a commander. Now in his mid sixties, Overkirk was palpably showing the strain. Prince Eugene, by contrast, seemed young, fresh and energetic. He was eager to return to Lille to resume control of the siege.

'It's decided, then,' he said, briskly. 'We can launch the major assault as planned.'

'It has my blessing, Your Highness,' said Marlborough.

'Your Grace's seal of approval is welcome.'

'Strike soon and strike hard.'

'There'll be a large butcher's bill to pay,' cautioned Overkirk. 'Every time we've attacked, we've suffered heavy casualties, especially among the British Grenadiers. They've been shot, stabbed, drowned, blown up by hellish bombs and drenched in boiling pitch, tar, oil and brimstone. Scalding water has also been poured down on them.'

'These are repulsive tactics,' said Marlborough, 'but we'll win through in spite of them. We may have lost men but so has Boufflers. I fancy that there'll be anxious debates inside Lille.'

'Deserters tell us that the townspeople want to sue for peace.'

'That won't influence the marshal. He'll make his decisions on military grounds not on sentiment. Besides, he's built his reputation on withstanding sieges. The only way to get him out of there,' said Marlborough, tapping the town plan in front of him, 'is to kill more troops and knock down more walls.'

Daniel spared a thought for the fate of his regiment. In any major assault, the 24th was likely to be called into action. The siege had so far been a battle of attrition. Every yard of ground gained by the Allies had been irrigated with their blood. Daniel hoped that Henry Welbeck and his other close friends in the regiment would come through the next engagement without mishap.

In the hope of making a significant impact, Prince Eugene chose to commit almost half of his entire force to the attack. Gathering fifteen thousand men in readiness, he concentrated his latest assault on the ravelin between Bastions II and III. Everyone in the Allied ranks knew the kind of fierce retaliation they could expect. Some of the corpses they'd had to bury had been in a hideous condition. Such grotesque sights served to harden their determination to strike back. Henry Welbeck weighed the possibility of success against the welfare of the men in his charge. It left him with a nagging pessimism. He took the opportunity to speak to one of the more amenable officers.

'We'll lose too many men, Lieutenant,' predicted Welbeck.

'Not if we make an early breach,' said Jonathan Ainley. 'The artillery will clear the way for us, then the cavalry can lead the charge. As for the enemy, we must have sapped their strength by now.'

'It's our own lack of strength that worries me.'

'Casualties have been unwarrantably high, Sergeant, I grant you. But we mustn't be deterred by that.'

'I've had to watch far too many of my men lowered into graves before their time,' said Welbeck, testily. 'Prince Eugene has a plan of the defences – Captain Rawson went into Lille to get it – yet he still hasn't worked out the best way to penetrate them.'

'I'll hear no criticism of His Highness,' warned Ainley.

'Dan might have saved himself all that trouble.'

'Show some respect to your superiors.'

Welbeck stifled his reply. The lieutenant was amiable but he wouldn't countenance any censure of a man he revered. In his opinion, Prince Eugene was an outstanding soldier. While he held the sergeant in great esteem – and knew of his exploits inside Lille – Ainley drew the line at too much familiarity. Welbeck's task was simply to obey orders and not to question them. He had to be kept in his place.

'Are there any tidings of fresh supplies?' asked Welbeck.

'They're on their way, Sergeant.'

'People have been saying that for weeks.'

'The situation remains unchanged.'

'In other words, the French have blocked our supply line.'

'That's not true at all,' said Ainley, hiding his own worries about the lack of supplies. 'On the other hand, we've stopped any relief getting through to Lille. Hunger and lack of ammunition will soon begin to tell on them.'

'It will tell on us as well, Lieutenant.'

'We are not under siege.'

'Well, it sometimes feels as if we are.'

'I don't care for your defeatist tone, Sergeant,' said Ainley, sharply. 'How can you inspire the men to fight if you suggest that the cause is hopeless? We have brilliant commanders able to exploit all the advantages we hold. I think you should remember Oudenarde. We were at a disadvantage there yet we still achieved a victory.'

'Luck was on our side that day,' argued Welbeck. 'We all know it. Had the Duke of Burgundy entered the fray, the result might have been very different. Even you must acknowledge that.'

'I'm not prepared to discuss it.'

'You were the one who mentioned Oudenarde.'

'And I'll not endure this impertinence from you,' said Ainley, raising a finger. 'I'll thank you to get about your business and leave me to get about mine.'

Turning on his heel, Ainley marched off. Welbeck was dismayed. As a rule, the lieutenant was a courteous and reasonable man with no hint of the arrogance common to many officers. If Ainley was feeling tetchy, it was a bad sign. He, too, must be having doubts about their ability to sustain the siege. Welbeck was not reassured. When he went off to his men, he had to conceal his deep concerns. On one thing only could he rely with any certainty. Of the men he was about to address, several would die unspeakable deaths.

The latest batch of recruits would be thrown into action again, marching beside battle-hardened veterans. Because of his injury, the one-eyed Harry Gaunt was excused, but Ben

Plummer and the others were already standing in line with muskets loaded and bayonets fixed. They looked frightened and forlorn. Welbeck was reminded of his own early days in the army when he'd been overcome by feelings of sheer helplessness on the verge of a battle. It was a hot day but some of the men in the ranks were shivering in anticipation of what was to come.

The siege guns had been pounding away hard and the outer defences of the town were wreathed in smoke. Some of the enemy had been killed by flying masonry, others burnt alive yet the survivors fought back with resounding cannon and raking musket volleys. The Allied cavalry charged at full gallop and the infantry went in behind them, marching to the beat of the drums. Welbeck was at the heart of the 24th Regiment. When men fell dead or wounded in front of him, he stepped over them and pressed on. If he saw anyone faltering through fear or trying to turn back, he urged them on with stentorian bellows. As they got closer and closer to the ravelin, the noise made even Welbeck's bellow redundant. Smoke in their nostrils and chaos all around them, the 24th fought on, firing, reloading, firing again then repeating the whole process as best they could in the glowing furnace of warfare. Musket balls seemed to be coming from everywhere.

Slowly and with great fortitude, they began to make ground, crashing through the breaches in the walls to fight at close quarters with the enemy and forcing a retreat. Instead of sniping from well-defended positions, French soldiers now offered their fleeing backs as targets. It was a rewarding sight for the Allies. Lille might still be intact but they'd captured most of the ravelin between the two huge bastions and established a base much nearer the town. Only after the last shots had been fired could they take an inventory of their losses. Over a thousand men in the Allied force had been killed or wounded. Scores of horses had fallen during the cavalry charge while others lay dying in their gore. The most significant casualty had been Prince Eugene. Hit above the eye by a musket ball, he'd had to retire from the field with blood streaming down his face. The man commanding the siege would take no further part in it.

'Would you ever consider living in England?' he asked.

'Yes, Sir John,' she replied.

'You've not been put off by this visit, then?'

'Not in the least – England has been a revelation.'

'So have you, Miss Janssen,' he said, seizing on the chance to pass a compliment. 'I see that I've been unkind to the Dutch. I always thought their womenfolk were rather plain and dowdy yet you give the lie to that. You could hold your own with any English lady.'

'You flatter me,' she said with a nervous smile.

'It would be virtually impossible to do that.'

They'd ridden around the estate together and paused beside the lake. Even on a dull day, they could see themselves and their horses reflected in the water. The serenity that Amalia had noticed on her first visit there was comforting. Two things had prompted her to accept his invitation to ride out with him. The first was that she felt obliged to Sir John Rievers for the boundless hospitality he'd offered them. The second and more important reason was that he held the key to the truth about Daniel. Thanks to his initiative of sending someone abroad, Amalia would know the full facts of the case. While she still believed Daniel to be alive, a few vestigial doubts flitted across her mind from time to time. Sir John would put an end to uncertainty.

'What has appealed to you about England?' he asked.

'Almost everything I've seen and everyone I've met.'

His eyebrow arched. 'Does that include Her Grace, the Duchess of Marlborough?'

'Evidently, we didn't meet Her Grace at the best of times,' she said, tactfully. 'But we were enraptured by Blenheim Palace. Father was thrilled to be able to meet the architect. Thank you so much for arranging that, Sir John.'

'It was the least I could do.'

'When the news comes – and when I know for sure that Daniel is alive – it may be possible for us to accept that invitation to dinner.'

'You and your father are always welcome at Rievers Hall,' he said, 'but it may not be quite so easy to entice Her Grace there. She's gone back to Windsor and we may have to wait a long while until there's someone else for her to upbraid at Blenheim.'

'We may not be here by then.'

He was upset. 'Oh? I thought you intended to stay for weeks.'

'That was the original intention.'

'Then what's changed it? Are you unhappy with the house? I can find you alternative accommodation, if you wish. You could move into Rievers Hall, for instance. Now that I've seen how thoroughly charming you both are, I'd be delighted to welcome you as guests in my own home.'

'We couldn't put you to that inconvenience,' she said.

'Where's the inconvenience?' he asked with a laugh. 'We have endless empty rooms that we never use and plenty of servants to wait on you night and day.'

'Father and I are not used to such luxury, Sir John.'

'Do you think you could *grow* accustomed to it?'

The directness of the question made her feel uneasy. Amalia was unsure if it were a serious enquiry or light-hearted one. Sir John's smile was ambiguous. He could either be declaring his love for her or teasing her about a world she'd never expected to inhabit. A glance at the lake helped to supply her with an answer.

'I'd feel like a fish out of water,' she said.

'Nonsense,' he countered. 'You could hold your own anywhere.'

'I'll never be put to that test.'

'We shall see.' His smile became more avuncular. 'Tell me about the visit to Somerset.'

'It rained for most of the journey there but we were glad that we'd made the effort. I was able to visit the farm where Daniel had been born and brought up. Had things worked out differently, he might still be there with his family.'

'And you might never have met him.'

'That would have been a tragedy.'

'Not necessarily,' he said, pensively. 'Surely it's better never to have met someone than to meet them and lose them. Not that you *have* lost Captain Rawson, of course,' he added, quickly. 'I was only speaking hypothetically.'

'How soon will we *know*, Sir John?'

'That depends on the North Sea. If it's in a bad mood, it can hold ships up for days or blow them right off course. I've been caught in a squall myself and know how hazardous it can be. We just have to grit our teeth, Miss Janssen, and be patient.'

'I don't think I have any patience left.'

He suggested that they walk around the lake. Leading their horses, they strolled side by side in a comfortable silence. Amalia was watching the swans on the lake while Sir John simply enjoyed being alone with her. They'd gone halfway around the perimeter of the lake before he spoke.

'Your father would prosper in England,' he observed.

'He does well enough in Amsterdam,' she said. 'Father is never without work. By the standards of most people, we are quite wealthy.'

'He'd have even more commissions here, Miss Janssen. Once his tapestry of Ramillies is hanging in Blenheim Palace, everyone who sees it will wish to employ him. Do you think he'd be happy here?'

'I'm afraid not, Sir John.'

'Is there any reason for that?'

'His heart is in Amsterdam.'

'What if *you* choose to live in England?'

'That's not going to happen in the near future.'

'One never knows,' he said, meaningfully. 'Fate has a strange habit of making decisions for us that we'd never before considered.'

'I have no control over that, Sir John. All I know is that I wish to be as close as possible to Daniel wherever he may be.'

'That's exactly how you should feel,' he said, feigning approval. 'Unhappily, it looks as if this war will carry on at least until the campaign season next year. There seems to be no earthly hope of a resolution.'

'Then I'll just have to wait,' she said, resignedly.

'We all will, Miss Janssen.' He stopped to look at her, his gaze roving her face before locking on her eyes. 'Remember what I said, won't you? As long as you're my guest, you can have anything you wish. You and your father can move into Rievers Hall tomorrow, if you choose.'

'I don't think we'll need to do that.'

'The offer stands open.'

'I'm grateful to you for making it, Sir John,' she said. 'There's only one thing I wish at the moment and that's to know for certain that Daniel is alive.'

'Even as we speak,' said Sir John, slipping an arm around her shoulders, 'your wish may be nearing fulfilment. I have the feeling that the man I sent abroad to verify the facts may be talking to Captain Rawson very soon.'

Andrew Syme had ridden into the main camp as part of the small but much needed band of reinforcements. It had not taken him long to find somewhere to stay and someone to bring him up to date with developments. He learnt that Daniel Rawson was no longer there. Since his injury made it impossible for him to continue, Prince Eugene had been forced to hand over the conduct of the siege to Marlborough himself, obliging the captain-general to attend on a daily basis. Daniel went with him. Syme was in no hurry. He was ready to bide his time until his quarry came within reach. Meanwhile, he was enjoying the experience of being back in an army that was constantly on the alert. News was coming in regularly of casualties sustained at the siege. As he settled into his lodging, Syme resolved to add a new name to the list of dead – Captain Daniel Rawson.

*　*　*

'He was the victim of his own bravery, Dan,' said Welbeck. 'There was no holding back for Prince Eugene. He rode at the head of his men and that was his undoing.'

'He'll be sorely missed,' said Daniel. 'The prince was more than a gallant soldier. He was a figurehead, an example to all, the very essence of a fighting man.'

'At least he was only wounded.'

'Yes, Henry, he'll be back in the saddle one day.'

Daniel had accompanied Marlborough on his visit to the siege that day and taken the opportunity to call upon the 24th Regiment. There was a subdued air in the camp. Everyone had hoped that they would have made far more progress by this stage and were chastened by the setbacks. Welbeck's evaluation of the situation was blunt.

'We made too many mistakes,' he said, bitterly. 'For all his courage in battle, Prince Eugene has his weaknesses. Neither he nor General Overkirk studied Vauban's plan of the fortifications with sufficient care. They should have realised how much effort it had taken you to get it.'

'It was a combination of effort, luck and help from others,' said Daniel. 'It was Guillaume Lizier who told me where to find it and his son who acted as my lookout. But the plan was not comprehensive. Other defences had been added to the original design.'

'Our early attacks were a form of suicide.'

'Did you lose many men?'

'Far more than we can afford, Dan.'

'But the latest attack has borne fruit.'

'I wouldn't call the loss of our commander a case of bearing fruit,' said Welbeck, 'but we did make advances.

We're now masters of that particular ravelin and we killed a lot of Frenchies. I suppose that resembles a form of victory. Now that Corporal John is in charge of the siege, we'll make further inroads.'

'Don't bank on that,' warned Daniel.

'Oh?'

'His Grace is not at his best. He's been troubled by headaches and weakened by some other malady. Having to come here every day has been an imposition on him.'

'What does he feel about the state of the siege?'

'He's disappointed, Henry.'

'I'd use a stronger word than that.'

'He blames the engineers,' said Daniel. 'He feels that they've let us down. They've been too slow and too uninventive. He hoped for some enterprise from them but it never came. Also, of course, His Grace is very concerned about our lack of supplies.'

'We're desperate for ammunition, Dan. And don't tell me it's on its way,' cautioned Welbeck, 'because I'm fed up with hearing that. My men are hungry, fatigued, shocked by our losses and wondering if this siege is really worth such an effort. It's a question I've asked myself.'

'The strategic importance of Lille can't be underestimated.'

'Will we have enough men left to garrison the town?'

'Of course,' said Daniel. 'Don't be so downhearted, Henry. It's not like you to want to walk away from a fight.'

'I'll fight until I drop,' retorted Welbeck. 'But I need ammunition to do it with and food to sustain me. Oh, no,' he moaned, as he saw a figure bearing down upon them. 'Here's one thing I *don't* need. What's she doing here?'

'I should have thought that that was obvious.'

As she got closer, Daniel could see the smudges of blood on her bare arms and on her apron. Like other women, Rachel Rees had been acting as an auxiliary nurse, cleaning and binding wounds at the behest of the surgeons. After tending a man who'd been badly burnt, she found a moment to go in search of Welbeck. Seeing that Daniel was there as well made her face glow with joy.

'How are you both?' she asked, cheerfully.

'I'm very well, thank you,' replied Daniel.

'And I'm not,' grunted Welbeck.

She was concerned. 'Are you ailing, Henry?'

'Yes, I'm dying for lack of peace and quiet.'

'Do you have an injury?'

'*You're* my injury, Rachel.'

She cackled merrily. 'You still have your sense of humour, I see.'

'Tell her, Dan, will you? I don't want her anywhere near me.'

'You might change your tune if you're wounded,' said Daniel. 'You'll need a nurse then and Rachel is very experienced.'

'I'd sooner perish in battle than submit to her nursing. In fact,' said Welbeck, 'I'll pass the word around the surgeons. If I am injured, she's not to be allowed within twenty yards of me.'

'But I'd look after you, Henry,' she said, softly.

'That's my fear.'

'You ought to be grateful to women like Rachel,' said

Daniel. 'They give freely of their time and energy. How many men would have died if it hadn't been for their skills?'

'They do useful work, I admit,' said Welbeck, grudgingly. 'But I still don't want to be carried into a field hospital and find myself looking up at Rachel.'

'No,' she teased, 'you'd much rather have me lying beside you. Anyway,' she continued over Welbeck's spluttering, 'I really came to tell you that I've finally had enough. I've been thinking over that idea I told you about, Captain Rawson.'

'You're going to return to Wales?' said Daniel.

'Yes,' she said, 'though not immediately, of course. As long as I'm needed as a nurse, I'll stay. But the moment that Lille is taken, I'll be heading home to Brecon.'

'Praise the Lord!' cried Welbeck.

'You could always come with me, Henry.'

'I feel safer being shot at by the Frenchies.'

'What made you reach your decision?' asked Daniel.

'I've seen too much blood and misery and horror,' she said. 'I'm ready for a quieter life. In a sense, Captain Rawson, *you* helped me to make my mind up.'

'How did I do that?'

'It was when you took me into Lille. I know I was only a serving wench for a short time but I loved every second of it. I felt at home. I was meeting new people, selling them something they wanted and working in a happy atmosphere. I can do all that back in Brecon,' she said, 'with no danger of being arrested and thrown into gaol.'

'It's a good decision, Rachel,' said Welbeck, smiling at her for once. 'I support it wholeheartedly.'

'And so do I,' added Daniel.

'Wales is the only place for a woman like you.'

'I haven't gone yet, Henry,' she said, eyes twinkling. 'There's still time for you to make me change my mind.'

When she returned to the house, Amalia found her father seated in front of the painting so that he could study it in detail.

'Are you still looking at that?' she said with slight mockery.

'I like it, Amalia,' he rejoined. 'I liked it when I first saw it. To be honest, I thought of returning to Oxford to buy it.'

'Sir John anticipated your wish.'

'I was amazed when I found it waiting for me.'

'His generosity is overwhelming.'

'That's what worries me,' said Janssen. 'I'd feel much happier if he'd let me pay for the painting. We don't deserve such favours. He's been treating us like close friends of his rather than strangers.'

'He's invited us to move to Rievers Hall.'

'Why should we do that? We have everything we need here.'

'That's what I told him, Father.'

Emanuel Janssen was a doting parent of an only child. When Amalia lost a mother and he lost a wife, they became even closer. Protective of his daughter, Janssen had been delighted when he saw her friendship with Daniel Rawson develop into something deeper and more lasting. He was, however, less certain about her friendship with Sir John Rievers.

'Did you enjoy your ride this afternoon?'

'I always enjoy it.'

'You seem to spend a lot of time in Sir John's company.'

'I can hardly refuse an invitation,' she said. 'Besides – and I don't mean this as a criticism of you – Sir John and I are the only two people who are absolutely sure that Daniel is still alive. His presence helps to reassure me.'

'I believe he's alive as well, Amalia,' he attested.

'You only do that for my sake, Father. I can see it in your eyes and it's the same with Beatrix. Both of you do all you can to bolster my spirits in spite of your misgivings.'

'We're bound to have some qualms. After all, Sir John told us that he'd seen Daniel's name listed among the dead in the *Gazette*. That's an official publication, apparently. It doesn't often make mistakes.'

'It did so in this case,' she said, firmly.

'I hope with all my heart that you're right, Amalia.'

'I *am* right. Sir John agrees with me. His only regret is that he told me the bad news when he did.'

'Yes,' said Janssen, 'I've been thinking about that.'

'He keeps apologising to me. He did so again this afternoon. Sir John believes that he should have been certain of his facts before he passed on such dire news. It's because he's feeling so guilty,' she explained, 'that he went to the trouble of sending a man abroad to investigate.'

'Why *did* he tell you when he did?'

'He'd promised to find any mention of Daniel that he could.'

'That's not what I'm asking, Amalia,' he said. 'Why did Sir John break such terrible news to you alone? I was there at the time. He'd just presented me with this wonderful painting. Can you understand what I'm saying? I should have been with you at such a moment.'

Amalia was jolted. 'That never occurred to me.'

'By the time that I came into the room, you'd fainted.'

'Luckily, Sir John caught me as I fell. What I think happened was this,' she said, thinking it through. 'I suspect that he didn't intend to give me such a shock like that. But knowing how eager I was for news of Daniel – and catching me alone – he couldn't stop himself from blurting it out. That's why he can't stop apologising.'

'Yes,' said Janssen, unconvinced by her theory, 'it's one explanation, I suppose.'

'Can you think of another one, Father?'

Face puckered with concern, she looked up at him. Amalia seemed so young and fragile. He simply could not bring himself to upset her by raising any doubts. For her benefit, his fears had to be suppressed. He glanced admiringly at the painting once again before manufacturing a smile.

'No, Amalia,' he said, 'I can't. Obviously, that must have been exactly what happened. And if you and Sir John are convinced of Daniel's safety,' he added with confidence, 'then so am I. The man sent abroad after him will find Daniel alive and in good health.'

Even though he knew that supplies were running short, Daniel was shocked to learn that ammunition would run out in less than a week. The continuous booming of the siege guns had eaten up their stocks of powder and shot, and the artillery were forced to retrieve some of the enemy shot aimed at them in order to reuse it.

'Food supplies are low as well,' said Daniel.

'Where food is concerned,' said Marlborough, 'we can always reduce rations and forage further afield. That's not the case with ammunition. If we don't have it soon, then the guns will fall silent and Lille will be able to breathe a sigh of relief.'

'I'll set out at once, Your Grace.'

'You know the route the convoy is taking. They'll have left Ostend by now and be well on their way.'

'Who's in command of the escort?'

'Major-General Webb and he's an ideal choice. Acquaint them with our predicament here and see when he's likely to arrive. Tell him that Cadogan is on his way with reinforcements.'

'We'll have to hope the convoy has not been intercepted.'

'That's always a possibility, alas,' said Marlborough. 'The enemy have enough troops in the area. I had planned for Major General Erle to move towards Bruges but we had reports of massive numbers being rushed there so the plan had to be abandoned.'

'The French would hate to lose Bruges.'

'They'd hate to lose Lille even more but that's what will happen. Once Lille has fallen, we can turn our attention to Bruges and Ghent.'

'But only if we have enough ammunition,' said Daniel.

'Quite so – that's critical.'

'I'll bring news as soon as I can, Your Grace.'

'May good fortune attend you!'

After trading farewells with him, Daniel left Marlborough's quarters and walked briskly across to his horse. His uniform was likely to attract the attention of the enemy but he was relying on his riding skills and his knowledge of the region to avoid any problems. While he was only acting as a courier, he was glad to be back in action again. After the excitement of his two visits to Lille, he'd spent most of his time beside Marlborough and, while it was always fascinating to see the captain-general exercising his command, it didn't provide the exhilaration that Daniel sought. He was pleased with the opportunity to be sent on an important mission. As he left the camp, the road opened out enticingly before him.

His task not only gave him the freedom of action coveted, it enabled him to speculate once more on the mysterious reference to Amalia in the letter Marlborough received from his wife. Who had died and how had Amalia reacted? Why had she not written to him about her loss? Where was she now? What could he possibly do to alleviate her suffering? When could he see her again?

With so many questions filling his mind, his concentration was affected. Daniel kept his eyes peeled on what was ahead and on both sides of him but he was too preoccupied to look behind him. Thinking about Amalia's plight and blaming himself for not being there to comfort her, he was completely unaware of the fact that he'd been followed the moment he'd left camp.

Andrew Syme could not believe his luck. After only a short time, he'd been able to gather a lot of information about Daniel Rawson and could now identify him by sight. Knowing that it would be far too risky to make an attempt on his life in camp, he'd devised a ruse. Syme had written a letter that purported to come from Sir John Rievers. It informed Daniel that, in addition to grieving over the death of a close friend, Amalia was seriously ill. Since she could not be moved, she was desperate for Daniel to come to her in England. Syme had fully expected that his letter would lure Daniel out of the camp so that he could be killed somewhere along the road. The ruse was no longer needed. Having kept him under surveillance, Syme was rewarded with the sight of his leaving the camp entirely on his own. As he trailed behind his target, there was a smile of triumph on his face. His task was going to be far easier than he'd ever dared to imagine.

The dog did Daniel a favour. It was a small, fierce, ragged mongrel that hurtled out of a farmyard and yapped madly as it danced around his horse's hooves. Frightened by the attack, the animal reared slightly and swung round. In that split second, Daniel caught a glimpse of someone in the middle distance, riding steadily after him. He knew at once that he was being stalked. Avoiding the dog, he galloped clear of the little farm. A mile further on, he came to a hill with wooded slopes. As soon as he'd crested it, Daniel looked for a hiding place among the trees. He dismounted, tethered his horse then took out his pistol. Choosing a vantage point, he waited until he heard the clip-clop of a horse.

When the rider came into view, Daniel saw him rein in his mount at the top of the hill and look down the open road. His suspicions were confirmed. Had the man been harmless, he would have ridden on his way without caring about anyone else. Instead of that, he was hovering as he tried to work out where the person ahead of him had disappeared. The man was close enough for Daniel to take a good look at him but too far away to be within range of a pistol. Tall in the saddle, he was lean and alert. Daniel could discern the air of a soldier about him, yet he was wearing the apparel of a wealthy English gentleman. He was an odd person to meet in such a place.

After a few minutes, the man shrugged and seemed to abandon his pursuit. Tugging on the rein, he turned his horse and vanished down the other side of the hill. Daniel was not tempted out of hiding. He waited a considerable time before he moved, keeping an eye on the crest of the hill throughout. But the man did not come back. When he felt it was safe to do so, Daniel mounted his horse and trotted back up the road. He reached the top of the hill and looked at the prospect below. Beyond the farm, he could see for another mile or more. If the rider had gone back in that direction, Daniel would certainly have spotted him. That meant he was concealed somewhere, lying in wait, ready to pounce if his quarry came within reach. Daniel didn't give him that opportunity. Wheeling his horse, he set off back down the hill. Whenever he glanced over his shoulder, he saw nobody in pursuit yet he knew that the man would be back.

It was a minor setback but Syme was not in the least worried. Lurking among the trees, he decided that it might actually be a good thing that Daniel Rawson was aware of him. It added spice to the situation and gave him an extra challenge. It had never been Syme's intention to shoot him in the back. He was too much of a soldier and a gentleman to resort to what he regarded as cowardly murder. When he killed Daniel, he'd intended to do so in some form of duel. He wanted to look in the man's face before he took his life. It was clear where Daniel was going. By talking to officers at the camp, Syme had learnt how low the stocks of ammunition were at the siege. A convoy was on its way from Ostend. Someone needed to find out where it was and how long it would take to reach Lille. Since he was part of Marlborough's staff, Daniel Rawson had been selected. That was what Syme assumed and his assumption had been supported by the route taken. Daniel was on the road north to Menin.

Coming out of his refuge, Syme mounted his horse and trotted once more to the top of the hill. From his eminence, he could see a rider in the distance, his sword glinting in the sunshine and his red coat standing out in vivid contrast to the green grass. Syme kicked his horse into a canter. The second stage of his chase had begun.

Unable to see him, Daniel nevertheless knew that he was there. It didn't matter if the man was a French spy or someone with a personal grudge against him. The only fact that Daniel considered was that he was being tailed by a professional and he reproached himself for not realising sooner that he was being followed. Danger was not only behind him. As he came out of a copse, Daniel saw a French patrol directly ahead of him. He took evasive action at once, swinging his horse to the right and galloping along the bank of a bubbling stream. The patrol gave chase immediately, half a dozen men each eager to be the one to capture or kill an enemy. Fanned out across a field, they were a couple of hundred yards away but felt certain that they'd be able to overhaul him.

Daniel could hear the drumming of the hooves behind him. He didn't waste time looking back. His gaze was fixed on the wood ahead of him. If he could gain the safety of the trees, he believed, he might somehow be able to shake off the patrol. They were slowly gaining on him. Veering sharply to the right, Daniel splashed across the stream and felt the cold water sprinkling his face. When he reached the wood, he plunged in and picked a way between the trees and shrubs. The further he went, the darker it got. In what seemed like only seconds, he could hear the patrol crashing through the undergrowth behind him and taunting him with calls. Their leader ordered them to spread out.

He was in a quandary. Unable to find a hiding place, Daniel didn't dare to break cover. Once out in the open, he'd be doomed. Divide and kill. That was his only option. The soldiers would be coming one at a time. Daniel was armed with his sword, pistol and the dagger given him by Rachel Rees. Three weapons would not be enough to account for six soldiers but they were all that he had at his disposal. Finding a thick, gnarled oak, he tethered his horse behind some bushes then climbed the tree. The first man appeared only a few moments later, sword in hand as he rode slowly along. Daniel waited until his target was directly below him, then he dropped from the bough on which he'd been resting and knocked the man from the saddle, hitting the ground before rolling over and using the dagger to slit his throat. One down and five to go – the fight for survival was on.

The commotion brought another French soldier within range. This time Daniel felled him with his sword, leaping out from behind the tree to hack at the man, then grabbing his arm to drag him to the ground. One thrust of the sabre despatched him but the man's cry of agony aroused the others. Taking to his heels, Daniel darted off through the trees to put distance between himself and the two corpses, but he could not outrun a horse. One of them pounded after him and he could hear it closing in on him. When he turned round, he saw a sabre raised to slice his head off. Daniel had the pistol in his hand instantly and put a ball into the rider's brain. As the man fell backwards and dropped his sabre, its point stuck in the ground.

No sooner had one horse cantered past him than another came into view. It was the leader of the patrol and he was pointing a pistol menacingly at Daniel. The precise moment the man fired, Daniel hurled the dagger at him and, as he felt a searing pain in his right arm, he saw the weapon bury itself in the Frenchman's chest. Trying vainly to pull out the dagger, the soldier gurgled helplessly, then fell from the saddle and writhed on the ground. Four men down and only two left – Daniel had the right to feel elated. Instead he had to stem the bleeding from the flesh wound in his arm. The pistol ball had missed the bone but grazed him enough to produce a lot of blood and severe pain. Tearing open the jacket of the man he'd shot, Daniel ripped off enough of his shirt to be able to bind the wound. However, he was given no time to tie it in place. Before he could even move, two other riders nudged their horses into view and looked down with horror at their fallen comrades. Both had sabres in their hands and murder in their minds.

Daniel was defenceless. He had no weapon in his hand and no means of escape. His arm was on fire. His mind was racing. All that he could do was to wait for them to attack.

CHAPTER FIFTEEN

They were in no hurry. Dismounting from their horses, they looked closely at the two corpses, their anger mounting as they did so. The captain of a British regiment would be a good prize but they had no intention of taking a prisoner. All that they wanted was revenge. They exchanged a glance as if deciding who should be first, then one of them raised his sabre to strike. Knowing that his chances were slim, Daniel got ready to dodge the blow, hoping that he could dive for one of the discarded weapons. His plan was never put to the test. Before the blade descended in a vicious arc, two shots rang out and both men pitched forward with a pistol ball in their brain.

Grinning broadly, Andrew Syme stepped into view.

'Always carry *two* pistols, Captain Rawson,' he advised, holding up his two weapons. 'It doubles your chances of escaping alive from this sort of situation.'

'Who are you?' shouted Daniel.

'That's rather an impolite tone to use on someone who's just rescued you from a very painful death.'

'You've been following me.'

'Yes – and it's just as well that I did.'

'What do you want?'

'That can wait. I suggest that the first thing I do is to bind that arm of yours or your sleeve will be soaked with blood. Come on,' he said, tucking the pistols into his belt, 'let me help you off with your coat.'

Daniel agreed but remained on the defensive. He let the man take off the coat, examine the wound then bind it with part of the French soldier's shirt. From the proficient way that his rescuer went about it, Daniel could see that he'd tended wounds before. His arm was still stinging but at least he was not losing any more blood. After thanking the newcomer for his providential help, he squared up to him.

'Now will you tell me who you are?'

'My name is Andrew Syme,' replied the other.

'You were an army man, I fancy.'

'I was a major in a cavalry regiment.'

'Why were you on my tail?'

'I have orders to kill you,' said Syme, picking up one of the sabres from the ground, 'and I couldn't possibly let a couple of Frenchmen do my job for me.'

Daniel was taken aback. The man had spoken with a quiet confidence that showed he had no doubts whatsoever about his ability to carry out his orders. Instead of being cut to ribbons by two angry Frenchmen, Daniel was now confronted by another threat. He sought to buy time by asking questions.

'Who gave the orders?'

Syme shrugged. 'Does that matter?'

'It matters a great deal to me.'

'You've never heard of the noble gentleman.'

'Why has he singled me out?' asked Daniel.

'I'm afraid that you singled yourself out, Captain Rawson,' said the other, suavely. 'You made the unfortunate mistake of falling in love with the wrong woman.'

Daniel blenched. 'Is this something to do with Amalia?'

'It has *everything* to do with the young lady.'

'Is she in danger?' asked Daniel, stepping towards him.

'Don't come any closer,' warned Syme, jabbing Daniel's chest with the point of the sword. 'You can hear me quite clearly from where you're standing.'

'Tell me about Amalia.'

'I've never had the pleasure of meeting her but – since she can excite such passion in two different men – I can see that she must be an extraordinary young lady. Unhappily, only one of you can enjoy her. Pick up your sword, Captain Rawson.'

'Wait,' said Daniel. 'This is pointless. Killing me will not send Amalia into someone else's arms. She'd never look at another man.'

'Every woman can be won over in time and the gentleman in question is well versed in the art. You're not the first person I've had to remove because he obstructed the way to a lady's bed.'

'Is that what you are – a hired assassin?'

'I prefer to see myself as a trusted friend.'

'But you served in the British army,' said Daniel, earnestly. 'You've known the camaraderie created in warfare.

Would you really attempt to kill a fellow officer?'

'That would depend on his price,' said Syme, easily, 'and yours is inordinately high. I, too, have needs, you see. I have to pay for my pleasures and settle some gambling debts. Killing you is a simple way of doing that.' He prodded Daniel again. 'Pick up your sword, Captain Rawson. I'm no cold-blooded murderer. I always give a man a fighting chance. And, yes, I know you've been injured but that won't impair you too much. Someone who can kill four Frenchmen entirely on his own is to be admired. You'll be a worthy opponent.'

'It's a pity I can't say the same about you,' declared Daniel, retrieving his sword from the ground. 'You're a disgrace to the uniform of the British army, Major.'

Syme laughed. 'I always thrive on insults.'

Trying to catch Daniel off guard, he lunged forward but his thrust was easily parried. The blades clashed again and again in quick succession, convincing Daniel that he was fighting an expert swordsman. Syme was strong, well balanced and light on his feet. He was also untroubled by any injury. Daniel, by contrast, felt a sharp twinge in his right arm every time their swords met. At one point, when he parried Syme's flashing blade, Daniel winced at the pain he felt on impact. He was put on the defensive, stepping backwards over the dead French soldiers and knowing that he could not keep his opponent at bay indefinitely.

As the twinges in his right arm became more intense, Daniel switched his sword to the other hand and went on the attack. Syme was momentarily confused and forced backwards for a few moments. He adjusted quickly to the left-handed assault and managed to graze Daniel's hip with a thrust. With two injuries to hamper him, Daniel realised that he had to end the duel very soon. Syme was stronger, faster and brimming with confidence. He began to taunt Daniel, even to toy with him. While barely holding him off, Daniel worked his way carefully towards his discarded red coat. As he did so, he pretended to trip over one of the corpses and lose his balance. Seeing his chance, Syme jumped in for the kill.

He was too slow. Daniel eluded his thrust with ease, bent down to pick up the coat and threw it into Syme's face. While his opponent tried to get rid of the obstruction, Daniel snatched up the French sabre that stood upright in the ground and, fighting with his left hand at first, he suddenly used the sword in his right hand to pierce Syme's guard, pushing the blade deep into his stomach before twisting it then pulling it out again. The duel was over. Syme's eyes widened with incredulity. He'd never even considered the possibility of defeat. Dropping his sword, he sank to the ground with both hands to his stomach.

'Always carry *two* swords,' said Daniel, mocking Syme's earlier advice. 'It doubles your chances of escaping alive from this sort of situation.'

'Damn you, man!' roared Syme, as the blood gushed out of him. 'You've killed me.'

Daniel dropped his weapons and grabbed him by the throat.

'Who *sent* you?' he demanded.

'I never thought it would be this big,' said Beatrix Udderzook as she looked around in wonder. 'It's enormous.'

'It's magnificent,' said Amalia, 'but it's also a little intimidating.'

'I so wanted to see it.'

'Are you pleased that we came?'

'This is the best day for me since we've been in England.'

The visit to London had fulfilled the maidservant's dearest wish and given Amalia something to take her mind off the subject that had been gnawing away at it. When the three of them first arrived from Holland, they'd caught a glimpse of the dome of St Paul's Cathedral as they drove through the capital. It was only when they were actually inside it, however, that they got a clearer idea of its dimensions and its proportions. Emanuel Janssen was entranced, wandering around in delight as he studied every detail of Wren's masterpiece. After well over thirty years, work on the cathedral had not yet been completed but the bulk of the edifice was finished, enabling the visitors to stand inside the biggest Protestant church in Christendom.

'I could never go up there,' said Beatrix, pointing up at the Whispering Gallery. 'I'd get too dizzy.'

'Think of the view you could enjoy from there,' said Amalia, craning her neck to gaze upwards. 'The stonemasons who built it must have been working on it for years.'

'I wouldn't last ten seconds at that height.'

'You'd be surprised what you can do, Beatrix.'

Amalia was glad that they'd been able to bring her maidservant with her. Since there was so little for Beatrix to do in the house, she was thrilled to escape from Oxfordshire for a while in order to see the sights of London. It was now almost half a century since the city had been destroyed by the Great Fire and it had been assiduously rebuilt in the intervening years. New churches, guildhalls, civic buildings, business premises and warehouses had sprung up, surrounded by new dwellings of every size and description. There was something of interest to see at every turn in the bustling capital but St Paul's dominated everything else.

'I think there's somebody up there,' noted Amalia.

'I can't see them, Miss Amalia.'

'Look over to the left.'

Beatrix shifted her gaze, then caught her breath when she saw two tiny figures moving around the rim of the gallery. It made her feel queasy just to watch them. What if they fell? The very thought made her twitch involuntarily. Yet the people seemed unworried by being up at such a height. They paused to look down and, seeing Beatrix below, gave her a friendly wave. Startled by their bravery, she raised a nervous hand to wave back. One of them called something out but the words were lost in the cavernous interior of the cathedral. When the two people moved out of sight, Beatrix looked up beyond them to inspect the dome itself, wondering how something of that size and weight could stay up there without crashing to the ground. As if anticipating such a disaster, she felt the urge to move away and she turned to speak to Amalia. But there was nobody beside her.

Beatrix looked around. 'Where have you gone?' she asked.

Amalia didn't even hear the question. She was kneeling at the altar rail in a side chapel, head bowed in humility and hands clasped together as she offered up prayers for the safety of Daniel Rawson.

He was miles from Wynendael when he first heard the sounds of battle and it made him kick his heels into the flanks of his horse. After his encounter with the patrol and his duel in the wood, Daniel was feeling much stronger. He'd bandaged the flesh wound in his hip with part of another French shirt, put on his coat, then hurried back to the stream so that he could douse his face with water and wipe the blood from his hands. When he returned to the scattered corpses, he gathered up a selection of weapons, making sure that he pulled his dagger out of the man it had killed. Rachel Rees's gift had helped to save his life. Reclaiming his own horse, he set off. The escapade among the trees had left him with mementoes. His wounds were smarting and he was filled with anxiety over Amalia but there was a far more important souvenir of the struggle. It was the letter he'd taken from Andrew Syme's pocket. It gave Daniel a name, an address and an urgent reason to get to England. Amalia was in jeopardy and he was needed there. There was, however, a prior consideration that could not be ignored. Daniel had to reach the convoy first. The increasing clamour ahead of him told him where he'd find it. Vital to the continuance of the siege, the convoy was making no progress at all. It was obviously under a concerted attack.

The French had been waiting to intercept them in a densely forested area near Wynendael. General Lamotte had some twenty-three thousand men under his command against an Allied escort of a mere six thousand men. The battle opened with a bombardment from French cannon that inflicted severe casualties on both the convoy and its escort. They would have been even more severe but for the order from Major General Webb for his men to lie on the ground and present less of a target. Ignoring the disparity in numbers between the two sides, Webb deployed his men with skill. When the French came up through the relatively narrow space between the trees, they were met by the sight of triple lines of men with a handful of mounted troops to the fore. The odds seemed to be heavily in favour of Lamotte and his army.

The advantage proved illusory. Because they were fighting in such a confined space, the French forces had to be crowded into twelve lines of units. Infantry were at the front, supported by four lines of dragoons and two of cavalry. They closed on the escort, only to be checked by the speed and accuracy of the Allies' volley-firing. It took Lamotte's men by surprise. Most of his regiments were composed of French-speaking Netherlanders with shifting allegiances. Tending to pursue their own interests, they were quick to discern where these lay. As the platoon volleys kept popping away with deadly effect, a wave of panic started to spread. The advancing French line began to fold and fall back to the right, getting entangled with the lines behind them and causing confusion.

There was a new menace to face. Webb had concealed some of his forces in the woods on both sides and these started firing from unseen positions among the trees. The French were falling in large numbers and impeding those behind them. Confident that he could still overpower the smaller force, Lamotte sent in his dragoons but they too were beaten back by the volley-firing. It was a ferocious encounter that lasted barely two hours and it was ended by the arrival of Allied reinforcements under the command of Cadogan. When he saw them approach, Lamotte gave the order to retreat and fled from the scene. Webb and his men had achieved an unexpected but well-deserved victory. They'd lost a sixth of their escort in the process but enemy losses were over three times that number. While the Allied general had every right to congratulate himself, his French counterpart was slinking away with his tail between his legs.

It had been a significant engagement. Though they failed to realise it at the time, the battle of Wynendael was a decisive turning point in the siege of Lille. Thanks to the bravery and professionalism of the escort, two hundred and fifty thousand pounds of gunpowder and several tons of shot had been saved. It was enough to keep the Allied guns battering the walls of Lille for an additional fortnight.

Daniel arrived in time to take only a limited part in the battle. Unable to join Allied lines, he hid in the forest and was able to shoot two of the fleeing French infantrymen before reloading in time to put a pistol ball into the eye of a dragoon. When the retreat was sounded, he'd remounted and, in spite of his injured arm, was prepared to take on an isolated cavalry officer. The man galloped off before Daniel could get to him and he was followed by the rest of the French forces. Daniel had to content himself with taking two prisoners and marching them back to the Allied lines. There was a general air of celebration. While officers gathered around Webb, their acknowledged hero, Daniel went in search of a commander he knew well.

William Cadogan was a big, ebullient, fearless man in his thirties, with a brilliant record as the Quartermaster-General of the Allied armies. He was notorious for his addiction to gambling but Daniel didn't hold that against him. For all sorts of reasons, he liked and admired Cadogan. By the same token, Cadogan had the highest respect for him.

'Dear God!' he exclaimed when he saw Daniel. 'What's happened to you, man?'

'I met with some difficulties on my way here,' said Daniel.

'Your sleeve is soaked with blood. Have one of the surgeons look at the wound immediately.'

'It's already been dressed. Besides, the surgeons have more than enough to do at the moment. My wound was not picked up here but in an earlier encounter.'

During his brushes with the enemy, Daniel had become quite dishevelled but it was the blood-covered tear in his sleeve that caught the attention. As Daniel explained what had happened, Cadogan listened with interest and sympathy.

'I came here too late to be of any real use,' he concluded.

'So did we,' said Cadogan, regretfully, 'though there's nothing to bring such cheer as the sight of a French army in open retreat. What will you do next?'

'I'll present my compliments to Major General Webb, then I'll ride back to camp with news of events here. His Grace will want to hear a full report. Only then,' Daniel went on, 'can I ask his permission for some leave to attend to more personal matters.'

'By Jupiter!' exclaimed Cadogan. 'There's no need to waste time doing that, Captain Rawson. I can send men of my own with a report. You're needed in England. I'll write a letter to His Grace explaining why.' He saw Daniel hesitate. 'What are you waiting for, man?'

'I was given very specific orders.'

'Well, I've just countermanded them. His Grace would be angry with me if I didn't do just that. We always have need of you here, Captain Rawson, but someone else has a first claim.'

Daniel was thrilled. 'Please apologise to His Grace on my behalf.'

'There's no point. He and I are married men. We understand the power of love and the responsibilities it brings. Be off with you at once,' ordered Cadogan, pushing him away. 'The young lady is waiting to be rescued – though I suspect she'd rather that you did it in a smarter uniform.'

On the same day as the battle of Wynendael, the Allies encamped around Lille had an unforeseen taste of action themselves. They were settling down at dusk when they saw a column of two thousand horse and one hundred and fifty Grenadiers approaching. Since the newcomers wore Dutch insignia in their caps, it was assumed that they were part of the besieging army. They were allowed through the lines until the point when one of the officers gave an order in French for his troop to close up. Henry Welbeck was one of those who heard the command and realised its import. The riders were French soldiers in disguise, each one of them equipped with a fifty-pound bag of gunpowder destined for the beleaguered garrison. For a town that was down to its last reserves of ammunition, the convoy was precious but it would not all arrive intact. Welbeck's voice was only one of many raised in anger.

'The bastards are French!' he yelled. 'Shoot them.'

Scrambling to their feet, men grabbed their muskets

and began firing at the interlopers. Some of the shots hit the bags of gunpowder, causing huge explosions that killed both horses and riders. Other members of the convoy were unwitting agents of their own deaths. Whipping their horses into a mad gallop, they made sparks fly up from the clattering hooves to set off further explosions. The whole camp was suddenly alight with a firework display. Well over a hundred men and horses perished, leaving behind charred remains scattered far and wide. Ben Plummer was sickened by what he saw.

'Look at that poor devil,' he said, indicating one corpse. 'He was burnt to a cinder.'

Welbeck was unconcerned. 'It serves him right.'

'Don't you feel sorry for him, Sergeant?'

'I feel sorry for the horse but not for its rider.'

'How many did we kill?'

'Not enough,' said Welbeck, angrily. 'Most of them got through to the town with their fresh supplies. What were our picquets doing, letting the buggers through like that?'

'What will happen now?'

'There'll be some stern questioning, that's what will happen. When you besiege a town for two months, you should have it by the throat. The last thing you should do is to let a convoy get through to it with relief supplies.'

'Have you ever seen anything like this before?' asked Plummer, tearing his gaze away from the hideous scene around him.

'I've seen the Frenchies play tricks before but never like this.'

'You have to admire the way they rode in, bold as brass.'

'I blame the Dutch.'

'Why is that, Sergeant?'

'It's a simple question of colours, lad. Because some of our Dutch allies wear blue uniforms, they're dressed in the same colour as the enemy. If everybody in our ranks wore red coats like us, this deception could never have happened.' Thrusting his pipe into his mouth, he looked shrewdly at Plummer. 'How are you finding army life?'

'I hate every second of it.'

'That will wear off in time.'

'Harry Gaunt has deserted and some of the others are talking about it,' said Plummer. 'We're scared.'

'You should be more scared of running away than of staying here,' said Welbeck, his face inches away from the recruit. 'Deserters are usually caught and they get short shrift. How far will Harry Gaunt go with one eye and no knowledge of the region? Desertion means ignominy. Staying here to fight gives you a chance of glory.'

'Is that what you call glory?' asked Plummer, pointing to the blackened corpse.

'Yes – if you happened to be the man who shot him.'

'At least he was killed instantly. We're dying a slow death.'

'I've got a feeling you'll outlast this siege, Ben Plummer,' said Welbeck, taking a step backwards. 'When I first clapped eyes on you, I didn't like the way you looked or the way you talked. As for the crime that got you here, I despise people who live off the proceeds of women like that.'

'You never met any of them,' said Plummer with something of his old impudence. 'I only employed the most succulent ladies. Even you would've felt a tingle of interest in them.'

'Close that foul mouth of yours.'

'If I had one of them to warm my bed right now, I might think that the army was not such an ordeal after all. Perhaps that's the answer,' he mused. 'I'll have to get myself wounded – though not too badly – then I can get to pick out the prettiest nurse and persuade her to tend to my needs.' He gave a snigger. 'Your own dear lady is working as a nurse, isn't she, Sergeant?'

Welbeck's punch sent him somersaulting across the ground.

The voyage was a test of his patience. A squall came up from nowhere to blow them off course and add another day to the crossing. All that Daniel could do was to wait for better weather and endeavour to remain calm. There was one source of consolation. The ship on which he'd embarked would have been the earliest that Andrew Syme could have taken with certain news of Daniel's death. Sir John Rievers might not make his move until he heard that news. Amalia was in the clutches of a dangerous and manipulative man but – until word arrived from the hired assassin – Rievers might stay his hand. Daniel was sure that Amalia would be unaware of her host's intentions. With her trusting nature, she'd be powerless against his wiles.

As he sat below deck, Daniel took out the letter he'd found in Syme's pocket. In the brief time before his death, the man had been unable to supply many details of his employer but he'd admitted writing the letter designed to lure Daniel out of camp. Had he read it earlier, he would certainly have been deceived. The neat calligraphy, the desperate plea for help and the plausible manner of the courier would have had the desired effect on Daniel. After securing permission from Marlborough, he would have ridden off unsuspectingly with the man paid to kill him. It was a chilling thought.

Reading it now, he was in a different frame of mind. Instead of being concerned by Amalia's plight to the exclusion of all else, he was able to study it carefully. An emotional response was superseded by a more critical one. If a close friend of Amalia's had died, a name would have been supplied. As for the claim of a serious illness, it had to be set against the fact that she was a healthy young woman in the prime of her life. While she might look delicate, Amalia had a very strong constitution and was rarely troubled by complaints of any kind. The deciding factor for Daniel was that the letter was apparently penned by Sir John Rievers. However bereaved and sick she might be, Amalia would never call upon her host to send for help. Her father would willingly have taken on that duty.

Everything about the epistle was false yet it might have succeeded in its malign purpose. Daniel was grateful that it had never been put into his hand. Folding it up, he slipped it back into his pocket and got to his feet. Before leaving the convoy, he'd managed to borrow another uniform, albeit from a different regiment than the 24th. He looked very smart in it. The ship's surgeon had dressed his wounds properly and they were already starting to heal. While his physical ailments were improving, however, his mind was still a cauldron of doubt and apprehension. Who was Sir John Rievers and why did he have designs on Amalia? What did Syme mean when he said that Daniel was not the first person to be killed at the man's behest? When would they reach England? Where was Amalia now? Would Daniel be in time?

A yell from above interrupted his meditation. The sound of feet running on deck suggested activity. Daniel went up the narrow staircase to investigate. All of a sudden, the breeze had stiffened markedly and the sails were flapping. Members of the crew were hauling on ropes or climbing the rigging as they sought to unfurl every piece of canvas on the vessel. It was as if a giant hand was now pushing them along. They sailed on through the white-capped waves with far more speed. Daniel crossed to the bulwark. With the wind plucking at his hair and with spray sprinkling his face, he scanned the horizon for a sight of land but all that confronted him was a vast expanse of sea. Somewhere in the far distance, Amalia was facing a terrible danger of which she was not even aware.

The very idea of her being molested made him burn with anger.

'I'm coming, Amalia,' he said under his breath. 'I'm coming.'

Sir John Rievers chafed at the delay. Amalia and the others had been away for days now. He'd offered to act as their guide in London but Janssen had politely refused the offer, feeling that he wanted to be alone with his daughter after so much time under their host's eye. Understanding that, Sir John took no offence but he missed Amalia the second she left his property. An early fear had disturbed him. He wondered if the visit to London would also be a search for news about Daniel Rawson. If they questioned the information given them by Sir John, they might wish to see a copy of the relevant *Gazette* in order to check the list of dead. When they saw that Daniel's name was not, in fact, there, they'd know they'd been duped.

On reflection, Sir John dismissed the notion. Amalia and her father were too naive to do such a thing. In awe of a member of the aristocracy, they'd never have the slightest suspicion of him. It was her effulgent innocence that made Amalia so irresistible. She was blithely unaware of his designs on her. Waiting for her to return only served to intensify his desire to possess her. The one barrier between them must have been removed by now. Andrew Syme would have obeyed his orders and be on his way back to England. There was no need to delay anymore. When Amalia finally returned from London with the others, Sir John was waiting for them.

'Did you see all you wanted to see?' asked Sir John.

'Yes, thank you,' replied Janssen. 'It was wonderful.'

'We could have stayed for a week,' said Amalia as she let Sir John help her down from the carriage. 'Is there any news?'

'Not as yet,' he said, 'but I expect it every day.'

'I prayed that we'd know the truth by now,' she said.

'When I was in church, I added my own supplication.'

He went into the house with them, leaving the servants to unload the luggage. Beatrix went off into the kitchen and Janssen begged to be excused because he was suffering from a headache. Without having to contrive it, Sir John was alone with Amalia. His eyes feasted on her.

'Do you feel tired after the journey?'

'No, Sir John, I feel as fresh as a daisy.'

'Then perhaps you'd join me for a walk. There's

something I need to discuss with you.'

Amalia was puzzled. 'Couldn't we discuss it here?'

'Walls have ears – and it's a very private matter.'

'Then I'll be happy to come with you.'

'It's a beautiful day for a stroll.'

She nodded in agreement. 'Where shall we go, Sir John?'

'Let's walk in the direction of the lake, shall we?' he suggested. 'That should enable us to stretch our legs.'

He stood aside so that Amalia could go past him. As they left the house, she adjusted her hat. They had gone riding together a number of times but they'd never been for a stroll together. Somehow it felt more intimate. Beaming at her, Sir John offered his arm. Amalia hesitated for a moment before taking it. Feeling her so close to him made his blood race. It confirmed his earlier decision. The time had at last come.

When the ship docked at Harwich, Daniel was among the first passengers to go down the gangplank. It was early evening but he didn't stay in the town. He hired a horse immediately and set off at a steady pace, riding through the night so that no time was wasted. On every other occasion he'd been in England, he'd made a point of visiting his father's grave. Somerset didn't even impinge upon his thoughts now. Daniel had only one object in mind and that was to reach Amalia as soon as possible. When the long continuous ride began to tell on his horse, he changed it for a new mount, snatching food and drink at a tavern before he resumed his journey. With fresh legs beneath him and with most of the distance already covered, he was able to push the new horse hard. Endless hours in the saddle eventually yielded their bounty. A signpost to Woodstock told him that he only had three miles to go.

It was a pleasant walk through the broad acres of parkland but Amalia was not entirely at ease. For one thing, Sir John was holding her arm too tightly for comfort. Then again, his manner had changed. He was much more familiar and confiding than he'd ever been before. What worried her more, however, was the subject of the discussion. When she'd asked what it was, he told her that he'd rather wait until they reached the lake. Having no idea what it could be, Amalia let all kinds of worrying thoughts fill her head. When they reached the lake, Sir John guided her along its edge until they reached an arbour. He released her arm so that she could sit on the wooden bench. Certain that they had complete privacy, he lowered himself down beside her.

'What did you enjoy most about London?' he asked.

'The visit to St Paul's Cathedral – it was overwhelming.'

'You've seen a lot during your stay in England. I hope that it's helped you to think well of us as a people.'

'I've never thought less than well of you, Sir John,' she said.

'Some foreign visitors are critical of the English character.'

'Well, I'm not one of them, I can assure you.'

'You like it here, then?'

'Everything we've seen of England has been a delight.'

'I hope that you include Rievers Hall in your praise.'

'We'll take away the fondest memory of it, Sir John.'

He smiled at her. 'What a sweet thing to say!'

'It's the truth.'

She looked so beautiful that he wanted to reach out and take a first kiss from her but that would only disturb her. Sir John knew that he had to take his time. Biting his lip, he turned away as if he was searching for words. When he faced her again, his expression had changed completely. He seemed to be sad and deeply upset.

'What is it?' she asked, anxiously.

'I said that I had something to discuss with you.'

'I've been wondering what it is.'

He took a deep breath before speaking. 'I lied to you earlier on, Miss Janssen,' he said, taking her hands. 'It was not the right place or the right time to tell you. I'm afraid that I have to pass on some grim news.'

Her whole body tensed. 'Is it about Daniel?'

'Unhappily, it is.'

'What happened? Tell me, please. Don't keep me in suspense.'

'The man whom I sent abroad – Andrew Syme – returned to England while you were away.'

'What did he find out?' she begged. 'What did he say?'

'Captain Rawson did not, in fact, fall in action.'

'Thank God!' she cried.

'But he is dead, alas.' Her face crumpled. 'It appears that he was killed in a duel.' He squeezed her hands. 'I feel dreadful at having to pass on such sad tidings but I felt that you ought to know.'

'I can't believe it,' she said, shaking all over. 'Daniel killed in a duel? Can this be true? No, no, Sir John,' she cried. 'I *know* he's still alive. Why are you trying to tell me that he's dead?'

It was too much for Amalia to bear. As the full impact of the news hit her, she began to sway to and fro, her eyelids fluttered, her mind went numb and her limbs slack. When she swooned into his arms, Sir John pulled her to him, embracing her warmly and covering her face with kisses. It was the first stage in a process that would take time that he was ready to invest. Until her grief subsided, he would be the reliable friend, gently ingratiating himself with Amalia and with her father. As soon as she began to recover from her loss, he would ensnare her as he'd ensnared other women before her, moving almost imperceptibly from being a friend to being a lover. Amalia was his at last. Pulling her even closer, he could feel her heart beating against his chest. He could also hear it pounding away.

Sir John was mistaken. The noise had not come from her heart but from the hooves of an approaching horse. He looked out of the arbour to see a figure in uniform coming around the rim of the lake. Amalia was starting to come out of her faint, shaking her head to clear it and trying to sit up. Sir John pulled away from her, using only one hand to steady her. His eyes were fixed on the stranger, heading for them with such obvious determination. Sir John might be unable to identify him but Amalia recognised him at once.

'Daniel!' she exclaimed, leaping to her feet.

Sir John gaped. 'That *can't* be Captain Rawson.'

'He's not dead, after all. Why did you lie to me? That was cruel. Daniel is alive. You can see for yourself, Sir John.'

She ran to meet him. When Daniel reached her, he reined in the horse, leapt from the saddle and embraced her. Amalia sobbed on his shoulder. After easing her head back so that he could look at her, he gave her a kiss, then put an arm around her as he led her back to the arbour. Having risen from the bench, Sir John struck an attitude.

'Captain Rawson, I declare,' he said, forcing a smile. 'By all, this is wonderful! You are most welcome, sir. We were misinformed about you. A report came in that you were dead.'

'It's your friend, Mr Syme, who's dead,' said Daniel. 'I had the supreme pleasure of killing him.'

Amalia was confused. 'But I thought that Mr Syme was sent to find out if you were still alive.'

'He was hired to kill me, Amalia, and there's his paymaster.'

He pointed an accusatory finger at Sir John, who remained quite unperturbed. Amalia was still in a state of disbelief. Daniel detached himself from her so that he could confront the other man.

'You are wholly despicable, Sir John,' he said.

'Clearly, there's been a misunderstanding here,' replied the other with an attempt at nonchalance. 'I would never pay someone to kill another man. The very idea is unthinkable.' His laugh was brittle. 'Why don't you both come up to the Hall and let me explain everything over a glass of claret?'

'I've had all the explanation I need,' said Daniel. 'You wanted me out of the way so that you could use your charm on Amalia. I'm told that she's not the first woman you've deprived of her man in order to take advantage of her.'

Amalia gasped. 'Is that what he was going to do?'

'Not at all, dear lady,' said Sir John. 'I'm a married man and a doting husband. You've seen the way I minister to Lady Rievers. I've devoted my life to her.'

'No,' said Daniel, advancing on him. 'You have other

interests in your life, Sir John, and you'll stop at nothing –
not even murder – so that you can enjoy them.' He drew
his sword. 'Find yourself a weapon. Only a coward sends
someone else to do their dirty work. If you really want me
dead, kill me yourself.'

Sir John abandoned his pose of innocence. He was
staggered to learn that Andrew Syme had failed for once.
Knowing of the man's expertise with a sword, he could not
believe that someone had beaten him in a duel. Evidently,
Daniel was an even better swordsman. If he dared to take
him on, Sir John would certainly be killed. He tried to bluff
his way out of the situation.

'Why don't you leave while you still may, Captain
Rawson?' he asked. 'We're within hailing distance of the
Hall. All I have to do is to raise the alarm and half a dozen
servants will come running to beat you to death with
staves.'

Daniel stood his ground. 'His Grace, the Duke of
Marlborough knows where I am and precisely why I'm here.
If anything untoward happens to me, you'll have to answer
to him.' He held his sword aloft. 'Give me satisfaction, Sir
John. Since you can't live as a gentleman, at least try to die
like one.'

'Don't you dare insult me!' yelled Sir John, flipping his
coat open so that he could pull a pistol from its holster. 'I
always carry this with me on the estate so that I can shoot
vermin. And that's all you are to me, Captain Rawson.'

Adjusting his stance, he took aim. Amalia flung herself
in front of Daniel to protect him, but he was not afraid. He
eased her away.

'Stand by my horse, Amalia,' he advised, 'and take hold

of the rein. If Sir John has the courage to fire, the noise might frighten the animal.' Sheathing his sword, he spread his arms wide. 'Well, Sir John, *do* you have the courage?'

'Don't provoke me, Captain.'

'Here I am, an easy target, and still you can't pull the trigger.'

'I can do it with the utmost pleasure,' warned Sir John.

'And what happens then?' asked Daniel. 'How will you account for my death to His Grace? How will you explain why you hired Mr Syme? What will you tell your wife about all this?'

'Keep her out of this,' snarled Sir John.

'It's too late. Everyone will *know*. Your family, your friends, your acquaintances will all know the kind of man you are when you're not pretending to be a loving husband. Shoot me, if you can,' said Daniel, 'but you'll have to tell the truth to Lady Rievers afterwards. You'll have to admit how far you were prepared to go in order to lure Amalia into your bed. You're a broken man, Sir John. And that's why you lack the courage to shoot me.'

Arms still wide apart, Daniel walked slowly towards him. Sir John's nerve began to fail. He was finished. His villainy had been exposed and there was no escape for him. He thought of all the people who loved and trusted him and who would now be horrified to learn of his murky secrets. As Daniel came closer, Sir John's hand began to shake and the pistol jiggled up and down. He longed to pull the trigger but knew that it would solve nothing. It was all over.

'Here I am,' said Daniel, stopping a couple of yards in front of him. 'Is that close enough for you, Sir John? Or shall I wait while you fetch someone else to shoot me in your stead?' He patted his heart. 'This is the place to aim. Let's see if you're man enough to do it.'

Sir John could take no more. Exposed as a criminal and humiliated in front of a woman he'd planned to seduce, he was filled with despair. He closed his eyes, thrust the pistol inside his mouth and pulled the trigger. Some of the blood spattered Daniel's face.

The loud report frightened the birds, startled the horse and made Amalia scream hysterically. Daniel rushed to enfold her in his arms, shielding her from having to look at the corpse of Sir John Rievers. For her part, she was caught between shock and relief, appalled by the suicide she'd witnessed yet grateful that it was not Daniel who'd been shot. Amalia was also horrified to realise how Sir John had exploited her, manipulating her emotions and making her reliant on him. She tried to look at his body but Daniel moved her several yards away from the arbour. It took a long time to soothe her. When she eventually calmed down, the questions poured out of her.

'You came all this way for me?' she said.

'I'd have come ten times the distance, Amalia.'

'What about the siege?'

'It seems to me you've been enduring one of your own.'

'When did you get to England?'

'I got here just in time, by the look of it.'

'Who was this man sent to kill you?'

'I'll tell you about him in due course.'

'How did you know where to find us?'

'I called at the house first,' said Daniel. 'Beatrix saw you leaving on foot with Sir John Rievers. You had to be on the estate somewhere.'

'He brought me here to tell me that you were dead.'

Daniel smiled. 'I had to disillusion him on that score.'

'What will happen now?' she asked.

'I'll take you away from here, Amalia. I'm sorry that your first visit to England has been blighted by all this. I hope it won't stop you from coming back here again one day.'

'I'd come if you brought me, Daniel.'

'That's exactly what I intend to do,' he said. 'Meanwhile, I have to get you, your father and Beatrix safely back to Amsterdam. When that's done,' he went on, using his thumb to brush back a stray hair from her cheek, 'there's the small matter of the siege of Lille.'

The bombardment of Lille continued unabated. On 22nd October, 1708, with his defences crumbling, Marshal Boufflers beat a parley. Three days later, he surrendered the town with the proviso that he and the surviving members of the garrison could retire to the citadel. Under constant attack, they held out there until the evening of 9th December when Boufflers signed the articles of capitulation. The Allied army finally took possession of Lille. The siege had lasted 120 days.